AN AMISH COUNTRY TREASURE 4-BOOK BOXED SET BUNDLE

RUTH PRICE

ISBN:152271541X
ISBN-13:9781522715412

TABLE OF CONTENTS

ACKNOWLEDGMENTS   I

AN AMISH COUNTRY TREASURE 1   1

CHAPTER ONE   1

CHAPTER TWO   7

CHAPTER THREE   13

CHAPTER FOUR   23

CHAPTER FIVE   31

CHAPTER SIX   37

CHAPTER SEVEN   43

CHAPTER EIGHT   49

CHAPTER NINE   55

CHAPTER TEN   61

CHAPTER ELEVEN   69

CHAPTER TWELVE   75

CHAPTER THIRTEEN   81

CHAPTER FOURTEEN	87
AN AMISH COUNTRY TREASURE 2	93
CHAPTER ONE	93
CHAPTER TWO	101
CHAPTER THREE	109
CHAPTER FOUR	117
CHAPTER FIVE	125
CHAPTER SIX	133
CHAPTER SEVEN	143
CHAPTER EIGHT	151
CHAPTER NINE	159
CHAPTER TEN	167
CHAPTER ELEVEN	173
CHAPTER TWELVE	181
CHAPTER THIRTEEN	187
CHAPTER FOURTEEN	195

CHAPTER FIFTEEN 203

CHAPTER SIXTEEN 213

CHAPTER SEVENTEEN 221

CHAPTER EIGHTEEN 229

CHAPTER NINETEEN 237

CHAPTER TWENTY 245

CHAPTER TWENTY-ONE 253

CHAPTER TWENTY-TWO 261

CHAPTER TWENTY-THREE 269

CHAPTER TWENTY-FOUR 275

CHAPTER TWENTY-FIVE 281

CHAPTER TWENTY-SIX 287

AN AMISH COUNTRY TREASURE 3 295

CHAPTER ONE 295

CHAPTER TWO 303

CHAPTER THREE 309

CHAPTER FOUR   315

CHAPTER FIVE   323

CHAPTER SIX   335

CHAPTER SEVEN   341

CHAPTER EIGHT   349

CHAPTER NINE   357

CHAPTER TEN   365

CHAPTER ELEVEN   373

CHAPTER TWELVE   381

CHAPTER THIRTEEN   387

CHAPTER FOURTEEN   395

CHAPTER FIFTEEN   403

CHAPTER SIXTEEN   409

CHAPTER SEVENTEEN   417

CHAPTER EIGHTEEN   425

CHAPTER NINETEEN   433

CHAPTER TWENTY   439

CHAPTER TWENTY-ONE   447

CHAPTER TWENTY-TWO   457

CHAPTER TWENTY-THREE   465

CHAPTER TWENTY-FOUR   475

CHAPTER TWENTY-FIVE   483

AN AMISH COUNTRY TREASURE 4   493

CHAPTER ONE   493

CHAPTER TWO   499

CHAPTER THREE   503

CHAPTER FOUR   509

CHAPTER FIVE   517

CHAPTER SIX   527

CHAPTER SEVEN   535

CHAPTER EIGHT   543

CHAPTER NINE   553

CHAPTER TEN   559

CHAPTER ELEVEN   565

CHAPTER TWELVE   573

CHAPTER THIRTEEN   579

CHAPTER FOURTEEN   585

CHAPTER FIFTEEN   593

CHAPTER SIXTEEN   601

CHAPTER SEVENTEEN   609

CHAPTER EIGHTEEN   615

CHAPTER NINETEEN   623

CHAPTER TWENTY   629

CHAPTER TWENTY-ONE   635

CHAPTER TWENTY-TWO   643

CHAPTER TWENTY-THREE   649

CHAPTER TWENTY-FOUR   657

CHAPTER TWENTY-FIVE   665

CHAPTER TWENTY-SIX   671

CHAPTER TWENTY-SEVEN   677

CHAPTER TWENTY-EIGHT   685

CHAPTER TWENTY-NINE   691

EPILOGUE   695

A LANCASTER COUNTY CHRISTMAS YULE
    GOAT CALAMITY   697

ABOUT THE AUTHOR   703

ACKNOWLEDGMENTS

All Praise first to the Almighty God who has given me this wonderful opportunity to share my words and stories with the world. Next, I have to thank my family, especially my husband Harold who supports me even when I am being extremely crabby. Further, I have to thank my wonderful friends and associates with Global Grafx Press who support me in every way as a writer. Lastly, I wouldn't be able to do any of this without you, my readers. I hold you in my heart and prayers and hope that you enjoy my books.

All the best and Blessings,

Ruth.

AN AMISH COUNTRY TREASURE 1

CHAPTER ONE

"Wait -- Jemima!"

Jemima King turned her head, but it was more out of habit than a real need to identify the voice. She would've known the sound of Mark Christner's voice in her sleep. They had lived next door to each other in the same Lancaster County community for 17 years.

He came running up and then stopped dead in the road. He bent double, caught his breath and laughed.

Jemima turned her eyes down demurely. Mark was always at her elbow these days. There was nothing new about that – they were childhood playmates – but Mark's reasons were different now.

She stole a glance at him through her lashes.

Mark was no longer the scruffy little boy of her childhood, and that was especially clear on a day like this one, when the sun gave his black hair a silky blue sheen, and made the curve of his cheek look as downy and smooth as a peach.

He was almost as tall as her father now. And his voice was nearly as deep. Jemima pinched in a smile. She would have to be made of stone not to notice that Mark had filled out nicely – especially when he flashed those beautiful white teeth in her direction.

She looked down at her feet. Their relationship was changing fast. The same Mark who had once irritated and teased her was – strangely -- becoming more solicitous by the day.

Maybe that was because *she* had changed, too.

Mark used to tease her about her red hair and green eyes. He had said she looked like an orange cat, and had made her cry.

But just the other day Mark had compared her hair to a maple leaf in the fall, and her eyes to the color of sunshine through leaves.

"I'll walk you home," he volunteered, and put a big brown hand out for her books.

Jemima smiled and gave them to him.

"What are you going to do, now that we've finished

school? What are you going to do on *your* rumspringa, Mark?" she teased him. "Are you going to dress in English clothes and turn all the girls' heads?"

He grimaced wryly, and shook his head. "I'd just as soon dress up in a monkey suit," he said bluntly, and Jemima laughed outright.

"I'm disappointed in you, Mark," she said mischievously. "I was hoping you'd shock us all!"

Jemima enjoyed his chagrined expression out of her corner of her eye. She really shouldn't tease him, but it was *so* tempting. Mark was so *easy* to tease. No one she knew was more staunchly Amish, or more conservative. Mark reminded her of something big and strong and immovable, like the face of a mountain.

Or, maybe, *dormant volcano* would be a better description.

Because underneath all that unyielding rock, there was definitely warmth on the inside. She glanced at him affectionately then tilted her head, considering.

Maybe there was even a little *lava* under that mountain. She had seen one or two things lately that…

"Jemima, slow down!"

Jemima came back to herself. She stopped walking and turned around. Her little sister Deborah had fallen behind again, and was trotting along the dirt road to catch up.

"You… never… *wait for me*," Deborah complained, as she huffed along. She finally caught up with them and bent over double, gasping for breath.

Jemima looked at her little sister pityingly. Deborah's sandy brown hair had worked its way out from under her cap and was flying all around her face like a swarm of gnats.

She couldn't keep her hands from reaching out to smooth it back again. "Mind your hair, Deborah," she said softly.

Deborah swatted her hands away irritably. "I know how I look!" she snapped. "Maybe it's because I had to run! Next time just *wait* for me, and we can *both* look good!"

"That's no way to talk to your sis, Debby," Mark chided gently.

Deborah said nothing, but shot him a look that said, *Oh, shut up* as clearly as any words.

Jemima sighed and turned to him. "Never mind her, Mark, she has the temper of a wildcat. I know she doesn't mean half the things she says."

"I do, too – I mean *every word*!" Deborah countered, "Why shouldn't I, when you leave me behind to *flirt with your boyfriends*?"

"*Debby!*" cried Jemima and Mark, together.

"Oh, just forget it," Deborah fumed, "I'll walk home by myself. That's what you two *want*, anyway!" She hoisted her books up in her arms and stumped off, muttering under her breath.

Jemima shot Mark an apologetic look. "You'll have to forgive her, Mark," she explained, "Deborah's at that awkward stage. I'm sure that once it's over, she won't be – mad *all the time*."

Mark tilted his head and watched Deborah as she disappeared down the road. "I don't remember *you* ever being that –" He cleared his throat and quickly amended, "I mean, I don't remember that *you* ever had a… hard time."

Jemima shook her head. "She's driving poor Mamm to despair. It's only a few years until Debby comes of age, and the way she's treating all the boys she knows, not one of them is going to court with her!"

"Well, at least your Mamm will never have that problem with *you*." Mark looked at her with transparent admiration, and she blushed.

They rounded a corner and the King homestead gradually moved into view. It was a large, white, two story house surrounded by several outbuildings, including the blacksmith shop where Jemima's father worked. Even from that distance, the faint sound of a hammer rang out over the fields.

There was a buggy parked at the front of the house, and Mark's dark eyebrows moved together. He shaded his eyes with one hand.

"Whose buggy is that?" he frowned.

Jemima looked at him uncomfortably. "It's probably Samuel Kauffman's," she murmured. "He said he'd be coming by this afternoon. His mother is sending Mamm some canning supplies."

Mark grunted suspiciously, and it was clear that he thought that Samuel Kauffman's mission was not primarily about preserving fruits and vegetables.

"Well, that sounds about right," he growled. "Samuel and your mamm are probably *trading recipes*."

"Mark!"

CHAPTER TWO

By the time they reached the front yard, it was clear that Samuel Kauffman was in attendance. His tall, slim frame was draped easily over one of the porch rails.

Samuel would have been at home at any beach in the world. He had a shock of bushy blond hair, he was brown as a nut, and his eyes were a sparkling blue. He greeted Jemima with a beautiful white smile and a wink that made her lower her eyes and go pink.

He acknowledged Mark with a cheery: "Well, look who's here! Sit down, Mark, you look exhausted. Can I get you a glass of water?"

Mark gave him a grim look, but replied: "I know you're *used* to doing that, but no thanks. We aren't at your folks' restaurant. Speaking of that – isn't it about time for you to put on your *apron*? It's getting close to dinner."

Jemima broke in hastily. "Samuel, it was very kind of you

to come all the way out here. I'm sure Mamm appreciates it."

Samuel beamed at her. "It's nothing, Jemima. Anytime! I'm always happy to do what I can."

"*That's for sure*," Mark mumbled under his breath.

Jemima's eyes moved uncertainly between the two of them. "Would the two of you like to – to stay to supper?" she ventured.

"Can't," Samuel lamented, and reached out to take her hand. "But give me a rain check, okay? I'd love to see you some *other* time."

Jemima noticed, with trepidation, that Mark's brow was gathering thunder, and he looked as if he was about to burst out with the accompanying lightning. So she hurried to reply, "Oh, I'm sorry you can't stay with us, Samuel. But yes, do drop by when you can," she smiled.

Samuel squeezed her hand and ran his thumb over her palm in a way that made it tingle. Then he smiled, bounded down the porch steps, and was driving away before she found the nerve to look up.

Mark watched him go with a scowl. "Why do you encourage that skinny little weasel?" he blurted.

Jemima went red. "Samuel is a very good person -- and you know it, Mark Christner!" she retorted indignantly. "I don't know *why* you take such a dislike to him, but he doesn't deserve it."

Mark turned to look at her, and his blue eyes were sad and reproachful. "Don't you, Jemima?" he asked softly.

Jemima couldn't meet his eyes, and felt her cheeks going hot. But she was spared the necessity of a reply by the sound of her father's heavy shoes approaching on the gravel drive. His booming voice cut off any possibility of a reply.

"Jemima, shouldn't you be helping your mamm with dinner?" he said pointedly, and directed a speaking look at Mark.

Mark's cheeks went a dull red. Jemima nodded, gave her visitor an apologetic look, and fled.

After she had gone, the six-foot-three Jacob King leaned against one of the porch posts and regarded his 17-year-old guest with a knowing look in his eye.

"How is your family, Mark?" he inquired gently.

"They're fine, sir," Mark mumbled.

Jacob nodded. "Good. I haven't seen much of them lately. Or of *you*, for that matter."

Mark looked out across the fields and bit his lip.

"And that's *not* good," Jacob sighed, running a massive hand through his rumpled red hair. "Because if a young man comes to this house to see my daughter, I expect him to come to see me *first*."

"Yes, sir."

"Just so long as we understand one another," Jacob smiled, and clapped his hand down on Mark's shoulder – hard.

Mark winced, but nodded.

Jacob smiled. "Staying to supper, boy?" he inquired gently.

"Ah – no. I have chores to do."

"Say hello to your folks for me," Jacob told him, and stood on the porch, watching, until Mark Christner's retreating form disappeared down the long dirt road.

Jacob King put both hands on his hips and laughed long and loud, and then turned and entered his house.

His wife Rachel was waiting for him at the door, with her arms crossed. "Jacob King, you should be ashamed of yourself," she chided gently. "Jemima is finished with her schooling now. It's *time* for her to be getting visits from young men. And Mark is her… *special friend*. He's plainly working up the nerve to ask if he can court with her. Why do you discourage him? Don't you *want* your daughter to find a good husband?"

Jacob leaned over and kissed his wife's pretty pink cheek. "You can set your mind at rest, Rachel," he assured her, "we'll never have to worry that Jemima will *lose* a man. Her danger is going to be picking the right one, out of the teeming horde!"

"Jacob, what a way to put it!" his wife exclaimed, but her lips curled up a little. "It's true that Jemima is *very* blessed, but how will she ever know which of her suitors is right for her, if she never gets a chance to spend time with them?"

Jacob sighed, and stretched his rippling arms. "Don't tire me with those silly pups, Rachel," he yawned. "I'm *hungry*. I've spent all day hammering over a forge, and I could eat a horse."

"Come to dinner then, Jacob," she smiled softly. "The table is laid."

Jacob's eyes lighted on a large cardboard box sitting on one of the dining room chairs. He lifted a canning jar.

"What's this?"

His wife assumed an innocent look, and shrugged. "Samuel Kauffman came by this afternoon to bring me some jars. It was a gift from his mother."

"Oh, *did* he now?"

Jacob met his wife's eyes, and raised his brows comically. She looked away, and pinched in a smile.

"Your dinner is getting cold."

Jacob sat down at the groaning dinner table, and rubbed his hands. But before his family bowed their heads to pray, he gave his pretty daughter a meaningful look.

"Jemima, the next time you see Samuel Kauffman, tell him *I'd like a word with him.*"

"Oh, Daed!" Jemima gave him a pleading look from her lovely eyes, but her father was the one male on earth who had found the strength to resist it.

"I mean it."

CHAPTER THREE

"You're so *lucky,* Mima," Ruth Yoder sighed. "I wish I had *your* problems."

The next afternoon, Jemima and her best friend were sitting in the woods just beyond the family garden, and were talking *boys*.

Jemima's friend rested her chin on her hands and raised impish blue eyes to the sky. *"Oh, Mark, stop it,"* she simpered. *"Samuel, you'll make me cry!"*

Jemima rolled her eyes. "If you say that again with a big scowl on your face, you'll sound almost like Debby," she sighed. "Does *everybody* hate me, then?"

Ruth giggled and relented. "Of course not, Mima. Everybody *loves* you. All the boys do, anyway, and the girls just wish they *were* you!"

Jemima eyed her friend ruefully. "I wish they didn't," she confessed.

"Why not?" Ruth replied, stretching luxuriantly. She looked up at the sky through the tree branches. "If you've *got* it, *flaunt* it, I say. I just wish *I* had it, so I could *flaunt* it, too!"

Jemima giggled, and then hushed her. "*Quiet*, Ruth! Be careful what you say! Debby is hanging around somewhere, and if she hears you, you'll find yourself having to explain to your parents! I love my sister, but she's the biggest tattletale –"

A rustling in the bushes, about a stone's throw away, make Jemima break off. Sure enough, Deborah's scowling face materialized out of the leaves.

"So that's where you're hiding! Mamm says come and help her with lunch, Jemima. And you, too, Ruth -- *since you're here*!" Debby added rudely, and stalked off.

Jemima went red with embarrassment. She turned to her friend apologetically. "I'm sorry, Ruth," she stammered, "she's just so... *mean* these days. I don't know what's come over her!"

Ruth stood up, brushing grass from her skirt. "*I* do!" she replied tartly. She looked at Jemima's distressed face and bit back the rest of what she'd been planning to say. "But I'll be glad to help *you* with lunch."

Jemima clasped her friend's arm warmly. "*Of course* you'll stay and eat with us," she pressed, and Ruth's expression relaxed. She nodded.

They hugged one another, and walked back to the house arm in arm.

But while they were in the kitchen, dutifully making sandwiches, there was a jaunty knock at the front door.

Samuel Kauffman stuck his head into the living room and smiled. "Knock knock! Is anybody home?"

"Why, Samuel," Rachel King exclaimed in a pleased tone, "come in! I hope everything is well with your folks?"

"They're fine," Samuel smiled.

The girls craned their necks to sneak a look at Samuel as he began to chat with Jemima's mother. Samuel towered over her, and he had taken his hat off in deference. His blond hair shone like summer wheat.

Ruth squeezed Jemima's arm in excitement, and they both smothered giggles.

"He's here to see you – lucky thing!" Ruth hissed.

Jemima blushed and smoothed her hair back, but to her consternation, her mother was saying:

"Well, Samuel, in that case, you'll have to go out to the shop and talk to Jacob. He won't let you court with Jemima unless you talk to him first."

Ruth hissed, "Did you hear that?"

Jemima put her hands over her mouth, and her heart began to beat oddly. She stopped even pretending to make sandwiches and inclined her ear to catch every word spoken.

"Thank you, Rachel," Samuel said in a respectful tone, and took his leave.

After the door closed behind him, Jemima's mother returned to the kitchen. She was trying hard to project a calm demeanor, but Jemima could see at once that her mother was on fire with excitement.

Jemima's eyes went to her mother's face. She searched it silently.

Rachel King broke down. "He wants to *court* with you, Jemima," she said thrillingly. "The second boy in as many *days*! Your father will be –"

But another quick knock at the door interrupted her words. They all turned to look through the kitchen door.

Another young man stood hat in hand on the doorstep.

Jemima looked at her mother worriedly. Her admirers were dropping by so often now that it was becoming almost *awkward*.

Rachel King took a deep breath, smoothed her apron, and went back out to greet their newest guest.

That evening at dinner, Jacob King put a forkful of potatoes into his mouth, and gave his lovely daughter a rueful glance.

"*Four* now," he told her, and Jemima turned a guilty red.

He turned to his wife. "What am I going to do with her?" he asked, with a twinkle in his eye. "If this keeps up, we're going to have to make them take *numbers*. I thought Samuel Kauffman and that what's-his-name Beiler boy were going to fight each other on the porch today."

Rachel smiled at Jemima. "Jemima is a *very* blessed young lady," she murmured happily. "Jemima, you should be praying every day for wisdom. You have an... unusual choice ahead of you. It isn't many girls who have so many suitors to choose from."

Deborah had been listening to the conversation in unhappy silence, but apparently she had endured her limit. She twisted her freckled face into a scowl and cried: "Jemima, Jemima, *Jemima*! If I hear one more word about *Jemima* and her *boyfriends*, I'm going to *throw up*!" She jumped up, flounced out of the room, and slammed the door behind her.

Jacob watched her, and frowned, but didn't seem disposed to interrupt his meal. He took another bite of ham. "Do you want me to get involved?" he asked quietly, and looked at his wife.

Rachel closed her eyes, but shook her head. "No. I'll take care of it. I know what it is. She's going through an awkward phase, and the boys at school tease her. It's hard for her, and then to be compared to Jemima -- But I *can't wait* until she's fourteen, and over this – this –" She gave a soft huff, rose, and followed her daughter.

That left Jemima alone with her father. She raised her eyes tentatively to his face.

His expression softened as he looked down at her. "Well, Mima, you've got all the boys in this county rushing to my door! Got any that you want me to throw *back?*"

He winked and laughed, and Jemima blushed and sputtered, "Oh, *Daed.*"

After dinner, Jemima went up to her bedroom and sat at the window. She brushed her glowing hair and looked out through the green curtain of trees. The window was open and a cool breath of air, smelling of mown grass, wafted in.

She really should be putting the finishing touches on her work. She had sewn three big boxes full of dolls to sell at the store in town. There was a big summer festival planned for the next morning, and she was going to have to get up early to get them to town before the shop opened.

Jemima sighed and looked down at the neatly stitched cloth dolls. There was a blank space where their faces would have been, as was Amish tradition.

She looked out through the trees again. She felt like a doll sometimes herself, only uncomfortably different – like the one *painted* doll in a box full of normal ones.

She put the brush down and sighed.

She couldn't concentrate on even the simplest task these days.

If she stared out the window long enough, she began to see faces – Mark Christner's strong face, and Samuel Kauffman's laughing one, and even Joseph Beiler's shy eyes.

Mark was strong and sure and steady and handsome and she knew him so well and was so comfortable with him.

Samuel was fun and easy to talk to and he made her laugh and he was always interesting.

Joseph was quiet and shy, but so handsome, and, she thought -- *very* smitten.

How could she choose between them? She couldn't bear the thought of hurting Mark -- *or* Samuel. And Joseph was so sweet and quiet.

She looked up at the soft twilit sky. Lord, what should I do? she prayed. I wouldn't hurt any of them for the world, but I'll have to, if I choose one over the others. Please show me what You want me to do.

She glanced back over her shoulder. She could hear the muffled sound of Deborah making noise in her own bedroom, across the hall. It sounded like she was muttering angrily and kicking something.

And please give me patience with Debby, Lord. Sometimes I have un-Christian thoughts about her.

There was a crash, and what sounded like a curse word, from across the hall. Then Deborah shrieked out, removing any doubt. There was a thunderous stomping sound, and Jemima's door burst open to reveal her angry sister.

"*Why* didn't you tell me that this clock you gave me was a piece of junk?" she demanded, throwing it down on Jemima's bed. "It just fell apart! I'm *tired* of getting all *your* old hand-me —"

Their mother appeared suddenly in the hall, her anxious eyes on Deborah's scowling face. "Deborah, that's no way to talk to your sister. I won't have you behaving like this. Go back to your room."

Deborah pinched her lips together and stomped out again.

Jemima met her mother's eyes ruefully, and they exchanged an unspoken comment before Rachel King sighed and closed Jemima's door after her.

Jemima turned to her work and closed up the big cardboard

boxes. Then she turned down the lamp and undressed for bed.

Tomorrow morning was going to start early.

CHAPTER FOUR

The next morning Jemima stood outside, shivering in the early morning chill. The lanterns on the buggy threw off a ghostly light in the predawn darkness.

Her father came striding out across the porch to the buggy, and his big shoes made a thunderous sound. When he climbed up into the driver's seat, the whole buggy leaned to one side.

He stuck his head out. "Hoist the boxes up, Mima," he told her, and held out his hands.

Jemima lifted up the boxes, and he stacked them in the back seat of the buggy. Then he extended his big hand, and Jemima took it. One pull from his muscular arm was all it took to catapult her into the seat. She shrieked, and laughed, and almost went tumbling into her father's arms.

"Steady on," he told her indulgently. "All in?"

She adjusted her cap and nodded, and he flicked the whip. Their dark chestnut, Rufus, swished his tail and started down the road at a smart clip.

"I have some business to do in town," Jacob told her, "But I'll only be gone for a few minutes. I'll park outside the store, and meet you there when I'm done. I should be there before you're finished."

Jemima nodded.

"Have you decided what you're going to do with the money, Mima?" he teased her.

Jemima shook her head. "Save it, I suppose," she told him.

"That's a smart girl," he replied approvingly. "You'll likely *need* the extra money before the year is out."

Jemima smiled, and went pink.

By the time they had reached town, the sun was just rising. At that early hour, the shopkeepers and festival organizers were the only ones in town. A few people were raising a big tent in the town square, and vendors were setting up tables in preparation for the crowd.

There was even a truck with a news logo on the door

parked on the far side of the block, and seeing it, Jacob muttered impatiently and turned Rufus' head. The buggy disappeared down a side street.

"You can knock on the back door of the shop," Jacob told her. "I'll stay until Mr. Satterwhite lets you in."

Jemima jumped down from the buggy and knocked softly on the back door. After a few minutes Mr. Satterwhite opened it and greeted her with: "Up early, eh, Jemima? Got some dolls for me?"

Jemima smiled and nodded.

"Well, I'll help you get them in. I expect they'll sell out quick, with all the folks expected in town today."

When they had carried all the dolls inside, her father raised his hand. "I'll be back in a few minutes, Jemima," he called.

Jemima put up her hand and then returned to the shop.

Mr. Satterwhite closed the back door behind her, and led her through the stock room up to the sales floor. He put the cardboard boxes on the counter. "So, three boxes, that makes 30 dolls this time, I guess," he muttered. "That's $150 American." He opened the cash register and counted out some bills.

Jemima drifted away from the counter as he talked. She let her eyes wander idly over the merchandise – mostly rustic knick-knacks, handmade quilts and crafts, like her dolls, and a smattering of antiques. She picked up a little stuffed rabbit with floppy ears and smiled into its button eyes.

"Here you go, Jemima," Mr. Satterwhite called.

She put down the stuffed toy and went to the counter. The elderly man counted the money out and put it into an envelope. "You do good work, Jemima," he told her. "If this batch sells as well as the others, I'll want three boxes every month."

Jemima smiled at him. "Thank you, Mr. Satterwhite." She tucked the envelope into a little bag. "Would you like me to open the front door for you?"

He craned his neck, looking out through the shop windows. "Thank you, yes, it is getting on toward opening. Go ahead."

Jemima walked to the shop doors and threw them open. The square was beginning to come alive with food and art vendors. Someone was setting up a P.A. system, and was testing the mic. The first festivalgoers were beginning to arrive.

She turned back, and her eye was caught by a small wooden wall clock sitting in a cardboard box by the door. It was plain and looked old, but it was made of a rich cherry wood, and the dial looked hand painted. Its fine, curving numerals scrolled delicately over the yellowed dial.

She picked it up, turned it over in her hands, and remembered Deborah's tantrum about her broken clock. She smiled ruefully. It probably *was* hard on her, to have to live with so many hand-me-downs.

She looked up at Mr. Satterwhite. "Is this clock for sale?" she asked.

He squinted. "That old thing? My wife got it at an auction yesterday. I haven't really decided what to charge for it. I can't imagine it would bring much. Why, were you interested in it?"

Jemima looked down at it. "I was thinking I might buy it for my sister."

"Well… I guess you could have it for five dollars, if you want it."

Jemima brought it up to the counter, and handed the shop owner a five dollar bill. He scribbled out a receipt, and she stuck it into her bag.

"To tell you the truth, I don't know why you want it," he said candidly.

"Oh, I don't know," Jemima answered softly. "I think it's pretty. It has a – a *look*. As if it's been worn *soft*."

"Hmm." He looked over her head and nodded. "Looks like your father is back."

Jemima turned to see the buggy parked on the street outside. She picked up the clock and nestled it in the crook of her arm. "Thank you, Mr. Satterwhite. I'll have your order for you next month at the same time."

He threw up his hand and she walked out of the store.

The square outside was coming alive with people. A band had started to pick out notes over the P.A. system, and the scent of funnel cakes sweetened the air. Jemima turned her eyes in the direction of the music, and took them off of where she was going.

A sharp, sudden collision brought her back to her surroundings – too late. She smacked into another pedestrian, *hard*. The clock jumped out of her arms, fell on the sidewalk, and cracked open.

Jemima put her hand to her mouth in dismay. "Oh *no!*" she wailed.

She lifted her eyes to the other person, and found two bright, humorous eyes trained on hers.

"I'm so sorry!" the man said apologetically. He bent down to pick up the clock. "I didn't see you coming. Here's your clock." He picked up the pieces and handed them to her. "It looks like the back popped off, but I don't think it's broken." His eyes returned to the sidewalk. "I think this came out, too." He bent down and picked up a folded piece of paper.

Jemima took it from his outstretched hand, and looked up fleetingly into his face. The stranger had light blue eyes shining from underneath bushy brown eyebrows, a wry, strong mouth, and a thick mop of curly, brown-blonde hair.

Her glance flitted down. To her horror, he was wearing a blue oxford with the logo of a local *newspaper* stitched into the collar.

She turned without a word and jumped up into the buggy, and her father whipped up the horse instantly. Rufus jumped into a canter, and the buggy lurched away. Jemima hugged the clock to her chest. Her heart was pounding.

But when she looked back over her shoulder at the shop entrance, the stranger was still standing on the sidewalk, staring after her.

CHAPTER FIVE

Brad Williams stood in the middle of the street, staring open mouthed at the retreating buggy. The delicate, luminous redhead riding away inside of it was quite possibly the most beautiful woman he'd ever seen in his life. His lips pursed in a soundless whistle.

They do grow everything better here, he thought wryly, and shook his head. Must be something in the water.

An irritable voice intruded on his amazement. "Don't block the entryway." An elderly shopkeeper was staring at him, hands on hips.

"Oh – oh, yeah. I was just coming in for a bite of breakfast.

You do sell food, right?"

Mr. Satterwhite jerked a thumb in the direction of the counter. "In the mini-fridge to the right. I have soda and some cheese danish."

"Coffee?"

"On the counter."

The young man sauntered to the front of the shop and poured black coffee into a paper cup. He took an appreciative sip and looked around the store. "I'm Brad Williams from the *Ledger*. Do you mind if I ask you a few questions about the festival?" he asked.

Mr. Satterwhite picked up a broom and started sweeping the floor. "Yes, I mind."

Brad looked at him and cracked a grin. "Have a little pity, friend. It's a slow day."

"And it will be until you leave," the elderly man replied bluntly. "Folks around here don't like reporters."

"Oh, I don't bite. Think about it, anyway. *Free publicity*."

"I don't need publicity, young man. My customers already know where I am."

Brad grinned again, took a danish out of the mini-fridge, and slapped a ten dollar bill into the man's outstretched hand.

"Now get along, you'll hex me," Mr. Satterwhite told him,

counting out change.

Brad took a bite of the cheese danish and sauntered out into the doorway. He stood there momentarily, chewing, and so was almost knocked down for the second time that morning.

A big man in a business suit came charging into the shop, knocking him to one side. He stopped in front of the store counter and stood there, flushed and breathless. When he caught sight of Mr. Satterwhite, he demanded: "Are you the owner here?"

The elderly man gave him a withering glance. "Yes, I am," he replied.

Brad called indignantly from the doorway: "Hey, buster, why don't you *knock me down* next time?" he objected, brushing frosting off his shirt. "I should send you the cleaning bill for this!"

The man ignored him. He sighed deeply, caught his breath, and trained his dark eyes on Mr. Satterwhite. "Did you buy a clock yesterday, at an estate auction in Marietta?"

The elderly man looked at him narrowly. "My wife bought a bunch of junk at an auction yesterday," he drawled. "I think there was a clock."

The man stared at him intently. *"Do you still have it?"*

Mr. Satterwhite shook his head. "Nope. I sold it this

morning."

The man stifled an impatient exclamation and asked, *"Who did you sell it to?"*

Brad, who was still brushing his shirt front in the doorway, looked up at this.

The elderly man bristled. "That's none of your business, mister," he replied, with a straight look.

The man shook his head. "I'm sorry. It's just that the auction was for my mother's estate, and the clock was important to me for sentimental reasons. I would be willing to pay whatever the person gave for it, and a little more. Do you know the person who bought it? Would you be willing to give them that message for me, or, tell me how to contact them, so I can ask myself?"

"I know the girl who bought it, but I'm not going to give out her name without her permission," Mr. Satterwhite replied coldly.

"So she lives around here?"

"Look here, I've answered all the questions I'm going to this morning," Mr. Satterwhite snapped. "Buy something, or get out! I have work to do."

The man held up his hands. "All right, all right. But I'm going to write down my name and number. Can you at least give her this, and ask her to call me, when you see her again?

I'd appreciate it."

Brad narrowed his eyes and walked back into the store. He leaned against one wall with his arms crossed.

The older man appeared somewhat mollified. "I'll take it, but I'm not promising you anything."

"Thank you. I appreciate it." The man put his pen back into his jacket pocket and glanced at Brad as he walked out.

"Sorry about the shirt," he apologized, and hurried off.

Brad watched him as he walked down the street.

"He sure was anxious to get his hands on that clock," he murmured, mostly to himself. He turned to Mr. Satterwhite. "That girl I bumped into when I first came in – the redhead – was that her?"

The older man shrugged, and refused to answer. Brad smiled and shook a forefinger.

"It *was* her! What's her name?"

The old man lifted angry eyes. "I'm not telling *you*, any more than I told him! Now beat it!"

"Okay, but at least tell me where she lives. Hey, you wouldn't give me an interview, at least help me get one for myself!"

Mr. Satterwhite set his mouth. "Okay -- if it will get you out of here! She lives ten miles away from town. You take

Yoder Road out to the river, and –"

"Wait, wait," Brad interrupted, scrambling for a pen. "Okay, what again?"

"You cross the river, and take the first right on the river road. You have to look close – it's an unmarked, dirt road. You follow it for five miles, and then take the second left – you'll know it by the big oak tree – and her father's farm is the third one on that road. A big house with green shutters."

"Got it." Brad snapped the pen and grinned. "Thanks!"

The old man nodded grimly, and watched his customer stride out and disappear into the crowd.

Then he laughed to himself, a dry, cackling laugh, and wiped his eyes.

CHAPTER SIX

Brad Williams moved through the crowd toward the company truck. His cameraman was still sitting in it. The other man looked up as Brad approached, and relief flooded his face.

"There you are! Where you been, man? I've been sitting here for thirty minutes! Do you have something lined up?"

Brad opened the car door and slid in. "I have a new lead. Here's the game plan. Get plenty of crowd shots, lots of generic local color, and I'll fill in the blanks when I get back."

"You're taking the truck? We're supposed to be working the festival!"

"I've got a lead on something more interesting."

The cameraman shook his head. "Man, Delores is going to have your hide."

Brad winked and grinned. "Delores loves me."

"Yeah, you're going to find out how much she loves you," the other man retorted, wrestling with his camera equipment. "I am so glad, that I am not *you*."

"I'll be back, Eddie!" Brad called after him.

"Wait, how long are you going to be gone?"

But the roar of the truck engine was the only answer he got. The cameraman slumped, and shook his head, and hoisted his equipment on his shoulder. He was still muttering to himself as he disappeared into the crowd.

It took fifteen minutes of crawling traffic to get out of the festival traffic, but once he was clear, Brad stuck the piece of paper on the truck dashboard and squinted at the handwriting.

"Yoder Road…where the heck…okay, okay, there it is." He made a left turn onto a long, straight two-lane road that plunged immediately into corn fields, and stayed there for fifteen minutes. The only signs of life on it were the occasional Amish buggy, and guys out working the fields.

He squinted at the paper again. "Stay on Yoder Road until

the river...what river? Where is the stupid – okay, coming up."

There was a wide, shallow river visible on the road ahead. There was a bridge, and barely visible beyond it, a tiny, unmarked dirt road. Brad thought dryly that it was just as well that the old man had warned him, because he never would have noticed it otherwise. He made a hard right turn and the truck plunged onto the dirt road, kicking up a trail of dust.

"Okay...follow it for five miles, and take the second left...big oak tree."

The truck bounced along the dirt road, jouncing over potholes and the occasional rock. The only things visible on it were a line of trees overhanging the river, on the right, and dense forest on the left. There wasn't even a house now.

At the five mile mark, just as the directions said, there was a huge old oak tree on the left side of the road, and a turning onto another, even smaller, dirt road. He turned left, and consulted the paper again.

"Third farm on the road...big house...green shutters."

He drove down the road, which was getting progressively worse. The potholes were getting bigger and harder to navigate. He craned his neck, looking for a farm, but there were only more and bigger trees, crowding more and more closely to the edge of the road.

At last he pulled the truck to a stop. The sign across the

road read, *Dead End.*

He groaned and pressed his head against the wheel.

An hour later Brad Williams walked into the Satterwhite Gift Shop, tired, rumpled, and grim.

"*Ha ha,*" he said sardonically.

Mr. Satterwhite smirked, and continued scribbling in a ledger. "I told you I wasn't going to give you information, boy," he said dryly. "You should learn to take a hint."

Brad slumped against the wall, and eyed him. "Look, what if that clock turns out to be something valuable, and your friend doesn't know it? That guy sure sounded anxious to get it back."

"What's your interest in it?" the old man drawled.

"A story, of course."

The old man shook his head. "You're new here, aren't you boy? None of the Amish folk are going to talk to you."

Brad sighed, bit his lip, and turned to go, but couldn't resist a parting shot.

"*You* can still do an interview though, right?"

"Get out!"

Brad walked out onto the street and into a running stream of tourists. He shielded his eyes, squinting. There might still be time to get a few good interviews before the festival was over for the day, and he had to go back to the paper. To report to his editor, *Delores.*

He bit his lip.

With yet another boring story about a vegetable festival in Amish country.

It was true that he was fresh out of school, a greenhorn reporter, but Delores hadn't assigned him anything more important than horse auctions and business openings since he arrived.

It was *past* time for something more substantial.

He rolled a pen between his fingers. The clock thing was intriguing, and possibly newsworthy, if his hunch was right. And if the clock turned out to be something old or valuable, a story about it might help him move up from the grunt assignments, to actual *news.*

His mind returned to the redheaded beauty. The old man at the store had been tough as an old boot, but maybe one of the other shop owners in town would know who the girl was, and be willing to give a name, at least.

And he had to admit, the prospect of seeing her again was hardly less pleasant than that of getting a good story.

He wiped his brow with one arm, straightened, and walked into the store to the left of the Satterwhite Gift Shop.

"Yes, she comes into town every so often to sell her dolls."

The woman behind the counter was plump, matronly, and, to Brad's relief, fond of talking.

"Do you know her name?"

"Oh yes, her name is Jemima King. Pretty little thing, all the Amish boys are wild about her."

Brad nodded pleasantly. "I guess she must be a local, then."

"Yes, her family has lived here for hundreds of years! Her father has a blacksmith shop about five miles out of town."

"Could you tell me how to get there?"

She giggled. "If you're hoping to get a date, young man, you'll be disappointed. Her father will never let her go out with a young man who isn't Amish!"

"Oh, it's not that," he smiled. "I just wanted to ask a question."

She shook her head and smiled. "You can try, but you'll most likely be wasting a trip." She looked at him amiably, and began scribbling out directions on a piece of paper.

CHAPTER SEVEN

The next morning, Brad tapped on the steering wheel of the truck and whistled as it zoomed over the back roads. The news truck was drawing startled looks from the Amish passersby, but there were few on the roads at that hour. Most were in fields or workshops at that time of day.

Brad consulted the directions the shop lady had given him, and to his relief, this time they were correct. As she had described, there was the King farm: an immaculate white farm house, surrounded by a green patchwork of garden plots and fields.

Brad pulled the truck into the long driveway to the farm, but to his surprise, there was already a car in the drive.

Even *he* knew that a car at an Amish house meant that *something was up*.

He pulled in behind the car and got out. There was movement on the farmhouse porch. The redheaded girl was standing there, looking even better than he remembered. But to his astonishment – and suspicion – the businessman he had seen at the store was there, too. He was gesturing earnestly toward the girl. Brad scrambled out of the car and strode up to the house.

"Hi there!" he called to her, putting up a hand. "Remember me? We met at the store yesterday, by accident. My name is Brad Williams."

He bounded up the porch steps and smiled big and bright. The girl's luminous green eyes met his doubtfully, and made his skin tingle in the places they swept.

The other man turned to him impatiently. "Look, kid, why don't you get out of here," he snapped. "This is none of *your* business, after all. This young lady was about to sell me my mother's clock." He stuck a handful of cash towards her.

For the first time, Brad noticed that the girl was holding the old clock that had fallen on the sidewalk. He frowned and looked up at her.

"Look, miss, I don't know you, but I came out here to ask you about this clock. Don't sell it just yet. Do you remember that when you dropped it, and the back popped open, that a paper fell out? I just wanted to ask you what it was. Have you looked at the paper?"

The girl frowned, and shook her head.

"Well," he added gently, "don't you think you *should* look at the paper, before you sell the clock? You never know. Sometimes little things like that turn out to be important." He shot a dry look at the other man. "Or *valuable!*"

"That clock is worthless to anybody but me," the businessman interjected. "I'm doing you a favor, young lady, by offering you a profit. I hope you don't plan to take advantage of the situation!"

Brad shot him an unfriendly glance. "You're awfully eager," he observed. "I wonder why?"

"Miss, we have an agreement," the other man said, in an irritated tone. "I expect you to honor your promise!"

She looked at him, and spoke for the first time. Brad was alarmed to discover that the sound of her voice was like velvet against his ear, and made it difficult to concentrate on what she was actually saying. He shook his head slightly, as if to recalibrate it.

"No, I didn't promise," she replied doubtfully. "You said you wanted to *see* the clock, and I told you I'd bring it out."

Her eyes moved back to Brad. "What do you want to ask me about it?"

His eyes lingered wistfully on hers. He smiled again, a bit crookedly. "I just want to know what the paper is."

"Why?"

"I work for a newspaper. There might be a story in it."

Instantly, he was conscious of having made a mistake. She pulled the clock to her chest, and for an instant he was afraid that she would run inside the house. She shook her head.

"No, I won't be in the paper. I won't have my picture taken!" she replied firmly.

Brad put up his hands. "Okay, I get it, I respect that," he answered quickly. "But can you at least just satisfy my curiosity? I'd really like to know what the paper is."

"You have no business being here at all!" the other man broke out savagely.

Brad met his glare steadily. "As much as you, friend," he replied through his teeth.

The girl looked first at the businessman and then back at him. Finally she looked down at the clock, and opened the back panel. A small, yellowed piece of paper fell out into her hands.

She unfolded it.

"It's a letter," she said simply and then frowned.

"From who?" Brad moved as close as he dared.

She was staring at the paper as if she couldn't believe her eyes. "*George Washington,*" she replied, in a stunned tone.

In spite of himself, Brad leaned over and snatched it out of her hands. He looked down at it in amazement. Sure enough, there was the signature. He raised his eyes to hers, and smiled apologetically as he handed it back.

"I'm sorry, miss, that was rude of me. It's just that – do you know how *valuable* this might be?"

"This is outrageous!" the other man exploded. "That clock belonged to my mother for years, and by rights, it belongs to me now! Take the money, and give me my clock!" He threw a handful of bills down at her feet.

With one swift step, Brad moved between the other man and the girl. "Hey, leave her alone!"

The other man suddenly stepped up and drew his fist back. The girl screamed, and Brad put up his arms to block the blow.

But he was spared the necessity.

A huge redheaded man suddenly loomed up behind the businessman, grabbed him by the shoulders, and flung him a good fifteen feet out onto the lawn. The man hit the ground rolling, scrambled up, fell, got up again, and ran for his life.

He jumped into his car. It roared to life and scratched off down the road in a frenzied cloud of dust.

Then the flame-haired giant turned around. He was wearing a grim expression that Brad had no trouble interpreting.

He eyes widened. He put up his hands. "Okay, I'm leaving. I am going *now*." He backed warily around the other man, and down the porch.

But as he left, he called out, "Miss, I'm telling you, you should have that letter appraised. If it's real, it could be worth a *fortune*! You might be rich —"

The older man made as if to come after him, and he turned and beat a hasty retreat.

But he turned at the car door and called out again. "*Have it appraised*!"

Then the big man came striding across the lawn after him, and he was obliged to beat the second hasty retreat of the morning.

CHAPTER EIGHT

Brad put a hand to his chest, and it reflexively fumbled for his shirt pocket before he remembered that he was trying to give up cigarettes, and that there were none there. He muttered under his breath.

His heart was still pounding from the adrenaline rush of a fight-or-flight morning, but it was also jumping with excitement. His instinct had been right: there *had* been a big story in that strange little clock.

He chewed his lip. Now if he could only get that girl alone, and convince her to have the letter appraised, it might be a story that could go viral. He could already see the headline: *Amish beauty strikes it rich.* Or maybe, *Local antique hides priceless find.*

Because that was probably the truth. Why else would that other guy have gone to so much trouble to track down an old, ugly clock? And why would anyone hide the letter in the first place, unless they *believed* at least that it was genuine?

He was already rehearsing his speech to Delores.

Delores, you won't believe what I just found.

No, that sounded eager.

Delores, I could be sitting on the biggest story this paper has seen for years.

His mouth twisted. She'd probably crack an obscene joke.

Delores, I have an intriguing lead. I want your okay to check it out.

Yes, that was better. She might go for that.

He reached for a cigarette again, didn't find one again, and mumbled in disgust.

"You *what?*"

Delores Watkins put her hand on one ample hip and tilted her head to one side in incredulous wonder.

"It could be *legit*, Delores. Think of it – a letter from George Washington, a national *treasure*, possibly worth hundreds of thousands of dollars, found in a local shop!"

"Are you crazy?"

"I saw it. It was on some kind of parchment-type paper, it was yellow, and the ink had gone brown. It looked *genuine*."

She closed her eyes, pursed her lips, and nodded her head. "Sure, sure. *Genuine*. Like the time you wanted to go with the story that the mayor might be descended from Teddy Roosevelt."

Brad looked away in irritation. "Can I help it if the guy falsified documents? And I wasn't the only one who believed him – it actually *ran* on Channel 3!"

Delores shook her head. "Let it be a lesson to you, to check it five times before you come to me." She turned and walked away.

Brad moved to keep pace. "And that's what I *want* to do with this story. I want the green light to follow up, to have it checked out. Let me go back there. If I can convince the girl to have the letter appraised, and it turns out to be genuine, we'll have something that could go *viral* online. If it's not genuine, who cares? It'll just be a few hours lost."

"*And* money. I'm assuming you want the paper to pay for this?"

"Hey, does the paper want me to work for free? I'm telling you, Delores, this could be huge. *I held the letter in my hand.*

The signature at the bottom read *George Washington*."

"And the tab on the back of my shirt reads *Valentino Tucci*. I bought it at a dollar store."

"Delores, just let me try. *Three days*. If she says no, I come back, and no harm done. If she says *yes –*"

His boss fixed him with ironic brown eyes. "--then we'll all be amazed," she finished sardonically. "Go back to your desk already, Brad. You're nuts."

Delores walked off, leaving him to stare after her. He bowed his head in frustration, and rubbed the back of his neck.

Then he looked up, and noticed that everybody else in the office was looking at him.

"Ah, shut up!" he mumbled good-naturedly, and giggling filled the room.

The next day, Delores Watkins looked up from her desk to see Brad Williams hovering over it.

"Delores, what if I foot the bill myself?" he asked, eyes on her face.

She looked up with a dry expression in her eyes. "I know what you make. You don't have *that* much money."

"I mean it. If I bomb, I eat the expense – the hotel, the

appraisal, everything. If I score – *metaphorically* speaking," he grinned "then the paper reimburses me for my expenses."

"That girl must be pin-up material," Delores observed, in an amused tone.

Brad flushed red, but rallied: "She's a gorgeous green-eyed redhead. She's photogenic as *he*– she's photogenic," he said quickly.

He leaned in close and hissed, "Picture the page views for *Amish Barbie Gets Rich*! I'm telling you, it will play like a Stradivarius, and all I have to do is get the confirmation that the letter is genuine. What do you have to lose?"

Dolores twirled a pencil between bright orange nails. "Okay, Romeo. Three days. Not that I believe it for a minute, but if you're willing to foot the bill – okay. *Go.* Knock yourself out."

Brad cracked a wide grin. "You love me, Delores -- admit it!" He leaned over and kissed her cheek.

She turned it toward him, but retorted, "I tolerate you. And guess what? I still expect you to finish your other assignments, while you're gone."

"I'm on it," he called, but was already backing out of the office. He pointed a jubilant finger at the older woman. "*You won't be sorry, Delores!*"

"I'm sorry already."

Brad hurried off to his desk and rummaged around in the upper drawer. He grabbed a thumb drive, and a camera.

Another reporter watched him with a jaundiced eye. "So Delores finally gave in, eh?"

"She knows I'm right," Brad told him.

"Fifty dollars says you'll strike out. No Amish woman is going to agree to meet a strange English man -- let alone a reporter!"

"You're on. And you're going to lose your money. You know why, my friend?"

The other man rested his chin on his hands. "Enlighten me."

"Because I'm going to help that girl get *rich*," he replied. He looked up and grinned. "*And* because women *love* me."

The other man threw an eraser at his head. "Get out of here!"

CHAPTER NINE

Brad closed the truck door, brushed the crumbs of his dinner off of his shirt, and surveyed the underwhelming exterior of Uncle Bob's Amish Motel. It was a long, low, red brick structure that looked as if was a remodeled '60s restaurant.

He sighed, locked the truck door, and went in.

The teenaged girl behind the counter was chewing gum and listening to an mp3. She brightened when he walked in, and pulled the earphones out.

"Hi, can I help you?" she smiled.

Brad dug out his wallet. "Yeah, I'd like a single room for three nights." He opened up the slender billfold and looked down at it despondently. "The chea— the most *economical* room available."

The girl dimpled at him, and consulted her computer screen. "I have a single room available for $50 a night, but it's next to the laundry room, and it may be noisy sometimes. Is that okay?"

"That's perfect. You have wi-fi, right?"

"Oh, yes."

He pushed a card across the counter, and her hand brushed his as she took it. She giggled and tossed her head slightly.

Brad glanced around. The lobby was spare, but looked clean, and the room beyond was, apparently, a *very* basic dining room. He tilted his head to the right. "Is breakfast included in the price of a room?"

"You get a Continental breakfast: coffee, juice, fruit and danish," she recited.

"That's great."

She handed him a receipt and a room key. "Your room is on the right, past the dining room. First turn to the left, and the fifth door on the left."

"Thanks."

"If you need anything, just call me," she sang out.

He smiled faintly, and waved.

When he opened the door to Room 205, he was greeted by the loud hum of an air conditioner, a blast of cold, and an aggressive floral scent that was certainly cheap air freshener. There was a single bed, neatly made, a desk with a chair, and a bathroom.

He walked to the desk and set up his laptop then pulled the curtains open with a *snap*. He was startled to see a black cow looking back at him. It stood there, eyeing him patiently, over the fence that separated the motel from the neighboring farm.

He unlocked the window and threw it open, and nodded to the cow. "Howdy there, bossy," he told it. "Got time for a few questions?"

The cow turned her head and looked off into the distance.

He nodded. "What is it with people around here, *hmm*? If I didn't know better, I'd say you were being unfriendly."

He plopped down on the bed, put his hands behind his head, and stared up at the ceiling.

Now that he had Delores's okay, the next step in his plan was to find a way to persuade that curvy redheaded girl to get the letter appraised.

He'd been so preoccupied with winning Delores over that he hadn't had time to think of much else, but he had to admit, the prospect of seeing that girl again was a distinctly pleasant one -- quite apart from the story.

Of course, getting her alone wasn't going to be easy.

He called her up again in his mind. Her eyes were the lightest, most startling green he'd ever seen. They were as big and beautiful as a cat's, ringed with thick black lashes, and slightly almond-shaped.

They stood out like – he couldn't think of the right words -- like *green jewels on white satin*.

He caught himself, and his mouth curled down. He was waxing *poetic*.

But still.

And the look in them had been so… soft. *Gentle*, that was the word.

He fumbled in his shirt pocket, and this time, there was a pack of cigarettes in it. He lighted one, and puffed contemplatively.

Yes, she was a beauty, all right.

Her dress seemed designed to cover up her figure – that Amish prudishness – but even so, it couldn't completely hide the fact that she was young, lissome, and graceful.

He blew a spout of smoke toward the ceiling.

But also, *extremely* shy. And guarded by an angry giant

who he assumed to be her father.

The memory of the man's expression gave him real pause. It didn't take a rocket scientist to know that if that guy caught him out there talking to his daughter, he was going to need his insurance plan.

But still, her father couldn't stay with her *all* the time. There had to be some window of opportunity, and he was determined to find it.

He frowned.

It was a beautiful place, that farm. Just setting aside what had happened there, or even that an uber-hot girl lived in it. It looked peaceful. Well-ordered.

And it was clear that the girl had a parent who was there all the time, and willing to protect her.

His face twisted. *Sweet setup.* Something like that would've been nice when *he* was a kid.

He crushed the cigarette butt into an ashtray.

If he could just find some way to get to that girl, to get her alone, he had a shot. She looked as if she'd be fairly pliable. If he could convince her that the letter might bring a lot of money, *and* that he'd pay the fee for the appraisal, she might agree.

The appraisal. He pulled his hands over his face. It was going to cost hundreds of dollars, money he didn't have.

But it was a risk he was willing to take.

Because if the letter proved to be real, it would make his name famous overnight and then maybe he could start getting the *real* assignments, and leave the boonies behind forever.

Wouldn't do that girl any harm, either.

Maybe then she'd be able to afford to see the real world, and get a life of her own.

CHAPTER TEN

Jemima clutched the clock to her chest, watching in consternation as the newspaper reporter twisted round in front of his truck and yelled to her:

"If it's real, it could be worth a *fortune*! You might be *rich*!"

She stared at him in amazement. To look at the stranger's expression, you would think that a tiny scrap of paper had created some terrible emergency – like the *world* was going to end somehow. Then her father had started toward him, and the young man had dived into the truck, cranked the motor, and drove off.

She watched the truck as it disappeared down the road, trailing dust.

Her father climbed the porch steps and paused in front of her. He put his big hands lightly on her shoulders.

"Are you all right, Mima?"

She looked up at him, and nodded mutely.

His whole body seemed to relax. He exhaled, and released her -- but planted his hands on his hips.

"Well, then, tell me -- *what* was *that*?"

She blushed, and shook her head. "I don't know, Daed. An English man wearing a fancy suit came out this morning asking to buy this clock –" she presented it to him – "the clock I bought in town, because he said it belonged to his mother. I went to get it, but before I could sell it to him, a newspaper reporter drove up and told me not to sell the clock, because it might be valuable."

Jacob King tilted his head to one side and studied at the clock doubtfully. "It looks plain enough to me," he observed, picking it up and turning it back and forth.

"Oh, but it's not the clock itself, Daed," Jemima said earnestly, "it's the letter that was hidden inside. *Look*." She handed the little yellowed note to her father.

He read it, and his frown deepened. He uttered a deep, skeptical grunt.

"Probably a prank of some kind. Pay it no mind, Mima." He handed the letter back to her. "The English are crazy, and greedy for money *always*."

He lifted his head, and gazed out over the fields in the direction that the strangers had fled. His expression darkened.

"But if any other Englishers come back, I want you to come and get me. *I'll take care of them*."

"Yes, Daed," Jemima murmured submissively.

"Now come and make me a sandwich, daughter," he told her, putting an arm around her shoulder. "Since my work has been interrupted, I may as well have my lunch now."

Jemima walked into the house arm in arm with her father. She set the clock down on the kitchen table, and the letter beside it then went to the refrigerator to make her father lunch.

Deborah walked in while she was doing it. Her quick eye fell at once on the clock.

"What's *that* ugly thing?"

Jacob turned to look at his youngest daughter with a warning glint in his eye. "That is the clock your sister bought for you with her own money, so you could have one to replace the one that broke," he told her sternly.

Deborah picked it up and flipped it contemptuously. "It'll probably be broken, too, in a few weeks," she complained. "It looks a hundred years old! I *never* get any new things!"

"Enough!" Jacob thundered, and stood up.

Jemima looked up at her father in dismay, and even Deborah knew better than to open her mouth when her father's good humor finally ran out.

"That's the last word of complaint from your mouth, Deborah," he boomed, "or next time, it won't be Scripture verses, but the *woodshed*! Don't think you're too old to be taken over my knee!"

Deborah shut her mouth with a snap.

"That's right!" her father told her sternly, and sat down, still glowering. "And because you spoke to your sister with disrespect, you can do her chores for the rest of the day."

Deborah's eyes looked as if they were ready to pop out of her head, but she remained silent. Jemima stared at her father in awed silence, and handed her sister the apron.

Rachel King came hurrying into the kitchen, drawn by the sound of her husband's voice. Her eyes went to his face, and she looked a question.

"I know what you're going to say, Rachel, and it won't work this time," he told her. "I've put up with the last bit of naughtiness from your daughter that I'm going to stand!"

"*My* daughter, Jacob?"

He looked at her, and the mild expression on her face seemed to weaken his resolve. "*Our* daughter."

She leaned over and kissed him, and he looked away, grumbling into his beard.

Rachel turned to Deborah.

"Deborah, you can make dinner tonight, too, as a reminder to watch your tongue," she said calmly.

Deborah swelled visibly, but one look at her father's simmering expression stifled the outburst.

Rachel's eyes moved to Jemima. "Jemima, you may do as you please until dinner is ready."

Jemima nodded, glanced almost fearfully at her younger sister, and moved to retrieve the clock, and the letter. She took them upstairs to her own room, and closed the door behind her.

She put the clock down on the little table beside her bed. Then she padded to the window and sank down on the floor in front of it.

She rested her head on the sill and unfolded the little letter. She hadn't had time to even read it. She had to admit that she *was* curious.

Flowing, graceful script covered the little page.

My Dearest Martha, it began, *Tonight I am thinking of our last words together before I left to begin this Great Adventure of which we are all a part. No words can express how keenly I felt the Ties between us, or how strong and entwining they are.*

Jemima put the note to her lips, smiling in surprise and delight. She had never expected a *love letter*.

A night does not pass that I do not see your Dear face when I close my eyes, or dream of you beside me. Though time and distance may part us, I feel your presence near me always, and the knowledge that your Thoughts are with me is my comfort in our present distress.

Jemima's mouth opened slightly. When and where he had written these tender words -- in a tent somewhere maybe – just before battle?

I leave to our God the outcome of our Great Struggle, and commend my soul to its Maker; but whether I go to Him tomorrow, or return to your dear side, know that your Name will be my last breath, and your face the last in my memory, when I close my eyes.

Yours ever,

G. Washington.

Jemima lowered the little note. Her mouth trembled, and

her eyes filled with tears.

It was beautiful.

Her eyes returned to the page. It was the soul of a man deep in love – a man who was unsure if he would live to see his sweetheart again.

She pressed it to her chest, closed her eyes and smiled. She imagined this man coming back to his home again, and his wife running to meeting him, laughing, arms outstretched.

Then she opened her eyes again, and looked back down at it.

Her father thought the letter was an English prank, a joke. But why would anyone make up such a letter, only to hide it away?

It was so tender, so loving. Did words like *these* come from a deceitful heart?

She ran her hand lightly over the paper. Wouldn't it be *wonderful*, if it was truly a love letter from George Washington, to his Martha?

She remembered her father's words -- but he hadn't commanded her to *destroy* the letter.

She got up from the window, and walked over to the opposite wall. She ran her fingernail over the wall panel, and pushed down on one point. A tiny bit of bead board popped out to reveal a hollow space.

Jemima placed the love letter into the secret space and smiled. She thought to herself that it might not really be genuine – but that she was going to keep it, *just in case*. She carefully replaced the cover.

She told herself that she might as well keep it secret. A calf-eyed love letter -- from *George Washington*? No one would ever believe her, if she told them!

Then she lay down on her bed, bit her fingertip and giggled.

CHAPTER ELEVEN

Jemima spent the next morning doing chores in the garden. Her mother had a vegetable patch that was an acre across, filled with the tomatoes and green peppers and onions and squash that their father loved, plus cucumbers for pickling, and pole beans.

She had a big basket, and was moving from row to row, harvesting vegetables for their meal.

A cool dawn had ripened into a perfect morning, not too hot, and slightly breezy. The air felt refreshingly cool for July, and the sky was filled with the billowy clouds of summer. Jemima shaded her eyes, thinking that they looked ripe, too – they were full and tall and blue-tinged, towering all the way to the edge of sight.

A voice from the house interrupted her reverie.

"Jemima!"

She put her basket down and smoothed her hair and skirt. It was Mark's voice.

"Here."

She could just see the top of his dark head on the other side of the garden. He waved, and came weaving through the rows of plants to reach her.

"How are you this morning?" he asked, smiling. "I haven't seen you in the last few days."

She looked down, and smiled. It felt *nice* to be missed.

"I was in town for the festival."

"You are coming to the sing this Sunday evening?"

She nodded, not looking up.

"Good. I was hoping we could talk."

She felt her cheeks going warm, but nodded again, and looked up. The shifting sunlight was moving over Mark's inky black hair, making it glisten blue.

His bright eyes were on her face. He stared at her for a long instant and then, to her surprise, he leaned over and kissed her. His lips were smooth and pleasantly warm, like the sun beaming through the dappled leaves. They moved over hers strongly, and with a steady pulse – like the thrumming of her own heart.

He took her chin in his hand. "I want to ask your Daed to court with you," he whispered. "Would you let me, Jemima?"

She looked up into his eyes. "I – I would, Mark. *But –*"

The sound of another voice calling made Mark straighten up suddenly.

"Mark Christner!"

It was her father's voice, calling urgently – and, it seemed to his daughter, a little suspiciously.

"Yes sir!"

Mark turned to her, and took her hand in his. "Remember, Jemima. This Sunday."

"I won't forget, Mark."

"Mark!"

"I have to go." He gave her a quick peck on the cheek then turned quickly and walked back to the house.

Jemima watched him go with a little smile playing on her lips. Mark was so sweet.

She put her fingers to her lips. She liked the way he *kissed,* too.

She shook her head, and smiled. She had meant to tell Mark that Samuel had asked to court with her, as well – but she hadn't had much of a chance.

She expected that Samuel would soon be coming by to ask her for *himself.*

She smiled again, and returned to her task.

She plucked handfuls of shiny, sugar-sweet tomatoes off of the vine and dropped them into her basket. She picked basil and rosemary from the little herb patch, and lifted a sprig to her nose.

She had almost filled up her basket when a strange sound startled her.

It was a *hissing* sound.

She looked around, but no one was there.

"Psst!"

She turned to look behind her, and almost screamed. The English reporter was *back* -- crouching in the bushes behind her!

"What are you doing here?" she cried, flushing in embarrassment. "And how long have you been hiding there!"

He stood up quickly, smiling. "I'm sorry, I'm not a stalker, I swear. It's just that this is the only way I could think of to talk to you again."

Jemima dropped the basket and began walking back toward the house. The man ran behind her.

"*Please,* don't run away – I'm not crazy, I'm a reporter. Look – here's my card!"

He hurried in front of her, and blocked her way.

She stopped dead, and her voice rose in panic. "If you don't leave me alone, *I'll call my father!*"

He was smiling, brows raised, his hands stretched out in a calming gesture. "There's no need for that! I'm going now. I just wanted to tell you that you need to get that letter appraised. It could be worth *hundreds of thousands of dollars.* I'm telling you, you might be rich! And I know where you can get it appraised. If you want to do it, I'll drive you there."

Jemima's eyes widened in terror. "I won't go anywhere with you!"

"My paper will *pay* to have the letter appraised. You don't even have to spend money, if you'll let me write a story about the letter. Just meet me back here on Monday, same time. I'll drive you to the appraiser's, and bring you back."

Jemima looked up into his face. His blue eyes were on fire with -- *something.*

His eyes flitted over her terrified expression, and he suddenly blurted: "I think you're the most beautiful woman I've ever seen in my life, and – and I don't even care about the letter, really. *Just let me see you again*!"

She screamed, picked up her skirts, and went flying towards the house.

He raised his eyes to the sky in despair, cursed himself, skipped backwards a few paces and then began to run.

CHAPTER TWELVE

Jemima bounded up the steps to the back porch, ran inside, and fled up the back stairs and into her own bedroom. She slammed the door behind her and leaned against it, heart pounding.

She closed her eyes. She had *never* been so frightened in her life!

Her bedroom window overlooked the garden, and she inched over to peer out, though she was careful not to show herself. To her relief, there was now no sign of the intruder.

She frowned, thinking that her father had been right: the English were crazy, every one of them, and greedy for money.

She shuddered, remembering the look in that reporter's eyes: like they were on *fire* with insanity.

She rolled her own to the spot where she had hidden the letter. That letter had caused her nothing but trouble since the day she had found it, even if it was sweet and touching, and possibly from George Washington.

Nothing was worth this much trouble.

She walked to the spot, and lifted the cover off of the hollow section. She grabbed the letter and took it in her hands, preparing to tear it into little pieces.

But the sound of her own name prevented her.

"Jemima!"

It was her mother calling.

"Jemima, you have a visitor!"

Her heart began pounding again, but this time with anger. She returned the letter to its hiding place, and opened the bedroom door.

If that crazy Englisher had come *inside the house*, she was going to call her father!

She ran swiftly downstairs, as outraged as she had ever been in her short life. But when she reached the living room, the person standing with her mother was only Samuel

Kauffman.

Jemima's mother turned to her with a smile, but it soon faltered. "Why, Jemima, what's wrong? You look as if you..." her voice trailed off.

Jemima looked down at the floor, suddenly conscious that her face must be advertising her anger. "Nothing," she said quickly. "I was just – I was –"

"Samuel has paid us a call," her mother intervened quietly. "Why don't you talk with him, while I make some sandwiches?"

Jemima looked up at Samuel, and he smiled at her.

She nodded mutely.

"Let's go out to the porch," Samuel suggested. "It's cool out there."

Jemima followed him. He settled easily on the swing, and patted the seat beside him. She smiled, trying to focus her thoughts, and joined him.

They began to swing gently, back and forth.

Samuel had his hands clasped in his lap. He looked over at her, serious now.

"Jemima, I talked to your father the other day," he said quietly. "I asked for his permission to court with you. He was kind enough to give it."

He reached over and took her hand in his warm, brown one.

"But what do *you* say, Jemima?"

"I – I would say *yes,* Samuel, but –"

There was a sudden rustling in the bushes below the porch, and Jemima jumped as if she'd been shot.

"*What was that?*" she cried, and put a hand to her mouth.

Samuel frowned, and turned his head to look. "It's... one of your mother's chickens."

Jemima closed her eyes and leaned back against the swing. "*Oh.*"

He searched her face, and added: "Is something *wrong,* Jemima?"

Her eyes flew open, and met his earnestly. "Oh *no,* Samuel, nothing's wrong! I'm *happy,* I am, but --"

His expression cleared. "Then, it's all right with you, that we court?"

"Oh, yes, but, there's something –"

The sound of footsteps on the porch steps interrupted her. Mark and her father had returned to the house.

Jemima looked over at them in trepidation. Mark's eyes were glued to Samuel's, and were filled with outrage; her father's were on her own face, and were at first puzzled then worried.

Her father spoke first. "Jemima, is something wrong?"

Samuel spoke first. "No, sir, she was just startled by a chicken, or something."

Mark burst out, "Is that right, Jemima?"

She went beet red, and her father interjected, sternly, "That's for *me* to ask." He turned to her and raised his brows.

"There – there was something in the bushes, it was nothing," she stammered, in confusion, "everything is all right now."

"*All right?*" Mark echoed incredulously, and she looked at him pleadingly.

"You heard her!" Samuel answered, and stood up.

Jemima put a hand up, appealing to them both: "Don't be so quick to –" she began, but Mark took a step toward Samuel, and Samuel closed the gap between them.

Her father quickly pushed between them and said in an exasperated voice, "The *both* of you, go home. Now! You two hotheads aren't going to disrupt the peace of this house. And in the future, if either one of you wants to court with my daughter, you'll behave yourselves respectful -- or you won't be coming back!"

Mark and Samuel glared at one another then looked away.

"That's right! Now get gone -- before I lose my own temper!"

Mark shot Jemima a reproachful glance, and Samuel a warning one then stormed out.

Samuel turned to her, and extended a hand. "Don't let him upset you, Jemima," he said seriously. "May I come back again?"

She looked up, and nodded.

He smiled, and his blue eyes sparkled. "I'll be counting the days," he told her, in a low voice, and seemed ready to say more, but her father's hand on his shoulder made his straighten.

"*Now.*"

CHAPTER THIRTEEN

That night Jemima lay in her bed, staring at the ceiling, until well past midnight. The hum of crickets wafted in through her window, but so far had not been able to soothe her to sleep.

It had been a terrible day. She had been accosted by a crazy and frightening stranger, Mark and Samuel had shown up at the house on the same day -- and at the same *time*. Mark was mad at *her* for seeing Samuel, and now they were both angry at each *other*.

The two of them *had* been good friends. She turned her face into her pillow.

And what about that letter, still hidden in the wall nook? The reporter kept telling her that she might be rich, but she could honestly say that she didn't care. All she had *ever* wanted was to live in peace with a good Amish husband, near her family and friends. If that dream came true, she neither needed nor wanted anything else.

But clearly, the reporter did. *He wanted that letter.* That thing he had said about wanting to see *her,* about thinking she was *pretty,* she dismissed as a trick to get it.

A new thought came to her. What if she just – *gave* it to him?

Yes, she could just *give* it to him. Then he and everyone else who might want it would go away forever, and *leave her alone.*

Her spirits rose, only to be quenched by a new thought. *How would she get it to him?*

She tried to remember the name of the paper he said he worked for, but she couldn't.

She sighed. There was only one other alterative – to try to forget that the whole ugly incident ever happened, and to call her father if the English fellow ever showed his face to her again.

She sighed and nestled into the pillow. She had no doubt that her father would convince him to *mind his own business.*

The next morning was fair and clear and sunny. Jemima took up her basket, and resumed her usual chore in her mother's garden – gathering vegetables for the day's meal.

She hesitated to go to the same spot where the Englisher had ambushed her. She was reasonably certain that he wouldn't try a second time, but even so.

She ventured as far as the last row of pole beans, but only on the side nearest the house, so that if he was crazy enough to come back, she'd have a clear path back.

She scanned the bushes narrowly, but there was no sign of an intruder.

She picked fuzzy green bean pods and red peppers, and was about to move to the lettuce patch when something in her peripheral vision caught her eye.

She jumped, and rolled frightened eyes towards the house – but it was just a little spot of white lying on the grass.

She looked at the bushes again, and moved to take a closer look.

She bent down to pick it up. To her surprise – and relief – it was a business card. It read:

Brad Williams

Reporter, Ledger-Inquirer

bwilliams@ledger.com

There was also the phone number, and the newspaper's address.

Jemima breathed a silent prayer, and tucked the little piece of paper into her apron. Now that she had the man's address, she could mail the letter to him, and The Nightmare of the English Letter would be over.

She turned back to the garden patch, and began humming.

That evening, when she had closed her bedroom door, Jemima sat down at a little table, took a sheet of paper, and began to write her letter.

Dear Mr. Williams, she began, *I do not want this letter, and I do not like people coming to my house without my permission because of it. If you want this letter, I will give it to you. I have no need to be rich, so you can be, if you want to be.*

Please do not come to my house again, or send anybody else.

Sincerely,

Jemima King

P.S. Or I will tell my father that you are there.

She folded the letter neatly. Then she picked up the old,

yellowed letter and tucked it carefully inside the first one, and slid them both into an envelope.

She sat back in her chair and sighed in satisfaction. She would go to the post office and mail it the next morning.

She propped the letter on the table, turned down the lamp, and went to bed, where she slept soundly for the first time in days.

CHAPTER FOURTEEN

August bloomed fine and fair and hot, and though her mother's garden was in riotous bloom, heavy with melons and berries and ripening corn, Jemima was still no closer to a harvest in her own heart.

She still couldn't decide who she loved the most, out of so many. Mark and Samuel had redoubled their efforts, and shy, adorable Joseph Beiler was beginning to send her love letters.

"Jemima!"

Deborah came striding out to her, holding an envelope in her hands. "Here, Jemima," she said in a disgusted voice, "another page of *puke poetry* from Joseph Beiler."

"*Deborah!*" Jemima chided her, but her irritable younger sister was already on her way back to the house.

She looked down at the envelope. *Poor Joseph,* she thought sadly, as she tore it open. He *did* try, and it was the thought that counted, but no one was ever going to mistake him for a...

She opened the letter and was struck-staring in amazement.

The letter wasn't from Joseph Beiler at all.

It was from that Englisher, *Brad Williams!* She put a hand to her mouth and read the letter in shocked disbelief.

Dear Miss King, it read, *I have taken the liberty of showing your letter to a reputable appraiser, and he in turn has shared it with several experts on Revolutionary War documents. I have enclosed his report on the letter you sent me. I hope you will read it, because I think will please you to know the truth about your find.*

Jemima flipped the letter over. There was another letter beneath it, on very heavy, official-looking paper. The letterhead read: *Cheever and Cheever Appraisers, Philadelphia.*

Her eye skimmed quickly down the page.

Dear Ms. King, the letter read, *It is our great pleasure to inform you that the letter that was presented to us by Mr. Williams is, in our opinion, a genuine and previously unknown letter from George Washington to his wife, Martha.*

Jemima batted tears from her eyes, and hurried on.

It is well known that after George Washington's death, his wife burned his correspondence to her in an effort to preserve their privacy, and letters such as yours are, therefore, exceedingly rare.

While it is, of course, impossible to arrive at a precise value, since we consider the letter a priceless piece of Americana, we are willing to hazard a conservative estimate that it could bring a million dollars or more at auction.

Jemima went completely still. For a few long seconds, she could scarcely feel her own pulse.

If you should wish to put the letter up for sale, we would be happy to help you. At Mr. William's request, our bank is holding the letter for you in its vault for safekeeping, and it is available to you at any time.

Please advise us as how you wish us to proceed, and congratulations.

With warm regards,

Jonathan Cheever

The page fell back from her nerveless hand. She returned

to the first letter, the one from Brad Williams. It read:

Thank you for offering to give me the letter, but as I told you earlier, my interest is in the story.

I would be very honored if you allowed me to tell this story for my paper, the Ledger. If you wish, I will not take any pictures of your face, or of your other family members. But I am convinced that our readership, and America at large, will be delighted by your good fortune, as I am myself.

Congratulations, and I hope to speak with you again. I have enclosed my number, if you would like to call. Should you choose to talk to me, I will be staying at Uncle Bob's Amish Motel for three weeks. You can send word to me there, if you like.

Cordially,

Brad Williams

Jemima dropped the letter and just stood there in the sunshine for several minutes. Then she looked up at the sky and spread out her hands in a wordless appeal.

She crushed the papers to her chest, bowed her head, and prayed hard.

Because she had the feeling that her life was never going to be the same.

THE END.

Thank you for Reading!

I hope you enjoyed reading this as much as I loved writing it! If so, there is a sample of the next book in the next chapter. You can find the whole book in eBook and Paperback format at your favorite online book distributors.

All the best,

Ruth

AN AMISH COUNTRY TREASURE 2

CHAPTER ONE

Jemima waited until night had fallen and the moon began its slow arc across the sky. When its smiling silver face appeared in the corner of her bedroom window, when the house had been quiet for hours, and when everyone else was asleep – she crept downstairs and out onto the front porch.

The moon was so bright that it cast shadows across the front yard, and the crickets hummed invisibly from the meadow.

Jemima sat down on the porch steps and looked out across the soft darkness, fragrant of mown grass and roses. She had always come to this spot as a child when she had been confused or upset because it was safe and quiet, and a good spot from which to watch the stars.

She looked up into the infinite night sky and questioned it

with her eyes.

The George Washington letter was worth a million dollars – that was what the experts had said. And she'd been sure that once she'd given it to him, Brad Williams, the Englischer reporter, would've grabbed the letter and run. She'd been sure that he'd have sold it and gotten rich and never bothered her again.

But he hadn't done that.

She was still in shock.

Instead – unbelievably – he had thrown it right back into her lap.

Jemima had a fleeting suspicion that his gesture might still be some clever reporter's trick, but what could he hope to gain by giving the letter back – and giving up a fortune?

She had been taught to be wary of the Englisch, but what could she say when the Englisch fellow could simply have taken the million dollars – and yet chose instead to give it back to her? Who would ever have guessed that an Englischer could pass up the chance to be rich?

A strange tingling danced down her neck. What if the Englisch reporter really did mean what he said about wanting to see her again – for her own sake?

She pressed her brow against her arms. But of course, that was impossible, and would be wrong, anyway. He wasn't

Amish, and so they had nothing in common.

Her thoughts returned to the thick, official-looking letters from the appraisers. They were a secret that she'd tucked away in the little hidden space behind her bedroom wall. She had told no one about them, not even her mother.

The ghost of a smile played across her lips. No matter what else happened, she was glad that the love letter itself had turned out to be real. It had been so sweet – so much the words of a man in love. Who would have thought it?

She wondered briefly if Martha Washington had been as pierced by its beauty as she had been herself.

Wouldn't it be wonderful to have a husband who wrote you such letters?

She looked up at the sky, and just because there was no one there but her and God, and because there wasn't another soul awake within miles, she allowed herself to dream.

A tiny star trembled in the unfathomable distance and she watched it wistfully. If only there was a man who would tremble like that when she kissed him.

And who would tell her about his feelings so she didn't have to guess!

She closed her eyes. That was why the letter had been so beautiful. It had been written by a lover, not just a husband. A man who knew how to make himself vulnerable. A man who was strong enough to risk showing his heart without any attempt to protect it.

There were many boys who were willing to chase her, to kiss her, and do things for her. But not one of them, so far at least, had been willing to be naked in front of her – emotionally naked – and wasn't that what it truly meant to be intimate?

Wasn't love all about becoming vulnerable? Wasn't that…how you knew what it was?

That was what she dreamed of, at any rate: a man who was strong enough to let love make him vulnerable. Who would open his heart and share his feelings. And none of the boys who were chasing her had made the faintest attempt. Clearly, that was because they didn't know that was what she really wanted.

But if she told them, then they'd all say what she wanted to hear, and she'd never know if it had been real or not.

Jemima opened her eyes. She knew that Mark and Samuel and Joseph were all capable of making themselves vulnerable to her. Maybe they were just too busy competing with each other to notice that she was looking for a man who knew how to lose his heart.

Not win a contest.

She sighed.

But, of course, that was just wishful thinking. Her mother had told her many times that romance was not the same as happiness, and Jemima knew that she was right. A man's integrity – his devotion to God and to his family – was what really made him a good husband.

And that was what made it so hard to choose between Mark and Samuel and Joseph. They were all good, they all had integrity, they all loved God and they would all be good providers.

And since they were all equally good, and all of them would likely make good husbands – would it be sinful of her to hope that she could find one who would make a good lover, as well?

Her mouth turned down gently. Not one, so far, had even told her that he loved her.

She had no doubt that all of them did – but they were Amish boys, and had been raised to show rather than tell.

Mark especially. She knew that he would do anything on earth for her, but he wasn't one to talk about it. Her lips curved, as she remembered all the ways he had shown her that he loved her: he never let her carry anything, he gave her candy and bites of his lunch and little gifts he had made with his hands – a carved wooden box, a tiny bird made out of copper wire, and pressed flowers. But Mark felt deeply, she knew.

And Samuel – he was far more likely to kiss her, than to murmur sweet nothings in her ear. But sometimes he looked at her with so much love in his eyes that it wasn't really necessary to hear the words. They were all there – right on his face. And when he took her hand, his touch was so tender and gentle that she would have had to have been a fool not to know that he loved her.

Joseph Beiler had big, melting brown eyes and thick dark hair and was as handsome as any movie star. But he was so shy that he was hardly able to string two words together in front of her – poor Joseph! Then he tried to make up for it by writing her poetry. She made a face, remembering his last effort: he had compared her to a beautiful cow. Her sister Deborah had been rude, but right: Joseph's heart was pure, but he was a terrible lover.

She looked up at the stars wistfully. Just now and then, it would be so nice to have a boy tell her what he felt when he looked at her. To let her see inside his heart.

And it wouldn't hurt at all, if he did it well.

Jemima brushed a tendril of hair out of her eyes. Her mother had told her many times that it was foolish to have your head turned by flowery words and pretty gestures.

"A good man shows love by what he does, Jemima," had been her teaching. "Not by what he says."

Jemima frowned. Her mother's wisdom had seemed so

clear and right just a few days ago, and she knew that it was the truth. But even so, she was confused.

Because by that reasoning, her childhood friends and current suitors weren't the only ones who loved her. A strange Englisch reporter that she hardly knew had just shown her love.

Sort of.

And that made no sense at all.

CHAPTER TWO

Five o'clock came far too early the next morning, at least for Jemima King.

She dragged herself out of bed while it was still dark, dressed, and helped her mother cook breakfast; but she nodded over the stove as she cooked the eggs.

"Mind your hand, Jemima!" her mother cried sharply, and Jemima jerked her fingers back just in time to keep them from being burned on the hot metal. "Good heavens, child, you're sleepy! Didn't you get your rest?"

Jemima looked up at her apologetically. "No, I-I didn't get enough sleep last night," she confessed, blushing.

"Are you feeling all right?" her mother frowned, and put a hand to her cheek.

Jemima nodded, and the cloud lifted from her mother's brow. "Well, you must go to bed earlier tonight," she told her.

"Now help me set out breakfast. We can't be late for worship."

It was a Sunday morning, and worship was being held at the home of Aaron Kauffman, Samuel's father. It was on the far side of their church district, and it would therefore be necessary to get an early start.

Jemima set out a platter of sliced ham, and a bowl of biscuits, and fried potatoes. She was grateful when it came time to sit down, but she wondered how on earth she would ever stay awake through a two-hour sermon when she was starting out so tired.

Jacob King came walking in, stretching and yawning. "Good morning, my girls!" he told them, and leaned over to give their mother a peck on the cheek. "Ready for worship? It's a fine, fair morning, and not too hot. Are we set to eat?"

Rachel nodded, and sat down quickly. They all said a silent prayer, and then ate. Everyone but Jemima seemed to be in a good mood. Even Deborah wore a neutral expression through the meal, and for her that was as good as a smile.

But Jemima was worrying about the letter and chewed her thumbnail instead of her food. She could hardly concentrate on eating, wondering what on earth she was supposed to do now that she owned a document worth a million dollars. Nothing like that had ever happened to anyone she knew, or to anyone she had ever even heard about. What was she supposed to do now?

It felt sinful and greedy to keep such a thing. Surely such an important letter should be in a museum somewhere, not hidden away in a bank vault in her name.

But it would also feel sinful and greedy to sell it. A million dollars! What would an Amish girl like her even do with all that money? She already had all she needed, and it wasn't right to want more than that.

But, on the other hand, she had already tried to give it away, and to her total amazement that hadn't worked.

"Jemima!"

Jemima came to herself with a start. When she looked up, everyone at the table was staring at her.

"I-I'm sorry, I was-I was daydreaming," she stammered.

"About one of those silly pups, I suppose," her father replied, shaking his head. "Never mind, Mima! Just come along. It's time to get on the road."

Jemima followed them as they left. She climbed up into the buggy, and settled into the back seat, and watched the passing countryside without seeing it.

Maybe she should ask her parents what to do. But she dreaded the scolding they were sure to give her about talking to the Englisch reporter in the first place.

Then, too, if she told them what had happened, it would be the end of her own choice in the matter: they would forbid her to talk to any Englischer, ever again, as long as she lived.

And she would never find out if the Englisch reporter had meant what he'd said – or not.

She nibbled off another corner of her nail.

When they arrived at the Kauffman's home, she drifted alongside her family, nodding in response to greetings and keeping her eyes on the ground.

But soon Samuel appeared at her elbow, looking love at her out of those beautiful blue eyes.

"I missed you," he smiled, and a tender look was on his face. "Is your family staying for lunch, Jemima?" he asked in a lower voice. "I was hoping you and I could talk somewhere privately afterwards."

She looked up at him, and was about to answer, when her father noticed them. "Good morning, Samuel!" he said loudly. He clapped Samuel on the shoulder, pushed right in between them, and smiled broadly. "Beautiful morning, isn't it?"

"Yes, sir," Samuel replied, much less enthusiastically.

"And so much friendliness, everywhere I turn!" he added, shaking Samuel's shoulder. Samuel looked up at him with a chagrined expression.

"Jemima, go and find your mother and sister a place to sit and hold it for them," her father commanded, and she nodded submissively. She shot Samuel an apologetic look over her shoulder, and was grateful to see that his eyes were still fastened to hers.

But when she looked back again, just before entering the Kauffman's barn, she saw with a sinking heart that her father was talking earnestly to Samuel, and that her handsome blond admirer looked as though he'd been rained on.

She found a nice empty spot at the end of a bench, and waited for her mother and sister.

And sighed.

Soon her mother and Deborah arrived and settled in beside her, and the benches began to fill up. Jemima noticed Samuel took a seat just across from them on the front row of the men's benches. His eyes were on hers, and she smiled at him faintly. His eyes sparkled, and he winked at her – just once. It was over like lightning, and she doubted that anyone else even saw it. She lowered her head, to hide her laughter, but when she looked up again, she noticed that her father's eyes were on her and she assumed a more pious expression.

The service started with the singing of hymns, and after they were over, the sermon. The minister opened his Bible and began talking.

Jemima felt herself beginning to zone out. She was sleepy, she was confused about the letter, and she was distracted by Samuel. Because now and then, when she looked up, he would catch her eye. And do something silly.

Like flick his tongue out over his lower lip, like a snake. And she would have to lower her head again and try not to laugh.

Or roll his eyes up toward the ceiling, as if he were about to pass out. That time, she had to bite her lip to keep from laughing.

But eventually her father noticed where she was looking and gave Samuel such a freezing look that he had to stop playing.

The preacher talked and talked, and to Jemima it seemed that the sermon would never end. But at some point, after she had gotten quiet and had settled down, the words that the preacher was saying started to reach her.

He was talking about being a good Christian, and how that meant being kind to the poor. Jemima sighed and crossed her legs and looked through a window at the beautiful summer afternoon outside. She had heard this many times before.

But suddenly he raised his Bible in the air, and said:

"What if a miracle happened? What if I suddenly had a million dollars and yet kept it all for myself? What kind of a Christian would let a neighbor stay hungry? Or cold, or sick, if he had the power to help him?"

Jemima gasped, and rolled stricken eyes to the man's face. He was looking right at her.

"It's the duty of a Christian to do as Jesus would do," the man said earnestly. "And Jesus fed the hungry, and took care of the sick."

Jemima's eyes filled with quick tears.

"If we follow Jesus, we must do those things, too."

Jemima felt herself going hot. She lowered her face, to hide the tears in her eyes.

The man's words had pierced her heart like a sharp arrow. It was like God had spoken through him, straight to her.

She had prayed to God, asking Him what she should do with the letter. And she hadn't heard any answer.

Until now.

Now it was crystal clear. This, this was her answer: she was to sell the letter, and give the money to people who needed it.

It answered everything. She would not be selfishly hiding the letter away; she would not be greedily spending the money on herself. The money could be used to feed her hungry neighbors, and help those who were sick and needed medical help.

And that would even explain why the Englischer had given the letter back to her against all reason: it had plainly been the will of God – a miracle.

She lifted her eyes to the ceiling and put her palms up, in a gesture of pure gratitude to God. She mouthed silent words of worship, and smiled to herself.

And when she opened them again, she noticed that Samuel Kauffman was staring at her face. The silly look was gone.

His eyes were dead serious now. And the look in them was that of a man who would run through fire.

CHAPTER THREE

After the service, there was always a light lunch served inside the house and outside on the lawn. Jemima, like all the other girls, helped serve her elders until it was her own turn to dine.

It was a fine, clear morning with a blue sky and green grass and white tablecloths and people talking and laughing. Many of Jemima's elders greeted her pleasantly as she brought plates or pitchers to their tables.

Most of the boys stole shy glances at her face. She dimpled, and smiled at them, and watched in amusement as their faces went pink.

Afterwards, she joined her family and listened in dutiful

silence as her father and their next-door neighbor talked crops. When she let her gaze wander, she noticed that Samuel was sitting at a table nearby. He was hard to miss when he took his hat off, his blond hair shone like corn silk against his black jacket. She noticed some of the other girls looking at him when he turned away, and she felt a little glow of gratitude. She was a lucky girl to have such a handsome young man pursuing her.

And he was pursuing her. It didn't take him long to sense her eyes on him. He smiled, and then got serious again and looked at her with such frank intent that she felt herself going hot. Samuel had beautiful blue eyes, and they expressed every feeling going through his heart as clearly as any sign.

She looked at him through her lashes. That was Samuel's charm – his glib laughter, and his carelessness, was all an act. He couldn't hide his true feelings – his eyes betrayed him every time.

And what his eyes were saying to her at the moment was probably best not said in a room full of people.

Jemima smiled faintly, well pleased, and dropped her own gaze demurely.

After everyone had eaten lunch, and she was free, Samuel appeared at her elbow. He whisked her away with him so quickly that even her father – who was talking to a neighbor about horseshoes – didn't have time to see them go.

Samuel took her hand and led her down a tortuous path that twisted crazily through a side door, down a few steps, through a narrow doorway, up a few stairs, and into a small sitting room in a hidden corner of their house.

Then he closed the door behind them and pulled her into his arms without another word.

Jemima went into them without a murmur and turned her face up to be kissed.

Samuel pulled her to his chest, twined his strong fingers in hers, pressed both hands behind her back, and kissed her with delicious tenderness. He was a delightful kisser – his lips seemed made for light, playful caresses, and he would pause mid-pucker sometimes, to pull back and look down at her until she opened her eyes. Then he would go on quirky kissing tangents, one kiss on each of her closed eyelids, lots of little kisses along her brows, and he might even plant a few stray kisses in the delicate, sensitive spot under her ear.

She giggled suddenly, and shook her head. "Oh, Samuel, that tickles," she laughed, turning her face away teasingly. "Didn't you shave your chin this morning?"

He looked down at her with a smile, and rubbed it with one brown hand. "Now that you mention it," he admitted ruefully, and his smile widened to a grin. "Tell me, does the scruffy look do anything for me?" He turned his profile, and she giggled again.

Then the smile faded from his lips. A serious look replaced them,

He pulled back, taking both her hands in his. "Jemima, I brought you here because I wanted to talk to you alone. I have something to say to you."

She held his gaze, waiting.

An uncharacteristic wave of shyness seemed to overwhelm him. "We-we've known each other a long time," he stammered.

"Yes, Samuel." She smiled, remembering the first time she had seen Samuel: he had been a mischievous little five-year-old boy making mud pies. He had looked up at her suddenly, his blue eyes and blond hair in stark contrast to a face covered in black mud. She had screamed and run away, and he had chased her.

He seemed to read the thought off her face. He relaxed a bit, and chuckled. "Yes, we go way back, don't we, Mima?" he said softly.

She looked up into his eyes and nodded, giving him her earnest attention.

"You know what kind of person I am, and I hope you feel about me, the same way I feel about you."

He massaged her hand gently, and half-smiled.

"After all – I asked to court with you, and you agreed."

Jemima's heartbeat quickened. She leaned in and looked deep into his beautiful eyes. Maybe Samuel was finally going to show her his heart. He might even tell her that he loved her.

And since he seemed to be shy, maybe she could help things along and give him a little nudge. Maybe she could gently remind him that there were other boys who might be willing to admit they loved her.

Maybe then he would confess his love, and pour out his heart, and make himself vulnerable – like in that magical letter.

She took a deep breath. "Yes, Samuel, we have been good friends. I agreed to see you. Not to see just you, but to go out. Just like you can see other girls, and not just me."

He raised his eyes to hers, and the look in them now was determined. Jemima's pulse quickened in anticipation. He was going to tell her he loved her at last. He was going to say it.

"I don't want to go out with any other girls, Jemima. And I don't want you to go out with any other men."

She held his eyes. "Why not, Samuel?" she asked gently.

Samuel looked pained. "Jemima, I-I–"

There was suddenly a thunder of pounding feet outside, and two little girls burst into the room, laughing and giggling.

"Abby, you're it!" shrieked a little pigtailed girl. "I caught you!"

"Count to ten!" the other one cried, and pressed herself against the wall. "One two three four…"

The pigtailed girl streaked out into the hall, only to collide with her outraged mother. "Ruth Beiler, stop that this instant! The noise you make – this isn't our house!"

She looked in and caught sight of the other child. "Abby Stoltzfus, is that you? Come out now, and stop this nonsense!"

The child obeyed in subdued silence, and the woman finally noticed Jemima and Samuel standing there. She looked embarrassed.

"Oh – I'm sorry," she murmured, and hustled the children out, but not before casting another curious, and frankly speculative glance at them.

After the door had closed behind the intruders, Samuel ran a hand through his rumpled blond hair, looked up at the ceiling, and then down at Jemima with a rueful sigh.

Jemima could have cried in frustration. There had been a confession trembling on Samuel's very lips, and it was slipping away – she could feel it. She pressed her hands against his chest.

"Oh Samuel, never mind them," she said earnestly, "you

were going to tell me something. Don't hold back – I'm listening! Tell me now."

He smiled, gave a self-deprecating shrug, and cupped her cheek with his hand. "Mima," he said tenderly, "I–"

He leaned close. Jemima searched his eyes with her own, but to her disappointment, no tender confession followed.

Unless she counted the gentle, softly rhythmic kiss that communicated so much.

And admitted exactly nothing.

CHAPTER FOUR

A week passed, in which Samuel called at the house again and used his handsome lips to kiss her much and confess little; Mark called at the house also, and also kissed her much, and told her even less; and Joseph mailed three regrettable pages of poetry in which he compared her to a large chicken, though she was fairly sure he was trying to say that she would make a good wife, in a very roundabout way.

She hadn't had much time to think about the letter, but the memory of it nagged at her. She had received what she believed to be direction from God to sell it, and the proper thing to do now was to call that Englisch reporter and get it over with.

But she dreaded it.

She counted it sheer Divine Intervention that he hadn't kept the letter for himself. That must surely be it, because she had no confidence in the fellow's ethics, or, to be honest, his sanity. He'd behaved like a madman the first day she met him. And his behavior hadn't improved – the last time she'd seen him, he'd jumped at her from the bushes in her mother's garden, like a wild animal.

He even pretended to be interested in her, though they were total strangers.

Still, it was her duty to sell the letter, and she supposed she'd better get on with it and have done. And since the crazy Englischer was the only person she knew that could help her, she guessed she ought to call him up.

Of course, it would all be very awkward, and not at all proper. As an Amish woman, she was not supposed to talk to Englischers and Englisch men in particular. But in a case like this, what other choice did she have?

She couldn't think of any other choice, anyway. But once the letter had been sold, and she had the money, no one would have to know what she'd done. She would just be an anonymous donor to people who needed help.

There was one possible problem, though: the Englisch reporter had said he wanted to write a story about her. That part did worry her. But since she didn't intend to see him again if she could help it, she supposed it would be all right to tell him her story over the phone.

There was little danger that her family and friends would ever find out. No one she knew read Englisch papers or visited their websites.

She sat on the porch swing, shelling beans into a big metal bowl. She still had the little card the reporter had given her. She could go out to the little phone shack at the end of their driveway and call. She would tell the Williams fellow to go ahead and put the letter up for auction.

Maybe she wouldn't even have to see him again at all. Maybe she could just tell him to take pictures of the letter, and tell him her story over the phone and tell him not to share her name.

Yes, that was it! She would give him permission to tell the story but not use her name. Then no one, not even the people who read the story, would ever know it was her.

Yes, that would be perfect. She smiled to herself, comforted by the belief that even if she had to do some unusual things at first, everything would be all right in the end.

Jemima put her plan into action early the next day.

At sunrise, she sat patiently on a small bench in the phone

shack. The phone rang and rang…four times, five, six.

She wondered why the Englischer didn't answer his phone. He had written that he was staying at the motel outside of town. Surely he was up by now – it was almost 6 a.m., and the sky had been light for almost an hour.

After the tenth ring, there was a fumbling sound, and a clunk, and more fumbling. A bleary, irritable voice snapped:

"Very funny, Delores! Six o'clock in the morning! I'm reporting you to Dapper Dwayne for employee abuse. He'll be sending you a list of my grievances."

Jemima frowned. "I must have the wrong number," she stammered, and prepared to hang up the phone.

There was a frantic fumbling sound on the other end, followed by: "No, no, um, yes, this is Brad Williams. I'm sorry – is this – is this Miss Jemima King?"

Jemima frowned. He was babbling like a lunatic, and she was seized by the urge to hang up the phone and forget the whole thing. But the remembrance of the sermon she had heard spurred her to take a new grip on her resolve.

She took a deep breath. "Yes, it is."

"Ah! Ah, I apologize, Miss King. I, ah, mistook you for someone else."

She set her mouth, and replied firmly: "I'm giving you permission to sell the letter for me. You can give it to those people, and they can put it up for auction."

"Wonderful! I'd be delighted to help you! Would you be open to meeting me in town and letting me drive you out to the auction house?"

Jemima frowned into the receiver. His voice sounded absurdly excited. She shook her head, thinking: Greed.

"I'm not going to meet with anybody," she told him firmly, "and I'm not going to the auction house, and I'm not going to get my picture taken. But if you want to ask me questions, I'll tell you about how I found the letter. But only if you don't use my name or my family's name."

"Ah." There was a split-second of silence, followed by: "I ah, appreciate that, Miss King! I would absolutely like to ask you questions about how you found the letter! Maybe I could come out to your house, it would only be for a–"

She shook her head vehemently. "No, I don't want anyone to come out to my house!"

"Okay, I understand," he replied quickly. "We can do it over the phone! I'll call you the day before the sale – when everything is ready."

"I'll call you," she told him.

"Or, you could call me," he amended quickly.

Jemima looked out the window toward the house. She only had a few minutes.

When she returned to the conversation, the reporter was saying, "Call me at this same number next Monday, about noon. I'll walk you through the small print, because there are some legal formalities. In order for us to sell the letter, you'll have to fill out some forms, and give the auction house your written permission to sell."

Jemima frowned. "Will they keep my name a secret?"

"If you want that."

Jemima nodded. "I do."

"I, ah, the appraisers recommended Brinkley's, is that all right with you?"

"Who's Brinkley?"

There was a long silence. "Ah...I'm sorry...Brinkley's is the auction house."

"As long as they keep my name private, and don't come out to the house or bother my family, I don't care who sells it," Jemima answered.

She looked up and saw her father standing on the front lawn with his hands on his hips. He was looking for her. Rufus was hitched to the buggy, and it was time to go back to Mr. Satterwhite's with the batch of dolls that she'd promised him.

"I have to go," she said suddenly. "I have to go to town."

"Wait – I mean, is it all right if I mail the documents to your home? You'll have to–"

But Jemima was no longer paying attention. Her father had stumped off to the garden, and she knew that once he missed her there, he'd be coming in the direction of the phone shack.

And she couldn't afford to be caught in it.

She dropped the phone and decamped, hoping that she could reach the lawn before her father returned.

Meanwhile, the phone receiver swung back and forth, as the reporter's tiny, agitated voice spooled out uselessly into the air.

CHAPTER FIVE

Delores Watkins nursed a large cup of steaming black coffee between two large, brightly-manicured hands. The rays of the rising sun dawned through the office window behind her. They tinged the back of her large brown bouffant hairdo like an orange halo, and glimmered off the backs of her earrings.

A green box suddenly appeared on her computer screen. She cursed softly and fluently, put her coffee cup down, and gingerly placed a headset on her carefully-coiffed hair.

"Hello?"

Brad William's voice was already running, non-stop, on the other end. She rolled her eyes up toward the ceiling.

"Stop. Stop, Brad. It's too early. What? No, slow down."

She lifted the cup and took another sip, frowning.

"So, she did call you. Congratulations.

"You promised her you'd do what? Now wait a minute. Yes, it's good; it has the potential to be – yes, yes. But you represent the Ledger. I can't just let you go running off to the most prestigious auction house in the country without–"

She took another sip.

"Yes, I was implying that. And posturing will get you nowhere.

"I never said no. But we're going to have to talk to Dapper Dwayne and do a little legal CYA before I'll even think about letting you call the auction house.

"I don't care.

"Cry me an ocean, Brad.

"Okay, you're lucky that I don't can you for that. Remember that there are plenty of other guys who'd be glad to --

The little box disappeared from the screen, and Delores rolled her eyes and removed the headset. Her assistant entered the room just then, saw her face, and looked at her quizzically. She shrugged and smiled.

"It was Brad on the phone," she explained.

The young woman grinned, and put a folder on her desk. "Oh. What is it this time?"

Delores took another pull from the coffee cup. "Oh, nothing.

"The kid may have the biggest story of the year – that's all."

Back at Uncle Bob's Amish Motel, Brad Williams was coming to much the same conclusion.

He sat on the edge of the motel bed, wearing nothing but a pair of boxer shorts. He held his head in his hands, and his mind was racing.

Delores was infuriating, but upon mature reflection, he had to admit that she was right to be cautious.

Because he couldn't be.

He had the mother of all feature stories. All he had to do was reel it in. Once they'd cleared the legal stuff with Dapper Dwayne – and he was convinced it was just a formality – he was going to have a hand in one of the biggest and most historic auction sales in American history.

The story was sure to go viral, especially if he could get that girl to change her mind about the picture. She was just made for the camera.

He allowed himself to picture it. That gorgeous face would sell the story instantly on social media. Every man in America would be seeing that face in his dreams, and every woman would be trying to recreate it with makeup – in vain.

He closed his eyes and conjured it up in his mind: the tiny curls just below the little cap, the smooth, placid brow, the light, perfectly arched brows. The huge green eyes, so effortlessly seductive in their beautiful innocence. The delicate nose and the plump, pouting lips that have haunted him since they'd first met. What would it feel like to be kissed by those lips?

He shook his head slightly, and forced himself to focus.

Of course, there was one big hitch. He'd promised not to take a photo of her face. He still had no idea why he'd promised her that. Probably, it was because she turned him into a babbling idiot.

He fumbled over the nightstand for a cigarette. He lit one, inhaled deeply, and stretched back out on the bed.

It must've been the thought of her lips on the other end of the line. Or that voice. He closed his eyes, remembering it. Her voice was smooth, and soft, and so gentle and feminine that it distracted him from what she'd actually been saying.

No, mostly he remembered – no names, no pictures, no appearance at the auction house, and no visits to her home from anyone else.

He took another drag from the cigarette.

Of course, he couldn't keep all those the promises he'd made to her. He felt a flicker of guilt about it, but he couldn't. He might as well just give up on the story, and he'd stuck his neck out way too far for that. He'd given up too much for that.

When he'd opened Jemima's letter, and a 200-year-old document, signed by George Washington had fallen out on the motel bed, it had taken every last atom of will power for him not to take it and cash in. He still didn't understand completely why he hadn't. It would've been technically ethical to accept – she had given it to him, after all.

But somehow, he couldn't. It was as simple as that.

Maybe it was the idea of taking money from a woman. And not just any woman – a young, gorgeous woman that, he had to admit, he wanted to impress.

Maybe it was ethics. Maybe he didn't want to think of himself as a creep or an opportunist. Maybe he wanted to make his own money.

Or maybe he just liked doing things the hard way. It was the story of his life, after all. It was why he was going to die poor, and probably young.

Delores' disgusted face popped into his mind, and he sputtered smoke as he tamped the cigarette out. Another of his bad habits.

And he had plenty. What was more, he was tired of being a good boy. He had just ruined himself and turned down a fortune, out of some quixotic idea of being his own man. Well, now that he was guaranteed rocky sledding for the rest of his life, he might as well steer the sled himself.

It was time to return to the real world.

He couldn't stay away from Jemima, not if he wanted the story. That decision was as simple as his decision not to take the money. He'd be risking everything, but without Jemima's picture, the story was going nowhere anyway.

Somehow, he had to get her to let him take a photo, and it wasn't going to be easy. It was against her religion, for one thing. She didn't know him, for another. He got the definite feeling that she didn't trust him and, possibly, that she might even be frightened of him.

Of course, that was because he hadn't exactly been Mr. Smooth so far. He had done everything wrong when it came to gaining her trust.

And that was a first.

He frowned at the ceiling. He didn't like to admit it, but that gorgeous redhead threw him right off his game. His decision to hide in the bushes at her house definitely hadn't been well thought out.

Which brought him to his reason for that choice: her volcano of a father. Her very mountainous, very fiery, very rumbling old man.

If the red giant caught him anywhere near Jemima...? Brad closed his eyes, and had a sudden vision of himself flying through the air and landing ingloriously, and in great confusion, on his rearward parts.

He had to get Jemima away from her father, and preferably from everybody else as well. And once he did – well, she'd laid down a lot of conditions over the phone, but he was confident that he'd be able to change all that, if he could just get alone with her.

At least, that was how it usually worked – when he applied himself.

He sprang out of bed and made for the shower.

CHAPTER SIX

Brad parked the company truck in a parking space as far away from the Satterwhite Gift Shop as he could manage. He didn't want to advertise his presence.

There was no sign of a buggy outside the shop, and he had no guarantee that Jemima would be there. But she had mentioned going to town, and if she supplied merchandise to that cantankerous old man, it was at least possible that today was the day.

He climbed out of the truck and scanned the street. There was no sign of her, but, he smiled suddenly, it looked like the store had a back door. He ducked into a cramped alleyway between the old buildings, and weaved his way to the street behind.

He came out on the backside of the building, amidst dumpsters and unpainted wooden steps and loading docks – the side of the business that customers weren't meant to see.

He cracked a delighted grin. He'd been right. Sure enough, there was an Amish buggy. And better yet, it was empty.

He weaved through the boxes and trashcans, rehearsing the speech he had made up in his head on the way over.

I'm sorry Jemima, but I had to talk to you again. I need some information before I can go to the auction house, and I didn't get a chance to ask you.

Yeah, that might work, especially if she felt a little guilty about hanging up on him. It might at least keep her from running away.

Then he would add: *I can only help you if you work with me. I'll do all I can for you, but I can't do everything by myself.*

Then, he thought, he might give her a soulful look. He was aware that he had nice eyes – or at least, he'd been told so by enough women that he considered it probable.

After he'd given her the old puppy dog look, he could say: *Please, can you compromise just a little? Just a tiny photo, only one, for the article?*

No, that was too direct. He'd have to lead up to that.

Maybe he could go with: *Would you be willing to let me come out to the house again, very briefly, so we could talk face to face? Would you–*

A clattering sound from the back door of the shop made him duck behind a stack of crates. He stood there, with his heart pounding.

The old storekeeper's bald head appeared in the doorway. He was sweeping dust out of the storeroom, and a choking cloud filled the air. Brad turned his face away as it descended on him.

The old man turned and addressed someone inside the store. "It's a shame. You can't turn around these days without being pestered by strangers. I wish things could go back to the way they were, before tourism ruined everything."

A big, booming voice answered from inside the storeroom, and Brad flattened himself against the back wall of the store.

"Yes, it's true," the voice growled. "I wish – but it doesn't matter what I wish, because wishing won't make it so. We can only go about our own business, and hope that other people do the same." Jacob King's enormous shadow fell across the back doorway. "I'll be back in a few minutes, Eli," he told the old man. "Tell Jemima to wait here for me." He strode out onto the loading dock, and the wooden boards groaned under his feet.

The storekeeper followed as Jacob King climbed up into

the buggy. "Tell Jed I need some baling wire when you see him," he called.

Jacob King raised his hand in farewell, and the buggy clattered off down the back street. The storekeeper turned and went back inside immediately.

Brad stayed in hiding until he was sure the old man was gone, and then followed cautiously.

He leaped easily onto the small loading dock, and peered around the edge of the doorway. The small storeroom was empty, and the door to the sales floor was standing open.

He could see the old man through the doorway. His back was turned; he was standing at the cash register. Jemima was facing him, her lovely eyes turned to the old man's.

"Your Poppa wants you to wait for him here," the old man said kindly. "Why don't you take a bottle of pop from the fridge in the back?"

Jemima smiled at him, and the sight of her face made something in Brad's chest turn over. Every detail froze in his memory: the little wisps of coppery hair floating around her face. The way the light from the front window cupped the curve of her right cheek; how smooth and soft it looked. Her eyes. Those luminous, innocent eyes that never failed to make him think very guilty thoughts. He cursed under his breath, but it was useless; she had the face of an angel, and even that black outfit she was wearing couldn't hide the fact that that she had the body of one, as well.

The light behind her just outlined the delicate curve of a breast, smoothed in to the tiny waist, and curved out again over the hip, like a caress. He'd never felt it before, but suddenly he realized that it was possible to be more stirred by imagination than stark nakedness. To Brad's horror, his body abruptly put him on notice – it hadn't signed off on his plan to play it cool.

He rolled his head against the wall and closed his eyes, trying to remember his speech. After a few seconds it came back to him – and not an instant too soon. The sound of an approaching footfall in the doorway made his eyes fly open.

Jemima's startled gaze took him in as he crouched against the back wall. He straightened instantly. What was his opening line?

He opened his mouth to say: *I'm sorry Jemima, but I had to talk to you again.*

But what came out, with a croak, was: "I'm sorry, Jemima!"

He seized her shoulders, crushed her to him, and dug his face into hers. Then he kissed her more crazily than he'd ever kissed any woman in his life.

Her lips were as silky, as full, and as yielding as he had dreamed. They melted against his like sugar dissolving on his tongue.

She froze in his arms. Her small hands curled up against his chest, and he could feel her sharp intake of breath.

Her body was as light as a feather against his, soft and tiny and beautifully fragile. He could feel her heart fluttering against his chest, like a snared bird trying to escape. His own was pounding like a hammer.

He was ruined, his life was over, and she'd hate him and take him for a lunatic stalker and a moron. Not only that, but he was going to be fired and he'd thrown away a million dollars and the story of a lifetime.

But oh, Duchess – it was all worth it!

And just for an instant, he could've sworn that something sparked between them. For a split-second, those heavenly lips moved.

Just before she clawed out of his arms.

"Oh, let go of me!" she hissed, but to his intense gratitude, she didn't scream. "Crazy Englischer–" she broke off into a long string of angry German-sounding words that really needed no translation.

Her almond-shaped eyes blazed. "I know what you were thinking, you – you Englischer reporter!" she spat, as if she could think of nothing worse. Her voice was low, but she was as angry as it was possible for a gentle girl to be.

"You want me to give you a big story, and you think that you can just kiss the simple Amish girl and make her do anything you say! Well, I've kissed plenty of boys before, and better boys than you, and they ask first, and kiss second!"

She jabbed a forefinger at his chest for emphasis: "And only if I say yes!"

Brad blinked at her. His face went hot. "You're totally right. I'm sorry, I shouldn't have done that," he stammered. He regained enough of his self-possession to attempt a pleading look, only to be captured by her eyes – again.

"It's true that I came here to talk to you about the story, but I-I forgot myself." He ran a hand through his hair in distraction. "I'm not like this, really. I'm a professional. It's just that you're – you really are the most beautiful girl I've ever met in my life."

The look in her eyes slowly changed. The anger swirling in them faded to puzzlement, and then to something that looked almost like–

He shook his head. "I am so sorry. There was no excuse for the way I behaved. I'll go away now and leave you alone." He glanced back over his shoulder, and bit his lip.

"I hope you don't let the – the way I acted keep you from selling the letter, though. I'll mail you the forms. Because I hope you get all the – the good things from it that you deserve. Here" – he scrabbled in his shirt pocket for a card –

"here's the number of the auction house. You really shouldn't miss that auction, you know. It's a once-in-a-lifetime thing."

She reluctantly took the card from his hand, and he gave her a sickly smile.

Annnd it was time to leave.

He started out the back door, only to be confronted by the sound of the returning buggy. He blanched. It was her father.

He was a dead man.

Something touched his shoulder. When he looked down, it was her hand.

"I'll go out to him," the soft voice was saying. "Stay here until we're gone." She looked at him again, shook her head, and brushed past him.

He withdrew into the shadows, and watched as the buggy stopped, Jemima stepped up lightly, and the vehicle clattered away.

He couldn't help watching it as it went, and to his surprise, Jemima turned to look back at him just before it rolled out of sight.

He exhaled and collapsed against the wall. His heart was pounding out of his chest, electrified by a combined near-love and near-death experience. He slumped there, weak and trembling, for a full ten minutes.

But after his pulse had calmed down – a long while later – when he'd had a chance to think, maybe he wasn't ruined after all. Sure, he'd been a thumping moron, he'd lost his mind, and he'd gone way, way off script. He'd risked the story of a lifetime and his whole career. But–

Jemima hadn't screamed when he kissed her.

She hadn't handed him over to her father, when that would've been easy.

Of course, there was no way to know what that meant – if it meant anything.

Except, maybe, mercy. The Amish were big on mercy.

He closed his eyes in despair. But Delores Watkins was not big. At least, not big on mercy. He put his head in his hands and groaned.

CHAPTER SEVEN

Jacob King cast a quizzical look at his daughter as they drove out of town and into the countryside.

"What's the matter with you, Mima? Aren't you feeling well?"

Jemima rolled startled eyes to her father's worried ones. "I feel fine," she stammered.

He gave her a shrewd look, and chucked her under the chin with one big knuckle. "You look almost feverish. Your cheeks are flushed, your cap is off center, your hair is mussed and you look as if you'd seen a ghost. If I didn't know for sure that those boys of yours were at work right now, I'd say you were suffering from a bad case of puppy."

She gasped, and turned her eyes down to her lap.

But her father only laughed. "I suppose your Mamm is right. I am too hard on you – my poor girl! I guess I do see a puppy under every bush. But it's only because, so far, there has been one under there. Every time!"

He looked at her, laughed again, and turned his eyes back to the road. "It's what I get for having such a beautiful daughter."

Jemima looked up at him, but he was gazing out over the road. "Don't let your mother know I told you that," he said, without turning his head. "She'll say I'm teaching you to be vain."

Jemima smiled just a tiny bit, and reached for his hand. "Thank you, Daed," she said gratefully.

By the time they got home, it was midmorning, and the day promised to be fair and hot. Her father unhitched Rufus and took him back to the barn, and Jemima went inside the house.

Her mother was heavily embroiled in a major baking project. She was bending over the kitchen table with her hair flying from under her cap and flour up to her elbows. She was rolling out dough with a wooden pin. She looked up and cried out in relief.

"Oh, Jemima, there you are! How I missed you this morning! You would have been willing to help me, but your sister ran away, and I haven't seen her since breakfast. Just wait until I see her again – I haven't spanked her for years, but that's about to change!"

She raised one arm and wiped perspiration off her brow. "Help me with the chores, Jemima. I have fifteen pies to finish before the bake sale tomorrow, and I don't have time to do anything else. Go out and gather the eggs, and get a basket of greens for tonight, and when you finish that I need you to make lunch." She paused and closed her eyes. "Oh! Why I ever agreed to do so many baked goods, all at once, I don't know! It sounded like such a good idea at the time!"

Jemima leaned in and kissed her mother's cheek. "It still is," she told her. "I'll wash up and start right away."

"Hurry," her mother sighed.

Jemima ran quickly up the stairs, ducked into the bathroom, and gave herself a quick cat bath in front of the bathroom mirror.

But when she met her own eyes in the glass, she gasped to see the girl staring back at her. Her father had been right: she looked a mess. Her cap was all crooked, and her hair was all over, her eyes looked wild and she was flushed. She put one palm to her cheek, to cool it.

She lowered her head and pinched her lips together

angrily, and washed her hands a little too vigorously.

Then she walked into her own bedroom and closed the door behind her. She dug out the money that Mr. Satterwhite had given her for the dolls and tucked it away in the little hidden panel in the wall.

She frowned. There were the official-looking letters from the auction house, just where she had left them. But the whole thing was trouble, and the sooner she could sell the George Washington letter and have done with it, the better she'd like it!

She took the little panel in her hand, but as she moved to fasten it, another piece of paper came fluttering out onto the floor.

She bent down to pick it up. It was the business card the crazy Englischer had given to her. Her eyes darkened, and on an angry impulse, she pinched the little card between her fingers and tore it right in two.

That gave her a certain pleasure, but then the thought occurred to her: she couldn't just throw the pieces away, because if someone found them, how would she explain them?

Jemima pushed her lip into a pout that would have driven her admirers to frenzy had they seen it, and reluctantly pushed the torn pieces in with the other papers. She could hide them there, until she could safely destroy them.

She replaced the panel with a bit more force than was required, and turned her lips down in distress.

Crazy Englisch reporter – the very idea!

"Jemima!"

Her mother's voice floated up from downstairs, and Jemima took a deep breath, and shook her skirts out briskly, as if shaking off a distasteful memory. Then she hurried downstairs, and put the thought of the morning's shocking events from her mind.

Or, at least, she tried to put them from her mind. She found, to her dismay, that it was easier said than done. Confusion swirled in her brain, making it impossible to concentrate on her work.

She collected a few eggs in the hen house, but soon had to stop. The bewildered prayer welling up in her had to come out.

Why, God?

Jemima closed her eyes and pressed her brow against one of the hens. It was downy and warm, but it gave her no answer.

Why did this happen? Didn't You tell me to sell the letter? Wasn't Your message as clear as day? And weren't You the one making the Englischer help me?

But if that's true, then why did this happen? It ruins

everything!

She opened her eyes, but she wasn't seeing the dim interior of the hen house. She was seeing a pair of bright blue eyes, glowing like electricity. Insane eyes.

Lord, what can I do? The wicked Englischer is the only person I know who can help me sell the letter. What now?

The soft muttering of the hens gave her no clue as to the answer. She shook her head.

When she had finished gathering eggs, she went and knelt in the garden on her hands and knees, and picked cherry tomatoes and carrots. Every now and then she looked over her shoulder and out into the bushes at the edge of the yard.

And imagined that she saw a branch move.

Then grumbled under her breath, and returned to work.

Jemima yanked a carrot out of the ground. The more she thought about the Englischer, the angrier she got. She had never been so shocked in all her life, or so outraged. Some people thought that they were so big and important, or maybe so handsome, that they could treat other people any way they liked.

But they were wrong.

She leaned back on her heels and swiped the dirt off of her hands.

Some people were so full of hochmut and – her eye fell on a wheelbarrow – *fertilizer* that they didn't care about other people's feelings, or rights.

Only their own.

She muttered under her breath and shook her head angrily. Her father had been right, the Englisch were crazy and greedy and you couldn't trust them when you were looking right at them, much less when your back was turned.

Her face went red, as that horrifying scenario flashed through her mind, and she yanked out another carrot.

CHAPTER EIGHT

The next morning was a perfect day for the bake sale: sunny, bright, and not too hot. At nine o'clock, Jemima was helping her mother set up a table at a neighborhood plant nursery. The owner had agreed to let their congregation hold the sale outside his shop.

Summer weekends were always good sale days, since those were the days that both locals and tourists came to the nursery to buy big, beautiful Amish garden plants.

And Amish-produced confections.

The congregation was holding the bake sale to raise money for little Adam Yoder who had fallen down a well and had broken a half-dozen bones. He had been in the hospital for days, and his medical bill was, reportedly, astronomical.

Jemima carried a sheet cake to the table and set it carefully between a basket of yeast rolls and a plate of blueberry muffins. Her mother had worked all day yesterday, and lots of other people from their congregation had as well.

But Jemima was depressed. She gazed out over the groaning tables and couldn't help thinking that it was a wasted effort. Even if the bake sale was a huge success, it could hardly raise the money that Adam's parents needed.

She thought of the letter gathering dust in the bank vault, and was pierced by guilt. The proceeds of that letter would be more than enough to relive Adam's parents of that crushing debt, and maybe, the debts of a lot more sick people, besides.

And here she stood, with all their neighbors, selling cakes that would bring ten dollars, at the most.

Jemima scanned the sale tables sadly. They had set them up outside the store, and those tables were now laden with every kind of temptation imaginable: her mother's mouth-watering blackberry pies and peach cobblers, friendship bread still warm from the oven, sticky buns, sugar cookies, and all manner of cakes. Some local farm families that made their own cheeses and hams were also selling their wares.

Including Mark's.

Jemima's expression lightened at the sight of him. Mark

was a welcome distraction from her guilt and her confusion. It was a comfort to see him. He was as strong and reliable as her father's watch.

He was already there, helping some of the other vendors unload their heavier boxes, since he was young and strong and – and muscular.

Jemima allowed herself the pleasure of watching him – discreetly – as he worked. Samuel was taller, and Joseph was more handsome, but Mark was by far the most well-built of her suitors. His arms were strong, his chest was broad, his hips were narrow, and his stomach was so flat that it actually curved in slightly.

He was almost a man now; he certainly didn't look much like her old childhood tormentor. But an old longing surged up inside her suddenly as she watched him – she longed to talk to Mark, like she had when they were children. She longed to get him alone and pour out her heart to him.

Mark didn't talk much, but he was a wonderful listener. She knew he would never betray her, not to anyone.

Of course she couldn't tell him about the letter, or the crazy Englischer, but – maybe she could just ask him what he would do – if something unexpected and – and difficult happened.

Mark had always been so practical and down to earth. He had so much common sense – and after the craziness of the last few weeks, she yearned for that.

Jemima looked around for her mother, and to her relief, she was facing in the other direction talking to some of the other women.

Jemima backed away from the table, and disappeared into the nursery, shielding herself behind racks of seedlings and big potted trees. She peered out, looking for Mark. He was unloading boxes about ten feet away.

She moved closer, still keeping herself out of sight, and when he passed close by, she called softly from behind a ficus bush.

"Mark!"

He stopped, and looked around in puzzlement.

"Mark, here!"

He stepped closer, frowning slightly. "Mima? What are you doing hiding in the bushes?"

Jemima felt her face going red, but she was committed now, and she had to follow through. She looked up at him pleadingly.

"I-I wanted to talk to you. Alone, someplace. Away from all these people," she begged. "Can you get away – just for a few minutes?"

He looked at her eyes, and his expression softened. "Of

course," he said, and put the box down on a table nearby. "Where do you want to go?"

Jemima was embarrassed to feel tears pool in her eyes. "Oh, anywhere," she told him, "just away from everybody. Just somewhere we can be alone!"

He looked at her again. "Okay." He put a hand lightly under her elbow, and guided her out through to the farthest edge of the nursery. He led her to a little nook, mostly hidden behind a row of potted evergreens, and they sat down together in a garden swing.

He looked into her eyes with a concerned expression. "What's the matter, Mima? Has something upset you?"

Jemima felt her lip trembling, and she looked away, irritated by her own weakness. She shook her head, and strove to control her voice. "It's just – something strange has happened, Mark," she said, keeping her eyes on a nearby tree. "Something very strange. And I don't know what to do."

She turned her eyes back to his, and looked into them pleadingly. "And I thought, maybe, you could give me some advice."

Mark took her hands in his and nodded. "Of course, Mima. You know that. Anything."

Jemima looked up at him. "Mark, I-I have a decision to make. A very important decision. I think, I believe, that I have guidance from God about what to do. But something just happened that – that has confused me, very much, and I-I'm not so sure anymore."

He was watching her intently, but at this, his eyes burned. "Has someone…has someone done something they shouldn't, Jemima?" he asked.

Jemima felt a wave of fire roll over her cheeks. Mark clenched his jaw, nodded angrily, looked up at the sky, and then back at her.

"I think I know what I should do, Mark," she whispered, looking up into his eyes, "but now I'm – I'm scared."

Mark was frowning now, and looked angry. "No one's hurt you, have they, Mima?" he demanded. "Or threatened you? Because if they have–"

Jemima shook her head. "Oh, no, Mark," she shrugged. "It's just that I'm so confused. If I do what I think I should, it will be wonderful and good things will happen, but it may also be unpleasant, at first, and some people might not understand, or…or be – upset, as well."

His expression changed. The anger faded, and was replaced by puzzlement – and then, dawning certainty. He pressed her hands warmly between his. "I think I know what you're trying to tell me, Mima," he said intently. "And I think you should do what you think is right, no matter what. And you don't need to be scared, not of anything. Not while I'm around."

He pulled her hands toward him. "Can't you tell me what you're afraid of, Mima? What – what decision you have to make?"

Jemima shook her head unhappily. "I-I can't, Mark. I'm sorry, not yet. But it's preying on my mind so. I don't like what I'll have to do."

His eyes were full of compassion. "Of course not. But you shouldn't let that keep you from doing what you think is best."

Jemima looked up into his eyes. "Oh, Mark, it's such a comfort to talk to you," she cried. "I haven't been able to talk to anyone about this – it's been all bottled up inside me, until I think I'm going to–"

But it was as far as she got.

Mark simply pulled her hands behind him, and then put his own around her, and before she knew what was happening, he was kissing her.

His lips were warm, and tender, almost reverent, but she shook her head and pulled away. She looked up at him almost in despair, and opened her mouth, as if to say something, but then shook her head.

"Just kiss me, Mark," she told him. "Kiss me hard!"

CHAPTER NINE

Jemima kept to herself, and said little to anyone, for days after the bake sale. She was usually very quiet and peaceful, never one to nurse anger or to act out like her sister. But to Jemima's dismay, all that had unexpectedly changed – because now she was angry and upset.

She was trying to stay away from other people because she was horrified by the idea that she might bark at someone, like her sister Deborah. She was angry with the Englischer, she was angry with herself, she was angry with Mark and Samuel and Joseph, and she was even angry at her parents – with her father, for grabbing every decision out of her hands, and even with her poor mother, for wearing herself out in a useless gesture that would help no one.

Because in spite of her confusion, one thing at least was depressingly clear: despite of all their neighbors' hard work, the total proceeds that the Yoders would receive from the bake sale had only been 351 dollars and 43 cents. About what it would cost for Adam Yoder's parents to take him to a doctor...once.

The Yoders were like every other Amish family – they didn't participate in traditional health insurance. And if their Amish neighbors couldn't help them, they had no way to pay their medical bills. Who had that kind of money?

Except...her?

It was on her now. She was the only one who could help the Yoders, and therefore she had a moral obligation to do it. The preacher had been right; it was sinful for her to have the means to help her neighbors and to do nothing, just because she dreaded the process of selling that letter, or the people she'd have to deal with.

But why did it have to be her? Why did she have to find that cursed letter? Why couldn't it have gone to someone else – anyone else?

She had no head for business, and no interest in business. She had no desire to go among the Englisch or to be rich. She was horrified by that crazy Englischer, and appearing in a newspaper – on purpose – well, it was the opposite of what a good Amish person should do.

Jemima mulled these things over uneasily as she sat, well hidden, in the loft of her father's barn. It was where she always ran to hide when she'd been small, and it was still a good place for that. Because since she'd grown up, and grown pretty, no one ever suspected that she'd ever return to such a dusty corner.

But it was perfect for thinking. It was quiet and cool and sweetly fragrant of hay. She closed her eyes and rested her head against a big bale.

She'd hoped that Mark would help her find a way out when they had talked at the bake sale, but she'd been disappointed. Or maybe she had just been naïve. It wasn't Mark's fault that he wasn't a mind reader – it was hers, for expecting him to be one.

She had sought advice from him because he was a childhood friend – as if she could hide from her problems by going back to the past. But Mark was no longer a child, and neither was she.

And because they were courting, he'd naturally assumed that she'd been talking about her choice of a mate, and had been anxious to show his sympathy. He'd tried to make love to her because they were alone, and because his way of expressing affection was almost purely physical.

She sighed, and was momentarily distracted by an old

grievance.

If only Mark would tell her that he loved her – just once! – instead of expecting physical closeness to say it all!

Because what did a kiss mean, anyway? It could mean anything, unless the person doing the kissing bothered to explain what it meant.

But that was another worry, a distraction that she didn't have the luxury to dwell on.

Her problem now, was the letter.

There was no getting around her duty. She had to call the Englischer, accept his help and sell the letter. It was a fate she dreaded, but there was one thing that was even worse – the thought of little Adam Yoder, and others like him, suffering for lack of the medical care that she could easily provide.

If she could only work up the nerve to do what she must.

Jemima looked out through a chink in the barn wall, out toward the garden. It was drowsing peacefully under a quiet summer sun.

She hated the thought of her home being invaded by strangers, of being stalked by some crazy, greedy newspaper reporter that she didn't know and didn't want to know.

It was true that he was very handsome, with that big bush of sandy brown hair. It was streaked with all different colors of brown and blond, like the sun had bleached it out, but not all the same.

And his eyes were bright and blue, and his eyebrows were bushy and wild and moved as if they were alive.

And he did have a strong chin, nice white teeth, and a strong…mouth.

A slow wave of heat crawled from her feet to the top of her head. She couldn't help it, the memory came surging back, of his mouth clamped down over hers, and how that had felt.

An electric thrill flashed up her spine and branched out into little tingling, sparkling threads along every nerve in her body. She shuddered, and shook her head and frowned. She had been kissed many times before, and by many boys. But she had never, never been kissed by a madman.

It terrified her.

It was true that he had apologized, looked sorry, and even called her *the most beautiful girl he'd ever met.*

Jemima put her chin on her knees and hugged them.

Then she frowned. But her mother was right, a man's actions were what counted, and the Englischer was a madman, and a wicked one, to treat her so disrespectfully.

She opened her eyes, and the look in them was troubled. But if so – then she must also be mad, and wicked. Because when the Englischer had taken her in his arms and kissed her, she had been – electrified.

She frowned again, and her mouth moved in silent prayer. But when she opened her eyes, she had no sense of the presence of God, and was downcast about it.

Maybe her heart wasn't right any more.

That made it all the more awkward and terrifying to call that madman, and to talk to him again. Because, with her own feelings so jumbled up, surely she should stay as far away from him as she could get?

She chewed her thumbnail. Maybe she should just tell her father everything, and let him deal with the Englischer. That would be safest, and perhaps best.

But even though she knew it was right, somehow – she couldn't bring herself to do it.

Her father would take the letter and the decision out of her hands, just as he always did. And that would be the end. But for once in her life, Jemima thought, she wanted to be the one to decide. Even if that meant that she had to take a risk and do something that other people might not understand.

Something that she, even, might not fully understand.

She bit her lip, looking out through the little chink in the wall, out to the garden. But the idea of seeing the reporter again made her very uneasy. There was no knowing what he'd do. That mad Englischer always surprised her.

Always.

He frightened her, he shocked her, he made her angry, and he amazed her.

And what was even more unsettling – maybe she liked that, just a little bit.

Jemima's beautiful eyes widened in fear. She frowned, pulled her knees to her chest and prayed even more earnestly.

CHAPTER TEN

Jemima craned her neck to peer out of the little window in the phone shack, but her father was nowhere in sight. She closed her eyes and drummed one foot nervously against the wall.

The phone rang and rang. Six times, seven times, eight. No one was answering.

The sudden click of the receiver made Jemima's heart jump up into her throat, and she almost dropped the phone when a voice on the other end said, cheerfully:

"It's a beautiful morning at Uncle Bob's Amish Motel. My name is Stessily. How can I help you today?"

Jemima swallowed hard, and forced herself to answer:

"Good – good morning, Stessily. I – I'm calling for a Mr. – a Mr. Brad Williams. Is he in?"

"Hmm, let me see." There was a tapping sound on the other end. "Brad Williams. Oh – oh, I'm sorry, miss. It looks like he just checked out this morning. But it was only a few minutes ago – if you can wait, I'll see if he's still here."

"Thank you," Jemima replied faintly. She hardly knew what to hope for – that she would catch the crazy Englischer, or that he'd be gone forever.

She had fought herself for days, had prayed earnestly, and had tried to look at the thing from every angle. And in the end she had just decided to call the Englischer, and pray that somehow, everything worked out in the end.

Not that it was likely to work out.

She could hear the girl's voice faintly in the background, calling. "Mr. Williams – Mr. Williams!" There was unintelligible discussion, and within seconds, loud fumbling on the other end. Then, suddenly, the voice she had learned to dread:

"Miss King?"

Jemima bit her lip in irritation. She'd caught the Englischer. Just her luck!

"Yes."

There was a small pause. "Thank you for calling back," he

said quietly. To her intense relief, and for once, he sounded almost...sane.

"I know that couldn't have been easy for you. And I promise, nothing – unprofessional – will ever happen again." There was a sound like a deep breath on the other end of the line.

"Now. How can I help you?"

Jemima's heart was pounding, and the little shack felt hot – like it was closing in on her.

"You-you said that I needed to sign some papers," she said evenly.

"Yes, you must give the auction house written permission to sell the letter."

"Will you send them to me in the mail?"

"I can, if you like."

Jemima nodded. "Yes."

There was more fumbling. "If you'll give me your address..."

Jemima recited the information with her eyes squeezed shut. In spite of little Adam Yoder, and the preacher's message, she had the awful feeling that she was doing something wrong somehow, and that it was going to blow up on her.

That feeling intensified when the reporter added: "And once Brinkley's has the signed papers, they can prepare for the auction. An auction is always very exciting, and this one – well, it'll be historic. One in a million."

There was another pause, and he added: "It'd be a shame to miss it."

Jemima shook her head, and said, in a strangled voice: "I will only sign the papers. I can't go to any auction!"

The tone of the reporter's voice was suggestive of a shrug. "Why not?"

Jemima pulled the receiver away from her ear and stared at it. She sputtered: "You-you don't know anything about Amish people, about what we believe!" she cried, and slammed the phone down on the hook. Then she gathered her skirts and ran back up the hill, but not to hide inside the house.

To run into the barn, climb up into the loft, and curl up in the shadows, and be upset and confused – again.

Brad Williams heard the click on the other end of the line, and handed the receiver back to the grinning receptionist.

He grinned back, crookedly, gathered the shreds of his dignity about him, and limped back out to the truck.

But when he closed the door behind him, he just leaned his

head against the rim of the wheel. There was only one thought pounding in his brain: She called back. She called back. She called back.

He just sat there, basking in his absurd joy. Because he was no longer ruined. He was no longer even on probation. He had his job and future back, and he still had a toehold on the story of the year.

The Duchess had called him back.

He flipped the knob on the radio and turned the volume up to blasting, beat his palms on the wheel, and sang at the top of his lungs like a lunatic all the way back to his apartment.

Once he was there, he flopped down on his couch with a bottle of soda in one hand and the phone in the other. Since the Ledger was springing for the sale fees, and had a hand in the negotiations, he was going to have to light a fire under Dapper Dwayne and get all this stuff fast tracked: the contract, the insurance forms, the commission agreements for the auction house, all the fine print.

He punched the necessary numbers on his phone, but to Brad's annoyance, the lawyer was out; he could only get his voicemail. But he was determined to get the show on the road as fast as humanly possible. It could take Brinkley's months to get such a huge auction advertised and scheduled.

And in the meantime, he had to be busy as well, keeping the lines of communication open between him and Jemima, so that when the time came, she'd maybe agree to attend the auction.

He already knew how he was going to do it. He wouldn't send her everything at once. He'd take her one form at a time, and deliver them himself. He was sure he could come up with some excuse that was at least plausible.

That would give him time to establish rapport, and hopefully, trust. Once that groundwork was laid, then he could bring up the subject of the article – and the photo.

What had she said – something like: "You don't understand what the Amish believe"?

He sipped his drink. It was a fair enough criticism – it was true. Maybe if he learned a little more, he could couch his requests in a way that would make the Duchess more likely to say yes.

Maybe even to requests that had nothing to do with letters or a million dollars or auctions.

He punched a few buttons on his phone and said: "Amish religion."

The little screen winked to life and pulled up a long list of links. Brad punched another button, took a long draught of his soda, and began to read.

CHAPTER ELEVEN

Brad spent the rest of that day, and a good part of that night, absorbing the long – and to him – depressing history of the Amish. They had been a minority religious sect in Europe, and had been tortured and murdered because of it. They came to the New World looking to escape religious persecution.

Brad pushed a pile of crumpled clothes off his bed. Then he stretched out on it in the dark and learned about the Amish by the blue light of his smart phone.

It was not the usual immigrant story.

The Amish settled mainly in the northeastern states, where they withdrew from the larger world because of their belief that it was "wicked" and that they were called by God to be "separate."

Brad pulled a hand over his jaw ruefully. *Great*. He was a part of the world. So, to Jemima, he was starting out wicked. He was wicked by definition.

But, on the other hand, that could work to his advantage. Some girls had a thing for bad boys.

In fact, maybe he should encourage that perception. He took a pull at the bottle and read on:

Farming and close-knit communities were integral to the Amish faith and way of life, and as 19th-century society embraced technological changes, the Amish began to reject certain advances as disruptive to the way of life that they had chosen.

Essentially, if a new gadget or technology tended to pull people, and especially families, away from one another, it was rejected.

If an advance put their community in direct contact with the wicked outside world – it, too, was rejected.

They largely rejected telephones until the 20th century and in many communities, still only allow them in "phone shacks" out at the end of the road, rather than inside the house, because phones are considered disruptive to family life, and are a line to the outside world. Television is still verboten for the same reasons. Cars are disallowed, because they give families the mobility to travel great distances and present them with the temptation to abandon their extended families and neighborhoods.

Brad and shook his head.

But even in these circumstances, many Amish communities make concessions: owning a car is forbidden, but riding in one is not, if it belongs to someone else. Electric power is forbidden, because electric lines are a direct link to the outside world; but solar power is not, because solar panels are self-contained.

Change in Amish communities happens slowly, if at all. Amish families are strictly traditional, with the man the undisputed head of the household, and a high value placed on the qualities of submission and modesty, not just for the women and girls, but generally. Divorce is discouraged and rare.

Brad's eye jumped to the section marked courtship. He raised his brows.

Teenagers of 16 and older enter a period called rumspringa, in which they are allowed to go out and experience the wider world before joining the church. Rumspringa is often a time of courtship. But this time of latitude is mainly offered as a way of giving the young a chance to make an informed choice about joining the church. Because, once a new member joins the Amish church, and takes their vows to God, serious and repeated infractions could result in shunning, and/or excommunication.

Brad ran a hand through his hair. So, if that was right, Jemima was, technically, on her rumspringa and eligible to be courted. From what he'd seen, that was already well under way. He'd seen her with one guy already, and a girl as beautiful as the Duchess was sure to have others.

But if what he'd seen was representative, she probably wasn't committed to any of them. They were probably good little Mamma's boys, and chicks never went for that.

He looked down at the article. According to its author, Jemima was also eligible to go out into the world and walk on the wild side. So to speak.

Brad grinned in the dark, thinking *I can arrange that.*

He might even be able to use it as leverage when it came time to really pitch for the photo. After all, he could say, you're on your rumspringa. It's now or never!

The now or never tactic got good results generally with girls. He'd have to remember this useful variant, for later.

He went back to the article.

The Amish believe the major tenets of traditional Christianity, but with emphasis on showing, rather than telling. They do not proselytize, at least not heavily, and place great emphasis on meekness, non-violence, submission to God, prayer, and hard work.

Brad flicked the phone off and tossed it onto his bedside table. He didn't really need to hear all that religious stuff. He thought he had a pretty good picture now. Good enough for what he wanted, anyway.

He put his arms behind his head and stared up at his bedroom ceiling. In a way, he was going to have a hard time getting his head around this Amish thing. It was as far removed from his own life as one pole was from another.

He tried to imagine what it would be like to live that life: to get up and dress in pilgrim clothes, and work in the fields like 100 years ago, and not even to have electricity. Poor Jemima! He felt sorry for her. No normal life. No pretty clothes, like a beautiful girl should have, no schooling past the eighth grade. No future, except the drab existence of a farm wife, condemned to wash clothes by hand and have a baby every year.

Thank heaven, maybe the letter would change that for her. At least, he hoped so. Maybe when Jemima understood that she had choices now, she'd choose to move away and live like a normal human being.

Still, he had to admit that there were some parts of her life that were pretty. Or at least, seemed pretty: the beautiful countryside where they all lived, with those endless, rolling green fields full of corn, and the antique farmhouses, and the buggies.

Even the way her old man stood guard over her, like a

giant Rottweiler.

He sputtered and reached for a cigarette. That part must be nice. He wouldn't know, because his own old man had left when he was five, and his mother had drugged herself into a coma – and him into foster care – by the time he was nine.

He pulled his lips down. She was dead now, and he didn't know if his old man was still alive or not. Not that he cared.

He allowed himself to wonder what it would be like having parents that actually did the fifties sitcom trip.

He laughed to himself and amended: No, the pioneer trip.

That part, he imagined, would be very nice. It would feel comforting and safe. And in the 21st century, that was a real luxury. Maybe it helped make up for the other things they were missing.

The religious part was a big minus, though – all that praying. They sang hymns that were hundreds of years old for hours. It was as if they were always repenting for something.

It made him angry, suddenly. A sweet, sheltered girl like Jemima – what did she have to repent for? But then, religion was only good for putting guilt trips on people who didn't deserve them. The world would be a better place if everyone forgot all that stuff and became agnostic, like he was.

It'd be a happier place, anyway.

Brad finished the cigarette, crushed it out on the table, and yanked off his shirt. He turned over and flicked a few buttons on the phone, and music blared from the speaker until he drifted off to sleep.

But his thoughts continued into his dreams that night. He saw himself running through an Amish cornfield, chasing a beautiful redheaded girl whose tempting smile was always half-hidden,   and   just   out   of   reach.

CHAPTER TWELVE

A week later, Brad began the first of a series of carefully-planned visits to Jemima's house. They were intended to help him build up friendship, trust, and eventually, an interview.

His first visit was a Hail Mary, and could have ended disastrously, but luck was with him. He arrived in the middle of the day, when the Duchess' old man was out somewhere, and she was working outside again.

It had been hard to get out to her place without attracting attention, but lucky for him, the place adjoined a piece of public land, an overgrown forest tract owned by the county. He had simply parked on the other side of that property, and hiked over.

By the time he had slogged to the edge of her family's farm, his slacks were torn by briars and he was covered in cockleburs.

He took a minute to pick the little prickly pods off of his clothing, before climbing over the fence.

He kept to the edge of the tree line, being careful not to walk out over the lawn. He had learned that the old man was a blacksmith and that if he was home, you could hear him from a distance away, but the house was quiet.

The red giant was gone.

Brad kept behind the bushes, working his way back to the spot where he had met Jemima before. It was an ideal hiding spot; he could see the whole house and garden without being seen himself. He returned to it, and sure enough, there was the Duchess, sitting in a little folding chair on one side of the garden. There was another, empty chair facing her.

He shot a glance at the house. The best he could tell, a big line of flowering bushes screened Jemima from the house, so if he stepped out from his hiding place, he should be safe, unless–

He ducked down. Unless, she had a visitor.

He crouched low, cursing softly under his breath. Some pretty farm boy had come out to see her. He sat down in the empty chair facing Jemima.

Brad grimaced. The guy was actually wearing a straw hat.

He was close enough to hear what they were saying, though he devoutly wished he wasn't because, of course, the guy was trying to romance the Duchess, and it was painful to watch.

The hat guy gave her a piece of paper. Brad craned his neck, wondering what it was.

Jemima looked up at him and smiled. "Oh, Joseph, another poem! This is so sweet," she murmured.

Brad shook his head. You're dying, buddy, he told the stranger. Sweet is for babies and lapdogs.

The guy looked down at his hands, as though he couldn't bring himself to lift his eyes to her face. "Read it, Jemima," he pleaded.

She looked startled, and Brad shook his head. Poor girl!

She cleared her throat, and coughed. "You are like a...strong mare, with a shiny red coat."

She looked up at him doubtfully, but he nodded encouragement, and she continued: "You are a hard worker, and work well with others. Yoke and...harness will be no hardship for you, because you are mild and gentle."

Brad laughed out loud, and Jemima's head jerked up suddenly. "What was that? Did you hear something, Joseph?"

Joseph shook his head, and his eyes returned to the paper.

She scanned the bushes again, and continued, less placidly: "Your road will be smooth and happy, and you will never run it alone."

Jemima finished, and looked up at the young man. "That's a – that's a lovely poem, Joseph."

Brad made a decision, and stood up suddenly. He stepped boldly onto the lawn, waved the forms over his head, and pointed to them.

Jemima's eyes met his over her visitor's shoulder. She shrieked and dropped the paper, and Brad ducked back into the bushes.

Joseph looked almost as alarmed as Jemima. He jumped up, and then sat down again, abruptly.

"What's wrong, Mima?" he asked earnestly.

Jemima's eyes scanned the bushes crazily. "I-I thought I saw something!" she stammered.

The young man turned and looked in the direction of her gaze. "I don't see anything, Mima," he said, in a puzzled tone. He turned back to her. "Maybe – you're a little nervous." The thought seemed to please him; he smiled a bit.

"Was I too – too ardent?"

Jemima uttered a choking sound that she abruptly

swallowed, and then pressed a hand to her head. "No, no, Joseph! It's just that – well, maybe you're right, I am a bit nervous today. I'm sorry."

Her visitor smiled serenely. He dared to pat her hand. "That's all right," he told her. "I won't press you, Jemima."

Jemima raised her head and cast a fiery look at the bushes. "I wish everyone had your courtesy, Joseph!" she cried.

He stood up, hat in hand. "May I call on you again – Mima?"

She was still looking out into the trees. "Yes, yes. Anytime you like! I mean – well, you'll have to ask my Daed." She raised her voice. "He'll be back any minute!"

Joseph nodded. "There's no hurry, Mima. I'll see you at worship Sunday." He leaned forward, and paused.

Jemima looked up at him, bit her lip, and allowed him to kiss her cheek.

After her visitor had disappeared around the side of the house, climbed into his buggy, and driven off down the road, she turned to the bushes, hands on hips.

Brad stepped out of them, laughing crazily.

"How dare you come out here when I told you not to!" Jemima cried, eyes blazing. "And you spied on me! How can you stand there laughing! You should be ashamed of yourself!"

Brad wiped his eyes and shook his head. "I'm sorry, Jemima," he sputtered. "I wasn't trying to spy, and I didn't mean to listen. I just didn't want to interrupt. I came out to bring you the auction contract. I figured it would be faster and safer than mailing it."

"Leave this minute!" she told him, pointing back to the bushes. "I specifically told you not to come. Don't you pay attention to anything that other people say?"

Brad raised his hands in the air. "Okay, okay," he shrugged. "Though it isn't very polite to insult me, after I took the trouble to make a special trip all the way out here."

That line of reasoning seemed to give her pause. Some of the fire died out of her eyes. She sputtered, "Just, just go now, before my father comes home. Because this time, I won't protect you!"

Brad looked up at her sharply, and grinned. She gasped, went beet red, stamped her foot, turned, and ran.

Brad set the contract down on the neatly-mown lawn, turned, and beat a strategic retreat. Because if there was any chance that she was right, he had better demonstrate the better part of valor.

Before he experienced the better part of a thrashing.

CHAPTER THIRTEEN

Jemima sat out on the front porch steps, looking up at the stars.

It was two o'clock in the morning, and she'd have to be up again at five, but she had long since given up any hope of getting any sleep.

That Williams fellow had popped up again in the bushes, for the third straight time in the last month. The first time, it had caused her to scream out, because Joseph was there, and she'd been terrified that Joseph would see the fellow standing there. The second time, he appeared early one morning, and

Deborah had almost caught them talking, and that would've been a disaster, because Deborah would gleefully have blabbed all she knew. But he was quick – she had to give him that. He had dived into the bushes like an expert.

It made her wonder if he had a lot of experience hiding in bushes outside girl's houses.

This last time had been at dusk, just before it was time to go inside. He had been bold enough to come out onto the lawn this time, and he had come quite close in the near-darkness. Uncomfortably close, really. She put a hand to her brow, and smoothed back a little wisp of hair. He had stood so close that she could feel his breath, and catch the scent of his clothes; they had been faintly fragrant of pipe tobacco, and that man scent. She couldn't quite describe it – it was a clean scent, equal parts salt, and soap, and skin.

She sighed and rubbed her arms against the evening chill.

He had wanted her to sign a paper. Every time he'd come out to the house, it was the same thing: sign this paper.

She bit her lip and looked up at the sky unhappily. It was odd that he didn't bring all the papers at the same time and have done with it. And she really should have told him to go away and never come back. He didn't listen, he was stubborn beyond all reason, and she was terrified that someone would see him, and ask her why he was there.

She couldn't figure that out, herself.

Unless, he wanted to be near her, like he'd said once.

She twisted the end of her long braid. She didn't like the way things were going. There was going to be trouble if things went on the way they were going.

She was beginning to understand that she'd been naïve to think she'd be able to keep the sale of the letter a secret. Once the reporter knew about it, well, she was pretty much ruined, and she had been silly not to admit that before now.

He had already gotten the story out of her – how she'd found the letter, what it had said, and even how she felt about what it had said.

She blushed, and looked down at her hands. How had he done that? She hadn't intended to tell anyone how beautiful she thought it was.

Maybe it was the way he had sat down beside her, and settled down and listened. The reporter boy listened better than anyone she had ever met.

Well, to her story at least. He didn't listen at all in the general way, when it came to things like keeping his distance and behaving like a gentleman. He had kept his promise, technically – the promise he had made to her in the store. He hadn't grabbed her up or tried to kiss her, or laid a finger on her, not even to shake her hand. He had been polite, and had stuck mostly to talking just about the letter, and the auction.

But he showed up at the house whether she liked it or not,

he laughed at inappropriate things, and he was always nagging her to let him take a picture. He had said that the world would want to see the girl who found the million-dollar letter.

And, that he wouldn't mind having a picture of her, himself. Then he had smiled again, and winked.

She would have dismissed that as nonsense, except she'd caught him staring at her, and not just at her face, especially when he'd thought she was looking somewhere else. Jemima tossed her head and looked out over the slumbering fields.

He was a typical barbarian Englischer and had no manners whatsoever.

But, she had to admit, there was another side, too. Because when it had come time to tell her story, then he had gotten very quiet, and settled down and listened very hard. He listened with his mind, which was the best way she could put it. Not just with his ears.

He had smiled when she told him that she'd been glad the letter was real, because it was a beautiful letter – very sweet and romantic. He had a wonderful smile, it was very warm, and it lit up his face.

Like he really…understood.

She had actually dreamed about him. And that horrified her, but she supposed she didn't have any say over that – or responsibility. She wasn't in control of her dreams, after all.

She had dreamed that the Williams fellow had climbed in through her bedroom window and chased her all through the house, with her wearing nothing but a cotton shift and her hair going all down her back.

And then, then she dreamed that he caught her and kissed her again, hard, just like he had in the store that day. And she screamed, and he jumped out through a window again, and broke all the glass out of it, like a wild animal.

And then she dreamed that Mark and Samuel and Joseph came running into the room and gave her flowers, and since she couldn't decide between them, she married them all, right there in the living room, in her cotton gown.

But when she turned to leave with them, she looked back over her shoulder, and the Englischer's crazy blue eyes were watching her from the broken window.

She woke up with her heart pounding, and she must have cried out, because Deborah had called out from across the hall for her to shut up, and go back to sleep.

But she hadn't slept. She hadn't slept for hours.

She chewed her nail.

This last time when he'd shown up, the Williams fellow had come as close as she'd let him, and looked into her face with those bright eyes. He had said:

"Tomorrow is the auction, Jemima. I know you're

reluctant to go, but please, give it serious thought. This is something that only happens once in a lifetime. You will never get a chance to see something this important again. It's – well, it's history – and it will change your life."

She had set her mouth, given him a direct look, and was on the point of telling him that it would not change her, but he had smiled, and nodded, as if to say "Yes, it will." He put out his hand, as if he would have taken her cheek in it, and then dropped it to his side.

He smiled, and added softly: "And Jemima, you shouldn't be afraid of that. It'll be a good thing."

Then he had added: "It's now – or never."

His voice had been as low and tender as if he had been talking to a baby. The memory of it made a ghostly tingle dance up her spine.

He wanted her to meet him in town tomorrow, and get into a car with him alone, and let him drive her to another city. It was unheard of – it was definitely not allowed – and if anyone ever found out that she did it, well, she couldn't imagine.

Only one thing was certain – it would be a scandal, and she would be in disgrace and very likely in trouble as well.

She bit her lip again and shook her head. There was definitely going to be trouble. Because she had already decided that she was going with him.

She believed that the end result was the will of God, and justified it to herself that way. But if she was really honest, she had to admit that she probably would have found a reason to do it anyway.

Because it was wicked and rebellious, but she wanted to see him again. She wanted to get to know him better.

Because only then could she get the answer to the question that had haunted her for months.

Why didn't you take that letter when I gave you the chance?

CHAPTER FOURTEEN

Just after four o' clock, Jemima freshened up and dressed. She could hear her parents stirring down the hall; they were always the first to rise.

She felt guilty already, because she was going to have to tell a story to explain why she was going to be gone all day. The best thing she could think of was to volunteer to deliver some preserves that her mother wanted taken to her sister, a few miles away. It was a long walk, and her parents would expect her to stay for some time, visiting her aunt, and then it would be a long walk back.

It was at least a plausible story, though she'd also have to make up a story about why she hadn't shown up at her aunt's house, as planned.

Jemima bit her thumbnail nervously, but to her dismay, there was nothing left – she had chewed it down to the quick. She knew that lying was wrong, but how could she possibly slip away for a whole day without giving her family some reason for going?

When she went down to the kitchen, her mother was already pouring out coffee, and her father was nursing a cup between his big hands.

Jacob looked up, and his expression softened. He grinned at his eldest daughter, but Jemima was stabbed by guilt, and could only muster a small, sickly smile in return. To her relief, he didn't seem to notice, and her mother pulled her aside.

"Jemima, start some bacon, please."

Jemima did as she was told, but shot her mother a surreptitious look as she carefully placed bacon strips into a fry pan. "Mamm – do you still want to send that basket of preserves to Aunt Priscilla? I could take them today, if-if you like."

Her mother looked at her. "Well – yes, I still do. I'd appreciate that, Jemima, if you're willing. But you'll have to walk. Your father is taking the buggy into town today."

"Oh, that's all right," Jemima answered quickly, and directed her attention to the stove. But when she raised her eyes again, she noticed that her sister, who had just arrived, was staring at her through narrowed eyes.

"Can I come with you?" Deborah asked suddenly.

Jemima's mouth dropped open slightly. Deborah never asked to come with her – anywhere.

Her mother smiled and nodded. "That's a wonderful idea, Deborah! Aunt Priscilla will be glad to see you."

Jemima bit her lip, and added slowly: "Yes! The last time I saw her, she told me that she wanted to teach you how to make her sauerkraut. Now you can learn!"

She didn't raise her eyes. That was another lie; she was getting in deeper and deeper.

But as she'd hoped, Deborah made a face and shrugged. "In that case, I'd rather stay here. I hate her sauerkraut!"

"Deborah!" cried both of her parents, at once.

Jemima finished the bacon, and helped her mother prepare the rest of breakfast. When everything was ready, she sat down meekly at the table, ate in silence, and kept her eyes mostly on her plate. She noticed, uneasily, that Deborah was watching her, and wondered if there was some look on her face that gave her away. Or – her blood ran cold at the thought – that she'd said something in her sleep that gave her away.

When breakfast was over at last – because to Jemima, it

seemed to last forever – she lingered behind to receive the jars that she was supposed to be carrying to her aunt. Her mother looked at her in surprise.

"Why Jemima, do you mean to go now?" she asked.

Jemima looked up at her. "Yes. It'll take a while to get there. I'd like to get there before the sun gets too hot."

Her mother nodded. "That's sensible. Here, I'll get them for you."

Jemima was alarmed to see that Deborah stayed behind at the table as well. Her suspicious blue eyes were still watching. Jemima finally bit her lip, and met them. She gave her sister a direct look.

"Is there something you wanted to ask me, Deborah?" she said, trying to keep her tone neutral.

Deborah narrowed her eyes again, but shook her head. To Jemima's intense relief, she pushed off from the table and went back upstairs.

Her mother returned with a half-dozen jelly jars, a loaf of bread, and half a ripe cheese in a basket. "Here, take these to your aunt," she instructed, "and give her a kiss for me! Be sure to tell her that I'm going to return her book, as soon as I've finished reading it."

Jemima nodded submissively, and felt more wretched than she could ever remember feeling in her life. Maybe she should just forget all about this thing.

But her mother was standing in front of her, with her hands on her hips.

"Well, scoot, girl!" she told her.

Jemima stood up, heart pounding, and carried the basket out through the front door. A rosy predawn light was in the east, and already the countryside was clearly visible. The sounds of early morning came faintly from across the valley: the sound of a barn door closing, a man calling to someone, a rooster's call.

Jemima moved quickly around the side of the house, and walked out to the garden. The Williams fellow had said that he'd be waiting for her in his usual place, but she'd learned that he was a very late riser. She had never seen him before 6 a.m., at any rate. But maybe this morning, he'd make a special effort.

He had promised to take her to his truck, and to drive her to the auction house. He had told her that it was scheduled at 9 o'clock, but the city was a good distance.

She walked out to the very edge of the garden. Her heart was pounding.

This was craziness. She shouldn't be travelling with a man she didn't know, not to the grocery store, much less to a city hours away. He was a crazy man, he'd proved it. What if he just drove away with her?

What if–

A soft hiss from the bushes brought her focus sharply back to earth. The branches trembled. Sure enough – there he was, just visible from her vantage point. She hesitated for a split-second, then walked quickly toward him, and followed into the underbrush.

But as she looked back over her shoulder, she was shocked to see that Deborah was standing on the front porch of the house, watching her as she went.

The Williams fellow took her hand and pulled her through the bushes until they reached the fence that separated the King farm from county land.

Then he turned to smile at her. He was beaming, and looked happier than she'd ever seen him.

"I knew you had it in you, Duchess!" he grinned.

Jemima frowned. "What did you call me?" she demanded.

"Duchess," he grinned, unrepentant. "You look like one. Now, we have to go over this field to get to my truck. I'll help you over the fence."

Jemima slapped his hand away. "I can climb over a fence by myself," she told him.

He grinned at her again, and waved toward it invitingly. Jemima set the heavy basket down in the weeds, hiked her skirt up, and climbed over. It was very awkward, and embarrassing, but she wanted to show this Brad Williams fellow that she was her own person, and not a helpless child.

Once she was over, he hopped over it easily, and then led her through the scrubby, overgrown field to a line of trees at the edge of the road. Sure enough, there was a white truck. He walked to the passenger side and opened the door for her gallantly. She gave him a long look before climbing in – carefully, and with great trepidation.

He walked quickly to the driver's side and climbed in. As he turned the switch, and the engine growled to life, he turned to her and smiled – that nice, warm smile.

Only – excited, too. She could see it.

"Don't worry, Duchess," he told her. "This is going to be the best day of your life."

As the truck pulled off down the road, Jemima shrank down in the seat, turning her face away from the window and covering it with her apron, in case she caught sight of anyone on the road.

If she was spotted riding in a car alone with an Englisch reporter, it was most definitely not going to be the best day of her   life.

CHAPTER FIFTEEN

It only took fifteen minutes for the truck to leave the green hill country behind, and soon they were zooming down the highway on the way to the city. Jemima watched the traffic with terrified eyes. She had only been in a car a few times before, and then only when she'd been sick. The trip had always been to the clinic in town, which was only a few miles away from her house.

But now the truck was hurtling down a highway as broad and wide as the road to destruction at lightning speed, barely avoiding other cars and larger trucks that suddenly appeared in front of them. Jemima clutched the armrest with white fingers, and finally had to close her eyes.

The Williams fellow had been quiet, but he started to hum to himself. Jemima frowned. She was trying to pray.

Then he started talking. "Now, when we get there, Duchess, I'll take you back to the waiting area. I've requested a room for us, so we can watch the auction privately. They've printed up a brochure for the buyers, all about the letter and its history. That might be fun to look at, while you're waiting. The guy from the appraiser's told me last week that he thinks the bidding is going to be fierce. You can't count on that, but the lady from Brinkley's – Miss Juniper, you'll meet her today – said that interest has been off the charts."

Jemima turned to look at him. "My name is Jemima. Not Duchess!"

He grinned at her, and she frowned again. "You don't care what I think, do you, Brad Williams?" she asked crossly. "You just want a story, to make yourself famous!"

He nodded placidly. "Of course I want a story. It's my job to want a story," he agreed. "Is that unfair?"

Jemima was nonplussed. She had never heard anyone admit a self-interested motive so readily. But then, he was an Englischer, and couldn't be expected to do anything else.

"Have you eaten breakfast?" he asked pleasantly.

She turned and looked at him. "Yes."

"Good. It'll take us an hour to get there, so you might be

hungry again. I've arranged for a light brunch before the auction, in case you are."

He was watching the road, and so she let her eyes linger on him. He had combed his hair back neatly, but it was still a big wavy bush, with twigs sticking out at odd angles against the stark light. His eyebrows were like...really, like the fuzzy blonde worms she had played with as a child, always moving, and curling up and down. He had a strong profile: a straight nose, a square jaw, and a stubborn chin.

"Why didn't you keep the letter?" she blurted.

The question seemed to take him by surprise. The fuzzy eyebrows shot up.

"Why? Well, I–" He was silent for a long minute, looked at her keenly, and then smiled and shrugged. "You know, I think you've got me there, Duchess. I don't really know why not. I have a few guesses. Most of them having to do with pride." He turned again and looked at her.

"And some of them, having to do with impressing a gorgeous redhead."

Jemima felt her mouth falling open, and shut it. She turned her eyes to the road ahead, and stared at it steadfastly.

But when she was sure he wasn't looking, she allowed herself the tiniest ghost of a smile.

An hour later, they crossed the perimeter of the city. Jemima gazed up at the skyline in wonder, and more than a little fear. The glittering buildings, towering up into the sky, seemed unlovely and ominous to her. They seemed the very personification of hochmut – of human pride and arrogance. They reminded her of the Tower of Babel – an attempt to climb to heaven without God.

Brad Williams noticed the direction of her gaze. He smiled. "Great, huh? Brinkley's is next to the convention center downtown. We should be there in twenty minutes, and with a little time to spare."

They exited the highway and turned onto broad, congested city streets that, to Jemima, seemed even worse than the ominous buildings. They were alive with people – all of them passing each other without so much as a glance or a nod, and most of them frowning or preoccupied with their gadgets. Lights flashed on and off garishly. There were no trees, only huge signs. And the noise – horns honking, the roar of busses and trucks, and exhaust smells that filtered in even through the car's ventilation system.

She cast a worried glance at her companion, but he seemed completely untroubled by the ugliness of their surroundings.

He glanced at her briefly. "Mind if I smoke?"

She shook her head, and he lit a cigarette, and blew a puff of smoke toward the ceiling. "Now, when we walk in, let me do the talking."

Jemima frowned at him again. "I'll do my own talking," she informed him, and he grinned at her, in that infuriating way.

"No need to get your hackles up. It's just that they know me. I've talked to them before. I can run interference for you, but if you'd like, I can leave it all to you."

He looked at her again out of the corner of his eye, raised his bushy brows, and stuck the cigarette up toward the ceiling.

Jemima bit her lip, and repressed the sudden urge to kick the underside of the dashboard.

Just as he had predicted, fifteen minutes later, the truck dived deep into the bowels of the Brinkley's building. Or at least, that was how it seemed to Jemima. They entered a huge, dark parking deck, as black as any cave, and to her at least, twice as frightening. It echoed with phantom noises and voices, ghostly puddles of light hid more than they revealed, and the low ceiling made her intensely conscious that there were tons of steel and stone overhead. It was all she could do to keep herself from reaching out for the Englischer's arm.

He pulled the truck into a tiny space, turned the engine off, and turned to her, his bright blue eyes glowing in the half-light.

"Show time," he smiled. "Ready to go?"

Jemima looked up into his face fearfully. He winked at her again, and grinned, and it made her feel a little bit better.

But only a little.

She stayed close to him as they walked through the echoing darkness to the elevator. Brad Williams pushed a button and whistled, seemingly unconcerned. When the doors opened he stepped right in; but Jemima hesitated at the entrance.

"Don't be shy, Duchess," he told her wryly. "The only other alternative is the stairs – six flights."

Jemima bit her lip, and stepped in reluctantly.

As soon as the doors closed, there was a huge hum and Jemima put one hand out to steady herself against the wall as the floor vibrated.

Within seconds, the doors opened again. Just beyond them was a glittering lobby with silver chandeliers, walls of glass, plush furniture and deep red carpet.

Jemima barely repressed a gasp. She had never seen anything like it before in all her life. It looked like – like Nebuchadnezzar's palace in Babylon.

She walked closely behind Brad Williams as he led her to another bank of elevators, but much fancier than the one they had just left. Jemima noticed, with a rush of self-consciousness, that some of the passersby were staring at her.

She put a hand to her cap.

The elevator doors closed behind them, and a little light on a console showed the floors as they passed, but this time there was hardly any sense of motion. The doors opened again.

This time, the doors opened onto a large, plush lobby ringed by entrances to smaller auction rooms. Jemima's companion led her out toward a large desk set up in the center of the room. A solitary woman sat behind it. Jemima noticed that she was young, smartly dressed in a business suit, and that her dark hair was swept back in a very professional looking updo.

She rose as they approached and smiled.

"Hello again, Mr. Williams," she beamed, and turned her eyes on Jemima. "And this must be Miss King? I'm Margo Juniper."

Jemima felt herself going red, but shook the well-manicured hand that the woman held out.

"Welcome to Brinkley's! We're so glad you decided to attend the sale, Miss King," Margo Juniper continued. "The auction will commence in thirty minutes, and the conference room is already full to overflowing. There's been incredible interest – we haven't seen anything like this letter in years."

Brad Williams turned to smile at her, and Jemima knew that he was saying "See? I told you so."

"If you'll follow me, I'll show you back to the private room. There's a television in it, so you can watch the bidding as it happens. I've set up the brunch you ordered, Mr. Williams, but if there's anything else you'd like, just let me know."

"Thank you."

Brad held out his hand in silent invitation, and Jemima followed the woman across the opulent lobby to a small door off to one side. When she opened it and stepped back, Jemima's eyes widened.

The little private room was the last word in Englisch excess. Three leather couches ringed an antique table covered in food. There was juice and tea in crystal glasses, coffee in china cups, plates of sliced ham and cheese, croissants, a jelly caddy, what looked like tiny cucumber sandwiches, steaming scrambled eggs, crisp bacon, toast, and pancakes with syrup.

She looked back at Brad William's face almost in consternation. But he just smiled.

"It's perfect, Miss Juniper!" he told her. "You've outdone yourself. Thanks for everything."

"You're welcome. If you need anything, you can just call me from the phone on the side table – extension 1."

"Will do."

She smiled again. "It was nice to meet you, Miss King,"

she said pleasantly. "Good luck with the auction, and thank you again for allowing us to help you with the sale of such an important document."

Then the door closed behind her.

CHAPTER SIXTEEN

As soon as she was gone, Brad Williams plopped down on one of the couches and poured coffee into a china cup. Not for her, Jemima noted, with a twinge of irritation – for himself.

"Sit down, Duchess," he told her easily. He reached for a small remote on the table and switched on the television. Instantly the conference room materialized, and it was evident that Miss Juniper had told the unvarnished truth: every last seat in the auction room was taken, and dozens of people were standing against the walls.

Jemima stared at the screen, round-eyed. She could see everything, just as it was happening, in the room next door!

Brad Williams glanced at her face between bites of toast and teased: "What's the matter, Duchess, haven't you ever seen a T.V. before?"

Jemima turned her eyes to his face, and was gratified to see him look temporarily chagrined. "Oh-oh, yeah. Sorry, I forgot. Well, at any rate, we'll be able to watch the bidding. It should be a real smackdown. They all seem to want that letter bad."

Jemima frowned and sank down onto the couch.

It was nothing but greed, all of it. It felt wrong, and dirty somehow, and she had to remind herself that she was – thought she was – obeying a direct command from God.

But obeying God had never been so confusing before.

Brad Williams collected some of the tidbits onto a plate and handed them to her. "Go ahead, eat. The auction may last for a while, and once we're out of here, the only other chance you'll get is the drive thru somewhere. As much as I'd like to spoil you, I can't promise you a spread like this on the Ledger's expense account."

Jemima took the plate from him, and nibbled morosely on a piece of cheese. She became aware that he was watching her, and she returned his gaze unhappily.

Brad Williams brushed the crumbs off his fingertips and leaned forward across the table. His bright eyes were intent. "Look, Jemima – I know what a big step this is for you. It can't have been easy to come all this way, and…with me." He looked down, and then up at her again. "It has to feel way strange, and maybe a little scary. But trust me – it's going to be fine. Really."

Jemima looked at him uncertainly. His eyes were full of that warm, sympathetic look again. Like he really did understand. Maybe, maybe God was using this young man to accomplish His will, even though he was an Englischer.

Brad smiled at her again. "Because, Jemima King, in another hour, you're going to be the richest Amish woman in history."

Then he cracked the devil's own grin.

Jemima put her plate down with a clatter, and reverted to chewing her nails.

After they had finished eating, Brad Williams had lit yet another cigarette, and she had decided – twice – to just get up and leave, and then didn't, the auction started. A man walked out onto a small stage and set the letter, now mounted in a clear plastic stand, up for all to see. The people in the crowd craned their necks.

After he had gone, the auctioneer walked briskly to the podium. He was tall, slim, youngish, and very smartly dressed.

He got right to the point. "We have here Item Number 10 in the catalog, a letter from George Washington to his wife Martha."

Brad Williams turned to look at her, smiling. Jemima returned a faint, tepid smile and raised her eyes to the television screen.

"I'm going to start the bidding out at $50,000. Fifty thousand dollars. Fifty thousand, do I have fifty-five. Sixty. Sixty-fi– Seventy, thank you sir. Can I have eighty thousand? Eighty, eighty-five, ninety."

Jemima watched in dumbstruck amazement. The auction had just begun, and already she had more money than she could imagine. Why did all those people want the letter so badly? It was sweet, it was even historically important, but it was just a letter, after all!

And if those rich people were that foolish with money – how had they gotten rich in the first place?

"One hundred thousand. Do I hear one hundred fifty, one sixty, one seventy." The auctioneer nodded toward a woman who seemed not to have made any motion at all. "One hundred eighty thousand. One hundred ninety, can I have two hundred? Two hundred, two hundred twenty-five. Yes, sir."

The auctioneer nodded toward a man talking on the phone. The man looked up at him and nodded. "Two hundred fifty thousand."

Jemima closed her eyes and leaned back into the luxurious leather cushions. This wasn't happening. She had never more than half believed those appraisers, and certainly had doubted Brad Williams when he told her that she was going to be filthy rich. She had thought she might get enough to help Adam Yoder with his bills, and maybe a few other people; and, if she was frugal, she might be able to sock a little away for her own family, just in case of an emergency. But this–

When she opened her eyes again, the auctioneer was no longer talking, but chanting in a fast, nasal sing-song: "Five-hundred fifty, five hundred seventy-five, can I see six hundred?"

There was a momentary pause, and Jemima held her breath. The auctioneer's eyes swept the room.

Then he nodded. "Six hundred. Can I hear six-fifty? Six fifty. Six fifty. In the back. Six seventy-five, seven hundred!"

Jemima rolled her eyes to Brad William's face. He was sitting on the couch opposite with his elbows on his knees, and his hands clasped. He was staring up at the T.V. screen with a look of such undisguised pain that Jemima felt suddenly guilty. Yes, of course he looked sick. How could he not?

All of this could have been his.

He hadn't noticed that she was looking at him. He was looking up at the screen with longing in his eyes, but to her surprise, Jemima saw no hint of regret. What was that he had said – something about pride – and wanting to impress a gorgeous redhead?

She felt so sorry for him suddenly that before she realized what she was doing, on impulse, she reached out and gave his hand a sympathetic squeeze.

He took her hand without missing a beat, as if it had been the most natural thing in the world for her to offer, and continued to look up at the screen. Jemima's eyes followed his. The auctioneer was now talking so fast that she could barely make out what he was saying: "Nine hundred thousand, nine-fifty. Nine fifty – thank you ma'am. One million dollars. One million. One – the gentleman in the front."

Jemima felt her heart throbbing in her chest, and closed her eyes again. She was never going to be able to hide this; she'd been lying to herself to imagine that she could. She was going to go home a millionaire, just as the appraisers had predicted, and she was going to have to explain everything.

But would her family understand?

And even more urgent – would Mark and Samuel and Joseph?

She shook her head, frowning. She would have to explain to her parents, and then most likely to the bishop. None of this was allowed, none of it had even happened to anyone else, and she was most likely going to have to repent.

She ticked off the list of infractions in her head. First and most glaringly, running off alone with an Englischer, meeting with him secretly beforehand, and not telling her parents about him at any point in that process. Then, not telling the bishop. Keeping the letter a secret, and not asking anyone else if she should sell the letter. Lying to her parents about going to her aunt's.

She opened her eyes. And watching a television.

She felt suddenly ill.

The auctioneer's voice rattled on: One million two hundred thousand. One million three. Thank you. One million four, one million five. One million six. One million six. Anyone?"

He looked around the room. "One million six. Last call. One million six." He brought a small gavel down with a bang,

Sold!" he announced, and the crowd broke out into applause.

Jemima stared at the screen in open-mouthed disbelief. One-million-six-hundred-thousand dollars.

She was dimly aware that Brad Williams was hugging her, and saying "Congratulations Duchess."

Then the door to the room suddenly burst open, and a camera flash went off.

CHAPTER SEVENTEEN

Brad Williams jumped up from the couch and thrust himself between Jemima and the intruder, but it was too late. His photographer had popped off five shots before he even had a chance to put up a hand.

He glanced quickly at Jemima, then scowled at the newcomer, and leaned in close to hiss: "Eddie, what're you doing? I told Delores I'd get the picture. She promised to do this my way!"

The young man smiled at Jemima, and then replied, through his teeth: "Delores says she gave you until the end of the auction. The auction is over. And so is this story, hot shot. Wrap things up, so we can run it!"

Brad's eyes widened. "Is Delores here?"

The photographer's lips pinched into a smug smile.

Brad ran a distracted hand through his hair. "Oh, no. Oh–" He grabbed the man's arm. "Is she outside now?"

"She called me from the parking deck. She's on her way up."

Brad frowned, looked down at the floor, and then hissed: "Go out and stall her for me!"

"Why?"

"Just do it. Or next week I'll write a series called '500 uses for pig dung' and send you out to Duluth for a 10-page spread!" He shoved the man's shoulder, and the photographer crashed against the door, shot him an evil look, and left.

Then he closed his eyes, took a deep breath, and turned back to Jemima.

Her green eyes were two big question marks. "Who was that? Why did he take my picture when I told you I–"

Brad ignored her. He sat down quickly on the couch and punched the button on the phone. Maybe he could get Jemima out of there before Delores arrived and picked her brain like a mad scientist.

"Hello, Margot? This is Brad Williams." He looked up at Jemima and tried to smile reassuringly. "Miss King has to go now, but she wanted to leave by a private exit.

"You understand – she doesn't want to be approached by the curious. Yes. Yes, I'll be happy to. No, we're in something of a hurry."

The secretary's voice buzzed faintly. "Really?" He looked at another door on the opposite end of the room. "Clever! And thanks, gorgeous. I owe you."

He put the phone down with a clatter and rose. "Well, that just about wraps it up, doesn't it, Duchess?" he said brightly, his eyes on the door. "There's a private exit, so you don't have to talk to anyone else."

Jemima frowned at him. "What's going on? You told me–"

Brad took her arm, pulled her smoothly to her feet, and propelled her across the room to the alternate doorway. He opened it and gave her just enough of a nudge to send her through.

The sound of the other door opening gave him just enough time to shut the door behind her, and lean against it, before the door to the outer hallway opened, and Delores Watkins walked in.

Brad crossed his arms. "Well, Delores – I didn't expect you here! How was the air traffic coming down Main Street?"

The older woman ignored him. She put her camera down on a small table and looked around. "Where's the girl?"

Brad shrugged. "You just missed her."

Delores' mouth thinned to an annoyed line. "Hmm... I wanted to get a juicy angle to pull in the millennials. Something about her love life. If she has one."

Brad raised his brows in mock regret. "Yeah, that's a shame. I just sent her back to 1845."

Delores gave him a narrow look. "On the Ledger expense account, I suppose."

Brad shrugged again, and smiled.

"Well, since she's gone, make yourself useful. What was the final sale price for the letter?"

Brad's smiled deepened. "One million six."

Delores nodded, and seemed mollified. "Good. Your story is ready to go, and now we have the photos. But I'd like to do a follow-up, if the story does well. And after what it's cost us – it had better do well."

Brad felt rotation in the small of his back. The doorknob behind him was turning. He leaned against it and laughed loudly.

"Trust me, Delores. Who loves you?"

Delores raised her heavily-lined brows and snorted. "The better question would be: who delivers? It had better be you, golden boy, if you want to grow up to be a real reporter."

"It can't miss, D. Fifty says a million hits before it's all over."

Delores shook her head and turned to the door. "You don't have fifty, Diamond Jim."

On this crushing parting shot, she departed.

He closed his eyes and slumped against the door, but the knob began digging into his lower back again. He turned and opened it.

Jemima stood in the opening, hands on hips. Her lovely eyes were bright with indignation.

"Why did you lie to that woman?" she demanded. "And why did you lie to me? You said you weren't going to take my picture!"

Brad stepped through the doorway, closed the door behind him, and ushered her down a narrow hall. "Trust me, if you knew Delores, you would understand instantly. And I didn't take your picture. That was my morally deficient colleague, without my knowledge or consent." He opened a door at the far end, which opened out to face a private elevator.

He pressed a button, and then turned to face her. "When I see him again, I'll object in the strongest possible terms."

The elevator doors opened, and he nudged her into the elevator. "I just talked to Margot Juniper, and she says that

Brinkley's will transfer the money to the bank account you gave them within 30 days. It will be one million six, less any applicable taxes, and of course, Brinkley's fees."

To his relief, this intelligence had the effect of silencing Jemima's objections. She frowned, looked worried, and began to chew a pink fingernail.

The elevator took them down to the garage level, and the door slid open soundlessly. They were in a glass-walled bay facing the parking deck.

He turned back to her. "Just stay here and I'll bring the truck around. That way, no one will see you walking out."

"Why are you scared that someone will see me?" Jemima objected. "I'm not hiding from anyone!"

"Of course not," he smiled, over his shoulder. "I'll be right back."

He walked quickly through the underground garage, weaving between cars and looking over his shoulder. The word was out now, and–

He slowed down, cursing under his breath. Sure enough, there was a gang of older reporters waiting for him around the white truck.

He looked down at the floor; but when he looked up again, he had firmly adjusted his game face and was smiling broadly. He sauntered out into the light, hands in pockets.

"Well, well! Am I throwing a party?"

Five hungry faces turned toward him. "There he is! Where's your little friend, junior? The Amish princess?"

"Oh, now, that's a sad story, friends. She left me for a guy with a beard." He fumbled in his pockets for the keys. "She said I wasn't hot enough."

"Come on, now, Brad. What happened to her? We'd like to get acquainted."

"She beat it back to the green hill country. Though I did my best to get her to run away with me."

They laughed. "Your sugar momma?"

"My insurance plan."

The reporters laughed again. "Too bad, Brad! Care to give the rest of us a shot?"

"You're on your own. I suggest you find some dungarees from the Civil War."

Another reporter leaned in and jabbed him in the chest. "You know where she lives. Come on now, tell us."

Brad smiled up into the other man's eyes. "I know where she used to live. With a million bucks in her bank account, I don't think she's going back to the farm. She did say something about going to a hotel, though."

"Which hotel?"

"Where? Here?"

Brad slid into the truck and closed the door behind him. He leaned out of the window. "I don't know. I'm off to indulge my grief. Anybody wanna loan me a twenty?"

They waved him away. "As if! Get out of here."

Brad cranked the truck and pulled away slowly. As soon as he had straightened the truck, rounded the corner, and the last reporter had faded from the rearview, he turned the truck sharply and made a beeline back to the private landing.

Jemima was still standing there patiently, and to his relief, she was alone. He leaned over and pushed the door open.

She hesitated again, bit her lip, and then slid in.

CHAPTER EIGHTEEN

He drove out of the parking deck as fast as he could, and did a few switchbacks on the city streets just in case some of those guys had spotted them. And was glad he did; while they were waiting at a light, he saw Channel 4's van go gliding down a side street like a shark patrolling the shallows. He nodded grimly. *Yes, their star reporter, Andrews: he was a smart one.* But, judging from the way Andrews was scanning the convention center, it looked like the little weasel had bought his story about the hotel.

And so he'd been thrown right off the scent by a college intern who wasn't even a real reporter yet. Brad exhaled with a sigh, and scanned the rearview. To his relief, he didn't see anyone else, but he didn't relax until he'd cleared downtown and was on the highway again.

Because he knew what would happen if one of his rivals got hold of Jemima. They'd dissect her like a lab specimen, and then spin every innocent thing she might say in the most sensational terms possible. God knew, he wasn't the most ethical man in the world, but at least he had stuck to Jemima's story, and what few things she'd said about it.

Not her personal life. And that was a big, fat, red dividing line between him and professionals like Andrews.

Not that Andrews was the only one. Even Delores would do it, if she could. He took another drag on the cigarette and frowned.

Jemima was watching him with a puzzled expression.

"Why did we drive around and around in circles for so long?" she asked. "Are we lost?"

He glanced at her. "No." He looked out the window, had a brief argument with his conscience, and lost. He turned to her.

"Look, Duchess – you're a very rich person. That's a wonderful thing, but you have to be a little more careful now than you used to be."

She frowned. "What do you mean?"

"I mean, there are people who" – he paused – "might try to take advantage of your good nature. Now that you're rich."

She crossed her arms. "Like who?"

He raised his eyebrows and looked at her ruefully. "Let's just say that I know some of them."

Jemima stared at him again out of those lovely green eyes. "Are you one of them?" she asked.

He winced inside – it was a reasonable question – but he met her gaze.

"No, I am not."

He was gratified to see her blush, and lower her eyes; but he wasn't entirely sure that he'd told her the truth.

"It's your life, and I don't have the right to tell you what to do. I'm just saying that it'd be smart not to make any new friends right now. Because there are going to be lots of people who will want to be your new friends."

Jemima looked troubled. "You mean people will be coming out to our farm." She turned to him. "Like you did."

This time it was his turn to go red, but he nodded. "That's right." He attempted a sickly smile. "But they won't have my sterling qualities – or my charm."

She felt quiet again, and didn't say anything else for more than an hour, during which time he chain-smoked and she sat quietly watching the countryside. The passing landscape slowly melted from skyscrapers, to smaller skyscrapers, to office buildings, to shopping malls, to suburbs, and then to open countryside.

Now and then he stole a glance at her out of the corner of his eye, wondering what she was thinking. It was hard to tell, and even harder to concentrate, because he could never look at her for long without his brains getting scrambled by her beauty. Today, it was the riotous curls of bright coppery hair. Even her severe hairstyle couldn't control them. Little curling wisps escaped all around the edge of her cap, and framed her face more poignantly that any painting. She looked like some Dutch Renaissance masterpiece. She had that dreamy beauty and melting feminine softness.

That could, unfortunately, turn in an instant to Puritanical indignation.

Suddenly, and apropos of nothing recent, she twisted to look at him, and her eyes were stern and unblinking. "You lied to me, Brad Williams. You told me, that you were only going to come out to my house once, and no more, and you came back and back. You said that you weren't going to take my picture, but you took it anyway – with that other man's hands! You told me that you were going to respect my wishes, but you've done just what you wanted to do, from beginning to end!"

Brad nodded dryly. That was the trouble with the Amish – they didn't understand ethical complexities or completely acceptable shades of gray.

"Now, Duchess–"

"And you call me some name that isn't mine, and why I don't know, because I never invited you to!"

By this time the truck was bouncing along the back roads just minutes from her farm. Rows of shoulder-high corn blocked the view on both sides. Brad felt his heartbeat quickening, and his face going red. He objected: "A friendly nickname. Why all the sturm und drang, Duch– Jemima?"

She was warming to her subject. "It's not a nickname. And when you call me this, it means you have no respect. No respect for what I say, no respect for my home, no respect even for my name!"

Now he was getting a little alarmed. She sounded really angry, and it was important not to let her get him stirred up, too. He put out one hand, as if to reassure her. "Sweetheart, please calm down, now…"

For some reason, those words acted on her like an electric shock. She straightened to her full height, and her eyes blazed.

"I am not your sweetheart," she cried, "I am not your Duchess, I am not a–" she struggled for words – "a doll without a face!"

He could feel his own face going red. He wasn't mad, but

yes, he was plenty – something. He told himself that it was important not to get stirred up. But a wave of heat surged through him from the bottom up and made his heart pound in his neck – and scrambled his brain.

Again.

"Why are you making me out the bad guy?" he sputtered. "Hey, I just helped you become the richest girl in the county! I would think I'd earned a little something – if not genuine gratitude, then at least a token thank you!"

She acted as if she hadn't even heard him. To his dismay, she wasn't even looking at him. She was staring out the windshield as if she saw some drooling monster on the other side of it.

"No, and you don't even have respect for me, for my – for my person! You even grabbed me and kissed me, without so much as a handshake or, or a question, much less permission! You're a-a–" she sputtered, and lapsed into angry German again.

He jerked the truck to a stop in front of her house and turned to face her. She already had her fingers on the door handle. In an instant she'd be gone.

He bit his lip. What the heck. If she was this angry with him now, she wasn't going to let him come back, anyway. And he couldn't bear to leave her without even a goodbye.

He grabbed her by the shoulders, looked down into those

blazing green eyes for a split-second, and gave her the kiss of his life. It was even crazier and more desperate than the last one, more fiery, more frantic, and more likely to ensure that she'd never speak to him ever again.

But he didn't care.

Mother of mercy, the lips – he'd never met anything like them, they melted like a receding wave into that silky mouth. His heart jumped into his throat.

That mouth that was kissing him back. Yes, yes, yes!

But that delightful moment suddenly came crashing down. The sound of an outraged voice boomed from outside. Brad raised his eyes over Jemima's head, and to his horror, the red-haired giant filled the window behind her. The giant grabbed the door handle, and when he found it locked, he simply ripped the passenger side door right off the truck. It peeled off the hinges with a hideous sound of tearing metal, and Jemima pulled out of his arms and shrieked crazily in German.

Jemima's father reached in and lifted his tiny daughter out of the passenger seat and set her down on the grass. Then he turned back.

Brad grabbed the wheel and gunned the motor, and the truck lurched over the dirt road with a roar. He sent it hurtling towards east Egypt without any clear idea of where he was going, or any real concern. He lifted terrified eyes to the rearview.

The giant was standing in the middle of the road with one hand on his hip, and the other clenched in a fist. He was shaking it.

Brad almost closed his eyes in relief. When he looked down at his hands they were trembling – whether from passion or terror, he couldn't tell. But one thing was for sure. He turned his eyes to the open cavity on the side of the truck. He was going to have a time explaining this to Delores.

CHAPTER NINETEEN

Brad Williams laced his fingers and stared at his computer screen. One last reading before it went to print:

Local Amish girl finds Washington letter worth $1.6 mil

Serenity, PA—Jemima King of Lancaster County was the lucky finder of a letter written by George Washington. Miss King's letter was verified by appraisers as a genuine and previously undiscovered correspondence from Washington to his wife, Martha, probably written during the Revolutionary War. It was recently sold at Brinkley's Auction House in Philadelphia for $1.6 million.

Miss King says she found the letter hidden in the back of an antique clock that she purchased at the Satterwhite Gift Shop in downtown Serenity.

"I didn't know what it was at first," Miss King said. "It was very sweet, a letter from a man in love. You could tell that he was worried that he might not see his wife again.

"I was glad that the letter turned out to be real, and that he got to come back again to Mrs. Washington. I like to think that they were happy."

The director of Brinkley's, William Danforth, says that interest in the letter was intense. "We haven't seen a letter like this for years," he commented. "The rarity of the letter, coupled with the intense interest, combined to push the price past a million dollars – a new high for this type of historical document."

Miss King says that the sale will have no impact on her way of life, and that she plans to save the money.

The anonymous buyer is a collector of American historical documents, and lives in Washington D.C.

Brad frowned, and bit his lip. His first major story in print.

He looked at the photo. It hurt his ego to admit it, but just as he'd suspected, the photo was what made the story. Jemima's beautiful, innocent eyes looked up at the camera like some adorable fawn's. She was such a fantasy girl that it was hard to believe she was really one of the "plain people."

He leaned back into his chair and sighed. He felt like an idiot, and he wouldn't want anyone else to know it, but he'd uploaded the other four photos Eddie had taken onto a thumb drive and meant to keep them, since he wasn't going to see her again.

He closed out the story and opened the photo file.

Eddie had been fast; there he was, giving the Duchess a celebratory hug when the sale figure had been finalized. Her little fingers curled over his back, and she was staring into space, as if she couldn't believe it.

Then, a split-second later, the two of them half-turned toward the camera. The Duchess was now looking stunned and a little scared; and his expression was one of dawning comprehension and anger.

In the third – the one they ran, and cropped to only show Jemima – she was looking full into the camera with that deer-in-the-headlights look.

And the last, a giant hand covering the lens. His hand.

Brad cursed under his breath. Eddie, I'm going to send to Duluth on the principle, you sneaky little weasel!

The sound of his office door opening made him close the file quickly and look up. Delores stood in the opening, hand on hip.

"Well, wonder boy, are you still game?"

He pursed his lips and reached back to open his wallet. He pulled out a bill and slapped it on the desk. "Fifty."

Delores smirked, and set another bill down beside it. "Well, we just went live. It's the moment of truth, hot shot. Let's see if you stay an intern -- or become a *reporter*."

Brad drew a deep breath and clicked over to the Ledger's social media page. There was his story, and that stunning picture of Jemima.

He dropped his eyes to the story's page views, and Delores moved behind his chair to look.

One view. Five, fifteen. Then...nothing.

Brad went very still. He could feel his heart beating in his throat. Come on, come on.

Sixteen views. One share, two. The first comment:

'Wow she's so beautiful!'

Followed by:

'Wow she's so RICH! Marry me, gorgeous!'

Brad exhaled and looked up at Delores. Her face was as unreadable as stone.

Twenty views, twenty-five. Five shares, thirty-five views.

More comments:

'Why don't I ever find anything like this?'

'Hey, I've been to that store!'

Fifty views. Ten shares, sixty, sixty-five views.

Brad glanced at his watch. They'd been live for less than five minutes.

Seventy-nine views, twelve shares. More comments:

'What did the letter say?'

Delores stirred behind him. "Put a link to the Washington letter at the end of your story."

Brad straightened and tapped keys. "There you go." His eyes returned to the page views.

And widened. Damn—just in that short time – two hundred sixty views, fifty-one shares. More comments:

'If I were her, I'd get on a plane and never look back. Aruba, baby!'

'She looks like a painting.'

'Think she'd turn English?'

Three hundred thirty-seven views. Sixty shares.

Delores' secretary walked in, smiling. "The Amish Barbie story just got picked up by Channel Four."

Brad frowned at her, but Delores only asked: "Did they credit us?"

"Yeah."

Delores relaxed and turned to look at Brad. "Well, it looks like you earned your wings, wonder boy. You were right. It's going to be big."

She placed a large hand on his shoulder. "You're now a full-time reporter for the Ledger. You just earned fifty dollars. And lunch, on me. I'm taking the office to O'Malley's to celebrate."

Brad looked up at her in relief and tried to smile, but his mouth wasn't working right. His lips felt like they were crooked.

"We'll talk about your salary and your new assignments tomorrow. No more yokum stories for you, my boy! Get your coat," Delores commanded, and swept out of the room like a ship casting off to sea.

The pretty secretary lingered and Brad noticed, with surprise, that she had a distinct gleam in her eye. She slid one hip over the edge of his desk and swung a shapely leg in his direction. "Looks like you've scored big. Congratulations, Brad."

He met her eyes. They were large and blue. One of them winked at him.

He smiled faintly, and then turned his lips down. Oh, why not. It might be good for him to get the Duchess out of his system. Or, at least try.

He picked up his coat and slung it over one shoulder, and extended an arm to the giggling blonde girl. "You're coming with us to O'Malley's, right?" he asked.

"Sure," she purred, and took his arm.

But after they had walked out, the comments continued to appear on the social media page.

'I'm in love!'

'She must be wearing makeup. Nobody looks that good naturally!'

'I bet the house where she lives is picturesque. I wish I could see it!'

CHAPTER TWENTY

Jemima looked up into her father's face fearfully. His expression reminded her of a huge, dark thunderhead just before a cloudburst.

"Daed–"

"Silence!" he barked, and she closed her mouth and looked down at her shoes.

They were standing out on the front lawn; he, with his massive arms crossed, and she, wishing she could make herself invisible. The mangled truck door was lying on the ground, just as it had fallen when her father had pulled it off of Brad William's truck.

Her father took a deep breath, and seemingly, got a new grip on his patience. "Now, Jemima," he said evenly, "we are going inside, and you are going to explain to your mother, and to me, why you did not go to your aunt's, as you told us. And where you were all day. And why you came back here in the company of an Englisch reporter." His voice gathered bass undertones, like a giant organ. "And why–"

Jemima raised her eyes. There were tears in them, and her lips were quivering. "Oh, Daed," she cried, "I'm sorry! But you don't understand! It was the will of God!"

He raised his brows, and tilted his head slightly, as if he mistrusted his ears.

"Oh, yes – if you'll only let me explain!" Jemima cried earnestly.

"You'll have plenty of chance to do that, young lady," he promised her grimly, and took her arm. He marched her up the front steps, and across the porch, and into the house. The screen door slammed behind them.

"Rachel!" he called. "Come and see what your daughter has done!"

Rachel King came down the stairs, her face a question mark. Jemima burst into tears, her mother held out her arms, and she went into them, sobbing.

Rachel met her husband's eyes over Jemima's head.

Her husband responded as if he had been severely rebuked. "Now, Rachel, it's no use to give me that look. You don't know what's just happened!"

"I know that our daughter is in tears, Jacob," she replied softly, looking down at Jemima's face. "What did you say to her?"

Her husband looked wounded. "Me? I am upholding standards in this house. Our daughter did not go to her aunt's house, as she told us. She has been somewhere else, all day long. I walked out into the yard just now to see her in the arms of a strange boy – an Englisch reporter!"

Rachel pulled back from her daughter and stared up into her face. "Jemima, is that true?"

Jemima nodded, and burst out into fresh tears.

Rachel looked at her husband again, and this time her eyes held worry. "Come, sit down at the table, Jemima," she said, and put an arm around her. "You can tell us what happened. We aren't angry, are we, Jacob?"

Her husband rolled his eyes, and threw up his hands, but followed her without objection.

Rachel helped Jemima into a chair, and then took one beside her. "Now, Jemima, tell us what happened," she urged.

Jemima sobbed into her apron. "When, when I went to the store a few months ago," she gulped, "and bought the little clock for Deborah, I found a piece of paper in it," she stuttered. "It was a l-letter."

"The letter you showed me?" her father interjected.

Jemima nodded. "Two Englischers came here to ask me about the letter. One of them wanted to buy it, and the other was the reporter." She was shaken by another gust of tears.

"It was a letter from George Washington. The reporter said it was worth a lot of money, and I should have someone look at it."

"And you gave it to him?" her mother asked.

Jemima looked up at her, her beautiful eyes swimming. "I tried to give it to the reporter," she whispered, "but he gave it back, and said he had showed it to the appraisers, and that it was worth a fortune!"

Rachel looked quickly at her husband, and he leaned close.

"Jemima – are you telling us that you – that you sold the letter?"

Jemima nodded, and burst out into guilty sobs.

Her parents looked at each other. Jacob leaned back in his chair, dumbfounded, and Rachel looked down at the table in stunned silence before recovering.

"Was that why you were with the Englischer?"

Jemima nodded. "He took me to the auction house today,"

she sniffed, and wiped her eyes. "I watched the people bidding on it, and they just wouldn't stop. They went on and on, until the letter sold." She looked up at her mother woefully.

"One million six hundred thousand dollars!" she whispered.

Jacob King burst out into startled German, and his wife covered her mouth with one hand. Their eyes met over Jemima's head.

There was a long, pregnant silence. Jacob took a deep breath and went on, slowly: "You still haven't explained, Jemima King, why I saw you with the Englischer, doing what no good Amish girl should do with a boy she doesn't know?"

Jemima's lips trembled. "It was just – he – was so understanding," she stammered, "and so helpful, and he didn't take the letter for himself when he could have, that I–"

Jacob nodded grimly. "Ha! An Englischer trick, to gain your trust! What did I tell you, Jemima, when you first found the letter? You would have done better to listen. Now, we must go to the bishop with this news of the letter, and see what he will say."

His eye returned to his errant daughter. "And why did you tell me it was the will of God?" he asked.

Jemima shook her head. "The Sunday after I got the news that the letter was worth so much, the preacher said, What if a miracle happened? What if I had a million dollars and kept it back from the poor? And I thought that God was speaking to me. And that He meant me to sell this letter. And to give the money to help the people who need it, like Adam Yoder, and his parents."

Jemima's mother reached for her, and took her into her arms. She looked at her husband through swimming eyes, and kissed her daughter's hair. "There, you see Jacob, her heart was right. I think that was a fine thing to do, Jemima. You're not in trouble. Everything will be all right, you'll see. Now go up to your bedroom, and wash, and get ready for bed."

Jemima sniffed, and dried her eyes, and looked up gratefully at her mother, and timidly at her father, and retreated.

After she had gone, Jacob crossed his arms and looked at his wife ruefully. "What good does it do for me to try to have discipline in this house, Rachel, when you pet our children so?"

His wife looked at him affectionately. "I know you, Jacob King," she smiled serenely. "You feel the same as I do, and you're right to try to keep them safe. But Jemima did no wrong."

"No wrong? You didn't see her, she was kissing that Englischer as if he was the last young man on earth. I don't know who he is, but it's plain he has designs on her – and the money he thinks he can get out of her! I don't want Jemima's life to be ruined and her heart broken, by some–"

His wife shook her head. "But Jacob, it's her rumspringa. It isn't good, I know, but if we make too big a fuss, we make it into something bigger than it is, maybe. Jemima has three healthy young Amish boys who are in love with her. One of them will make her forget this Englisch boy, you'll see."

"Well–"

"And the money, Jacob," his wife insisted, leaning toward him – "we must tell the bishop, yes, but Jemima hasn't joined the church yet, and she isn't bound to do what we would. The money is hers, Jacob. We can't force her to do anything with it."

Her husband looked at her grimly. "She's a 17-year-old girl, Rachel. She doesn't understand how to deal with money wisely. Do you want to see your daughter in Englisch clothes, and wearing makeup, or buying a television – or a car?"

His wife frowned, and shook her head. "No, Jacob," she replied simply. "But we must trust her, and trust God. He will help her to do the right thing."

Her husband's expression softened and he threw up his hands. "This is why I never win an argument with you, my Rachel," he sighed, and then leaned over and kissed her ruefully.

CHAPTER TWENTY-ONE

The next morning found Jemima out in the back yard of her parent's home, hanging clothes on the clothesline. It was still early; there was mist still hovering in the low folds of the hills, and the air was still pleasantly cool.

Jemima picked up a wet dress and draped it over the clothesline. Breakfast had been subdued and mostly silent. Her parents had said nothing about her embarrassing predicament. She wasn't sure if Deborah knew what had happened, because she, too, had been silent.

Jemima frowned, wondering why Deborah hadn't told their parents about seeing her walk off into the bushes with a stranger. But to be honest, she wasn't really worried about it –

just grateful.

She had other and much bigger things to be worried about.

It was only a matter of time now before someone saw the story in the newspaper, and the word got out in the community that Jemima King was a rich millionaire. She wondered if people would think that she was greedy for money and full of hochmut. She wondered what they would make of the fact that she'd talked to an Englisch reporter, and had gone all the way to the city with him, alone.

Or, more specifically – what Mark and Samuel and Joseph would make of it.

She shook her head, and stamped her foot and cried. It was that Englischer reporter – if he hadn't done what he'd promised not to do, if he hadn't grabbed her and kissed her again, she would've had time to get inside before her father caught them, and at least she could've had a few days of privacy before everyone found out. But now, even that was gone.

She grabbed up another dress and slapped it over the line savagely. Brad Williams was a liar. He had done only what he had wanted to do; he had no concern for anyone but himself.

And the thing that upset her most was that she was never going to see him again.

The sudden sound of her father's voice brought her sharply back to the present. His voice was raised in outrage and – yes – it was unmistakably anger.

It was coming from the front porch.

Jemima dropped a shirt onto the grass and ran around the side of the house. She was just in time to see a white truck scratch off down the road in a cloud of dust. She looked up at her father.

He was watching the truck as it left, and muttering in what her mother sometimes called "Low German."

When he turned back, and saw her standing there, he put his hands on his hips and regarded her with awful irony.

"So, here you are, hoping to see that hound again? No, my addled daughter, it wasn't him!" he said tartly. "It was a man from another such Englischer rag, full of questions about things that are none of his business! Now go back to your chores, and pray to God to be healed of silliness in the head!"

He relapsed into ominous muttering, and Jemima turned her eyes to the road. The truck was still visible, a tiny white dot speeding back to the city.

"Oh, Daed," she objected, but he waved her away, and retired to the house in disgust.

Jemima settled back into her chores, and they had quiet for

all the rest of that day. But soon after nightfall, when they were all in bed, there was a loud rapping on the front door.

Jemima got up out of bed and went to the window that faced the front yard. There was a van parked outside and several people climbing out of it. Jemima's heartbeat quickened. There was a big "Channel 10" logo painted on the side of the van. For an instant she hoped that Brad Williams would be with them – but no, he worked for a newspaper, not a television station.

One of the strangers lit a giant lamp, and the whole front of the house was suddenly flooded with blinding light. Jemima gasped and closed the curtain.

She could hear her father stomping down the stairs, and pulling on his pants as he went. The door creaked open, and Jemima could clearly hear a woman's voice:

"Hi, I'm Pamela Harrison with Channel 10 News – ah, that's a news station out of Philadelphia – and I was hoping to ask you a few questions about–"

Her usually-civil father cut her off. "We were all in bed, and we have nothing to say to anyone, about anything. Please go away, and leave us alone."

He shut the door with a bang.

But, Jemima was quick to note, he did not come back upstairs.

Voices muttered unintelligibly from below; the strangers seemed to be holding a conference of some kind. Then there was the sound of footsteps on the porch steps. She moved gingerly toward the window again, taking care not to show herself in it.

A group of four people were standing on their lawn in front of the van. Their silhouettes were razor-sharp against the huge light. The woman was very smartly dressed in a pantsuit and heels, but the others – photographers, she guessed – were dressed in oversized shirts, baggy pants, and sneakers.

Suddenly, the woman's voice boomed out over a microphone: "Jemima, we know you live here. We'd like to talk to you. Please call us at Channel 10 News."

Jemima turned her head. Now she could hear her mother's bare feet rushing downstairs, and she knew why: it was to keep her father from bursting out the front door.

She could hear her mother's low, pleading voice downstairs, followed by her father's – the bass organ sound was very strong now – followed by a soft scuffling sound, and her mother's voice again, very urgent.

To Jemima's relief, the painful brightness suddenly died. The intruders packed the lamp up again, and slowly climbed back into the van.

The van's lights flicked on, and the motor growled, and the van slowly rolled away over the long dirt road.

Jemima slumped against her bedroom wall and closed her eyes. Her heart was pounding with a mixture of fright, and deep embarrassment.

Because every other family in the valley had heard the woman's giant voice calling for Jemima King to "come out and talk."

She put her face in her hands and cried. But before long she heard her father's big feet climb the stairs, and then pause outside her door.

It swung open gently, and his tousled head of red hair appeared in the opening.

"Mima, are you all right?"

"Oh, Daed!" she sobbed.

He held out his arms and she went running into them. She wept on his shoulder as he patted her back with one huge hand.

"There now, Mima, my girl," he soothed, "there's no reason to be upset. We all know that Englischers are crazy in the head. They are doing what they do. But soon something new will happen, and they'll forget all about this, and leave us alone. Eh?"

He looked down at her. "Come now, let me see a smile, my brave girl."

Mima swallowed, and looked up into his face, and

mustered a weak smile. A tender light dawned over his face, and he smoothed her hair back.

"That's what I like to see. Now go back to bed, and don't worry. Your father is here, and he won't let anyone bother you."

He gave her a quick peck on the cheek, helped her back into bed, and pulled the covers up around her chin.

Then he smiled down at her reassuringly, walked out of the room, and closed the door softly behind him.

But after he was gone, Jemima bit the sheets with her teeth, and squeezed her eyes together, and wept again. Not entirely from fright, as her father had supposed.

Now she was angry, too.

CHAPTER TWENTY-TWO

The next Sunday, Jemima stood next to her mother and Deborah at worship. It was a beautiful midsummer's morning, a temptation to wandering eyes, but her eyes, and her mother's eyes, and Deborah's eyes, were all glued to the floor of Silas Yoder's barn.

Because that morning, Jacob King was one of the penitents making a public confession of sin.

He stood next to the bishop, hand in hand, head bowed, as the bishop asked him gently:

"What sin do you confess, Brother Jacob?"

Jemima stole a glance at her mother. She had closed her

eyes, and appeared to be praying.

Her father cleared his throat, and intoned: "I confess the sin of anger."

The bishop nodded. "And how did you commit this sin?"

Her father cleared his throat. "I tore the door off of a man's truck."

The bishop looked momentarily startled, and added, faintly: "Was that the only sin you wish to confess?"

Jacob shook his head. "No."

"What other sin do you confess, brother?"

"I brought down a flying camera that was taking pictures of my home. With a rock. And," he coughed, "I chased a couple of men with a shovel, and drove them off of my property."

The bishop nodded. "Is there any more?"

"Yes."

Jemima looked at her mother again. Her eyes were still closed, and she was frowning slightly.

Jacob cast an apologetic glance at his wife. "I – ah, I threw a woman into a pond. And her camera."

The bishop bit his lip, and nodded.

"Are you truly penitent, brother?"

There was a long moment of silence. To Jemima's astonishment, her mother coughed aloud, and Jacob sighed: "Yes, um, yes I am."

"Very well, brother."

Jacob nodded to the bishop, and returned to his seat on the men's benches, and the bishop led the closing prayer.

After the service, Jacob rejoined his family, and Rachel put her hand on his arm in a rare public display of affection. She beamed at him, and he pretended not to notice it, but Jemima noticed that he sometimes looked at her mother out of the corner of his eye, and smiled such a tiny smile, that no one who wasn't looking would've seen it.

But to judge by her smile, Jemima was fairly certain that her mother had seen it.

They sat down at long tables for lunch out under the sky, the eldest first, as always, and Jemima busied herself helping. But she was shy and didn't try to meet her neighbor's eyes, because this was the first Sunday since her embarrassing problem had become common knowledge, and she was nervous.

No one had been unkind; in fact, many of them spoke to her in what sounded like sympathetic tones, but she knew without having to ask that everyone knew everything.

Because her new fame had become a problem for the whole community.

The bishop and a group of elders had been obliged to go to local government and request a police presence in the first frantic week after the story became public because it had generated not just local, but national interest. All kinds of people were streaming to the area uninvited: the press first, followed by the rest of the world – tourists, the curious, men who claimed to be in love with her, people who wanted her to give money to their cause (or to them) and even those who were plainly mentally ill.

Deborah had been scared out of her wits by a man who had appeared out of one of their haystacks like a ghost; but she had been so outraged, and had given him such a fierce tongue lashing, that he had run away.

One of Jemima's geese had been stolen from its pen, and had later appeared on an online auction site advertised as "The million-dollar Amish goose." It had reportedly sold for five times its true value, and had acquired its own web site on the Internet, where, she had heard, thousands of people visited every day to see the goose wear funny hats, and ride a skateboard.

Her own mother had even been accosted in their backyard by a woman with a camera who shot video of her without her permission, until her father had arrived.

And that had resulted in this morning's confession. Jemima

thought, with a pang, that there were probably more confessions to come for her poor father, because there was no sign of the frenzy slowing down, much less stopping. Her father had been forced to barricade the driveway to keep cars and trucks from rolling right up to their door, and he hadn't had time for his work, because it had become necessary to guard the property from intruders all day long, and all night, too.

But what was just as bad, at least in Jemima's mind, was that she hadn't heard a word from any of her suitors since the scandal broke. It was odd and not like them at all, for all three of them to neglect her for a whole week.

She had seen no sign of any of them so far that morning. But when it was her own turn to sit down at the table, she saw with gratitude that at least her friend Ruth Yoder was the same. She came and sat down beside her at the table, and scooted over so that she could giggle and whisper to Jemima about the boys they saw.

And to Jemima's intense relief, Ruth didn't ask her lurid questions about her money, or about the handsome Englischer reporter, or about the circus that had rolled over the entire countryside for the last seven days.

She just sat there, munching jam and bread, and giggling, and pointing out the cute boys, just like always. And at first, that was a tremendous comfort.

Until Jemima noticed that Mark Christner, Samuel

Kauffman and Joseph Beiler were, in fact, in attendance that morning.

They just weren't attending her.

Jemima's mouth dropped open in amazement. All three of them – all three – had abandoned her for Miriam Zook.

It wasn't possible!

But she couldn't deny what was right in front of her eyes – there they were, clustered around another girl like bees around a hive of honey. Mark was offering Miriam a bite of his toast, and Samuel was laughing at something she had said, and even poor, shy Joseph was staring up at her with his big calf eyes.

Of course, Miriam was a beauty with her white-blonde hair and coffee-brown eyes, and she was a sweet girl. Jemima set her lips, and made herself admit it: Yes, Miriam was a – a very sweet girl.

But a pang of something so like jealousy stung her, that she was forced to admit that she didn't much care if Miriam Zook's righteousness floated her all the way up to heaven, like a big blonde balloon.

Ruth caught sight of these sad defections an instant later, and she leaned close to whisper, not unkindly: "Close your mouth, Mima! And don't stare. You don't want them to think that you care what they do."

Jemima closed her mouth then, and trained her eyes on her plate. But the rest of the day was ruined for her, and she was intensely conscious that she was now an object of pity as well as of wonder, because she feared that all the teenage girls there, and probably their mothers too, were shaking their heads and saying sadly:

"Poor Jemima King! It turns out that all the money in the world can't buy you love."

CHAPTER TWENTY-THREE

That night, Jemima curled up in a little ball in her favorite chair. It was her Daed's big stuffed chair, the one she had always crawled up into as a child when she wanted to sit on his lap. It was a deep, satisfying, oxblood red, and soft as a dream. And it had that comforting Daed scent of pipe tobacco, and a whiff of fire and steel.

The chair was in his little study, a room that he went to sometimes, all by himself. The chair faced a big stone fireplace, and in the winter, it was the coziest place in the house.

It was too warm for a fire in the middle of summer, but the idea of a fire appealed to Jemima that night. She hugged herself unhappily.

The door creaked open slowly, and when Jemima looked up, her Daed was standing there, looking at her sympathetically. He walked over, pulled up a chair, and crossed his arms over its back. He looked a question.

Jemima looked at him. "Did you mean it, Daed?" she asked quietly.

He raised his eyebrows. "Mean what, Mima?"

"Did you mean it today, when you said you were sorry?" she asked softly, and turned her eyes on his face.

He looked back toward the doorway, and seeing it empty, turned back and replied: "Mima, there are some things we must do if we feel them, or not."

"So you aren't sorry for those things you did?"

"I didn't say that." He looked up at her face briefly. "If you ask me, do I feel sorry, then no; I feel angry. But I know in my mind that anger is wrong, and we must all repent for wrong things."

Jemima digested this. "If it all happened again, would you do things the same?" she asked.

He looked at her, and set his jaw slightly. "I don't know."

"Because I feel angry, too, Daed," she whispered. "So angry! Angry at the Englischer reporter for lying to me, and for being selfish. Angry that he hasn't come back. Angry at the other Englischers for all coming here at once and making us trapped in our own house." She felt tears burn her eyelids, and looked away. "Angry at Mark and Samuel and even Joseph for going after Miriam Zook, and leaving me alone."

Her father's big hand appeared and gently turned her chin to face him. His eyes were sad and sympathetic.

"My poor Mima," he said quietly. "This is your first taste of trouble, my girl! But it won't last for long, you'll see."

"You should have seen them, Daed," she complained, "mooning over Miriam Zook as if she was the only girl on earth, and feeding her things, and laughing like she was so funny, and staring at her like she'd dropped down from the sky. It was horrible to watch!"

Her father's expression had taken on a tinge of amusement. "I did watch it, Mima."

Jemima looked at her father in surprise. "You noticed?"

"Of course I did," he replied. "And do you know what I saw?"

She shook her head.

"I saw three young pups with very bruised feelings, sending a message to a certain young lady. And do you know what that message was?"

Jemima pinched her lips together, and looked away.

"The message was, 'Two can play that game.' Or in your case, my poor Mima – three."

Jemima stared steadfastly out the window, frowning.

"Think of how you'd feel, Mima, if you saw that Mark Christner had gone from courting you one day, to running off to the city with a beautiful Englisch woman, the next."

"It wasn't like that at all!"

"Or that Samuel Kauffman had found something as big as a letter from George Washington, and that he didn't share the news with you. When you thought that you were important to him."

Jemima felt the tears coming back, and frowned.

"Or that Joseph Beiler had suddenly become rich. So rich, that now you were afraid to come near him, because he might misunderstand."

"Oh, Daed –" Jemima whimpered, and looked up into his face "–do you really think so? I never thought of how what I did – how all of this – must have made them feel."

Her father gave her a contemplative peck on the brow, and sighed. "That play-acting with Miriam Zook may have been silly, Mima, but it was a real warning, just the same. Those boys are telling you that you can't take them for granted."

He looked down at her face. "If I were one of them, I wouldn't let you do it, either. You've gotten used to being the queen bee around here, Mima. Maybe you've gotten a little too used to it."

Her father took her into his arms. "Maybe you should stop to think about their feelings, before you make another big decision. At least, you should, if you want one of those pups for a husband."

He sighed, and his big blue eyes looked rueful. "Though it would make things easier for everyone, if you could figure out which one of them you wanted."

Jemima put her arms around her father and frowned. He was right: what she had felt earlier was jealousy, pure and simple. And you couldn't be jealous over someone you didn't love.

She hugged her father closer, and closed her eyes. He had been right about something else, as well. She had been playing fast and loose with something very precious to her: the love of her friends. Mark and Samuel and Joseph were at least that, if not much more, and it had been wrong of her to shut them out.

She looked up at her father. "Do I need to repent, too, Daed?" she whispered.

Her father considered. "Maybe a little, Mima," he said, smiling. "But young men are always very forgiving of a pretty girl. And if they love her – well, she'll hardly have the words out of her mouth, before all is right again."

Jemima smiled, and snuggled back into his chest. "I love you, Daed," she murmured, and closed her eyes.

He rested his cheek on hers. "And I you, little girl."

CHAPTER TWENTY-FOUR

The media frenzy took more than two weeks to calm down enough for Jemima to be able to go out in public without fear of being mobbed; and only then because the local police had begun to jail trespassers and repeat harassers.

But little by little, Jemima began to take small excursions to places besides worship; to her friend's houses mostly, because she still wasn't bold enough to attempt to make her doll deliveries in town. And she wasn't sure she had the heart to do it, anyway. She'd been told by her friends that some of the shops were selling red-haired "Jemima" dolls to the tourists, and that they were outselling even traditional Amish dolls.

Jemima watched the countryside zoom past as their car rolled down the road. The last month had been a nightmare, but the money from Brinkley's had finally arrived in her bank account. Now that she was able, Jemima was determined to make at least one good thing come out of all this mess: she was going to the hospital to tell Adam Yoder's parents that they didn't have to worry about his medical bill.

Her father had asked Mr. Biggams, one of their Englisch neighbors, to drive them to the hospital in his car. Mr. Biggams was one of the few Englischers that her father trusted; he was a kind man, a hard worker, and minded his own business – three traits that her father very much admired.

He was also sympathetic. Jemima noticed that he was careful to take the back roads for as long as possible, and to Jemima's relief, the only other traffic that they saw was their neighbors' buggies.

Jemima was hopeful that she and her father would be able to get to Adam's room unnoticed. Mr. Biggams had warned them against using the main entrance to the hospital, and had promised that he knew a back entrance, closer to the elevators, that would give them privacy.

Her father shared the back seat of the car with her, and occupied four-fifths of it. He filled the space so completely that the girl at the parking lot tollbooth couldn't have seen Jemima if she'd tried, and when Mr. Biggams parked the car right next to a small door, and they all hurried through it,

Jacob King was a more effective shield for his daughter than a cloak of invisibility.

The way that Mr. Biggams knew seemed to be one that visitors weren't meant to use, but the best possible one for their purposes. It wound through a narrow maze of labs, small offices, and examination rooms, most of them empty. The few people they saw were nurses or techs, and all of them were too busy to take notice, and unlikely to ask questions if they did.

Mr. Biggams' indoor trail led at last through a pair of double doors that faced a small elevator. To Jemima's relief, it was already open, and empty, and they hurried in.

"What floor is he on?" Mr. Biggams asked, adjusting his glasses.

"The fourth," her father replied, and their neighbor pushed the button.

When they arrived on the fourth floor, it, too, was relatively empty and quiet. They made it to Adam Yoder's room without notice or comment.

Jacob King knocked softly on the door, and a voice from inside said: "Come in."

Mr. Biggams tactfully declined to enter, and remained outside, but Jemima and her father walked in.

When they entered, Jemima's eyes were drawn like a

magnet to Adam Yoder. The little blond boy was hardly recognizable because most of him was inside a body cast. One arm and two legs were lifted by slings.

His parents were sitting by his bedside, and looked to Jemima as if they hadn't slept in days.

Adam's father, Benjamin, stood up and extended his hand to her father. "Hello, Jacob," he said earnestly, and nodded to Jemima. "Thank you for coming."

Adam's mother, Hannah, smiled at Jemima, and she smiled back, trying not to show the pity that she felt. Her heart went out to them suddenly. It must be awful to be going through such a crisis. She was suddenly ashamed of her own self-pity; her own troubles were nothing in comparison.

"Won't you sit down?" Benjamin asked, but Jacob shook his head.

"We won't stay long. But we wanted to come by and see Adam, and to pray with you. Jemima also wanted to tell you something."

He turned toward her.

Jemima felt her face going red, but she looked full into Benjamin Yoder's face and set her mouth. "I guess you heard about what happened to me," she said steadily. "I just wanted to say that – whatever your hospital bills are, I will pay them. Because, I want to. And I can."

Hannah Yoder burst into tears and covered her mouth with her hand. Benjamin Yoder's eyes moved incredulously from her face to her father's. Jacob nodded.

He shook his head. "I don't – I don't know what to say."

Jacob shook his head. "There's no need to say anything." He looked back at his daughter's face and smiled.

And Jemima allowed herself to smile back. She hadn't expected to feel such pleasure, but she did. In fact, she hadn't felt such pleasure in a long time. She literally felt – warm.

"God bless you," Benjamin said softly, "Jemima King!"

On the way home, Jemima noticed that her father kept looking at her. He didn't say anything, but he was wearing that expression that always meant that he was secretly pleased. No one outside his family would have recognized it – it was too subtle – a certain tilt of his jaw, and the way his eyebrows rode high over his brow.

Jemima looked down and suppressed a smile. Because these were unmistakable signs.

Her father was proud of her.

CHAPTER TWENTY-FIVE

When they got back to the house, Jemima went upstairs to her own bedroom and closed the door behind her. She walked over to the window that looked out over the garden.

The afterglow of her father's approval still lingered; it was like the feeling she had when she had been out in the sun for an hour or two.

She looked up into the fluffy white clouds floating over the fields. Or, maybe, she was feeling something more than just her father's approval. She smiled to herself.

There was so much else she could do, besides just helping the Yoders: she could give money to her parents, so they could have something in case of an emergency. And she had always meant to give a good bit of the money to the community fund, to be used for neighbors in need.

She was still thinking about it, when voices from downstairs interrupted her train of thought. They were coming through the open window – the window directly over the front porch.

She could hear the porch swing groan and creak. Her father's voice called out: "Well! Good afternoon, Mark Christner! We haven't seen you in a while!"

Jemima's heart jumped into her mouth. Her first reaction was joy: her second, was to bite her lip. Her Daed was reminding Mark of his defection, and she was sure that Mark would take his point.

"Good afternoon," Mark's voice replied. His voice definitely had a chastened sound. "Is Jemima home?"

The swing groaned again, as if her father had crossed his legs. "She was here, but the other fellow came by a few minutes ago, and they went for a walk. I couldn't say when they'll be back."

Jemima opened her mouth in shock. How could he?

Then she giggled.

Mark's voice had an edge now. "The other fellow?"

Her father blew his nose, and sniffed. "Yes, the blond one,

I think. There are so many nowadays, I can't keep 'em straight."

Mark's voice was now hard with suspicion. "The blond one! You mean Samuel Kauffman?"

Her father's tone was lazy and nonchalant. "Or, maybe, the boy from Marietta. A guest of her aunt's, they've really hit it off." He coughed. "Shall I give her a message?"

"No. I mean, yes, if you would. Just tell her that I – I came by."

"I'll do that, Mark. Say hello to your folks for me."

Jemima crept to the window and looked down over the porch roof. Soon she could see Mark's black head, followed by his body, walking down the driveway, and out along the road.

He reminded her of nothing so much, as a rooster who'd just lost a fight.

Later that afternoon, she was sitting in that same swing, helping her mother shell beans. Deborah had been commanded to go to the mailbox. She returned and tossed one of the envelopes into Jemima's lap with a grimace.

"Well, he's back," was her disgusted assessment.

Jemima opened the envelope, and three pages of

handwritten poetry came tumbling out into her lap. She smiled, well pleased. Joseph was so sweet. He hadn't deserted her, after all!

She picked up the letter and read:

I know that you have fled away from me, for a little while, like a mare that jumps the fence and runs away. But now you have come back to your true pasture.

Her smile faded into a puzzled frown.

You were tempted away by a deceiver with an apple, and have chewed the fruit of the world. It tastes like honey in the mouth, but is bitter in the entrails.

Jemima's frown deepened.

But now you are returned, to a good and pleasant land, with green fields and an abundance of hay.

Jemima's mother was watching her face. "Is something wrong, Jemima?"

She looked up at her mother and hurriedly folded the letter. "Oh – no, no." She tried to smile. "It's from Joseph."

"Good," her mother replied, approvingly.

The next day, just after lunch, the last wanderer returned to the fold. Jemima was in the garden again, picking tomatoes, when two hands went over her eyes. She jumped and shrieked, but Samuel Kauffman's laughter put her instantly at ease.

She turned to face him. "Samuel! You scared me to death!"

He laughed at her, and then went quiet, and pulled a little tendril of hair out from underneath her cap. "Then we're even, Mima," he said softly.

Jemima looked down at the ground, and he took her hand. "Why didn't you tell me about all of it, Mima?" he asked. "I would have understood."

She lifted pleading eyes to his face. "Oh, Samuel, I wanted to, but I was – I was scared. Nothing like it had ever happened to anyone, and I didn't know what to do."

He twirled her hair between his fingers. "And the Englischer – he told you what to do."

Jemima nodded, and looked down again.

She could tell that he tried, but Samuel couldn't keep a tinge of jealousy out of his voice. "Don't let yourself get fooled, Mima. An Englischer man will take advantage of a girl like you. They are out in the world, they have no honor."

Jemima looked up at him gratefully. "You're very sweet to be worried about me, Samuel," she told him.

He took her in his arms. "I can't help it," he smiled. "I care about you."

He was going to tell her he loved her. Jemima gasped and searched Samuel's eyes. They held hers steadily – but to her disappointment, he said no more.

She smiled and hugged him anyway. After the awful month she had endured, she had learned a painful but valuable lesson. Namely, that it was wisest to be happy with what you had, instead of reaching for what you didn't.

All three of her suitors were back in the fold, and she didn't intend to do anything to drive them out again.

At least, not until she knew which one of them was her husband.

CHAPTER TWENTY-SIX

Mark Christner returned to the house two days later, and this time her father gave him admittance. Jemima had to cover a smile, to see what a timid return Mark made. He was normally so self-confident!

"Mima, may I see you outside?" he asked humbly.

Jemima smiled and nodded, and he led her out past the front porch, out across the lawn, and down to the edge of a little pond that fronted the road. There was a willow tree there, and a swing, and they sat down in it.

Mark looked out over the water a long time, and Jemima felt sorry for him. Words had never been Mark's strong suit, and she could see that he was struggling with them now. Finally he turned to her, with those beautiful blue eyes, ringed by dark lashes. And just said:

"What happened, Mima?"

For some reason, the way he said it went through her like a spear. Jemima felt tears in her eyes, and shook her head.

"It was too big for me, that's all, Mark," she murmured. "It got out of hand so fast. I met the Englischer reporter at Mr. Satterwhite's store when I bought the clock. He bumped into me, and the letter popped out of the back, so he saw it. And he saw another man wanting to the buy the clock very badly. I guess he just – guessed that the letter might be worth money.

"And they both came to the house and were arguing. And the reporter kept shouting that the letter was worth money. And it all got so confusing that I-I just mailed the letter to the reporter, Mark. I just wanted it to go away."

She raised troubled eyes to his. "But what was strange, Mark, was that – he didn't take it. The Englischer reporter didn't take the letter, or the money. He wrote me back, and told me he'd had it appraised, and that they were holding it for me. He promised to help me sell it."

She looked down at her hands again. "If only I would – let them write a story about it."

Mark was frowning, looking out at the horizon as if he saw it on fire. He nodded. "I can see what happened, Mima," he said angrily. "The Englischer was using you."

He turned to her, and added earnestly: "There's more than one kind of greed, Mima. You can be greedy for fame as much as for money. And some people are. They're sick with hochmut." He shook his head solemnly. "The Englischer used you, Mima."

Jemima felt her lower lip trembling – because she knew he was right. Mark had always had more common sense than most people, and he was right. He had seen instantly what she was only just realizing.

The reporter had used her.

Mark's eyes took on a sympathetic look. "I hope he didn't hurt you, Mima."

Jemima looked up at him, and smiled, and shook her head. "Oh, no!" she said stoutly, "the idea! It's true that he – liked to flirt, but it was very plain that he did that all the time, with every girl he met. Oh, no," she assured him. "I wasn't hurt."

And, she thought to herself, it was true. She wasn't hurt, at least not anymore. She was angry.

Mark relaxed visibly. He seemed to exhale.

"I'm glad," he said simply. "I hate to think of you being hurt, Mima." He reached out and twined his brown fingers in hers.

He looked at her again. "What are you going to do now?"

She met his eyes unhappily. "I don't know," she moaned. "I let the Englischer talk me into selling the letter, because I prayed to God, and I thought He was telling me to give the money to people who needed it. So, I am. Doing that, I mean."

Mark looked at her affectionately. "I figured you would." He put her hand to his lips. "You've always had a big heart."

His smile faded, and he looked down at the ground. "But until you finish, it gives me a problem, Mima."

She looked a question, but he didn't meet her eyes. "I can't court with a millionaire," he blurted.

He looked up again. "Mima, you know how I feel, but I can't. I won't have people saying, that Mark Christner is tagging after Mima King for her money. I won't do it."

Jemima sucked in her breath. Her Daed had been right. She raised her eyebrows, and sputtered: "B-but, Mark, it wouldn't make any difference. Nothing has changed. I haven't changed."

Mark's eyes took on a keen look, almost like pain. He shook his head. "Yes, you have, Mima. You used to be a beautiful girl. Now, you're a beautiful millionaire."

Jemima looked down at the ground, and shrugged painfully. "But I just told you, that – that I never meant to keep it. I mean to give the money away."

Mark squeezed her hand. "I know, Mima. Tell me when you're done." He leaned over to kiss her, and then got up and walked away.

Jemima sat staring at the water for a long time after. She felt as if someone had punched her in the stomach, but Mark hadn't meant to be cruel. Just the opposite – Mark was just trying to be honest, to let her know that he wasn't after her for her money. It was noble, and admirable, and good.

And she bowed her head, and cried bitterly over it for well over an hour. Because she knew now that it was only a matter of time before she had this conversation again with Samuel, and even with Joseph. They were Amish boys, they'd been raised right, and they would never let anyone think they weren't honest.

Especially when it came to love.

After a while her father came down to the lake and settled down in the swing beside her. He put his big arm around her shoulder and let her rest her head on his chest.

Her father looked up at the sky. "He told you he wasn't going to court with a rich girl, didn't he, Mima?"

Jemima nodded, and cried: "Why didn't you tell me, Daed?"

He leaned down and kissed her. "Would that have made it

any easier?"

She sniffed, and shook her head.

"No. Well, Mima, you're just going to have to choose. No decent boy will let people think he wants a girl for her money. None of your pups is going to stand for that, at least, not if he's worth having. I'm glad that at least one of them proved that he is worth having."

"Oh Daed," she replied indignantly, "Samuel and Joseph are too, and you know it!"

He chuckled. "Do I? I suppose. But let them prove it. You know, Mima, all of this may have a silver lining after all. It will show you which of those boys mean business about you, and which love you just for yourself."

Jemima buried her face in his shirt and nodded. "Maybe so, Daed," she mourned, "but right now, it just feels awful."

"I know," he soothed, and patted her shoulder. "Come inside, my girl, and stop moping out here. We're in sight of the road. You don't want to be in the papers again, do you?"

"Oh, Daed!" she cried, but then sputtered out a little laugh.

Her father looked down at her tenderly. "That's what I like to see. You're going to be all right, Mima – I promise. Come."

Jemima took her father's hand, and let him lead her back up the hill to the house. But she set her mouth into a hard, thin line. There was only one question in her mind:

What was the world's fastest time, for giving away a million dollars?

Because she was about to beat the record.

THE END

Thank you for Reading!

And thank you for supporting me as an independent author! I hope you enjoyed reading this book as much as I loved writing it!

In the next chapter, there is a FREE sample of the next book in the series, An Amish Country Treasure 3. You can find it at your favorite online booksellers in eBook and Paperback format.

All the Best

Ruth

AN AMISH COUNTRY TREASURE 3

CHAPTER ONE

"But *Daed*!"

Jemima King's lovely green eyes pled with her father's implacable blue ones, but when it came to a battle of wills, it was no contest. The head of the house sputtered an incredulous *whoof*, as if he couldn't believe what he'd just heard, and Jemima quickly lowered her eyes in defeat.

But Jemima's mother dimpled, and reached out to caress her oldest daughter's cheek. "Your father said *no*, and *no* it is," she told Jemima. "But it was very sweet of you to offer. It shows that your *heart* is in the right place." Rachel met her husband's gaze, and a look of approval passed between them.

Then Jacob raised his table napkin and wiped his mouth – a signal that the discussion was over.

"Well, *that's* that! Are we ready to go?" He trained his

bright eyes on Jemima's face.

She looked up at him pleadingly and made one last try. "But *Daed*! It doesn't make sense for me to give that much money to the *Yoders'*, and none to my *own* –"

Her father's answer was to slap his hands on his knees, stand up suddenly, and announce to the room at large: "Well, I'm going now! Everyone who wants to come with me had better shake a leg."

He made good on his threat immediately; he strode across the living room, opened the front door, and walked out.

Jemima's mother turned to her with a smile. "He's *proud* of you," she said softly and put her coffee cup to her lips. "And so am I."

Jemima met her eyes unhappily. "I may not be all that good. I want to give the money away, at least partly so I can see Mark and Samuel and Joseph again! All of them told me that they couldn't court with me anymore. Or at least, not while I'm so rich." She sighed, and kicked one of the table legs with a small foot.

Her mother reached for her hand. "Well, after today, everything will be back to normal," she reassured her. "When you give the money to the community fund, all of this will be behind you, and your – your *admirers* will be back over here every day, giving your father headaches."

Her mother laughed, and Jemima finally broke down and

joined in. It was such a wonderful thought that she couldn't help dwelling on it – the prospect of getting this Englisch *letter business* over for good.

And getting her young men back!

She took one last sip of coffee and patted her lips with a napkin. "I guess I need to go," she sighed. "The sooner I begin, the sooner it'll be *done!*"

Jemima followed her father across the living room, and out the front door. She paused on the porch steps, and breathed in the cool morning air, and let her eyes wander over the vista.

It was overcast: low, heavy clouds scudded over the green fields and veiled the hills. The mild breeze was fragrant of rain. It was pleasantly cool, a reminder that fall wasn't far away.

But another, less pleasant sight met Jemima's eyes too: one that she hadn't expected. Instead of her father waiting patiently for her in the buggy, he was standing beside Rufus, hands on hips. He was staring at a line of cars, parked by the side of the road, about 300 yards away.

Roughly a stone's throw away.

The strangers were smart to keep their distance, Jemima thought grimly. While the trespassers had never respected her family's privacy, they'd quickly learned to respect the fact that her father was a good shot with a rock.

Jemima pinched her lips into a straight line. She could tell at once that the people in the cars were reporters. They were standing beside their opened doors, resting their cameras on the car roofs. No doubt those cameras had long-range lenses – they were probably being photographed at that very moment!

Jemima looked up at her father. She could tell that he was wrestling with the same question that was troubling her: should they cancel the trip or go to the bishop's house anyway, and arrive surrounded by a gaggle of photo-snapping reporters?

Disappointment welled up in Jemima's throat and stuck there, like a big, hard lump that would not be swallowed. She'd looked forward to this day, she had prayed for it, and now that it was here –

For the thousandth time, she wished that she had never met Brad Williams. This was *his* fault. But he hadn't stuck around to see the misery he'd caused -- the coward!

While they were standing there, another car crested the hill, passed the reporters, and stopped just outside their driveway. A small, wizened man poked his head out of the window.

Jemima's father had built an impenetrable and multi-layered barricade of old anvils, hay bales and rocks, and the man was obliged to get out of his car: but get out he did.

When he skirted the barricade, Jacob strode down to meet him, calling:

"This is private property. You're trespassing -- get out!"

The man came ahead, and fixed his eyes on Jemima. He called out to her: "Are you Jemima King?"

Jemima stared at him in wonder. He was a shriveled stick of a man, with a pinched, mean face: but he had courage, she had to give him that. Anyone else would be running away by now because her father had quickened his pace and was rolling up his sleeves. But she nodded slightly.

The man pulled a sheaf of rolled-up papers out of his jacket, lobbed them at her, and turned to flee. He was surprisingly nimble, but he was obliged to dash to the hay bales – and to jump over them – to avoid being caught by her angry father.

The man landed on his feet and turned at the door of his car. "Jemima King, you've been served!" Then he tried to get back into his car, but the reporters had been watching, and some of them were nimble, too. They mobbed him before he was able to get in.

Jemima was able to hear just enough to be sure that they got the whole story out of him before he slammed the car door and sped away.

Jacob stayed at the barricade and scowled at the reporters who were brave enough to linger.

"Mr. King, is your daughter being sued?"

"Who's suing Jemima, Mr. King?"

"What's she being sued for?"

Jemima was amused to see that when her mighty father made as if to climb over the barricade, even the boldest of their tormentors fled back to the safety of their cars. His Amish beliefs notwithstanding, Jacob King was not a man to be tested.

When he was satisfied that he had chased the enemy from the field, Jacob climbed the hill again. As he came, he bent down and picked up the papers that the intruder had dropped on the lawn.

Then he handed them to Jemima.

She opened them reluctantly. They were written in very formal, very legal-sounding terms, but even she could see that the papers were telling her that she was being sued.

For $1.6 million dollars.

By a man named Caldwell C. Morton.

She looked up at her father. He put an arm around her shoulder, turned her, and walked back to the house.

"Come."

They walked back inside, and Jemima could tell by the way her father looked at her, that he expected her to burst into tears. A few months ago, she would have.

But not now.

She sighed and looked up at her father's face disconsolately. "I guess I'll stay at home today, Daed," she told him, and went to seek solitude.

CHAPTER TWO

Jemima retreated to her father's study and collapsed into his big red chair. She opened the sheaf of ominous-looking papers and flipped through them. Most of them might as well have been written in another language. She was able to glean that Caldwell C. Morton was suing her because he claimed that she'd promised to sell him the George Washington letter for $10 and was claiming that she had gone back on her word.

Yes, of course – he was the angry Englischer, who had tried to buy the letter from her that first day. If only she had *let* him!

Now, he was trying again to get the money, by accusing her of *lying*.

Jemima tossed the papers on the floor at her feet. Then she pulled her knees up under her chin and hugged them.

She stared into the empty grate, imagining a crackling fire. How good it would feel to burn the papers up -- and her troubles with them!

Jacob and Rachel followed softly, a few minutes after. Jacob pulled up a chair for Rachel, and another for himself. They sat down and sat with their daughter in supportive silence. Jacob's craggy face wore an uncharacteristic softness, and Rachel's doe eyes sparkled with sympathy.

After a long pause Rachel suggested: "We should pray, and ask God what to do."

Jemima didn't turn her head but instead shook it. "I already know what God wants me to do."

Rachel exchanged a wordless look with her husband, then replied: "What do you think God wants you to do, then?"

Jemima stared glumly into last year's ashes. "He wants me to keep the money." She turned to look into her mother's questioning eyes. "He wants me to *fight*. And that means I need to *get a lawyer*."

Rachel gasped audibly. Her expression plainly showed that this was the last answer she had expected.

"But you *can't!*"

Jemima set her small jaw and returned her mother's gaze. "Yes, I can," she countered, "and I will. I'm *not* a liar. That *Englischer* is the liar.

"And I've suffered too much for this money, to have someone steal it away, like a fox snatching a chicken!"

Rachel stared at her daughter in patent horror. "Jemima, it isn't *right* to resist! It's God's will for us to accept what comes, and *submit*." She turned to her husband for confirmation. "Not – not *go to court!*"

Jacob met his wife's gaze sympathetically, but his silence told his eldest daughter that he wasn't ready to agree with her. Jemima grasped the opportunity.

"I haven't joined the church yet. I can make my *own* decision," she insisted firmly.

Rachel stared at her as if she'd grown a second head. "What's come *over* you?" she wailed. "My beautiful, modest daughter – going to *court*, to *sue* a stranger over – over *money!*

"What will people think?" she cried. "What will your friends think? Oh, Mima, what will your young men say, when the girl they love goes out among the Englisch, *again*, and this time, to fight with them for *money!* They will wonder who she is. They will wonder if they still know her!" Rachel clamped her hand over her mouth in anguish.

At this, Jacob stirred. "Jemima is being sued, Rachel. She can't help *that*."

His wife turned to him. "She wants to get *rid* of the money, Jacob. She told me so herself! So why not just let the man *have* it since he wants it? Why go to court, in front of the Englisch, and, and all that nonsense with the reporters? Just let this man have the money, and –" she turned back to Jemima – "go back to living *your own life!*"

Her mother's gentle rebuke weakened Jemima's resolve. It was hard to be strong with those pleading eyes on her, and even harder to explain what she felt. But she met her mother's gaze.

"I'm *tired*, Mamm," she quavered. "I'm tired of being *bullied* over this money. And I won't let anyone call me a *liar*." She felt tears welling up, and blinked them away impatiently. "It's true that I don't want the money. I *never* wanted it. It's been nothing but a headache to me, from the first day I got it!"

"Then why not get *rid* of it?" her mother pleaded.

Jemima set her mouth. "I *am* getting rid of it," she replied. "But I believe it was God's will that I *get* that money, so I can *give* it to the people who need it, like the Yoders. Not this, this *Caldwell C. Morton*, whoever he is. He doesn't need the money. He's just greedy!"

"You don't know that," her mother objected. "God allowed this thing to happen. We should accept it."

Jemima shook her head. "But he's *suing* me. I have to go to court, and at least explain that I've given half the money away, and that part is *gone*. I gave some to the Yoders, and some to the Millers, and some to the Beilers, and a little to Grandma Sarah Fisher. And they spent it up."

Jacob looked at Rachel, and his silence was an unspoken comment. His wife shook her head and cried: "It's no use to look at me that way, Jacob King! You're not the *only* one who tries to uphold *standards in this house*!"

Then she turned to her daughter, and her usually tranquil face was wrung with anguish. "And you, Jemima – you should pray, pray *hard,* before you decide to do this thing. You'll drive away the boys who love you, *and* your friends, *and* displease God, if you turn to *fighting* and *warring*. That's the Englisch way! I can see now what this money has done to you – my poor girl!"

Then she lifted her apron to cover her face, and fled upstairs, weeping. Jacob gave Jemima a long, but sympathetic look before leaving the room to follow her.

Jemima sighed and fell into a depressed silence. But to her surprise, Deborah had been listening from the doorway. She walked out into the study, munching an apple. She looked at Jemima steadily.

"Don't let it faze you," she said. "It's your money. I say, *fight* the sucker."

Then she drifted off again, leaving Jemima to stare after her.

CHAPTER THREE

A faint tapping disturbed Jemima's dream. She turned her head on the pillow, murmuring, but she couldn't recapture it. The dream slid away from her, and slowly formed again.

Only this time, it became the darkness of her bedroom.

Moonlight slanted in through the window. There was no sound except for the faint echo of her father's thunderous snoring, from far down the hall. Jemima turned, sighing, and settled into her pillow again.

But the tapping came again. This time, sharp and loud, like something hitting her window.

She opened her eyes. It *was* something hitting her window.

Her heart began beating oddly. *Someone was outside on the lawn.* Was it a reporter, or, some crazy stranger, or even –

She frowned and set her mouth, and threw the covers back. She put two bare feet on the bare floor, threw a knitted shawl around her shoulders, and went to the window.

The moonlight flooded the lawn below with light. A man was standing below her window, looking up.

It – it looked like *Joseph Beiler*!

For an instant, astonishment wiped every other thought out of Jemima's mind. Joseph Beiler, on her lawn at midnight? He was the shyest boy she had ever known. Something was surely wrong! The sudden fear that something terrible had happened, urged her to dress quickly, and go down to meet him.

When she opened the screen door and stepped out onto the porch, he was standing at the corner of the house, waiting for her. She moved quickly down the porch steps, and across the lawn to meet him.

She searched his face anxiously. "Why, Joseph, what's wrong?" she whispered. "Why are you here? Has something *bad* happened?"

To her amazement, his answer was to grab her by the shoulders, crush her to his chest, and give her the third-wildest kiss of her young life. Her eyebrows shot up, but after the shock wore off, she didn't make a serious effort to get out of his arms. To her amazement, it seemed that Joseph wasn't *nearly* as shy as he seemed. He was actually an *excellent* kisser -- when he applied himself.

When he released her, she paused to catch her breath, and looked up at him. "Why, *Joseph*! I'm surprised at you!"

He seemed to take her breathless comment as a rebuke. He hung his handsome head, and said, softly: "I'm sorry, Jemima. I know what I said. But I couldn't stay away. I had to see you!"

Jemima smoothed her hair, and tried not to smile. "I understand, Joseph."

He took her hand warmly. "I *knew* you'd forgive me." The thought seemed to overwhelm her gentle suitor. He looked down at the ground.

"I shouldn't have come. I still stand by what I said before."

"Oh, I know, Joseph – and I *understand*. I mean to give away the money, and I understand that we can't see each other until it's gone. But it may be a while, Joseph. Something else has happened, and there may be a – a delay."

He looked down into her face. "What delay?"

She nodded unhappily. "A man came by the house and gave me papers. He said that I'm being sued for all the money by a strange Englischer. The Englischer says that I promised to sell him the letter, and lied!"

Joseph said nothing, but seemed shaken by a burst of anger. He pulled her close in a protective embrace, and pressed his cheek tight against hers. He rumbled angrily: "*Er ist verrückt!*" and for an instant, the deep bass note almost reminded Jemima of her father.

"Now I have to go to court and tell them that I don't have all the money anymore," Jemima whispered. "I've given almost half of it away already."

Joseph pressed her close. "My beautiful *maus*, don't be afraid. I'm here for you, don't let it make you afraid." Joseph kissed her brow, and tightened his hold around her.

Jemima allowed herself to be comforted. Joseph was tall and muscular and sweet and strong. He had silky brown hair and beautiful brown eyes, like a deer. His skin was tan and his teeth were white. And after all she'd been through in the last few days, Joseph's arms were a very welcome haven.

Jemima snuggled into them, thinking that Joseph really was, overall, the best-looking of all her suitors, and certainly the most sensitive. And after that astounding kiss, he had *a third* thing in his favor.

Now if he would only confess that he *loved her,* and give up writing poetry, she could see herself…

"I'll stand by you, Mima, no matter what you decide to

do," he told her suddenly. "Even if you go to court!"

Jemima looked up at him, startled out of her thoughts. "*Really,* Joseph?"

He nodded. "Yes, Mima," he said simply, and closed his eyes in a determined frown. "It isn't fair that you should suffer any more than you *have*."

Jemima looked up at him hopefully. Maybe *now* Joseph was going to do more than kiss her. Maybe he was going to tell her that he *loved* her. Maybe he was even going to *make himself vulnerable.*

"I'll go to the courthouse with you, if you like," he told her, opening his eyes again. "I'll help you find a lawyer, if you want one."

Jemima stared at him in the darkness, crestfallen. She had hoped that Joseph, of all people, would say *something* at least about love. Why did men always refuse to share what they felt?

She shook her head and tried to bring her mind back to what he was saying.

"That's wonderful of you, Joseph," she replied, "but my father will help me -- I think."

Joseph looked down at her. "Then promise you'll tell me as soon as the way is clear," he whispered. "Every day apart from you feels like a lifetime!"

Jemima's hope revived. "Oh, Joseph, that's so *sw*…"

But he turned and kissed her again so delightfully that Jemima quite lost her train of thought. In fact, she lost even the desire that Joseph would share his heart, just so long as he didn't *stop*.

Eventually Joseph pulled back from her, and cupped her face in his big hands. "I'll go with you to the courthouse, Mima," he smiled. "I'll be there for my *maus*, to lend her strength.

"And then, when all this nightmare is over -- we can get *married*!"

CHAPTER FOUR

Jemima was silent at the breakfast table the next morning. So was her mother, who showed distressing signs of having spent the night in tears; and also her father, whose sagging shoulders suggested that he had also been up late, trying to console her.

They ate in heavy silence, except for Deborah, who filled the void by complaining about the lack of discipline at school. Deborah said that she'd been the target of hateful boys who had suggested that she needed "a broom and a black hat."

"I don't know what they're *talking* about," she exclaimed, extending her hands. "*No one* is more patient than I am!"

This startled Jemima out of her depression, and she lifted her eyes in wonder to her sister's face. It seemed to irritate Deborah even further.

"What are *you* staring at, fright wig? And stop chewing your nails – you look like a four-year-old!"

It was a measure of their parent's preoccupation, that no one corrected Deborah for this rudeness or made the slightest mention of the woodshed: a fact that Jemima noted with some bitterness. But she had more important things to think about, than *Deborah*.

She had already decided to go find a lawyer and had planned to ask her father to drive her to town; but one look at her mother's face told Jemima that her father wouldn't be helping her *that* day.

She could drive the buggy herself, but it would be risky. The reporters could reappear at any time.

The thought occurred to her that she could ask Joseph to drive her into town, since he supported her decision: but his family's farm was clear across the valley, not close at all. And anyway, she didn't want Joseph to press her to *marry him* again. She couldn't make such a big decision when her life was upside down, and she'd told him so last night. But he hadn't paid much attention.

Maybe she could *walk* to town unnoticed, if she cut across country instead of using the road. Of course it would be a long, tiring trip, but the corn was tall in every field, and it would keep her out of sight, most of the way.

Yes, *that* was the best.

Jemima rose from the table, picked up a basket, and went outside to *pretend* that she meant to do her daily chores: gathering eggs, and vegetables, and working in the garden. But when she saw that no one was watching, she turned and walked out into the garden. She kept walking into the bushes at the edge of the garden, and through the woods beyond, all the way to the fence at the edge of their property.

Jemima looked this way and that, hiked up her skirt, and climbed over the rail fence. That put her into their neighbors' corn field, the first of many on the way to town. Jemima walked into it and was instantly swallowed up in the green rows.

After having been in the spotlight for so many months, there was something deliciously secretive about disappearing into the fields – going where *no one* could find her. Once she was inside the cornfield, there was nothing ahead, to either side or behind, except green stalks stretching into infinity.

And it was a beautiful day for walking -- a fine, bright morning, with the high white clouds of late summer sailing over the earth. Jemima stopped now and then to shade her eyes, and look up at them through the waving green leaves. She saw and heard nothing else, except the faint call of birds, and the equally faint hum of farm equipment somewhere across the valley. Occasionally her approach startled some small animal. A rabbit that she hadn't guessed was there suddenly jumped into the air and rocketed away: and a field mouse scurried across her path and disappeared.

They were the only living things she saw for a long while.

Halfway through her route, she climbed over a pasture fence and crossed over into the Christener's fields. The land belonged to Mark's family, and Jemima played with the idea of paying a quick visit, but decided against it. Mark had made it clear that he didn't plan to see her again until she had resolved this issue.

She crossed the entire breadth of the Christner's corn field without incident, but when she stepped out of it and prepared to cross the fence to the farm next door, she was mortified to see Mark standing not ten yards away – staring.

"*Oh!*" she shrieked and climbed down from the fence.

Mark's expression was as puzzled as his voice. "*Mima?* What are you doing way out here?" He put down a pair of pliers and took off his work gloves. Jemima noticed, with deep embarrassment, that she had managed to pop out of the field at the very point at which Mark had been mending their fence.

A full-body wave of heat began to crawl up from her toes. "I—that is – I'm walking to *town*."

Mark looked at her doubtfully. "Through the *fields*?"

Jemima nodded and looked down at her feet.

There was a heavy silence. Mark finally shrugged and sat down on a tree stump. "What's wrong, Mima? You'd never go hiking across country unless something was *bad* wrong. What is it?"

Jemima bit her lip and looked at him unhappily. "I'm going to town to get a *lawyer*," she murmured.

Mark's dark eyebrows shot up. "A lawyer? *You?* Are you in some kind of trouble?"

Jemima turned pleading eyes to his face. "Yes – big trouble! An Englischer is suing me for all the money I have! A man came and gave me papers and said I had to appear in court! The Englischer claims that I promised to sell him the George Washington letter – *and that I lied*!"

Mark's brow gathered darkness. He stood up, came over, and put his arms around her. Jemima pillowed gratefully on his chest.

"Mamm is unhappy with me," she murmured. "She says I should just let him have the money, but I *can't,* because I've already given half of it away! And if I don't fight, it's like admitting that he was right and that I'm a *liar*!"

"No one who knows you could *ever* think such a thing, Mima," Mark assured her, and kissed her cheek. "And it doesn't *matter* what outsiders think."

Jemima frowned. "It matters to me!" she said and pulled out of his arms. "And I'm not going to let him just *take* this money from me when he has no right, and when God *told* me to give it to others. It isn't fair!"

Mark's eyes were dark and troubled. "I think your Mamm is right, Mima," he said slowly. "I think you should let the Englischer have the money. It would end this trouble, and everything could go back to normal again. Don't you want that?"

Jemima felt her lower lip trembling and bit it. "Oh, of course I do!" she cried, "but not like *this*! I won't have people saying that I *lie* when I can prove that I *didn't*. And I won't let this greedy man come and steal from me!"

Mark ran a hand through his black hair and sighed. "All right then, Mima, have it your way. But I still think you'd do better to let be.

"And you still haven't told me -- *why* are you in our cornfield?"

This time, the tears were dangerously close. "Because we can't go out of our house!" Jemima cried. "There are reporters parked on the road outside our driveway, waiting for me like *vultures*! And Daed won't drive me because Mamm is upset! I don't want to drive *alone*, and if I walk through the fields, maybe they won't see me, and I can go to town in *peace*!"

Mark gave her a look that said he saw the tears underneath, and he took her in his arms again and kissed her hair. "All right, Mima. Come inside with me, and have something to eat, and rest. Let me change out of my work clothes, and I'll drive you into town if you're determined to go."

"Yes, I *am*. Thank you, Mark," she replied doggedly, but the tears trembling just underneath her words pooled up in her eyes and formed a knot in her throat. She was grateful that Mark asked her no more questions. Grateful that he just held her until knot had loosened somewhat and she could breathe without embarrassing herself.

CHAPTER FIVE

Jemima followed Mark back to the big white farmhouse that had been built by his great-great-grandfather 100 years before. It was white, with a green roof, spotlessly clean, and, apparently, temporarily empty.

Mark's mother Elizabeth was out doing chores and was nowhere to be seen: so Mark invited Jemima to sit down at the kitchen table. He poured her a cup of coffee, served her a piece of *snitz* pie, grabbed one for himself, and then went upstairs to change.

Jemima ate the pie gratefully. It was past noon now, and the walk had made her hungry.

When Mark came back downstairs, he was holding a big bonnet. He held it out to Jemima. "This belongs to my Mamm. If you wear it, no one will be able to see your face." Then he went outside to hitch up the buggy.

A few minutes later they were riding down the driveway and out onto the road.

They sat in silence. It was a good five miles to town from the Christner's farm, and Mark, as always, preferred silence to speech. But to Jemima's relief, it was the comfortable silence of long friendship. Even though the money had put a barrier between them, the money was still the only barrier there was.

It was also apparent that the bonnet was doing its job. It was far too big for Jemima and hid her face completely if she turned away from the road. No one they passed on the road took a second look at her. If they knew Mark, they supposed her to be his mother; if they didn't know Mark, they probably thought the same. Jemima figured that since the reporters didn't know him, they'd see him as just another young Amish man. But she was careful to look away when cars passed by, and to her great gratitude, no one took any notice of them.

Mark drove her, via sleepy side streets, to the office of Barfield Hutchinson, a lawyer who was trusted and sometimes hired by Amish folk in the area. Jemima had chosen him because he was frankly the only lawyer she knew and because she had once heard her father speak of him approvingly.

When Mark stopped the buggy outside his office, he threw the reins aside, turned to her, and took her hands solemnly.

"Mima, are you *sure* about this? Maybe you should think about it some more. This is a big step."

Jemima looked into his frowning eyes. She knew he was genuinely worried for her.

"You're so sweet, Mark," she whispered, and kissed him. His lips were warm and strong and delicious on hers – they tasted of snitz pie, and *protective*. But when they parted, she looked him dead in the eye.

"I've decided. I am going in there, and I -- I am going to *hire* him. I have no *choice*."

Mark sighed, and shook his head. "You're changing, Mima," he murmured, half to himself, and Jemima shot him a frightened look. Her mother's warning came back to her with terrible force, and she was shaken by the sudden fear that she might *lose* Mark.

"You don't hate me – do you, Mark?" she whispered.

He looked shocked. "Of course not, Mima," he sputtered and leaned in to kiss her reassuringly. "Hate you! Never. It's just that – well, you never used to be this – *brave*."

Jemima digested this and decided that she would take it as a compliment. "I've *had* to be," she told him grimly, then gathered her skirts, and climbed down from the buggy.

Mark opened the door for her, and they walked into the lawyer's office. It was housed in a two-story red brick building, the kind found in any small town square -- except this one was on a tree-lined side street.

The interior was elegantly furnished in colonial antiques – a highly polished grandfather clock ticked softly in one corner, what looked like a Persian rug covered the floor, and even the lobby furniture was upholstered in leather.

Jemima looked uncertainly at Mark, and he took her elbow. They walked to the receptionist's desk.

A young, attractive Englisch woman sat there. She was well-groomed and well-dressed but didn't seem especially well-disposed toward visitors. She smiled politely – but coolly, Jemima was quick to note.

"Good afternoon. Can I help you?"

Jemima nodded. "I'd like to hire Mr. Hutchinson," she said firmly.

The woman smiled broadly, and Jemima went red to the roots of her hair.

"Do you have an *appointment*?" she asked blandly.

Jemima shook her head.

The young woman smiled again. "I'm afraid Mr. Hutchinson is busy today," she said smoothly, "but if you'd like to make an appointment, he might be able to see you---" she glanced at her desk calendar "– two weeks from Friday."

Jemima looked at Mark helplessly. His lips were pressed into a thin, straight line. He said nothing, but he took hold of the bonnet and gently lifted it from her head.

The woman looked up and froze. Her eyes widened.

"This is *Jemima King*," Mark told her.

The woman stared, and then recovered her poise. She smiled again, and this time the expression touched her eyes.

"Let me buzz Mr. Hutchinson," she said. "I'm sure he'll want to see you, Miss King." She picked up the phone and pressed a button.

"Mr. Hutchinson, there's a *Miss Jemima King* to see you." She looked up at Jemima's face. "*Yes*. All right."

She put the phone down again. "Mr. Hutchinson will be right with you."

Jemima glanced at Mark gratefully, but she had no time to do more. There was a faint bumping sound on the other side of a polished door, and it opened to admit Mr. Barfield Hutchinson. He was a tall, distinguished-looking elderly man, with a thick head of long white hair, bright blue eyes, a trim mustache, and a broad, handsome mouth.

He smiled to reveal a full set of white teeth, and gestured in welcome.

"Please come *in*," he smiled.

They walked into his spacious office, and Jemima sank into one of two seats facing an ornate antique desk. The wall behind the desk was covered in law books that looked as if they dated back a century at least.

Mr. Hutchinson sat down in his leather chair, folded his hands on top of his desk, leaned forward, and smiled at Jemima.

"Now what can I do for *you*, Miss King?"

Jemima glanced over at Mark, but if she had hoped for encouragement, she was disappointed. Mark's stoic expression told her that he still thought their visit was a mistake, and that he wished neither of them was there. She set her mouth and turned to the lawyer.

"I want to hire you," she told him. "I'm being *sued*."

"Ah." The smiled faded from Mr. Hutchinson's face, to be replaced by an expression of mild concern. "And *who* would be suing such a charming young lady?"

Jemima dug into her bag and pulled out the sheaf of legal papers. She handed them to Mr. Hutchinson. "A man named Caldwell C. Morton," she frowned.

The lawyer took the papers and scanned them. He

mumbled under his breath and flipped the pages briefly. "*Hmm*. Yes, I've heard your story, Miss King, like most everyone else in the country." He looked up at her and smiled. "Congratulations on your historic find! Do you have any proof that you purchased the letter, to establish ownership – a receipt, witnesses?"

Jemima nodded. "I bought the letter at Mr. Satterwhite's Gift Shop on the square," she told him, "and I think I still have the receipt. I'll have to look. But Mr. Satterwhite sold the clock to me, so he knows I bought it. And there was someone else, who saw me take it out of his shop, and who saw the letter fall out of it."

"Who would that be?" the lawyer asked, scribbling on a notepad.

Jemima felt herself going red. She was very conscious of Mark, sitting at her elbow. She coughed a little. "A reporter, from the *Ledger* newspaper, named Brad Williams."

The lawyer nodded. "Yes, of course. The young man who broke the story! It's been very well documented, so I don't think I need to get that part of it from you."

Jemima looked down at her hands, and could *feel* Mark scowling.

"And – forgive me, Miss King –" the lawyer was smiling again – "but just for the record, are you certain that you never signed anything to the effect that you would sell the clock or the letter to this Morton fellow? You never promised that, in any way?"

Jemima shook her head vehemently. "*No*. He asked me over and over, but I never signed anything, and I never promised him I would. He's *lying*!"

"Is there anyone who can back you up on that, in court?"

Jemima bit her lip and looked down at her hands again. "Yes," she replied unwillingly. "After I bought the clock, the Englischer came out to my house and asked to buy it. Then Brad Williams came out, too. He told me that the clock could be valuable, and *not* to sell. Then the Englischer threw money on the porch and demanded I sell the clock to him. And said I had *promised* to sell. And I told him that no, I had *not* promised to sell, only to show him the clock. And – and Brad Williams was there when I said that."

Mr. Hutchinson scribbled again. "Good."

Jemima raised fierce eyes to his face. "But I don't want you to call Brad Williams, or to talk to him at all because I don't want to see him again!"

The lawyer looked at her. "Why not, Miss King? It seems to me that he could help you a great deal."

Jemima felt suddenly flustered, and huffed, "*Because*, because he was the one who got me into this mess, and I never want to see him again!"

The lawyer looked down and scribbled again. "I respect your wishes, Miss King, but I'm bound to tell you that it will make my job harder if he doesn't appear. Assuming he was the only witness to that conversation?"

Jemima bit her lip and nodded.

Mr. Hutchinson sighed. "Well, Miss King, I'll *still* be happy to represent you. Try hard to find the receipt, and if you do, send it to me."

"There's something else," Jemima told him reluctantly. "I don't have all the money any more. I've given it away to different people. I only have half of what he's suing me for!"

The lawyer paused, pulled his glasses down his nose, and stared at Jemima over them. "You mean to say – you've *given away* half of the money?"

Jemima looked down, and nodded.

"Do you mind telling me – to *whom*?"

Jemima looked up at him uncomfortably. "Well – to the Yoders – their little boy fell down a well, and broke almost all his bones, and he was in the hospital, and they couldn't pay their bills, so I gave them $200,000. And then there was the Millers, John Miller had a heart attack in January and the family's bills were terrible, and I gave them $150,000 for that. And I gave about as much to the Beilers for their premature baby, and a little to Grandma Sarah Fisher for her last trip to the emergency room, when she had the mini-stroke and had to stay overnight."

Mr. Hutchinson frowned, and closed his eyes, and shook his head slightly. "So – you're telling me – you gave all of that money to *other people?*"

Jemima met his eyes. "Yes."

"Would they be willing to be deposed?"

Jemima shook her head, and he added: "Would they come and tell me that themselves if they knew it would help you?"

Jemima nodded. "I think so."

Mr. Hutchinson tilted his head, and added: "You've certainly been very generous, Miss King! Would you tell me, please, how much of this money you've spent on *yourself?*"

Jemima raised her eyebrows and shrugged. "Why, *nothing*. I'm healthy, and my family does well. I don't need *anything*.

"But do – do you think I'm in very much trouble?"

Mr. Hutchinson smiled again, very broadly. "Oh, my dear," he told her, "don't worry about *anything*. Just leave everything to me." He rubbed his long hands and muttered, half to himself: "Morton will probably drop the suit, because if we go to a jury trial, I'll *destroy* him."

Mr. Hutchinson looked up at Jemima and smiled again. "What I mean to say is, of course I'll do everything in my power to see that you prevail."

CHAPTER SIX

Jemima moved uncomfortably in the buggy seat as they drove back from town. It seemed to her that the *tone* of Mark's silence had changed. On the way into town, his silence had been peaceful and relaxed. After their visit to the lawyer's office, she sensed -- something *else*.

After a while she turned to Mark and asked: *"What?"*

He looked away, out over the fields. To her relief, he didn't ask what she meant.

"I hate to hear you talk about that Williams Englischer," he blurted. "I hate to think of the two of you together."

Something about the way he said it melted Jemima's heart.

Poor Mark! She reached out and grasped one of his hands.

"You don't need to worry, Mark," she told him softly. "I didn't like having to talk about Brad Williams, either -- I wish I'd never *met* him.

"If it makes you feel better -- sometimes I really think that I *hate* him!"

Mark glanced at her, with a look almost like pain. "That's what I mean, Mima," he murmured. "It *doesn't* make me feel better, because – that's *new*. I've never seen you like that before."

Jemima pulled back her hand and sighed. "That's because no one has caused me so much *harm* before!" she replied.

"So that's what it is, Mima?" he asked. "Anger? I need to know. Because every time you talk about him, you look – I don't know – *stirred up*."

"You'd be stirred up, too, if he'd done this to *you!*" Jemima answered tartly, and then almost gasped aloud -- because she sounded so much like *Deborah*. But to her relief, Mark sputtered out a reluctant laugh.

"Fair enough. I know you have good cause to be mad at him." He turned to look at her. "But I'd hate to think that he'd gotten to you somehow, Mima."

Jemima raised her eyes to his and held them. "*Why,* Mark?" she asked pointedly.

He shrugged. "I just *would*, that's all."

"*Oh.*"

Jemima hoped that Mark would hear the disappointment in her voice, and understand what it meant. It was one thing to be reserved. But if you were a *lover*, sooner or later you needed to *say so*.

She toyed with the idea of just – telling him that. But instead, she lapsed into silence herself and gazed out over the cornfields as they passed.

When they reached the Christener farm, Jemima would have walked home, but Mark wanted to walk back with her. She tried to object – she felt guilty about interrupting his day – but he insisted. So she waited while he unhitched the buggy, and put the horse back in its stall, and returned to her.

They walked back the way she had come, though Mark did twitch his mouth to one side, and say that it felt strange to be in a field without a *team of horses*. Jemima laughed because it was funny, and when he held out his hand, she took it.

They walked back to her home hand in hand, as they had sometimes done when they were children, and to Jemima it felt natural and right. They said nothing because they didn't need to talk to feel comfortable, but she enjoyed his company and knew that he enjoyed hers.

That was the thing about Mark: he was so *easy* to be with. He made no demands on her, and yet he was always there, sensible, strong and reliable. He made no attempt to entertain her, but she felt no need to be entertained. They just *liked* each other and were comfortable together, and it was enough.

When they finally reached the fence that bordered her parent's farm, Mark lifted her in his arms and sat her down on the topmost rail of the fence. He held her there with his hands and looked into her questioning eyes.

"I think it was a wonderful thing you did, Mima. Giving all that money away to the Yoders, and the others. The man was right. That was very generous."

Jemima smiled, and looked down, and went pink. Mark's praise pleased her out of all proportion.

Because Mark had never been one to gush – when he praised you, he *meant* it.

"It's your rumspringa. You could've spent all that money on yourself, on a car, or a trip somewhere, or lots of pretty Englisch clothes." He raised a brown hand and brushed a tendril of hair back from her brow. "You would look so beautiful then, that *no one* could resist you."

"Oh, Mark!" she sputtered and shook her head, but he didn't back down.

"It's true, Mima. You're the most beautiful girl I've ever met. The most beautiful girl I ever expect to meet. And not just on the outside."

Jemima became very still. She raised her eyes to Mark's, searched them, hoped that he'd say the words that *should* come next.

The dappled sunlight played over his shoulders, turned his hair to black silk tinged with blue. His eyes were dark as sapphires, ringed with a smudge of black lashes. He smiled faintly and leaned in to kiss her, soft and sweet and warm.

Jemima received his kisses gratefully, savored them for the precious things they were, rolled them over her tongue like a favorite taste. But to her disappointment, Mark *still* did not use his tongue to form the words she longed to hear.

He pulled back from her at last, and kissed her again just on the edge of her mouth, and played with her ear.

"I want you to ask you something, Mima," he said quietly. "When all of this is over, and things have settled down, I'm going to come back to your house and ask you a question. I think you know what it's going to be. I want you to promise me you'll think about it, in the meantime."

Jemima felt a strange sensation: love and exasperation, simultaneously.

Exasperation won -- slightly. She spoke kindly but gave him an arch look. "How do I know what to think about, when you won't even tell me what the *question* is?"

Mark smiled but shook his head. "Don't play with me, Mima. I'm serious." He looked up into her eyes. "Promise."

Her exasperation melted. It was impossible to resist those beautiful blue eyes.

"*I promise*, Mark," she whispered.

"It wouldn't hurt, if you promised not to say *yes* to anyone else, before you talk to me," he added, only half-jokingly.

Jemima met his eyes and smiled apologetically. "There *are* other boys who are asking me -- *questions*," she confessed. "It's only fair you should know."

He twisted his mouth down. "I'd have to be pretty dumb not to guess," he told her wryly. "But I do have a chance, don't I, Mima?"

Jemima looked up at him, startled. "Of course you do – Oh, *Mark*!" She took him in her arms and hugged him. "How could you think any *different*?"

She could feel him relax. He put his arms around her and kissed her one last time.

"That's all I wanted to know, Mima," he told her. And before she could answer, he had released her and had disappeared into the rustling leaves.

CHAPTER SEVEN

When Jemima returned home, it was already late afternoon. She hurried to finish the chores she had left undone and tiptoed back into the house. To her relief, her mother was busy cooking dinner, and her father was still out in his workshop, and there was no sign of Deborah.

Her mother was standing at the kitchen sink. Jemima quietly piled the vegetables on the kitchen table, and would have crept upstairs, when her mother said, without turning:

"You went to the lawyer today, didn't you, Jemima?"

Jemima froze and hung her head. "Yes."

Rachel nodded, still without turning, and Jemima knew

without having to look that she was fighting tears.

"It's your decision. You're on your rumspringa, and you're free to choose. I just wanted to let you know that…I am *not* upset with you."

Jemima looked up at her. "You're *not?*"

Her mother took a deep breath and nodded, "Everything is all right. Go upstairs and wash up for supper. It's almost done."

Jemima batted back quick tears of her own. Hurting her gentle mother was the *last* thing she wanted to do. And it was the first time, ever in her *life*, that she had gone against her wishes.

But on the other hand, she saw no way to do differently than she *had* done so it would be dishonest to apologize. She stared at her mother's back unhappily.

"*Thank you, Mamm,*" she murmured and fled upstairs.

That evening dinner was subdued, but not as uncomfortable as Jemima had feared. Her mother was as good as her word, and her father was unchanged. Jemima suspected that he agreed with her decision, deep down; but in any case, he didn't scold her, except to ask how she had gotten to town.

Jemima told him, quite truthfully, that she had walked, and

had gone across country. Her father raised his bushy red eyebrows, and told her not to go alone next time: but said no more than that -- and she was grateful.

Deborah, however, was worse than ever. She complained about the food, accused Jemima of running off to meet boys instead of going to the lawyer's, and even talked back to Rachel when she rebuked her for her rudeness.

This stirred up her father's parental wrath, and to Jemima's guilty satisfaction, he took Deborah by the back of her apron and pulled her out to the front porch. Rachel and Jemima picked at their food and pretended not to hear the sounds of repeated *thwacks*, their father's booming voice, delivering a lecture, and Deborah's howls.

Jemima cleared her throat. "Do you think it will do any good this time?" she whispered.

Her mother pinched her lips into a straight line, and shook her head. "I *hope* so." The sound of renewed howls, interspersed with curses, assaulted their ears.

She returned Jemima's glance. "*Pray* for your sister."

Jemima raised her brows and thought that she would rather pray to be delivered *from* her sister: and immediately felt guilty for the uncharitable thought.

For a few days afterward, Jemima enjoyed relative peace.

Her parents, apparently having agreed to extend the olive branch, said no more to her about the lawyer; her suitors gave her rest; and Deborah, no doubt fearing retribution, maintained a resentful and much-appreciated silence.

Then one day Samuel Kauffman came knocking at the door.

Jemima was sitting in the living room, trying to soothe her jangled nerves by working on a quilt. Her mother had suggested that it might help her to work on something that required her concentration, and so far that morning it had worked.

But then there was a soft knock on the screen door, and when she looked up and saw Samuel standing there, so tall and handsome, every other thought flew out of her head. He had taken off his hat, and his beautiful blonde hair reminded her of wheat waving in the sun.

"Can I come in, Jemima?" he asked.

She dimpled and stood up immediately, and the quilt fell forgotten to the floor. "Of course, Samuel! What a question!"

He seemed unusually subdued – he didn't even smile -- but Jemima was so glad to see him that she didn't care. She gathered up the quilt and threw it over a chair.

"Come and sit with me." She sat down on the sofa and patted it.

Samuel came and sat down immediately, and she noticed that he was holding something. It looked like a newspaper, and that was odd because most people she knew didn't read Englisch newspapers.

But he set it down on the couch and turned to her. He took her hands in his and looked at her as if someone had died.

Jemima's smile faded. "Why, Samuel, what is it? You look as if something *terrible* has happened!"

His blue eyes searched hers. "I need to ask you a question, Mima," he said gravely.

Jemima's heart jumped into her throat. She couldn't trust herself to speak, but nodded, looking up at him expectantly.

He looked down at her hands as if he was gathering his nerve, and then said: "Joseph Beiler is going around town telling everyone that the two of you are – are *engaged*. Is it true, Mima?"

Jemima felt her mouth dropping open. "*Engaged?*"

"Everyone in the valley is talking about it. But – but I had to hear it from *you*. Is it true, Mima?"

Jemima felt her face going warm. Joseph *never* listened very well. She had told him that she needed time to *think*, not that she agreed to *marry* him! Poor Joseph, he was too much of a romantic, he always let his hopes outrun...

She remembered Samuel and bit her lip. "No, Samuel, it

isn't true," she told him firmly. "It's true that Joseph asked me to marry him, and that I promised to *think* about it, but I haven't given him any answer yet."

Samuel relaxed visibly. He closed his eyes briefly and leaned back against the couch, and revived. For the first time since he walked in, he smiled – a little ruefully, but with the same charm as always.

"I should've known," he confessed, running a hand through his hair. "Joseph gets carried away. But Mima, you – you couldn't say *yes* to anyone but me – *could* you?"

He grinned again, with that boyish charm, and Mima laughed in spite of his cheeky joke. She knew him well enough to know that he *was* making a joke – Samuel never took *anything* too seriously -- even himself.

But his question sent a wave of delight coursing through her. She looked down primly. "Why, Samuel, are you asking me to marry you?" she smiled.

When she ventured to look up again, Samuel's face looked startled. He cracked a confused grin, and then broke out into infectious laughter. "Yes, I guess I *am!*" he admitted, and Jemima had to smile with him. Samuel was *so* adorable – if she married him, her life would be full of fun and laughter, because he was so full of mischief – and so *terribly* handsome.

He pressed her hands between his, and became serious

again. His bright blue eyes questioned her. "*Will* you marry me, Mima?" he asked.

Jemima looked up at him, and as soon as their eyes met, he kissed her. It wasn't the playful, exploratory kisses that he usually gave her, and that she loved. It was a sober, serious kiss, full of the love that Samuel had never been able to bring himself to *say* but had never failed to *show*.

When their lips parted, Jemima looked up at him longingly but shook her head. "I can't answer you now, Samuel," she said softly. "I need time to pray and to think. But something *bad* has happened, and I'm so caught up in it, I *can't* think. I can hardly even *pray!*"

Samuel looked crestfallen, and her heart went out to him, but she had no other answer to give.

He nodded, and then reached for their town newspaper. "The *something bad* -- does it have anything to do with *this*?" he asked.

Jemima looked down at it. To her horror, there on the front page was the blaring headline: *Local Girl Center of $1.6 Million Lawsuit*.

She clapped a hand over her mouth and felt her self-control begin to slide away. Samuel's expressive eyes radiated compassion, and he took her in his arms.

"It never *ends,* Samuel!" she told him hopelessly, and he whispered comfort as she broke down and gave full vent to her feelings.

CHAPTER EIGHT

Delores Watkins sauntered into her star reporter's office and tossed a newspaper down on his desk with a *plop*. She tilted her head, put one hand on her hip, and drawled: "Do you mind telling me why I had to see this in some *other* newspaper? I thought this was your signature story, wonder boy!"

Brad Williams had a phone to his ear, but he swiveled in his chair and picked up the paper. It was a copy of the *Lancaster Farmer's Friend*, the tiny community paper from Serenity, Pennsylvania. The headline read: *Local Girl Center of $1.6 Million Lawsuit.*

Brad frowned and spoke hurriedly into his phone. "I have

to go. I'll call you back." He pushed the mic arm up and scanned the story.

"Somebody's suing *Jemima King*?" He looked up into Delores' ironic brown eyes and snapped his fingers at her. "*I know who it is* – it's that guy who was trying to buy the letter off her! Am I right?"

"Congratulations, Sherlock," Delores replied dryly. "It's the second graf down."

"What is this – *this morning's* edition? Has anybody else seen this yet?" he asked.

"I don't know," she replied. "But I do know *this*: if you'd been following the story, instead of romancing my secretary, *we* would've been first with this, instead of playing catch up."

Brad set his mouth as if he was preparing a reply, but Delores didn't give him time to deliver it. "You and this other guy were both there at the girl's house, on the same day, weren't you?" she demanded.

"That's right."

"Perfect. I want you to go back out and re-establish contact with the Amish girl. Let her think you'll testify on her behalf at the trial. It'll make her more likely to talk to you. I want an exclusive for the *Ledger*."

Strong, conflicting emotions swirled in Brad's chest, but he smashed them down. Delores, of all people, must never suspect that he had *feelings*.

He put on a cynical expression and raised his brows incredulously. "You *do* remember that the last time I was out there, her father ripped the *door* off my truck?"

"It was the *Ledger's* truck, and I could hardly forget," Delores replied dryly. "But you could be really useful to that girl right now if you testify. It might persuade her to talk to you. Anyway, I want you back out there tomorrow morning, bright and early."

Brad pulled his hands over his face and sighed heavily. Delores smirked and added: "Tell Sheila she'll just have to live without you for a week or two."

On that depressing note, she turned and left.

Brad sat there, with his hands over his face, for at least five minutes after. The thought of going back to Lancaster County was not a welcome one, and not even primarily because he might be murdered there.

He'd never *expected* to go back. He'd never expected to even *see* the Duchess again. In fact, he'd arranged his life around his deep belief that he would never, *ever* see her again.

Going back now would be messy. Very, *very* messy.

In the first place, Sheila would be upset because he'd be going away for two weeks at least, and she wouldn't be able to go with him.

Although, if he was really honest with himself, some *alone* time might be kind of refreshing. Sheila was high maintenance.

But as for trip itself – he was in trouble. The thought of going back to Lancaster County, of facing the Duchess again after the way they had parted, and everything that had happened since –

Messy. Unpleasant. Uber challenging. He was going to have to be at the very top of his game if he hoped to get Jemima King to talk to him again. Because after everything that had happened -- she probably *hated* him.

Any return there was fraught with danger. Her father, who beyond all doubt wanted to kill him. That boyfriend of hers, or maybe more than one, who'd probably want to fight him. But most of all, above everything – *the Duchess herself.* She had almost *supernatural* power. Power to make him destroy himself. Power to make him do crazy things, things he'd never *dream* of doing in cold blood.

Without even trying. Without even knowing that she was doing it.

He shuddered. That that was the really scary part. She was unconsciously hypnotic, like a force of nature. Like one of those sirens from Greek mythology.

All she had to do was *look* at him.

He groaned and pulled his hands over his face. Facing her again was going to be like leaning over the edge of a cliff, and praying that the wind didn't blow.

But so far, right up to that very hour, his luck with the Duchess had been nothing but bad.

Brad opened the door to O'Malley's Restaurant and strolled into the lobby. He and Sheila had gotten into the habit of having dinner there together after work. He noticed that Sheila was already there, in their usual booth. He braced himself, because when she found out he was leaving it wasn't going to be a happy evening.

She scooted over to let him slide into the seat. "Want a bite of my appetizer?" she asked, holding up a nacho.

"*Please.*"

She handed it to him, and he took a bite. Sheila snuggled in close and gave him a peck on the cheek.

"How was work today? You must've been busy because you stayed holed up in your office. You didn't even *call* me."

He turned his eyes to her smiling face. He might as well get it over with.

"Ah – about that, Sheila. Delores has decided to send me back out to the boonies for a follow up to the Washington letter story. I'll be gone for a couple of weeks, starting tomorrow."

Sheila pulled back. Her voice sounded stung. "A couple of *weeks*? What am I supposed to do in town all alone?"

Brad took a deep breath and switched his face to its *reassurance* setting. "I know, Sheila, but it won't be *too* long. Can't say no to my boss, after all," he shrugged, smiling. "I have to eat."

She straightened suddenly. "Delores could send me, too!"

"Oh, well now, I wish that were possible," he chuckled, "but Delores might have something to say about that. You're her right arm."

"No, I could ask her!" Sheila countered. Her eyes had taken on the determined look that told him she was already planning their agenda.

"Ah, *hah* now Sheila, I'd just love to have you work the story with me, but it isn't going to work out this time. It's a work trip, not play. We'll do something when I get back, I promise."

Sheila snapped back to the present with shocking suddenness. She pinched his cheek, and then slapped it smartly.

"Don't *patronize* me, you scheming rodent," she said sweetly, and the conversation ended abruptly.

That night, Brad lay awake in bed, staring at the ceiling. He was thinking that he should probably lie to Sheila about which hotel he was using because he was *really* looking forward to a little solitude.

He bit his lip. Sheila was on the high side of average in his young experience: pretty, fairly smart, self-interested, and hunting for a husband, though she knew better than to admit it. He'd grown fond of her because they were *alike*.

He considered himself the high side of average, too. He was good looking, fairly smart, self-interested, and absolutely *not* planning on marriage, though he, too, knew better than to admit it.

They suited one another. They got along, they liked one another, and neither of them was fooled by the other's nonsense. In short – they had a pleasant, mutually beneficial understanding.

He found that he really didn't want to do anything to mess that up.

He reached over to the nightstand, shook a cigarette out of the pack, and lit one up. He lay there, blowing gentle spouts of smoke toward the ceiling, until well past midnight.

CHAPTER NINE

To Brad's relief, his success with Jemima's story, and his improved status inspired Delores to spring for slightly more upscale accommodations than Uncle Bob's Amish Motel.

So at 9 a.m. the next morning, Brad was able to pull the company truck into the parking lot of the Lazy Daze Hotel and Dairy Bar just outside Serenity. It looked like a refurbished chain hotel, because unlike Uncle Bob's, it boasted a pool with a diving board, a sit down restaurant that served three meals a day, and a small store that sold a wide variety of "wholesome, organic Amish-made dairy products."

The teenage boy at the desk gave him a room on the second floor, overlooking the pool, and Brad made the weary trudge up a flight of flimsy metal steps. But when he opened the door to his room, he was rewarded with a blast of arctic air, and that indefinable *clean hotel* aroma that was equal parts guest soap, *very* faded cigarette smoke and refrigeration.

Brad dumped his gear on the big bed and collapsed face down across it. He lay there for a long while, recovering from his far too early morning.

As he lay there, he began to game out several possible scenarios by which to approach the Duchess. None of them were especially promising, but Delores had given him no choice. He told himself that forethought *now*, might preserve his teeth *later*. So --

Scenario Number One: He would drive up to the King's front door in the company truck in broad daylight, walk up the steps like a civilized man, knock on the front door, and pray that he got the woman of the house. If so, he'd fall on his knees and beg her with tears in his eyes, to *let him talk to Jemima*.

If he got the red giant -- he'd jump into the truck and gun it for parts unknown.

Scenario Number Two. He would park on the edge of the adjoining property, like before, hike across an acre of brambles, jump the fence, and hide in the bushes at the edge of the garden until Jemima came outside.

If she came outside.

Scenario Number Three. He would approach some sympathetic intermediary and beg or bribe them to contact Jemima and make his case *for* him. This seemed like the best option available, except that he didn't know anybody in Serenity who also knew Jemima, except for that sadistic geezer at the store who'd sent him on a snipe hunt.

Scenario Number Four. He would mail Jemima a letter, and beg her to meet him. And hope that she: got the letter; got it in time; didn't ignore it; didn't show it to anyone else; or send someone else, like her *father*, to the proposed meeting.

Scenario Number Five. He would call the number she gave him once and hope that somebody happened to be inside while the phone was ringing and that they cared enough to answer the call.

He beat his head against the pillow.

After a while, having failed to think of anything cleverer, he got up and stored his things, turned on the TV, and raided the mini bar. He pulled out a soda, cracked it open, and took a long pull.

The TV was playing the local news. All-too-familiar stuff – he'd covered it all – a county fair, a proposed stoplight to prevent collisions with buggies, a new business opening.

His cell phone buzzed, and when he looked down, it was Sheila. His mouth twisted into a sly grin. She had found out that he'd lied about his hotel, and that he'd turned off the geolocator, so now she was calling to figure out where he really was. And, it wasn't going to work, but it would be fun to play with her.

"Hello?"

"Hi, Brad. I was just calling to see that you got there okay."

"That was thoughtful. I'm sitting here with a tall cold one, watching TV."

"Where are you?"

He bit his lip. "Oh, I had to find another hotel besides Uncle Bob's. Some mix up with the credit card. I'm going to give Delores grief when I get back."

"Oh, how irritating. So where did you have to go?"

I'm at the Happy Acres Hotel in Marietta."

"Do you miss me?"

He rolled his eyes to the ceiling. The faint tapping sound in the background was Sheila, doing a quick Internet search, but she would soon discover that the Happy Acres Hotel, true to its Amish neighborhood, did *not* have a website.

"Sure do."

And…cue the cursing, in three…two…one….

A faint grumbling was just audible on the other end of the

line, and Brad grinned.

"Look cupcake, I have to go. Delores is calling me."

"But –"

"I'll be thinking of you."

And *click.*

He laughed to himself and pulled at the soda again. Sheila would check his story with Delores tomorrow, but he had already bought Delores' silence. Which meant that he was golden -- at least for the next few weeks.

He stretched out. It felt oddly luxurious to be alone for a few days, or at least without Sheila. Fond as he was of her, he had to admit that it was a relief to take a vacation from the games they played.

He let his eyes drift back to the TV. The news was still on. It was a story about quilting. He laughed and pulled the restaurant menu off the bedside table.

But when he looked back up again, the picture had changed. There was a distinguished older man talking to a reporter. He looked directly into the camera, smiled, and gestured elegantly with one hand.

The caption beneath him read, *Barfield Hutchinson, lawyer for Jemima King.*

Brad grabbed the remote and turned up the volume.

"...of course, being Amish, my client was reluctant to enter into a dispute such as this, but she sees it as an opportunity to vindicate herself from the accusations brought against her."

"Is it true that Miss King has given away more than $500,000?"

The lawyer smiled and shrugged gracefully. "It *is* true that my client has donated more than half of her windfall, *already*, to friends in need. True to her faith, she has spent her money helping others. She is an inspiration."

Brad felt his mouth dropping open. *Five hundred thousand dollars?*

He shook his head. If it'd been *anyone* else, he wouldn't have believed it. But having met the Duchess, he could buy it. She was crazy that way. Even from the beginning, she'd shown no interest in the money. It would be just like her to give it *all* away.

An unseen reporter stuck a mic in the lawyer's face, and the big, bright Channel 1 logo was clearly visible. Brad shook his head, cursing. Channel 1 -- that meant that *Wellman* had arrived -- and that he'd hit the ground running.

Brad was hoping he'd be able to get out ahead of the sharks, but apparently, no such luck. Now his job was exponentially harder. And, with pros like Wellman on the story, it meant that it was open season on Jemima King –

again.

He set his jaw. There was something about the Duchess that made him want to protect her from guys like Wellman. It was none of his business really, and if he tried, he'd probably get his chops busted for his pains.

But even so.

He took another sip of his drink and rolled his eyes up at the screen. Barfield Hutchinson was looking directly into the camera.

"Mr. Morton claims that my client promised to sell the letter to him, and then reneged on her promise. I'm hoping that if anyone witnessed their conversation, that he or she will *come forward.*"

Then he smiled again, with all his teeth.

CHAPTER TEN

The next morning, Brad forced himself to rise *obscenely* early
– it was hardly 7 o'clock – and beat it out to the overgrown
tract of land that adjoined the King farm. To his relief, no one
else was there, so he parked the truck and hoofed it across the
field of prickly vines to the property line.

He had spent the previous day calling Jemima's number,
since it was a low-risk strategy, but as he had feared, they
weren't answering their phone. So now it was on to the next
scenario – the one that seemed at least plausible, since it had
worked before.

Brad skirted the garden, taking care to keep out of sight
behind the bushes. He peered out, and his heart jumped up

into his throat. There was a young woman in the garden. Her face was turned away from him, but it had to be –

She turned her head, and his shoulders sagged. *It wasn't Jemima.* It was a plump, sharp-faced preteen with sandy brown hair and freckles. She was picking onions and putting them in a basket.

He bit his lip and cursed silently. As long as she was there, he couldn't get hold of the Duchess.

The girl worked her way closer to the edge of the garden, but never glanced his way. Brad looked closely at her. She was as ordinary as the Duchess was dazzling, but there was something about her – the way she moved, maybe – that suggested she might be a kid sister.

He was trying to decide whether or not to enlist her help when the girl settled the matter for him. Without turning her head, she said, just loudly enough:

"I see you standing there. What do you want?"

Brad's mouth dropped open. *Why, the sneaky little...*he straightened and looked around before answering: "I want to talk to Jemima."

There was a sputtering sound that might have been laughter. "You and everybody *else* in the world. What's it worth to you?"

He cocked his head to one side. *"What?"*

"You heard me. What's it worth to you? You won't get her without my help, I promise. The driveway is barricaded, and all I have to do is call my father, and you're busted."

Brad glared at her, torn between surprise, and the urge to laugh. He fished in his pocket. "I don't carry much *money*," he told her.

She shrugged, and made as if to walk away.

"Wait, *wait!*" he hissed and dug in his wallet. "How about a twenty?"

"You've got to be kidding me," she replied dryly.

He shot her an impatient glance and dug deeper. "Okay, a *fifty*. But it's all I've got."

She pretended to drop the basket and to retrieve the onions rolling across the lawn. He stuck the fifty out just far enough for her to grab, and she took it. She put it in the basket, and covered it with vegetables.

She turned her head slightly. "Wait here. I'll send her out to you." Then she made her way back to the house – slowly, and with many leisurely detours. She walked up onto the porch, and disappeared inside.

Time passed. Brad stood sweating in the bushes, craning his head for any sign of life at the front door. There was nothing.

He cursed under his breath. He was beginning to think that

the girl had played him when the screen door squeaked open, and someone stepped outside. He couldn't see who it was.

His heart began to pound, and he cursed again. Even after all these months, the Duchess did crazy things to his pulse, but he couldn't let her, not this time. He had to be at the top of his game. He made himself look down at the ground and tried to clear his mind.

When he looked up again, Jemima was walking out to the garden, her coppery hair framed by the new light shining through the trees. She was backlit by the morning sun, with a network of shining strands floating around her head like a red halo. Her eyes were that vivid, unearthly green, and her delicate profile was dreamy and soft.

She knelt down in the garden and dug in the soft earth with her small white fingers. He watched her, fascinated. She was like a Flemish painting come to life somehow, a...

He shook his head. It was happening *again*. But he wasn't going to let it throw him.

He shot a quick glance toward the house, saw no one, and took a deep breath. It was *now or never*.

He moved toward her quickly, hoping to close the distance before she noticed him. And it worked: he was at her elbow before she looked up. But when she did, his plan went south -- disastrously.

For a split second, she stared at him as if she couldn't

believe her eyes. And then her green eyes blazed.

"*You!*" she gasped. "How do you *dare* to show your face to me again, after all you've done to *me*, and to my *family*!" She put her hands on the ground and pushed up to her feet, and squared off against him, hands on hips.

"I haven't had a *moment's* peace since I sold that hateful letter! I've been hunted like a rabbit, I have no privacy even in my own *home*! All because of you, and your – your *lust for fame*!" Her angry eyes impaled him. "You *used* me, Brad Williams, and I – I –"

He tilted his head apologetically to one side. "I'm sorry it turned out the way it did, *truly*, Duchess," he told her, and oddly enough – he meant it. "But I wasn't the one who hounded you, was I? Is it fair to blame *me*, for what other people did?"

She turned and began to walk back toward the house. "You and your slick words! But I won't listen to them anymore! You are a *liar*, and you *used* me, and you've *hurt my family*, and *stolen our peace*! You're an evil, *crafty* man!"

He moved to follow. "Listen to me, Jemima! I'm here to *help* you. I saw your lawyer on the TV yesterday, he was asking for witnesses to come forward, and –"

She whirled to face him. "Leave me alone! Leave, and *never* come back! How plain do I have to make it? Go away!"

She turned again, and he grabbed her shoulders in

desperation. "Listen to me Duchess," he said urgently, looking down into her face. "I can testify at your trial. *I can help –*"

But she twisted in his arms, turned her face away from him, and cried out in frustrated German.

The next thing he knew, two big hands twisted him around. He had a split-second glimpse of some black-haired guy, and then, *fist city.*

Weren't the Amish supposed to be pacifists?

Brad went sprawling into the cabbage bed, rolled, scrambled up, and lobbed a haymaker at the stranger's jaw, sending the guy flying back into the dirt.

Brad's fist throbbed, but fear and adrenaline kept him from focusing too hard on the pain.

"*Oh halt es, bitte,*" Jemima sobbed, clawing at his shoulder. He stopped long enough to look back at her, and saw that her eyes were now on the house. He followed the direction of her gaze.

Oh, no.

Brad backed away as he caught sight of the red giant – Jemina's father -- and turned to run. Jemima screamed something in German, but her father kept coming. Brad didn't want to count on this man's pacifistic tendencies, not after how the other Amish man had slugged him. Instead, Brad vaulted through the underbrush, and when the fence loomed up in front of him, jumped it like a race horse.

He plowed through the brambles as hard as he could go, scrambled down the bank to his truck, flung open the door, and jammed the keys into the ignition. The engine roared to life, and he gunned the motor.

There was suddenly a shattering *crack*, and when Brad looked into the mirror, the rear window had a hole in it.

And even more unsettling: there on the passenger seat was a rock the size of a baseball.

CHAPTER ELEVEN

That evening, Brad Williams stretched out full length on the bed in Room 321 with a glass of water in one hand, and an ice pack in the other.

He pressed the ice to his swollen jaw, swirled the water between his teeth, and closed his eyes. To judge by the way his jaw was throbbing, he was sure that he was now the proud owner of a hairline fracture. He hoped with all his heart that the other guy had at *least* a broken tooth.

Although, to be fair, that guy had probably been one of the Duchess' slaves and had just been trying to protect her.

He inhaled sharply, and closed his eyes against a new wave

of pain.

His cell phone buzzed suddenly, and he would've ignored it, but the name on the display read *Delores Watkins*. He cursed but pressed the phone gingerly to his good ear.

"Hello?"

Delores' musky voice rumbled through the speaker. "Hello, wonder boy. How's life in the green hill country?"

"*Great*," he mumbled sardonically.

"How's your story coming?"

"Here's my headline for today," he mumbled. "*Amish People Hate Us.*"

"That's cute," Delores commiserated. "Meanwhile, did you notice that Channel 1 snagged an interview with the girl's lawyer?"

"I saw."

"Is that all you can say?"

Brad inhaled again. "For the moment."

"What's wrong with your voice? You sound like you've got cotton in your mouth."

"I got slugged."

"*Hmmm.*" Delores' voice sounded strangely unsurprised. "Well, be sure to ice it down tonight, because I don't want you looking like a piece of beef tomorrow. You're the face of the paper right now."

"You're all heart, Delores."

The other shoe suddenly dropped. Brad could practically see the light dawning on the other end of the line. "-- *Tell* me the truck is still in one piece, Brad!"

Brad groaned and hissed: "*Sssss* --- the pain! I have to go, Delores – can't talk anymore!"

He pressed a button, tossed the cell phone weakly onto the bed, and took another careful sip.

The cold drink made him suck in air, and grimace. Every muscle in his body ached, and his jaw throbbed. He was as muscular as the next guy, in fact he'd been told that he had a very nice body. He'd had *plenty of* energy last year in high school. He was something of an athlete; he'd pitched on the baseball team, he'd dated a bevy of girls, he'd hardly slept.

But something about this business today had drained him. Maybe it was the excitement of seeing the Duchess close up – as goofy as that sounded – and the adrenalin rush of a near-death experience.

But no matter where it came from, the charge he'd been running on was wearing off. He had to admit to himself that he was *exhausted*.

That dark-haired guy had nailed him with a dead-on shot to

the chops. His ears were still ringing. Even the arm he'd used to block the second shot ached.

Of course, blasting across more than an acre of brambles, at top speed, with the Duchess' father right at his heels had cost him a little something, too. He felt as if he could sleep for a week.

He closed his eyes, and tried to relax. His hotel room was quiet, and thankfully, he had no near neighbors. The only sound he could hear was the faint chirp of birds outside, calling to each other as the light faded.

Gradually, the pain in his jaw receded enough for him to drift off into a twilight sleep. The Duchess was in his arms again, but this time, she wasn't impatient, and didn't try to pull away. The sound of her dulcet voice whispered in his ear. She was still angry, she was still telling him to beat it, but she was doing it in such a soft voice that even "get lost" sounded hot.

He dozed for a few hours, and when he woke up again, it was early evening. The sky outside was dim, and lights shimmered over the blue pool water.

He sighed and stretched. He couldn't remember what he had dreamed, if he had dreamed anything, but for some strange reason -- he woke up thinking about what happened to you, when you died.

For the first time in his life, he wondered if he really might

-- as several people had suggested – *be headed to hell.*

He remembered the Duchess' angry eyes, and hoped devoutly that the decision wasn't up to *her.* He reached for the glass on the bedside table, and took another sip.

He'd never really given an afterlife any serious consideration, and probably wouldn't have now, except that he was in Amish country, where they thought about that sort of thing all the time. Plus, he had almost been murdered that afternoon, and it was sort of a reminder that he could, well -- actually *die.*

The thought was creepy, and he shook it off, but it was persistent.

What would happen to him, if he died?

Nothing, probably – he'd just cease to exist. Or at least, he'd always assumed that was true. Neither of his parents had made any mention of what they thought on the subject, and since they'd *both* been deadbeats, he wouldn't have paid attention if they had. Brad took another careful sip of his water.

His friends at school hadn't talked about it, either. He'd assumed that they were agnostics, like he was himself; at any rate, they lived as if they didn't believe in any God. Even the religious kids at school had been pretty much like everyone else -- no important difference that he'd noticed.

Jemima was the only person he'd ever known who acted

like she really believed all that religious stuff. She was the only person he'd even *heard* of who would give away half a million dollars of her own money, without spending a dime of it on herself.

That was pretty crazy, when he thought about it. But also – he had to admit it – pretty *amazing,* too.

Of course, Jemima hated him right now, and maybe she had a right to hate him. In his own defense, he really *had* believed that getting rich would be great for her, but maybe it hadn't been so great after all – at least for an Amish girl, who wasn't into *things.* Maybe it had just complicated her life.

And maybe she was even right about his motives. Maybe he *had* used her, a little, to get a job at the paper. Another pain hit him suddenly. It was sharp, and deep, but this pain wasn't in his jaw. It felt like it was somewhere under his ribcage, somewhere too deep to soothe with an ice pack.

Jemima had accused him of lying, and using her, and not caring about what she thought, or wanted, or even needed. She had called him everything except a child of God.

He twisted his lip. Maybe she was right. Maybe he *wasn't* one.

He glanced over at the bedside table. He'd noticed that someone had stuck a Bible in the top drawer, and he reached out and opened it.

It was a plain brown book. It looked inexpensive, and it

was written in some impenetrable medieval dialect.

But he opened it anyway. He'd heard of it all his life, but had never cracked it open before.

He flipped through it idly, and stopped at a random point near the front. The text read:

"And the LORD said unto me, Say unto them, Go not up, neither fight; for I am not among you; lest ye be smitten before your enemies.

"So I spake unto you; and ye would not hear, but rebelled against the commandment of the LORD, and went presumptuously up into the hill.

"And the Amorites, which dwelt in that mountain, came out against you, and chased you, as bees do, and destroyed you in Seir, even unto Hormah."

Brad pinched his lips into a straight line, looked up at the ceiling, and hurriedly flipped the book closed again, as if he'd been stung.

CHAPTER TWELVE

The next morning, Brad stared at his face in the hotel room mirror. The swelling had gone down to the point that his jaw looked almost normal, but now he had the *mother* of all bruises.

He tilted his head, studying it. It was going to be a *beauty*. It was roughly the size and shape of an apple – or a *fist* – and was already a dusky purple, shading to black at the point of impact, just below his lower lip.

The only way that he could hope to hide it was with massive amounts of face makeup, but there were some things he refused to do, even for his career. He didn't care if some other male reporters did it, and he didn't care if Delores *fired* him -- he wasn't going out with *makeup* on his face, like a girl.

He sighed and splashed his face with cold water, and dried it off.

Since his attempt to contact the Duchess at her home had blown up, and had almost resulted in his murder, now he had to fall back on the only other viable alternative he had left – trying to reach her through somebody else. And luckily for him – now he had a *prospect*.

Approximately 20 minutes later, Brad parked the truck outside the office of Barfield Hutchison, attorney at law. The prim brick two-story was standard issue lawyer digs: an upscale mansion from 100 years ago, suggestive of wealth and success. Brad glanced at his jaw in the rearview mirror and grimaced, but got out of the truck and entered boldly, nevertheless.

The fetching brunette sitting at the desk inside swept him with her long lashes. Her smile communicated approval, more than a bit of speculation, and even – if he wasn't mistaken – a certain amount of interest. "Good morning," she purred. "*May I help you?*"

Brad gave her his card. "I'm Brad Williams from the *Ledger* Newspaper. I was hoping to talk to Mr. Hutchinson about the Jemima King case."

The semi-flirtatious look vanished from the woman's face.

Her smile froze for an instant. She shifted her weight, cleared her throat, recalibrated, and smiled again. "I'll check. Please sit down, Mr. Williams."

Brad nodded his thanks, and settled into a leather chair a few feet away from the secretary's desk. He crossed his legs and tried to look patient and professional, but his pulse was thrumming in his neck. This was crunch time. If Hutchinson refused to play ball, he was out of luck, because the old shark was his last chance to get in touch with Jemima.

But to his relief, Barfield Hutchinson seemed perfectly willing to *play ball*.

The secretary's phone rang, and she murmured into it briefly and hung up. She looked up at him and smiled again. "Mr. Hutchinson will see you now," she informed him.

When he entered the lawyer's office, the older man was sitting behind a massive antique desk and was reading documents through horn-rimmed spectacles -- the very picture of a prosperous small town lawyer.

Hutchinson looked up at him and nodded toward a chair. "Well, well, good morning, Mr. Williams! I don't need to ask who *you* are and what you do – the whole country knows your name! Please sit down."

Brad sank into a leather chair and looked into Hutchinson's face. He didn't have time to beat around the bush.

"I know that Miss King is being sued for a lot of money,"

he said, without preamble. "I've come here to make you an offer."

The older man looked up, smiled, and raised his snowy brows. "I see," he said gently. "And what sort of *offer* are you making me, Mr. Williams?"

"I was there when Caldwell Morton talked to Jemima King about the antique clock," Brad told him. "And I'm willing to testify in court that she did *not* promise to sell it to him. I can also testify that he tried to bully her into selling it to him, and that it didn't work."

Mr. Hutchinson nodded, but his blue eyes were very bright and sharp. "I'm assuming there's a condition?"

Brad returned his smile. "There's a condition. I want to be able to talk to Miss King again, alone. I want to talk to her here, in your office."

The older man frowned faintly. "I'm not sure I follow you, Mr. Williams. You do realize that I can just subpoena you?"

Brad set his jaw. "If you do, you'll get nothing from me."

"What do you want to talk to my client about?"

Brad felt himself going hot, but he stared the older man down. "I want another interview," he replied evenly.

"Well, I'm sure you know that I can't promise that my client will agree to your conditions, Mr. Williams. Have you" – his eye fell on Brad's jaw – "talked to Miss King *yourself*?"

Brad struggled to keep his tone even. "I can't talk to Miss King at her own home for various reasons," he replied. "I won't bore you with them now. But I'd like to talk to her here, at your office, alone, for just a few minutes. If I can just do that -- I'll testify."

Hutchinson's expression was an unspoken comment. He shrugged slightly. "I'll pass your offer along to my client, Mr. Williams," he sighed, "but I can't make any promises. It's a very unusual request. *So* unusual, in fact, that I don't mind telling you that I'm tempted to advise her against it."

Brad pinched his lips together and leaned across the desk. "Just so long as you *give her the message.* Here's my card. I'm staying at a hotel in town. She can call me at this number, day or night."

The older man took the card, smiled thinly, and nodded. "I'll make sure she gets it, Mr. Williams."

Brad rose and turned for the door, but before he had reached it, the older man added smoothly:

"You'll forgive me, Mr. Williams, but no one can fail to notice that my client is a remarkably lovely young woman. For years, lovely young women were the reason for most of the lawsuits I saw. And they are routinely – you could almost say, *monotonously* -- the downfall of ambitious young men."

Brad swallowed the reply he wanted to make, flung open the door, and slapped it closed behind him with more force than was strictly necessary -- or politic.

CHAPTER THIRTEEN

Jemima King lay full length on her bed with her face crammed into her pillow. The only light in her dark bedroom was a narrow yellow bar underneath the door.

There was a soft knock, and Jemima lifted her face.

"Who is it?"

"*Mamm.*"

Jemima hurriedly wiped her eyes. "Come in," she murmured.

The door opened slowly and her mother appeared in it,

framed in light. She crossed the distance between them and sat quickly on the bed.

She held out her arms wordlessly and Jemima went into them, sobbing.

"There, now," her mother smiled, caressing her hair. "It's been a hard day, I know."

"Oh, Mamm, why does everything I do go so bad *wrong*?" Jemima cried. "I'm being sued for money I don't have, and the reporter is *back*, and now Mark has done what he shouldn't, and gotten hurt -- and it's all my fault!"

Her mother made a soft *hush* sound. "*None* of those things are your fault," Rachel soothed. "They're not your fault -- my poor girl. You will understand that better when you're not so upset." She kissed Jemima's cheek and smiled. "And everything is going to be all right."

Jemima shook her head. "I don't see *how*. I wish I could go back and – and *undo* everything I've done this summer!"

Her mother took her hand. "See now -- the Englischer sued you because he chose *money* over telling the truth. That young reporter is back because he wants another story. And Mark is hurt because he did what he should *not* have done. He lost his temper, and forgot who he is, and struck another human being with his fist. Mark is the one who will have to repent of that, my Mima. Not *you*."

"But he did it because of me," Jemima whispered.

"That may be," her mother replied, "but you didn't tell him to do it."

"No," Jemima shuddered. "It was *awful*! They were hitting each other and fighting like wild animals! But even that wasn't the worst," Jemima sobbed. "*Daed* chased Brad Williams all the way to the fence, and over the fence, and across the field next door, and – and I think he would have *hit* him, if he'd caught him!" She broke down into fresh tears, and her mother looked up at the ceiling.

"Your father –" she paused, coughed, and began again – "your father *also* did what he should not have done. He lost his temper, *too*, and forgot who he is." She looked down at her daughter's face tenderly. "When you have a daughter of your own, my Mima, you will understand better."

Jemima grew quiet in her mother's arms. "I forgot, too, Mamm," she whispered. "I was *upset* with Daed, for treating Brad Williams with such anger. But, I was angry with Brad Williams myself, and I said mean, hateful things to him. I called him a liar, and a user, and said he was *evil,* and it wasn't even the first time! Then I – I told him to go away, and never come back!"

She broke down into tears again. "But he said he wanted to *help* me. He makes me so angry sometimes, that I *forget* how much he's done for me. That he gave up a million dollars -- so I could have it!"

Rachel's face grew grim. "I think that young man helps

himself first, Mima," she replied carefully. "He's here because he wants a story for his paper. He told you that -- didn't he?"

Jemima stared over her mother's shoulder and said nothing.

"I know that you're on your rumspringa, Mima," her mother said gently, "but just because you're free to do what you please, doesn't mean that you're free of the consequences that will come from what you choose. I don't know what you feel toward that boy, Mima, if you feel anything. But I do know this: That boy is an Englischer. He lives in a different world. He thinks differently from you, he *believes* different things, and he *wants* different things. If you lose sight of that, you could be very bad hurt."

She smoothed Jemima's rumpled hair back from her brow. "That's what we worry about, your father and I. We want you to be happy, Mima. But more than that, we want you to be useful, and good, and right with God. The man you choose can help you be all those things."

"Or hinder you."

Jemima said nothing and kept her face buried in her mother's shoulder. Rachel kissed her again and then patted her shoulder.

"Come downstairs, and talk to your father. You owe him an apology, too, you know, after the things you said to him."

Jemima nodded wordlessly.

"I was *surprised*, Jemima, I have to say," her mother chided gently. "I've never heard you talk to your father in such a tone before. He loves you very much, but you've hurt him with your thoughtless words."

Jemima fought back tears. "I'm sorry, Mamm," she whispered. "It's just that – I was scared what could have happened if Daed had caught Brad Williams. Would he have hit him, like Mark? It frightened me, and it made me angry, too. Daed should ask me before he – before he – just decides!"

"Your father doesn't trust reporters," Rachel answered, "and he's wise. Most of them have been nothing but trouble to us. That boy was trespassing, and not for the first time. When your father arrived, he was fighting Mark! He's behaved very strangely all along, Mima. Your father was right to chase that boy away -- he's only trying to protect you."

Jemima fell silent, and her mother took her hand. "Come downstairs now, Mima. You have something important to say to your father."

Her mother put an arm around her waist, and Jemima allowed herself to be led out and downstairs. Her mother accompanied her to the door of her father's study but left her at the door.

Jemima looked after her wistfully, but turned the knob and went in.

Her father was sitting in the big red chair. He was leaning forward, with his elbows resting on his knees, but he looked up as she entered.

It only needed one glance at his wounded expression to make Jemima break down.

"I'm *sorry*, Daed," she whimpered.

Her father stood quickly and opened his arms. Jemima ran into them.

"I'm *sorry* I said such mean things to you," she cried. "I didn't mean them. I was just – scared that you were going to *hit* Brad Williams -- like Mark!"

Jacob closed his big arms around his daughter and smiled his forgiveness, but his eyes remained troubled. "I lost my temper, it's true," he told her. "That was wrong of me, and I'll have to repent -- again." He paused, and a dissatisfied expression flitted briefly across his face.

He returned to his daughter. "But that makes no difference for *you*. It isn't right for you to *disrespect your father*, Jemima King," he added firmly, looking her in the eyes. "You did wrong, and you'll have to be punished for it. Your mother and I, we've – we've decided that you will not attend any Sings or frolics for two weeks. It will give you a chance to think about your behavior."

Jemima nodded, and hugged him. "All right, Daed," she murmured.

Jacob relaxed visibly, as if he'd been worried. He tightened his arms around his daughter, and closed his eyes.

"Now run off to bed," he told her. "Morning comes early, and you've had a hard day."

Jemima smiled, and kissed him, and slipped out; and after she had gone, Rachel appeared in the doorway, entered, and closed the door after her.

"How did it go?" she asked softly.

Jacob frowned. "She apologized, and I know she meant it."

Rachel smiled. "I knew she would. She adores you, Jacob."

Jacob did not seem comforted. "I was never worried about that part." He frowned, and bit his thumbnail.

Rachel looked a question. "Why, are you worried about something else?"

Jacob looked up at his pretty wife. "Yes. I'm worried that she cried about that Englischer boy *all day*, but only asked once about Mark!"

CHAPTER FOURTEEN

It was now early fall. The sky was bright blue without clouds, and the air had turned crisp and cool in the morning. The hills around the King farm were spattered with pale greens, and golds, and blush pinks that would deepen to reds. Every field was full of corn, or wheat, and the trees were heavy with fruit. It was harvest time, and the sounds of harvest wafted faintly across the valley every afternoon.

Jacob King was a blacksmith, not a farmer, but he, too, was busy. He had returned to his smithy, and the sound of his hammer joined the other sounds in the valley the next morning, as Jemima began her day.

Jemima found some comfort in the rhythm of daily work.

She washed clothes, and hung them out to dry on the line. Then she spent the afternoon helping her mother put up vegetables, fruit, jam, soup, and sauces against the approach of winter. Rachel's root cellar would soon be packed, with row on row of shining glass jars filled with good things to eat.

At mid-afternoon, they took a break. Rachel and Jemima went to sit in the swing on the front porch, and rock, and drink iced tea for a few minutes before finishing up the last batch of creamed corn. Jemima sank gratefully onto the swing, and took a long drink, and sighed. A cool breeze moved the air, and she closed her eyes. After hours of kitchen work, it felt *good.*

Deborah walked up the steps as they sat there and tossed the day's mail down into Jemima's lap. Rachel fixed her with a kindling eye.

"Where have you been all morning, Deborah?" she asked. "I needed you to help us with the canning!"

Deborah shrugged, and Jemima looked down at her feet. She foresaw another whipping in her sister's future.

"Oh, Sarah Lapp asked me to come over to her house today," she replied lightly.

Her mother pinched her lips into a straight line. "Well, never mind. But make yourself useful now! Your sister has done both her work and *yours*, all morning. So you can take over from now on. Go upstairs and get washed up."

"But –"

Rachel answered with unusual firmness. "Do as I say!" she cried, and Deborah was so surprised at this rebuke, that she closed her mouth and actually *obeyed*.

Rachel set her glass down on the porch and gave Jemima a rueful glance. "And you, Jemima, you may do as you please this afternoon, because you helped me this morning."

Then she set her mouth, and followed her errant youngest daughter inside.

Jemima watched them go, sighed, and turned to the sheaf of mail on her lap. Most of the letters were for her father, but two of them were addressed to her.

Jemima smiled. One of them was unmistakably from Joseph. She would recognize his broad, looping handwriting anywhere.

She tore the envelope open and unfolded the letter. Its contents expressed a certain amount of agitation.

"My maus," it began, *"I was very surprised to hear Samuel Kauffman say that you told him that we were not engaged. How can that be? After our night of passion –"*

Jemima frowned in faint puzzlement. He must mean the night he came to the house, and *kissed* her so pleasantly.

"—how could we be anything but engaged? I know that you return my feelings, my sweet maus, and could never have said what Samuel claims."

Jemima closed her eyes, and put a hand on her head, because it had begun to ache. In all the turmoil, she hadn't had a chance to talk to Joseph. One *more* thing gone wrong – one more thing she would have to set right, if she could.

To Jemima's dismay, the letter continued: *"I consider you my wife already, Jemima, just as if we were standing in front of the bishop. And I have made it plain to Samuel Kauffman, and certain others, that we are engaged, and that I will not look kindly on any of them coming out to your house, or trying to court with you."*

"Oh!" Jemima put a hand to her mouth, closed her eyes, and shook her head. Really, sometimes Joseph Beiler was so - - *so* – she just wanted to *shake* him.

"I will be coming to see you again. I know that you depend on my strength, my maus, and I will soon be at your side."

"Oh, *Joseph*!" Jemima exclaimed, in exasperation. How on earth had he gotten *all that*, out of their last meeting? But on the other hand, how on earth could she tell him *anything*, when she wasn't sure whether she wanted to be free – or to *let* him tell the world that they were engaged?

And then there was Samuel, waiting for an answer to *his* proposal of marriage. And Mark, who'd asked her not to say *yes* to anyone, until after the trial, when he had hinted that *he'd* propose, as well!

Jemima shook her head in misery, and looked up at the sky. *Oh Lord,* she prayed, *Please help me! I'm in so far over my head, I don't know what to do!*

She sighed, and put Joseph's letter aside, making a mental note to call him later, even though she wasn't yet sure what she would *say.*

She picked up the other letter. It was heavy, and slick, and the envelope was professionally printed. It was from Barfield Hutchinson – the lawyer. It could hardly be *good* news, but Jemima made herself open it in spite of the dread she felt.

When she unfolded it, the neat, typed contents read:

"Dear Miss King:

A few days ago I received a visit at my office from a young man named Brad Williams."

Jemima's heart jumped up into her throat and throbbed there.

"Mr. Williams asked me to relay a message to you, and I agreed to do so. He says that he is willing to testify on your behalf in court, but only on the condition that you meet with him at my office, alone. I leave this completely to your own discretion. As you know, your court date is fast approaching. Mr. Williams' testimony could be very useful to us in court,

because he says he is ready to swear that he heard you tell Mr. Morton that you wouldn't sell the clock, and that Mr. Morton tried to intimidate you.

"However, should you decline Mr. Williams' offer, we will most likely still prevail. It is my opinion, based on years of experience, that Mr. Morton is bluffing, and that he is trying to bully you. He clearly believes that you will settle out of court, because of your religious tradition. But he can ill afford a jury case, and his lawyer at least will be aware of that.

"I have enclosed the card that Mr. Williams left. Should you choose to meet him here, please call my office to inform us of your decision.

"Yours sincerely,

Barfield Hutchinson, P.A."

Jemima let the letter fall out of her hands. A dozen conflicting emotions swirled up around her like birds startled from cover. They circled around her, fought, fought again, entwined, and then exploded into a burst of feeling that was almost like color, like bells.

And that vibrated deep in her heart for long afterwards.

She looked down at her lap. Just below the letter was the business card that she remembered. She picked it up, ran a small thumb over the stiff, heavy paper.

She turned her head toward the house. Kitchen sounds came through the screen door: the clink of glass jars, her mother's soothing voice, and occasionally, Deborah's sharp voice, raised in complaint.

She listened for a minute and then turned her head toward her father's smithy, next to the barn. The sound of hammering and the hiss of fire drowned in water, wafted faintly from the open door.

She looked out across the yard, and beyond it, across their meadow, further to the road, and beyond it to their neighbor's fields. There wasn't another human face in all that expanse: just the golden light of late afternoon, slanting across endless acres of corn.

Jemima turned the card in her fingers again, as if she were memorizing its texture. Then she stood, glanced at the screen door, and moved silently across the porch and down the steps.

CHAPTER FIFTEEN

Jemima got out of the cab and turned to pay the Englisch driver, who smiled, nodded, and slowly pulled the car away.

Jemima watched it disappear down the tree-lined street, and then turned to her destination. The elegant, two-story brick mansion that was the law office of Barfield Hutchinson looked just the same as it had been the last time she had seen it. It was still opulent, still a reminder of fighting and conflict, and still – *very* intimidating. She took a deep breath, shook out her skirts, and walked quickly up the cobbled driveway.

The grandfather clock in the corner was chiming when she stepped in. It was just three o'clock, and she was right on time.

The secretary looked up as she entered, and smiled politely. "Good afternoon, Miss King! You'll find Mr. Williams waiting for you in the consultation room. It's through that doorway, second room to the left."

"Thank you," Jemima nodded.

She walked across the plush carpet, noting that her feet hardly made a sound on it. The ticking of the big antique clock sounded loud in the stillness. She turned into a small hallway, and approached the second door on the left. It was closed.

Jemima paused outside of it, praying silently. Then she turned the knob and walked in.

Brad Williams was sitting at a big table, but stood as she entered. There was a big picture window behind him, and afternoon light flooded through it. His wild sandy hair seemed outlined in white light, and his light blue eyes looked almost on fire in his shadowed face.

But her eyes zoomed straight to his chin. Brad Williams' chin was still stamped with the imprint of Mark's fists. There was a horrible, purplish stain on one side of his jaw that spread all the way to his chin. In places, it looked *black*.

She gasped out loud. "*Oh*! *Es tut mir leid , das ist alles meine schuld...*"

He grinned a little crookedly, and lifted his hands. Jemima shook her head and reverted to English.

"Oh, your face! I'm so sorry!" she cried. She sank down into her chair and stared at him in horror.

He grinned again, and shrugged. "No worries, Duchess. I'm a big boy. It's an occupational hazard."

Jemima took a breath before she replied: "I'm *so sorry* that this happened to you. I know that Mark will be sorry too, when he has had time to think."

Brad smiled and rubbed his jaw gingerly. "Is that his name? Well, it's apt. He sure left one."

Jemima burst out into a sob, swallowed it, and put a hand to her mouth.

"Hey now," Brad objected, rising from his chair. "It's not as bad as all that, I promise! It looks pretty ugly, I admit, but it's not painful. See, I'll show you."

He came to the end of the table and knelt down beside her chair so that she was looking into his eyes. He smiled again.

"Go ahead – poke it," he told her.

Jemima stared at him in consternation, wondering briefly if he truly *was* mad. She shook her head.

"Go ahead. I promise I won't yell."

Jemima looked doubtfully into his eyes. He looked as if he was just going to *stay* there until she did, so she slowly and hesitantly extended a finger, and briefly touched his chin on the least-damaged-looking spot.

He squinched his face into a dreadful comic knot, with his eyes squeezed shut and his mouth puckered up. He looked so silly that she couldn't help feeling relieved, and sputtered out just a *tiny* laugh.

He winked at her. "That's right, Duchess. No worries." He pulled up a chair beside her and turned it so that he could face her. "So, now that we've established that I'm *not* murdered -- let me tell you why I asked you here."

He leaned forward and looked earnestly into her face. "What I was trying to say to you before, Duchess, is that I'm willing to testify on your behalf. Since I was there that day, when the guy was trying to get the clock from you. It might help you win in court."

Fresh tears dazzled her eyes. She shook her head and looked down into her lap. "I'm so *sorry*, Brad Williams," she said, "I said such mean things to you. You've been so kind *always*, you've always helped. It's true that things have been...sometimes hard since I sold the letter, but that wasn't *your* fault. You're not to blame for what other people do. I was wrong to take out all my anger on -- on *you*."

She peeped up at his face. His eyes looked solemn, and a little sad.

"Don't worry about it," he said quietly. "If anyone here is apologizing, it should be me. I should've thought more about how all this would affect your life. I made the mistake of assuming that a million dollars would be great for you. But I guess that's not what you're all about, huh?"

Jemima shook her head.

"And don't start feeling bad about me," he added, looking down. "I wanted a full time job at the *Ledger*. Your story helped me get it. That factored in, too, Duchess. I'm no victim."

She looked up at him again, and this time, she held his gaze. "That's why you did what you did?" she asked.

He bit his lip, but nodded.

She looked down into her lap, and then raised her eyes again. "Is that why you did – *everything* you did?"

He looked at her for a long moment, but finally shook his head. "*No.*"

Then he took her chin in one hand and held it perfectly still as he leaned in and kissed her. His kiss was softer than a sigh, barely tangible, and yet it electrified her in a way that she could hardly describe. Every nerve ending in her body strained toward that faint, soft contact, and every nerve registered its exquisite, *barely-thereness.*

He pulled back, released her chin, and smiled down into her eyes. "And call me *Brad.*"

He reached down along her arm, in a faint caress, and

grabbed her hand, squeezed it. "Let's get out of here, Duchess. We can grab a sandwich in some drive thru and go have lunch. I know a pretty spot down by the river that has a picnic bench. *Come on.*"

He smiled at her winningly, and looked so handsome, in spite of his bruises, that she smiled back.

"Because I want to hear your life story, from the *day you were born, until now*. I want to know what you think, what you hate, what you love, and what you want. I want to know *everything* there is to know about you."

Jemima stared at him, but his expression was so gentle, and his eyes so warm, that she let him pull her to her feet and lead her away.

CHAPTER SIXTEEN

The experience of being inside a car was a rare one for Jemima. She associated it with illness, or emergencies. The idea of a *pleasant* car ride was new to her.

But that afternoon, she enjoyed riding in Brad Williams' truck as much as she'd enjoyed anything in a long time. The way he drove the truck reminded her of a hawk swooping down to catch a fish: *zoom.*

He took them through a drive thru and bought everything on the menu that she even looked at: coffee, and danish, and salad, and sandwich, and fries, and shake, and ice cream. When she protested, he'd only grinned, and told her that it was his treat.

He drove her out to a little park outside of town, and they took their improvised picnic to one of the tables overlooking the water. It was a bright, sunny afternoon, with white clouds sailing in a blue sky. The river was clear and shallow, and made a pleasant *hush* sound as it flowed over the rocks. There were a few families relaxing nearby, and children ran back and forth on the grass.

Brad Williams' light eyes met hers across the table. "So tell me your story," he said, pointing at her with a french fry. "Who is Jemima King?"

Jemima colored, and shrugged. "Nobody," she answered. "At least, nobody different from anybody else." She looked up at him. "I sew a little, I bake, I cook. Any Amish girl can do the same."

He half-smiled, and tilted his head, as if he couldn't quite believe her reply, but it had been the truth. She took a bite of her hamburger to spare herself the necessity of answering another immediate question.

"How old are you?" he asked.

She took a sip of cola. "Seventeen. Eighteen in November."

"I saw a younger girl in your yard this last time," he told her. "Was that your sister?"

Jemima nodded. "Yes, Deborah. She's my only sister. I have no brothers. My father is a blacksmith, and his father and his father's father were blacksmiths. I think he was a little disappointed that he didn't have a son, to carry on the tradition."

Brad fell silent and took a big bite of pie. Jemima realized, with a pang, that the mention of her father could hardly be pleasant for him.

"I – I'm sorry that my Daed chased you, Brad Williams," she told him, in a chastened tone.

"*Brad*," he corrected quickly. She smiled and amended, "*Brad*" – though it felt very strange to call an Englisch man by his first name.

"My father is a good, gentle man, *truly*, but there have been so many people at our home since I sold the letter. Reporters, who come out at night and shine lights on our house. And people who come to steal things from us, to sell. Some of the people have been *wahnsinnig* – crazy in the *head*!" she told him earnestly. "*They* were so many, and my father is only *one*. He – he has had a very hard time."

To her surprise, Brad's face flushed – unmistakably, with embarrassment. He shook his head. "I'm sorry, Duchess," he told her. "really. It sounds like this whole thing has been a nightmare for you, instead of the amazing thing I thought it would be. Any Englisch person would've been over the moon. But I guess that's the difference between being Englisch, and being Amish," he concluded ruefully.

Jemima ate her lunch and refrained from a reply. There was nothing she could say to soften that because it was true.

He looked up at her, sighed and smiled a white, lopsided grin. "So -- what do you do for *fun?*" he asked jokingly.

She looked up at him. "I go to sings, after Sunday night worship," she told him, "and frolics, and sometimes volleyball, or softball. But I just watch," she confided. "I'm not very good at *sports.*"

He raised his bushy, woolly-worm eyebrows and smiled. Jemima colored, thinking that her life must seem unbearably dull to him – a reporter, who had seen so much, and had gone to so many places. She hurried to change the subject.

"And – what about *you?*" she asked shyly.

He gave her a lopsided smile. "Me? I'm a reporter for the *Ledger.*" He seemed disinclined to say any more, and it made Jemima tilt her head.

She regarded him curiously. "Yes, but -- you have family, don't you?"

Brad went red again, and he looked out into the trees suddenly, as if the question made him uncomfortable. "Actually, no. No, I don't, at least, not any family that I care to claim." He brought his eyes back to hers. "My father left us when I was small, and my Mom – well, she did drugs. She died years ago. I lived with my grandmother for awhile, until she died. But by that time, I was a senior in high school and old enough to look out for myself. So I got a scholarship to a city college, and a part-time job at the paper."

Jemima dropped her gaze to the table for fear that they would betray the shock and horror she felt. She couldn't imagine what it would be like to have *no parents*, and to be forced out into the world *alone*. She tried to keep her voice light.

"Where do you go to church?"

He raised his brows politely, and Jemima felt herself going red. Evidently, the answer was, *nowhere.* He looked like he was stifling laughter.

"Ah – I don't. I'm not the religious type, I'm afraid. Though I have no problem with people who are," he added, with a smile. "Live and let live, that's me."

"Oh."

"Isn't that what the Amish say?"

Jemima looked up at him. "Oh, *yes,*" she assured him, "live and – and *let* live."

He put his elbows on the picnic table and trained his bright eyes on her face. "Am I asking too many questions?"

Her mouth formed a small O. She shook her head. "It's just that, there's not that much to *tell*," she smiled. "I live a very quiet life."

His smile faded, but his eyed remained warm. "Have you ever thought about living a different kind of life?" he asked. "Say – going out into the world?"

Her eyes flew to his. "Oh, no! I could never leave my family, and my friends, or change what I believe!" she said earnestly. "No, I'm very happy. All I've ever wanted is –" she broke off suddenly, and looked down.

But he made her finish. "Is what?" he pressed gently.

She shrugged, and kept her eyes on the table. "What every Amish girl wants. To get married, to build a family. To live quietly, to be useful, to worship God in peace."

He watched her wistfully. "That last part is important to you, isn't it?" he asked.

She raised her brows in puzzlement. "Of *course*."

He took a drink, and coughed, and looked away. "And that guy Mark – is he a friend of yours?"

Jemima went hot, and looked down, and didn't reply. Brad smiled at her expression. "I just figured, since he objected so strongly to my visit."

Jemima pinched her lips together, and raised her eyes to his. "I have many friends," she told him evenly. "Mark is one of my oldest. I've known him since we were children."

He held her gaze. "Is he your boyfriend?"

Jemima looked at him in exasperation. He was beginning to irritate her again. She decided suddenly to push back, just a *little*.

"He's one of them," she replied calmly. "There are *three* boys who've asked to court with me."

He frowned faintly. "*Court* with you?"

Jemima repressed a smile, and told him teasingly: "It's almost like being *engaged*."

She had half-hoped for him to be dismayed, but to her surprise, he laughed outright. "You mean you're engaged to *three* guys?" he sputtered. "I'm not *surprised* you have that many guys who want to marry you, Duchess, but –"

She felt herself going hot. "No, of course I'm not engaged to them *all*!" she replied warmly, "just that they've *asked* me to be!"

He grinned at her. "Are you gonna marry one of them?" he asked.

She stared at him. He was shamelessly curious – bordering on rude. No one she knew would ever have *dreamed* of asking such a personal question. She hadn't expected it, and for an instant she was speechless. "I – I haven't decided," she sputtered.

To her amazement, he seemed *delighted* by her reply. He pressed a napkin to his mouth, leaned back, and regarded her with a wide grin. He pointed at her with a plastic fork.

"I wouldn't be afraid to bet $100 that you won't marry any of them," he announced.

"What!"

He stood up and brushed crumbs off of his lap. "That's right." He came over and sat down beside her, very close. Then he turned and looked her in the eyes.

"Because when you like someone *that* much, Duchess, you know *right away*."

Then he took her in his arms, and kissed her again, in front of God and everybody.

CHAPTER SEVENTEEN

"*There* she is!"

Jacob had been sitting at the kitchen table, but he rose and put his hands on his hips as Jemima walked in the front door. "Where have you *been* all day, young lady?" he demanded.

"Are you all right, Jemima?" Rachel added. Her anxious eyes were glued to Jemima's face. "*Look* at her, Jacob!"

Her father walked up and lifted her chin to the light. "You're right, she looks flushed." He covered her brow with one big palm. "Not running a fever, though."

Jemima lifted troubled eyes to father's face. "I feel fine," she told him.

Deborah raked her with a shrewd glance. "*Pffft*! She's been with one of her boyfriends," she scoffed and went back to her dinner.

Jacob's expression darkened. "Is that true, Jemima?" he demanded sternly.

Jemima cast her eyes down. "I went to the lawyer's office," she stammered. "He sent me a letter." She soothed her guilty conscience by telling himself *that* part was true enough.

Her parents exchanged a wordless look but seemed to accept her explanation, to her relief.

"What did the lawyer say, Mima?" her mother asked.

Jemima put her bag down and went to sit at the table. "He says he thinks my chances are good because Mr. Morton is bluffing and wants me to settle out of court," she replied. "He says that he thinks he'll *destroy* Mr. Morton if the case goes to a jury," she replied literally.

Her mother frowned her disapproval. "*That* is why we don't go to court, Jemima," she chided, "Fighting and talk of beating, of *destroying*! It isn't right to do such things!"

Jacob half-turned. "We've talked about this before, Rachel," he said quietly, and she fell silent; but not before giving him an unhappy look.

"Mr. Hutchinson says that my appearance is next week,"

Jemima continued. "He says he'll send a car to pick me up, and drive us to the courthouse. And not to be worried."

"I hope you told him that we are *not* worried, no matter the outcome," Rachel replied. "Now eat your dinner."

Jemima obeyed and said little else. She helped her mother clean up after, and joined her family for evening prayers, but once when she opened her eyes, she noticed that Deborah's sharp eyes were open, too – and watching her.

When prayers were done, they all went upstairs for the night. Jemima closed her bedroom door behind her, and changed into her nightgown, and plaited her hair. But she didn't even bother to turn down her lamp, because there was *no* chance that she would drop off to sleep, not for a long time.

She reclined on her bed and closed her eyes. In an instant, she was in Brad Williams' – *Brad*'s arms again, and his kisses were sending shivers up and down her spine. No matter how guilty it made her feel, she couldn't help reliving it. No one else had ever made her feel so – she couldn't describe it – so deliciously *burned up*.

Because somehow, Brad Williams was on fire, from his crazy eyes outward. He did insane things, like he had no fear, and maybe he was an Englischer, and maybe a madman, too, but when he kissed her, he kissed her like it was the last time, like the world was ending, like they were both going to die.

No one, not Mark, not Samuel, not even Joseph, had *ever* made her feel like Brad made her feel.

And that was a *problem*.

There was a soft knock at the door, and Jemima opened her eyes. "Come in," she called.

To her surprise, when the door opened, Deborah stood in it, braiding her long hair. She closed the door behind her, swung her braid behind her, and put her hands on her hips. "So, you like the Englisch reporter," she said, matter-of-factly. "What do you plan to do with Joseph, and Samuel, and Mark?"

Jemima frowned. "What I do is my own business, Deborah King," she said, with uncharacteristic tartness, "--not yours!"

"Fine," Deborah replied blandly, "but you can calm down. I'm not bashing your choice. I have to admit, he is a very nice-looking guy. Maybe not as good-looking as Joseph, or as well-built as Mark, but close. He's got plenty of nerve, I'll say that, he's smart, and he's *way* cooler than the other three.

"Are you planning *not* to join the church, and go Englisch, then?"

"Oh, for heaven's sake!" Jemima exclaimed crossly, "I'm not planning anything, and Brad Williams is not my choice, and I don't understand why you even brought him up."

Deborah smirked, "Please. I may be 14, but I'm not blind. I saw your face when you came back. After all your other romances, I know the *kissy face* look, and since Mark and Samuel and Joseph were all at work today -- it had to be the Englischer boy."

Jemima's mouth dropped open, and Deborah nodded, "*Mmmm-hmm.*"

Jemima swallowed, and tried not to look worried. "Why are you saying all this?"

Deborah shrugged. "I just wanted to tell you that I know and that I *approve*. In fact, I'll help you, if you like. I can talk him up to Mamm and Daed. You'll need that if you decide to keep seeing him."

Jemima frowned. "Why are you doing this? You're not – well, you don't *usually* –"

"I'm not usually *nice* to you," Deborah agreed. "True. But, maybe I've changed my ways."

Jemima frowned and gave her a narrow look: but Deborah only smiled angelically and walked out.

Jemima watched her go, then fell back onto the bed and gnawed her fingers. Now she was in Deborah's power -- as if she didn't already have enough troubles!

But even that danger couldn't distract her for long. After a few fretful minutes she drifted back into her dream: of being locked in Brad's embrace, of being kissed by that handsome madman, of feeling like they were all alone, like nothing and no one else *even existed.*

He had closed her in his arms and crushed her to his lips, in spite of the pain she knew it had cost him, and kissed her like a wild man. He had murmured in her ear, crazy things, had made her lose her breath, cry out even though they weren't alone, and made her promise that she'd meet him again after the trial. He had even promised to come back to their *house*, and she knew he was capable of doing it, in spite of the danger.

He might be an Englischer, but Brad Williams was a brave man, and a good and kind man. He had been amazingly unselfish, in spite of his talk about wanting a story for himself.

There was no *future* in Brad Williams, she knew that, but as long as he was there, as long as he kept coming back and holding out his hand, she would keep taking it. She frowned because it wasn't fair to Joseph, or Samuel, or Mark – but she couldn't help what she felt.

She trembled inside, thinking that maybe Brad had been right. Maybe if you loved someone – you knew *right away.*

She looked up at the ceiling and tried to pray, but God felt far away and remote. She had the guilty sense that she was doing wrong, or at least, doing *stupidly*. It wasn't wise for her to see an Englisch boy, because once she joined the church, she would only be able to marry another church member – not an outsider. And Brad Williams was *definitely* an outsider.

Her mother was right. She was setting herself up to be hurt. *None* of this was going to end well.

But as long as she could put off the painful ending, *she didn't care*. Jemima leaned over and blew out the light.

CHAPTER EIGHTEEN

Brad Williams unlocked the door to Room 321, took a running start, and jumped onto the bed with his arms flung out. Then he rolled over, stretched out, folded his arms behind his head, and laughed.

His cell phone buzzed, and he reached for it.

"*Hello, Brad,*" Delores' dry voice greeted him. "*You're the one who's supposed to be calling me – remember? So how's it going? Have you talked to the girl yet?*"

"I talked to her today, for a long time," he answered. "It wasn't an interview, but I'm back in. I'm pretty sure she'll tell me later if I ask."

Delores' voice sounded irritated. "Why didn't you just get the interview, while you *had* her? After all the trouble you've had making contact –"

"Trust me, Delores, I have to finesse this thing. The last time I saw her, she all but cussed me out. I'm coming in cold, after a long absence, and after a lot of bad things have happened. If I hit her again with a big request too soon, she'll bail, and we're out of luck."

There was a long, pregnant silence on the other end of the line. Brad could almost hear Delores' brain turning his words over, sniffing them.

"This wouldn't have anything to do with the fact that she's – what was the word you used – *photogenic* -- would it, Brad?" Delores drawled. "Because if I get the idea that you're stringing this assignment out to romance that girl, I'll –"

"I *promise* you, Delores," Brad replied smoothly, "I'm on the job. Just let me do things my own way."

Delores grumbled on the other end of the line. "You're taking a lot of chances, hot shot. You'd better be right."

"I've been right so far, haven't I?"

"You've been lucky. Meanwhile, Wellman at Channel 1 is running quotes from everyone in town who's ever *seen* her, and we have nothing."

Brad's smile faded. "Wellman has stories because he

makes up half of them," he retorted. "I'm handicapped, Delores. I have to wait until people actually *say* things."

To his surprise, she chuckled. "You're wasted on us, hot shot. You should work in PR. But remember – my patience is running thin. The public is interested in this story, but that will *only* last until the end of her court case. You have until then. Don't disappoint me."

There was a *click*.

Brad tossed the phone onto the bed, rolled his eyes up to the ceiling, put his hands on his head, and exhaled. He told himself that he *liked* to talk to Delores, because the end of the conversation always gave him a *near-death rush*.

He reached for the TV remote and the television winked to life. The local station was on commercial break. A car salesman named "Honest John" had dressed up as an Amish farmer and was poking "high prices" with a pitchfork.

Then the commercial ended, and the local news came on. It was the five o' clock broadcast.

To Brad's irritation, Wellman from Channel 1 was standing there with a mic to his face. Wellman was a tall, handsome specimen dressed in the reporter's uniform: a sports coat, a tie, slacks -- and a big gold ring. Brad noted that he had a more than *usually* bad case of reporter hair.

"And how do you know Jemima King?" he was asking. A teenaged girl was standing there, squinting into the camera.

"I saw her when she came to the hospital," the girl replied, smiling nervously. "I work in the gift shop, and she walked right past me. I recognized her because of her clothes. And her red hair."

"That was the day that she came to visit her friends, the Yoders," Wellman clarified, smiling directly into the camera. "Would you have guessed that she was there to give away *$200,000*?"

The girl shook her head. "I just thought she was there to see a doctor or something," she confessed.

Brad laughed out loud, and Wellman looked temporarily nonplussed. "Have you ever seen *anything like this before*?" he pressed, and the girl shook her head obligingly.

Finally, to wrap up the segment, he had the girl hold up a cloth doll. It was a red-haired Amish girl with angel wings. "What's this?" he asked, smiling into the camera.

"It's our 'Jemima' doll," the girl explained. "We can't keep them on the shelves."

"Well, she certainly does sound like an angel," Wellman replied. "And Channel 1 will be here to cover the $1.6 million dollar lawsuit being brought against her next week. Back to you, Monica."

Brad cursed under his breath and flicked a button on the remote. The TV went dead.

Brad closed his eyes and expelled all the breath in his body in one long, tired sigh. It was dinnertime, and he'd didn't feel like going down to the restaurant, so he grabbed the menu off the nightstand and picked up his phone again.

"Is this room service? Good. This is Room 321. Yeah, I'd like the steak burger meal. Sure, thirty minutes will be fine."

It was still early, but he was *in* for the evening. He was tired, mentally and physically, and he needed to recharge his brain if he hoped to get the scoop that Delores lusted after -- and that would save his job.

He pulled his hands over his face. He probably owed his job to the fact that he'd been able to charm Delores into giving him chances that no one else got. He had already missed one deadline.

Why *hadn't* he just gotten an interview from Jemima, when he had the chance? It was a fair question, and he didn't have an answer that made any sense to *him*, much less one that would satisfy Delores.

He opened his fingers and stared out through them. The truth, of course, was that being close to the Duchess had scrambled his brain, and he'd forgotten what he was supposed to be doing. He had forgotten why he was even *there*, and everything, in fact, except the urgent need to grab her and pick up where they'd left off.

It was a funny thing, too, because he wasn't the caveman type, usually. He liked to use his wits with women.

Except that when he was with the Duchess, he couldn't *find* them.

He shook his head. It was stupid, this whole thing: he was a moron, and he needed to get his head on straight, or he'd find himself in the unemployment line – as Delores had strongly hinted.

He put the phone back on the nightstand. The plain brown book was still lying there, where he left it. He picked it up idly and put it on his lap.

Jemima's soft voice echoed in his mind as he remembered their conversation:

I want what every Amish girl wants. To get married, to build a family. To live quietly, to be useful, to worship God in peace.

That last part is important to you, isn't it?

Of course.

He opened the plain brown book again. This time, it fell open more or less in the middle. He raised it just high enough to read: *"Who can find a virtuous woman? For her price is far above rubies. The heart of her husband doth safely trust in her...She will do him good and not evil all the days of her life."*

Brad let the book fall down again. He remembered his Mom, strung out on meth, slumped against the living room wall with her eyes rolled up to the ceiling and her mouth hanging open. His mouth twisted to one side.

But he couldn't get Jemima's soft voice out of his head. He heard it again, even when he closed his eyes and pulled a hand over his face:

I want what every Amish girl wants. To get married, to build a family. To live quietly, to be useful, to worship God in peace.

That last part is important to you, isn't it?

Of course.

CHAPTER NINETEEN

The next morning Brad went down to the hotel restaurant and enjoyed a leisurely breakfast and the morning paper. After a few days in Lancaster County, getting up *after* sunrise felt positively decadent.

He purused the front page of the *Lancaster Farmer's Friend*. It was a tiny local paper that had fallen into a big story by accident, but seemed to be playing it for all it was worth. The Duchess' upcoming court case was headline news, and the local slant was heavily in her favor. Brad noticed, with some satisfaction, that no one, even locally, had snagged a recent photo relevant to the story, except an extremely long-range shot of the King farmhouse.

Brad put down the paper and pulled out his smart phone. A quick scan online verified his hunch that it was the general trend. No one, not even Channel 1, had a picture of the Duchess, unless they had paid to display the one the *Ledger* had taken.

Brad took a sip of coffee and smiled to himself. He was on the brink of scooping even the networks because *no one* had the access to the Duchess that he enjoyed.

He sputtered suddenly and had to put the coffee cup down because a deep pain in his chest gave him an unholy jolt. It was that same pain he'd suffered before – the one deep down. It coincided with an intense feeling of guilt, but he pushed it away. *Guilt* was a luxury he couldn't afford, not if he wanted to keep his job.

He brushed coffee off of his shirt. But he had to admit that he did feel bad about – about what had happened earlier. If he'd had any sense, he wouldn't have tried to kiss the Duchess, or make her promises, but it was what always happened. He was an idiot.

Anyway, surely even an *Amish* girl had to understand that it was impossible for them to have anything more than a brief dalliance. She *had* to know that he was in this for the story. He'd told her often enough.

But he was looking forward to seeing her again. Or, to be honest, to seeing her for *one last time*. True, he'd screwed up, he shouldn't have made things *personal* between them, but maybe he could fix it. Maybe he could tell her that he'd been joking, or something, and encourage her to go back to her farm boys, so she wouldn't get the wrong idea.

But on the other hand, maybe she wouldn't *care* if he left. She'd told him that three other guys had proposed to her, so he probably wasn't even on her radar, at least not seriously.

He rubbed his jaw gingerly. Though, to be honest, he didn't *like* the idea of the Duchess ending up with that dark-haired guy. In fact, the mental image of the Duchess with anybody else was *No*, although he had the clarity to admit to himself that jealousy was insane. They hardly knew one another, and they weren't going to see each other at all after the court case.

In fact, Delores had been right – the sooner he got this interview *over with*, and himself out of Lancaster County, the better for everyone.

He paid his tab and returned to his room. He had just freshened up and was preparing to go out again when there was a soft knock on the hotel room door.

He frowned. He couldn't think of anyone who *should* be knocking.

He went to the door and opened it. To his amazement -- *Sheila* was standing there, in all her blonde glory.

"*Surprise*, Brad!" she purred, smiling from ear to ear. "*Guess who* just got assigned to help you on this story?"

Brad gaped at her. When his brain began to work again, it ran a frantic inventory of all the ways that having Sheila in his hair would destroy his chances of seeing the Duchess again. And one look at her face told him that Sheila *knew it.*

Brad pulled his mouth into a smile. "Sheila! What are *you* doing here? And what do you mean, *help me with this story?* You're *Delores'* assistant – aren't you?"

Sheila breezed past him and perched on the edge of a chair inside his room. "I'm *your* assistant now, Brad! Delores was so *sweet*, Brad, you wouldn't believe it. She said that she could see that I was *pining* for you, so she gave me permission to come here and help you with the story. She said that *you* need me more than *she* does – Wasn't that thoughtful of her?"

Brad laughed and nodded. "That Delores! Yeah, *that* – that Delores!" he agreed, looking up at the ceiling.

"And you know what's even better, Brad? The boy at the front desk was able to get me just a few doors down from you. So we can see each other all the time, for as long as we're here!"

He stared at her, and shook his head, and put his hands on his hips, and looked down at the carpet.

"That's – that's really great, Sheila!" he stammered.

She lifted her big blue eyes to his face. "So, Brad. How can I help you? I can see you've gotten into trouble already."

She lifted her hand to his chin and turned it carefully. "Poor thing! How did you get this shiner? Did one of the *Amish* people hit you?"

"Actually, *yes*, that happened. It's a long, strange story, Sheila, and I'd love to tell you all about it, but –"

Sheila nodded shrewdly. "But you have an urgent meeting and have to go, and why don't I just relax and wait for you back in my room?"

Brad mustered a sickly smile. "I knew you'd understand, Sheils," he told her warmly, "you're such a sport!" He made for the door, but she grabbed his tie as he passed.

"Nah, I want to come with you," she told him pleasantly. "So much more fun, don't you think? You can show me the back 40. Isn't that what they call it out here?" she giggled, and nibbled his ear.

He switched to another tack, "Ah – you know, this was a bit of a surprise, Sheils, but it works out *perfectly*! Because I was going to spend the morning at the library, doing research, but it would be time better spent getting interviews. Could *you* maybe spend the morning at the library? I'd want articles about former lawsuits in Lancaster County. I would *really* save me time."

She ran her hands through his hair.

"Not so fast, handsome. Because the last thing that Delores told me – bless her! – was that I'm supposed to stick to you

437

just like glue until you get the Amish Dolly interview and *write your story.*" She tapped his nose with a manicured finger. "And that's just what I intend to *do.*"

Then she put her arms around him and kissed him with lips tasting of spearmint and strawberry gloss. Brad allowed himself to experience Sheila's kiss. He told himself that he and Sheila had a lot in common, that he was fond of her, they got along, he found her attractive.

And -- he still wished she was a *thousand miles away.*

And as for *Delores* -- Brad lifted his eyes to the ceiling. He had to give it to Delores, she was scary smart. She was crafty.

And he was going to get even with her for this, if it was his *dying act.*

CHAPTER TWENTY

The court case was scheduled for the following Monday, and there were a few days left before Brad would be called up to testify. He had hoped to talk to Jemima again, but instead, he found himself using the time to entertain Sheila.

She rapped on his door at 9 a.m. the following morning. Brad wiped shaving cream off of his chin, pulled on his belt, and stepped into his shoes. She was kind of early, but then, *early* was a relative term. If there was one thing he appreciated about Sheila, it was that she did *not* require him to battle the world before sunrise.

He opened the door, and Sheila was standing in the opening with one hand on the frame, and the other set jauntily on one hip. She smiled at him, and jingled her car keys.

He allowed himself to admire her. Sheila was a beautiful girl. On that particular morning, her hair was pulled back into a sleek ponytail, and she was wearing a little red number that hugged every curve. And Sheila *did* have the curves.

She was wearing a little more mascara and lipstick than he liked, but there was no denying that he was a lucky guy. Kind of.

Because Sheila required *attention.*

"Let's grab some breakfast," she was saying. "I saw a cute little B&B on the way in, and you can bring me up to speed on the way over."

He assumed an innocent expression. "Oh, there's *really* not that much to tell, Sheila," he said apologetically. "Actually, it's been kind of *dull*, out here in the green hill county. Not much to do," he laughed.

She gave him a shrewd look. "Yes, I can see that," she drawled, flicking his bruised chin with her finger. "You never *did* tell me how you got that mark."

Brad gave her a big, cheesy smile and cast about in his mind for the least damaging way to explain. "I met a stranger *by accident*," he joked.

"Good grief, Brad," she teased, "do you mean that one of the *locals* popped you? They're incredibly boring, but they aren't supposed to be *violent!*" she laughed.

He rubbed his jaw gingerly. "You'd be surprised," he muttered.

"*Hmmm.* Well, if I had to guess, I'd say it had something to do with the Amish Dolly," she sighed and smiled. "And we can't have that, now – *can* we?"

Then she leaned over, gave him a kiss, and pulled him outside by his tie.

They spent the better part of the morning at the Happy Daisy Rest B&B outside of town. The Happy Daisy Rest was a two-story white clapboard farmhouse that had been tricked out in frilly gingerbread trim, lavishly landscaped, and turned into a bed and breakfast by a retired couple.

Sheila ordered the full breakfast. It was overpriced, served on bone china, skimpy by the generous local standards, and slow to arrive because the owners insisted on serving it in five stages. It was a touch that seemed to delight Sheila, but that Brad found pretentious and irritating.

Sheila devoured a cheese and spinach quiche about the size of a half-dollar, dabbed her lips, and cast an approving glance around the dining room. "You know, Brad, I can almost see it, why people come here. It's like taking a vacation to 1875. It might actually be *relaxing* for a day or two when things get crazy in the city."

Brad nodded silently and popped a biscuit that was small enough to be eaten in one bite.

"But I would think that after that, you'd just *lose your mind* with boredom," she added, taking a sip of coffee.

Brad smiled, nodded, and raised his own cup.

He was mostly silent, but since Sheila more than filled the gap with office gossip, he wasn't required to come up with much conversation. That was a relief: because there wasn't much he could *afford* to tell her.

Sheila continued to talk. After a leisurely half hour they finished their meal, and the owner brought the check. Brad reached into his wallet for his card.

Sheila picked up the tab, glanced at it, and giggled. *"We're in luck!"* she whispered. *"Look – they forgot to charge us for the second meal. Score!"*

Brad raised his eyebrows. He would've thought nothing of letting it slide a month ago, back in the city. But here, in the middle of Amish country, the small dishonesty seemed glaringly wrong.

Brad smiled awkwardly, because his reason sounded lame, even to him. "I can't stiff them, Shiels," he told her and raised his hand. *"Sir?"*

Sheila leaned in and hissed: "What are you doing? It was overpriced – you're blocking karma!"

But by that time, the owner had come to the table. Brad looked up at him sheepishly. He felt like a fool but made himself say: "Um – our bill was only for one meal, instead of two."

The man peered at it and gasped. "You're right – and *thank you*! I appreciate your honesty!"

The man hurried off to correct the mistake, and Sheila gave him a disgusted look. "What's wrong with you? You could have saved the paper some money!"

He shrugged sheepishly. "Must be something in the water around here," he told her, and got up to go.

Brad soon discovered that Sheila had a full itinerary for the day, and after breakfast she drove into downtown Serenity for some shopping. She hinted strongly that he should come, *too*.

Brad smiled and told her *no* as politely as he could muster. "People know my face around here," he shrugged. "I don't want them to mob me about Jemima."

Sheila raised her brows. "*Oh* yes – the Amish Dolly. She's the hometown hero here, isn't she?" she drawled. "That must be so irritating for you, Brad! I guess you're counting the days until you can get *out* of here, and back to *civilization*. Well, it won't be too long now – poor darling!"

She leaned over to give him a peck on the cheek. "Don't

go too far now! I'll meet you back at the gazebo in the square, in an hour."

Brad nodded, and waved, and Sheila teetered off on her three-inch heels. She had soon disappeared into one of Serenity's many gift shops.

And as soon as she was gone, Brad turned into an alley between buildings and dug in his pocket for his cell phone. He opened his messages and searched down them with a hungry eye. He'd given the Duchess his cell phone number and asked her to call him if she thought she could get away. To his disappointment, there was no message.

He sighed. Jemima's court case was going to be a media zoo, and he wanted to get the interview with her before then if he could. First and foremost, because Delores had threatened his job if he didn't; and secondly, because he had the feeling he might not get the chance to see Jemima afterward.

And he *really* wanted to see her one last time.

Of course, it was a lunatic desire: The Duchess was probably off with one of her farm boys at that very moment. She might even have decided which of them she wanted to *marry* by now. And it made perfect sense. They could give her what she wanted – a safe, quiet life and a family.

For an instant he allowed himself to picture what that would be like: living in the gorgeous green hill country, leading the simple life, turning his back on the 21st century with all of its noise and tension. No crushing deadlines, no games, no cutthroat competition. One day of peace melting into another, with familiar faces all around.

And for just an instant -- because he couldn't keep himself from doing it -- he imagined waking up to the Duchess' angel face every morning, of having her soft voice be the first sound to touch his ear. He closed his eyes and smiled.

After a long, pleasant moment, Brad opened his eyes again, turned the phone off and put it back into his pocket, frowning. He twisted his mouth sardonically. He'd never known anything even *close* to that pleasant dream. And if the truth were told, the Amish hinterland probably wasn't as perfect as it looked from the outside. Most things weren't.

And then, too, the Amish had all that religious guilt. They had to worship all the time, and their faith required endless hand-wringing about "sin." Even though, comparatively speaking, they probably needed to repent the *least* of anyone within a thousand miles. Or, the *particular* Amish person that he was thinking of, anyway.

He sighed and looked up at a small sliver of sky between the alley walls. No, Sheila was right, Delores was right, and *he* was right – in his moments of clarity. The Duchess was nothing but a beautiful mirage.

And a heck of a good *story*. The sooner he started thinking of her that way, the better.

But when he turned to leave the alley between the two stores, he happened to pass one of the display windows. There, with its big green eyes looking out at him, was the innocent Jemima doll, with its wispy red hair and angel wings.

CHAPTER TWENTY-ONE

It was still dark when the cell phone alarm went off in Brad's ear. It felt like no time had passed at all from the previous night. Brad groaned and pulled his hands down over his face. For about five minutes he told himself that it wasn't all that big a deal to get away from Sheila, But six minutes was all it took for him to think better of that, and to plant his feet on the floor.

He hated getting up early, and he'd have to find some way to play it off with Sheila later, but *one day* was all that he was willing to spend on shopping and overpriced food. And he was reasonably certain that Sheila didn't rise before the sun.

He stumbled to the bathroom and took a quick shower,

shaved, and dressed. He felt half-alive, but by local standards it wasn't even all that early. In the Englisch world, it might still be the night before, but at 5 a.m., Lancaster County was open for business.

When he was shaved and brushed and dressed and combed, Brad quietly locked his hotel room and padded down to Sheila's door. He pushed a small note under it, then descended the metal stairs to the breezeway, and walked out to the truck. He slid in, cranked the engine, and escaped to the freedom of the open road.

He rolled down the windows on the truck and let the cool air of early fall come pouring in. The hotel was well outside of town and mostly surrounded by rolling fields. They were beautiful at that time of year, thick with corn, and even at that early hour, there were boys out in them, driving teams ahead of a harvester.

He turned his head to watch them as the fenceposts flashed past: they were sitting up on the rigs, holding the reins. From where he was, it almost looked as if they were sailing across endless green waves.

He shook his head, smiling. It was picturesque, he had to admit it. He was going to miss that part when he went home to his studio apartment in the city.

He pulled the truck into the parking lot of a little cafe on the outskirts of town. It was already crowded, even though the sun was just rising, and he was lucky to find a window booth. The prospect faced out onto one of those endless fields, brushed by the new gold of the dawning sun. A pretty waitress came over and smiled at him. "Good morning! What can I get for you?"

"*Coffee*," he replied instantly, "*black* coffee. Ham and gravy biscuits, scrambled eggs with cheese, hash browns, and – let's see – a side of bacon."

"Coming up." He reached into his pocket and pulled out his smart phone. To his surprise, there was an instant message from Sheila. It read: *Ha ha, Brad, very funny.*

He grinned but declined to answer: because when he did, he was going to have to strike just the right balance of groveling apology, and firmness, and truly *creative* replies took time.

To his surprise, and delight, the waitress brought his order back in less than five minutes – platter after platter of good, solid farm food, trailing fragrant steam. He set to immediately, and almost closed his eyes in deep appreciation. This part of the country understood food.

He gave the plate his undivided attention for better than 15 minutes. That was another thing he was going to miss when he left: good, simple food, and plenty of it.

His phone buzzed, and he picked it up, thinking that Sheila must have thought of something else, but the message was from the lawyer, Hutchinson. The old shark wanted him to come in for a *briefing* before Jemima's court cast – legalese for "coaching." He took another bite of ham.

He was about the shut the phone completely off, but there was another notification on his call list. It was sandwiched in between the other two, and he almost missed it. But there, in black and white, was the number he'd almost forgotten.

The call had been from *Jemima.*

He coughed, and spilled coffee on himself, and cursed, and brushed it off with his napkin. He fumbled with the phone and pressed it to his ear.

Her voice was so soft that he could hardly make it out over the background noise in the diner, and he cupped his hand over the phone. He could just make out:

"...might not see you after, so I thought we might talk one more time. You can come to the same place as last time, in the garden. My parents are going to town so no one will see. I will be there today."

There was a long pause, and then, even fainter than before, two unintelligible words, then a click. He cursed and played the message back again, and they were still unintelligible. He played it a third time, and this time he was able to hear them.

"Please come."

He sat there, with his mouth open, not quite believing his own ears. Then he played the message back a fourth time.

There it was -- faint but real.

"Please come."

He stared at the tabletop without really seeing it. His pulse was beating in his neck, his mouth was dry, and the brain was blank.

"Please come."

He came to with a start, checked his watch. It was just coming up on 7 o'clock – midmorning, in these parts.

He slapped a $20 down on the table, took a quick sip of coffee, and left.

It was a fairly short drive from town to the King farm. Brad took his usual route, parking next to the overgrown tract of land next door, and hiked over the bramble bushes to the fenceline. He gave the yard and the house a quick sweep. There was no one visible, and no sounds of hammering, so he jumped over.

He made his way through the undergrowth, and so almost walked right into Jemima. She was standing there in the deep undergrowth beyond the garden – well hidden from anyone who might be watching from the house.

The suddenness of her appearance took his breath. He

pulled up short, mustered a lopsided smile, and tried not to look as goofy as he felt.

"*Duchess!*" he exclaimed -- absurdly. She was standing there, bathed in golden morning light, like some flame-haired pre-Raphaelite vision, and framed by a curtain of golden fall leaves. He wanted to stare at her but forced himself to concentrate.

"I *–um* -- I got your message," he stammered. "I'm glad you called. I wanted to talk to you, *too.*"

He lifted his head and looked around. "Where can we talk?"

She smiled at him softly. "We can go to the house. My parents are gone. *Come.*"

To his amazement, she reached out and took his hand. Hers was soft and warm as a kitten's, and almost as small.

He followed her across the lawn, past the garden, and up the porch. She led him to the porch swing and sat down on it. He sat down quickly beside her.

She released his hand, and put her own in her lap, and looked down at them without speaking for a long while.

In that long silence, his brain slowly woke up. He had to keep his head on straight. He had to remember Delores' warnings; his *job* was riding on whether or not he could get this interview. He hated to do it, but he *had* to do it.

He reached down into his pocket, and gently pushed a spot on the phone screen. The recording app kicked in.

Jemima looked up at him with those soft green eyes, the one that tilted up at the edges, the ones that seemed bottomless.

"I wanted to thank you," she said at last. "For everything. And to say I'm sorry for the bad things that happened to you. It's hard to us to trust outsiders. So many of them have not been kind."

Guilt twisted in his chest. He smiled a sickly smile. "It's alright," he assured her.

She added: "We won't be seeing much of each other after next week, maybe." She paused, as if waiting for him to refute it, but he forced himself not to answer. It wouldn't be fair to her.

She bowed her head and went on: "So I will tell you what happened. Mr. Morton came out ahead of you that day, and he only told me that he wanted the clock. He was very impatient. But I never promised to sell it to him."

He nodded. "I know."

"After you left, I thought about what you had said. About the letter being valuable, maybe. But I didn't see why that was so important. I didn't see why everyone was so excited. So I sent it to you. And I thought that you would take it."

She paused again, not looking up.

"But you didn't take it. And I was very surprised. So I – went along, with what you said. Mostly because I – I wanted to know *why* you hadn't taken the letter."

Brad looked up at the ceiling and tightened his lips to a thin line.

"I *still* don't know why you didn't take it."

Brad looked down at her, mustered a smile. "Call it *hochmut*, Duchess," he said gently.

She nodded and went on. "And when we went to the city, when we were watching the auction, and the price kept going up and up, I could see that you were thinking about the letter. And about giving it up. It must have been very hard, to give it up."

Brad pulled back, crossed his legs, coughed. He knew that he needed to start asking her questions, to begin guiding the conversation in the direction he needed it to go, but somehow he couldn't bring himself to do it.

"And after the auction was over. I think I know what you did, when we were there," she murmured, "*now*. You were taking me away before the *other* reporters could come, and – and take pictures, and shoot videos, and ask more questions."

She lifted her eyes to his face. "Isn't that right?"

He tried to make his mouth move into a smile, but it

wouldn't obey. He looked down and didn't answer.

"When the story came out, and all the people came here, it was very hard. I didn't understand why they thought it was so important, to have more money than everybody else. As if I had done something *wonderful*, when I had only bought a clock."

She picked at the fabric of her apron. "The elders had to go to the police, to ask them to block the roads, so many people came here. All because of the money. People I had never met, writing letters, and calling on the phone, and coming out to the house. Daed had to protect us, or they would have come inside our house."

"I can't tell you how sorry I am for that, Jemima," he said quietly.

She tilted her head to one side and shrugged. "It wasn't your fault. You only wrote a story. The rest was other people."

She sighed, and straightened. "Then one day a man came out and asked for me. He threw some papers at me and ran away. The papers were about the lawsuit. And that was hard, too. Because I don't have all the money anymore. I gave a lot of it away already. And I thought about it and prayed about it.

"We're not supposed to sue, you know," she told him. "And my Mamm was very upset, when I told her I was going to get a lawyer. But I believe that God told me to *give the money to other people.* And I can't do that if I don't have it anymore."

She looked up at him with those doe eyes. "What do you think?" she asked.

Brad didn't trust himself to reply. He coughed again, and looked away. "I think you're right," he said at last.

She nodded. "So I'm going to court. And that will be hard, too. But, I'm very grateful that you – came forward to tell the judge about what you heard. It was very nice."

Brad looked off into the distance and shrugged awkwardly.

"I'm sorry that I said mean things about you, and that I thought them. Because you really have been very – *kind*," she said firmly.

She looked up at him again. "I would offer you the money again, if I thought you would take it," she sighed. "But because I know you will *not*, I'll give you something else you want.

"I'll give you what I just said. I know that you're taping me somehow, Brad Williams. But I make you a gift of it."

Then she leaned forward, put a hand to his chin, and kissed him. Then she rose and went inside the house, leaving him to stare after her.

CHAPTER TWENTY-TWO

Brad spent that evening holed up in his hotel room. He locked the door behind him, sat cross-legged on his bed, and opened his laptop. Then he reached into his pocket, pulled out the phone, and pushed a button. Jemima's soft voice trickled out into the silence of the room.

"I wanted to thank you for everything. And to say I'm sorry for the bad things that happened to you."

Brad stuck a cigarette into his mouth and started to type and chain smoke. He typed and retyped all through the night until the laptop was hot enough to make it a fire hazard, and the ashtray on the bedside table was overflowing.

By the time the sun was rising, Brad had finished. He hit the "send" button, sighed deeply, and stretched out across the bed, where he instantly fell deeply asleep.

He woke up hours later, roused by the shrieks of children playing and splashing in the pool below his bedroom window. It was broad daylight – *noon*, in fact.

He opened the laptop again. His inbox was overflowing with messages, mostly from Delores, which he ignored. But there was one message from Sheila, and after long hesitation, he opened it.

Dear Brad,

I read your article. I'll say this for you, you're creative. This has to be one of the most unusual Dear Jane letters I've ever read. But I do understand that's what it is, as least as far as it concerns me. It made me shed a tear, even, and that doesn't happen often. But don't worry – I'm not a girl who mopes around.

Well, handsome, it was fun, and it was worth a try. If you ever change your mind, I'll be around. You can give me a call anytime.

XOXO,

Sheila

Brad stood up and took a few paces to the window. Sure

enough, her car was gone. He sat down on the bed, sighed again, and pulled his hands over his face. Sheila's beautiful blue eyes shimmered in his imagination for an instant, then faded.

Then he opened his eyes, scrolled down to his employer's messages, and read them, one after another. Delores' emails were much more to the point.

Brad,

If you don't get that article to me within the next 24 hours, you'll be reporting to the unemployment office.

Brad,

What's this I hear about you testifying in that girl's trial? If I find out that you're trying to make yourself a name by becoming a part of this story, I will fire you.

Brad lit another cigarette, blew a puff of smoke to the ceiling and frowned. How had Delores found *that* out?

Brad,

You've got exactly three more hours. Don't make me come down there myself.

Brad,

Finally! I'll message you when I'm finished reading it. After all the time you spent on this, it had better be good.

Brad,

This is in the wrong format. It's supposed to be a feature article, not an editorial. But it's brilliant, so I'll let you get away with it, just this once. We'll see how it plays, but my guess is that it'll go wildfire, like the other one. Congratulations, wonder boy.

P.S. Clever of you. An editorial doesn't require another photo – don't think I didn't notice the trick!

P.P.S.

I expect you in the office on Monday morning, bright and early.

Brad sputtered, and a wavy line of smoke curled out into the air. He was going to be in court on Monday so Delores would have to be patient. He turned back to the laptop and scrolled down further. There was also a message from the lawyer.

Dear Mr. Williams:

This is to remind you that you have a consultation with Mr. Hutchinson on Friday at 12:30 regarding the Jemima King trial on Monday morning. Mr. Hutchinson looks forward to talking to you then.

Regards,

Law Office of Barfield Hutchinson

Brad closed out of the email window, checked his watch, cursed, and jumped up from the bed. He only had a few minutes to shower, shave and dress.

In less than ten minutes he had shrugged into his coat, jumped into his shoes, and slammed the hotel room door behind him. But the laptop on the bedside table was still open to a file titled "Jemima King."

My Epiphany

by Brad Williams

"As a reporter, it's necessary to be objective – to distance yourself from the events that you describe. To some extent, it's like being a doctor or a nurse: you have to step back, or the ugliness that you witness will make you numb, and eventually, useless.

But how do you remain objective to beauty – to exquisite, transcendent beauty? This reporter has been trying to do that for months now, and can testify that it's impossible.

When I was first assigned to cover the remarkable story of Jemima King – the Amish girl who became a millionaire when she discovered a rare letter – I thought it would be just another story. I didn't think that it would change my life. But it did.

Ledger readers will remember that this Amish girl sold the letter at Brinkley's for $1.6 million dollars. What they don't know is that this historic sale almost never happened.

Because this Amish girl really doesn't believe that having a great deal of money is all that important.

Don't believe it? I didn't either, at first. But I quickly learned that Miss King meant what she said. In fact, at the beginning of our acquaintance -- and after she understood how much it was worth -- Miss King tried to give the letter away.

To *me*.

She offered again yesterday when I spoke to her about her upcoming trial. You see, Miss King is being sued for the whole $1.6 million by a man who claims that she promised to sell the letter to him and reneged. Not everyone is as indifferent to a million dollars as Miss King.

Jemima King has been in the news recently, and deservedly so – she has donated more than half a million dollars to neighbors and friends whose medical bills far exceeded their ability to pay. She has been rightly praised as a generous, selfless person. And yet, when I spoke to her, she seemed puzzled.

She told me: "I didn't understand why (people) thought it was so important, to have more money than everybody else. As if I had done something wonderful, when I had only bought a clock."

I tried to think of an answer to that, and couldn't. Because while there may be nothing praiseworthy about receiving a sudden windfall, it is extraordinarily selfless and remarkable to spend hundreds of thousands of dollars on others in need.

Anyone who has seen Miss King, or even her photograph, will observe that she is physically beautiful. Yet she is one of those rare people who is also beautiful on the inside.

Which brings me to the title of this editorial. Meeting Miss King was an epiphany for me, in the truest sense of the world. Before I met her, I was an agnostic. But I have changed my views.

Because I have confirmed the existence of an angel, I must therefore now concede the corresponding existence of a God.

How is it possible to remain objective to beauty, to remain unmoved by ineffable grace and generosity? I have discovered that it's impossible, and amid all the scandals and wars and tragedies of our world, this is the most hopeful news that I have ever been privileged to report."

CHAPTER TWENTY-THREE

Brad Williams shifted his weight from one leg to the other and looked up into the grave blue eyes of Barfield Hutchinson.

It was Monday morning, and the courthouse was jammed. Brad scanned the courtroom. Just beyond the big double doors, the press, a good deal of the Amish community, and hordes of curious paparazzi-filled the halls outside.

Inside, the benches were full as well – at least on Jemima's side of the room. Caldwell Morton and his attorney sat on one side, and Jemima, her family, and what looked like at least forty Amish friends and family filled the other side.

"How did you meet Miss King?" Hutchinson asked, clasping his hands behind his back.

Brad leaned toward the microphone in front of the witness box. "I was in downtown Serenity to cover a fair for my employer, the *Ledger* newspaper."

"You're a reporter there, are you not?"

"That's right."

"And what happened on the day that you first met her?"

"I went into the Satterwhite Gift Shop to grab a bite to eat before the fair opened, and Miss King was just walking out. We bumped into one another by accident, and the clock she was holding fell to the ground and a piece of paper fell out of it. I reached down and picked them up for her."

"But neither you, nor Miss King, saw what the paper was?"

"I didn't, and Miss King didn't even look at it. She took the clock and left immediately."

The lawyer nodded. Brad allowed his eyes to wander momentarily. Jemima was sitting on the defendant's bench. Her huge father – who seemed crammed into his black coat – and her mother, a very pretty blonde woman, were in the row immediately behind her.

Brad's glance flitted beyond them, to the people sitting on the back rows. He noticed the guy with the black hair and was gratified to see the remains of a truly epic shiner on his left eye. The guy with the silly straw hat was also there, and a third guy – a blonde – looked as if he might be the last of the Duchess' admirers.

Because *all* of them were staring at him like they wished they could jump the rails and swing at him.

"And what happened after Miss King left?"

Brad cleared his throat. "I went into the shop and bought something to eat. There was no place to sit, so I stood in the doorway. Then Mr. Morton came in, and nearly knocked me down."

"And why was that?"

"He was in a hurry," Brad replied, throwing Morton a dry glance. "He asked the shop owner if he'd bought an antique clock recently, and the man said he had. Morton was very anxious to get it. He asked the shop owner if he could get the name of the person who had bought it, but the man wouldn't give it to him."

Brad paused, and glanced over at the jury to see how his words were going over. The people in the jury box looked like local people, and to judge from their expressions, they were sympathetic to Jemima. Though Brad couldn't imagine how anyone could *avoid* that.

He glanced at her. She was sitting with her hands clasped in her lap. She hadn't looked up at all during the previous testimony, but her eyes had been trained on his face from the moment he sat down in the box.

Hutchinson pursed his lips and nodded. "So it was clear that Miss King had bought the clock earlier?"

"Yes."

"And that Mr. Morton wanted the clock urgently?"

Brad shot Morton a withering glance. "Oh yeah."

"What happened after that?"

"Morton left, and I thought it was funny that he wanted the clock so badly. I figured there might be a story in it, so I asked around for the directions to Miss King's house. I wanted to see if the clock was valuable, or something. I suspected that was why Morton wanted it."

"And so you went out to the King farm?" Hutchinson pressed.

"Yes."

"What happened then?"

"When I got there, Morton was ahead of me. I saw Miss King and Morton standing on the front porch of her house. He seemed agitated. He was talking loudly and pointing to the clock. When I got closer, I introduced myself and asked if I could talk to Miss King."

"How did Mr. Morton react?"

"He got mad. He told me that it was a private matter between him and Miss King and that he was about to buy the clock from her. I told her that she shouldn't sell it until she at least found out what the paper was. That made Morton even more upset. He said that Miss King had promised to sell the clock to him."

"And what did Miss King say?"

"She told him that she had *not* promised to sell the clock to him. Only to show it."

Hutchinson lifted his eyes to the jury box. "Can you repeat that, please, Mr. Williams?"

Brad leaned to the mic and stared into Caldwell Morton's face. "She said that she had only promised to *show it to him*."

"How did Mr. Morton react?"

"He flipped out. He threw money on the floor and said that the clock had belonged to his mother, that was rightfully his. When I told him that she had a right to keep it, he came at me."

Hutchinson raised his snowy eyebrows and affected surprise. "Mr. Morton became physically violent?"

"He pulled his fist back like he was going to slug me. I probably would've had to fight him, if her father hadn't shown up and thrown him out."

"I see. Thank you, Mr. Williams," Hutchinson smiled. "I

have no more questions."

He walked away and sat down beside Jemima. He leaned over and whispered something in Jemima's ear. She nodded.

Mr. Morton's attorney stood up. He was a small, thin man, with iron-gray hair, square glasses, and a mustache. He walked over and seemed to be reading from papers inside a manila folder.

"You said that you're a reporter for the *Ledger*, Mr. Williams?"

"Yes."

"Would you call yourself an objective reporter?"

Brad looked up at him. "I try to be."

"How well would you say you succeed?"

Brad gave the man a direct look. "I don't understand the question."

The lawyer lifted a newspaper over his head for the room to see. "I am holding a copy of the *Ledger* newspaper from last Friday. It contains an editorial entitled, 'My Epiphany.' Did you write this editorial, Mr. Williams?"

Brad looked at him. "Yes."

The lawyer walked over and placed the folded paper on top of the witness box. "Would you be so good as to read it, so we can all hear it?"

Brad could feel himself going red, and shot Hutchinson a questioning look, but the older man remained unmoved. Brad took the paper reluctantly, uncrossed his legs, and cleared his throat.

"As a reporter, it's necessary to be objective – to distance yourself from the events that you describe." He coughed, and slowly read the entire editorial in a voice that he hoped sounded neutral. It was odd, but it had been far easier to write those words for the whole world to read than to read them in front of Jemima and her family.

When he was finished, he looked up, folded the paper, and placed it back on top of the witness box. The lawyer walked over, took it in his hand, and held it up again.

"Mr. Williams has just said that it's important to be *objective*," the lawyer told the courtroom. "But it doesn't sound as if he's *at all* objective about Miss King! In this editorial" -- he adjusted his glasses – "he calls her an 'angel,' a 'generous, selfless person,' 'remarkable,' and 'physically beautiful.'" The lawyer turned to face him.

"You did write those things, didn't you, Mr. Williams?"

Brad met his eyes steadily. "Yes, I did."

The lawyer turned to address the jury. "And yet, you expect us to believe that a young man so clearly smitten with Miss King can be a reliable witness in a case that concerns her?"

Hutchinson stood up. "*Objection -- argumentative!*"

The judge turned to face the lawyer. "Sustained."

The lawyer nodded slightly toward the judge and shrugged. "Mr. Williams, you admit that Miss King tried on two occasions to give you a great deal of money?"

Hutchinson bounced up again. "*Objection!*"

The judge glanced at him. "Overruled."

Brad set his jaw. "She told me at the beginning that she had no wish to be rich, and mailed me the original letter, as a gift, and without any conditions attached. And just last week, she offered to give me the rest of the money she had."

"That *is* remarkable," the lawyer agreed. "An Amish girl offers an outsider a *fortune*, when it's unusual for an Amish woman to even *speak* to a non-Amish man. Why do you suppose she did that, Mr. Williams?"

Brad turned to look at Jemima. Her face was raised to his, and her eyes on him were like stars, like green gems glittering under a jeweller's lamp.

"I have no reason to doubt her own explanation," Brad replied. "She has no desire to be rich, and her actions since then have proved it on multiple occasions."

"I see. But isn't there another, equally simple explanation, Mr. Williams? One that would certainly explain her desire to give you gifts, and your willingness to come here, and to testify on her behalf? Isn't it possible -- and in light of this information -- even *likely*, that Miss King is smitten with you?"

Hutchinson rose again, wearily. *"Objection!"*

"Sustained."

The lawyer glanced at the jury, smiled, and sat back down again. "I have no further questions, your honor."

CHAPTER TWENTY-FOUR

Brad stood up and walked to the back of the courtroom. He could feel Jemima's eyes on him as he passed, and he tried hard *not* to imagine what she was thinking.

His testimony had been the last, and he sat down on the back bench and settled in for the closing arguments. He figured that he was already in it up to his neck with Delores, so a few extra hours, more or less, would make little difference.

Morton's lawyer got up and argued that Mr. Morton's family had owned the letter for hundreds of years and that it had been lost by accident. He said that Jemima had acquired it through a mistake and that she promised to sell the letter to his client, and had reneged. The lawyer also claimed that his *own* eyewitness testimony was suspect because he was besotted with Jemima and therefore not a trustworthy witness.

Brad pulled his hands over his face, imagining how *that* was going to play back at the office, and how it would affect his reputation as a reporter. Not well, that was for sure, but he told himself he'd made the choice to do it, and he wasn't sorry.

After Morton's attorney was finished, Hutchinson stood up and, in Brad's opinion, destroyed the prosecution by arguing that Jemima had the receipt proving she bought the clock legally; that by the testimony of two witnesses, she had been in possession of the letter at the time of dispute; and that, according to his own testimony, she had not promised to sell the clock.

Hutchinson stood facing the jury and pointed dramatically to Jemima as she sat in the defendant's box. "Ladies and gentlemen of the jury, I ask you," he said grandly, "if innocence could reveal itself to the naked eye, could it wear a clearer face than the one you see before you?"

In spite of his feelings toward Jemima, Brad lowered his head and smirked into his shirt. Hutchinson should've had his own TV show, but in this case, Brad figured that even overripe rhetoric couldn't blow Jemima's chances. One look at her face, as Hutchinson had claimed, really *was* it all it took.

Hutchinson finally sat down, and the jury left the room to deliberate. Brad sighed and dug into his pocket for the smart phone. It might be hours before they came back. He checked his email messages. To his dismay, they were almost all from Delores.

Brad,

Where are you? I told you to be here this morning bright and early. If you're where I think you are, you can turn in your badge!

Brad stifled a groan and scrolled down.

Brad,

On second thought, if you're at the trial, make yourself useful. If you can get me a blow-by-blow by noon, I'll forgive you, but only if you get it to me fast.

Brad,

Are you reading your mail?

He sighed, turned off the phone, and stuck it into his pocket. Time passed.

Brad amused himself by studying his neighbors. The people around him were mostly local folk, and a good many were Amish. The row he was sitting on was empty except for him, but the others were filled with primly-dressed men and women. They were talking softly in that near-German dialect he'd heard Jemima use.

His gaze wandered, and he noticed that one of the black-clad figures was staring back at him. It was the tall blonde guy that he figured for one of Jemima's boyfriends, the one who'd been giving him the dead eye. The guy looked even more disapproving now -- if that was *possible*.

On an evil impulse, Brad made eye contact, cracked a wide grin and winked at him. The other young man scowled, drew himself up, and stood briefly, just before the door opened and the jury returned.

The young man was forced to sit back down again, but he gave Brad such a speaking look that Brad began to wonder if he'd been smart to push him. Still, it *had* been hard to resist. He chuckled to himself, shook his head, and rubbed his hands together.

He checked his watch; the jury had been gone almost no time at all – less than 20 minutes. It was either some technical glitch or they'd decided in record time. Brad took a look at their faces, and decided it was probably -- record time.

The judge addressed the foreman. "Have you reached a verdict?"

A portly middle-aged man stood up and nodded. "We have, your honor."

"How do you find?"

"We find in favor of the defendant."

Brad grinned and turned to leave. He brushed past the bailiffs, opened the doors a crack, and was promptly mobbed by the reporters who were waiting outside.

Amish Millionaire Cleared in $1.6 Million Suit

By Brad Williams

Serenity, PA – In a 12-0 decision, a jury today rejected Caldwell Morton's claim that Jemima King, the Amish millionaire, had promised to sell him a letter written by George Washington. The jury, made up of six men and six women, took only 20 minutes to clear Miss King of the charge.

The jury heard arguments from the prosecution lawyer, William Harwell, that the Morton family had owned the letter for hundreds of years, and that Miss King had obtained it when the clock had mistakenly been included in an estate sale.

Defense attorney Barfield Hutchinson countered by arguing that Miss King had produced a receipt for the clock, and that according to the testimony of several witnesses, was in lawful possession of the clock at the time of the dispute.

Several witnesses testified on behalf of Miss King, including Eli Satterwhite, the owner of Satterwhite's Gift Shop in Serenity, Penn.; who said that he sold Miss King the clock; John Maxwell, of Brinkley's Auction House in

Philadelphia, who testified that Miss King had produced valid evidence of ownership prior to the letter auction; and Brad Williams, of the *Ledger* newspaper, who testified that he had heard Miss King refuse to sell the letter to Morton when asked.

Miss King has given more than $500,000 to help local families pay medical bills, and has expressed her intention of giving the rest of her windfall to people in need.

Back in his hotel room, Brad hit the "send" button and checked his watch. It was 11:55. He'd saved his job with five minutes to spare.

He smiled, thinking that testifying on Jemima's behalf was the one thing he'd done since coming to Amish country that he felt completely good about. At least now, he'd done something that really *helped* her.

The rest – well, it was probably better to chalk it up to experience. His time with the Duchess had shown him little more than that he could be reduced to babbling idiocy by a pretty face, that he wanted what he thought he couldn't have, and that he didn't have the sense to keep a girl that he actually got along with, and who understood him.

Now, after all these reverses, it was time to return to the real world, and get back to his own life. He pulled his suitcase out from underneath the bed and opened it beside him.

His smartphone buzzed, and he glanced down at it. Delores had sent him an email.

Brad,

Great article. Here's something that will make you laugh: your editorial has gone viral on social media. You are now the lovelorn boy. Go and see what women are offering to send you in the mail, Romeo!

Brad raised his brows and sputtered out a laugh. He was about to put the phone down again, when the phone buzzed a second time. This time, it was a call.

He picked it up. "Hello?"

There was a long pause on the other end. "Brad?"

He sat up straight. Every nerve in his body was suddenly on alert. *It was Jemima.* How had she gotten hold of a phone?

"Yes, I'm here."

There was silence again. "I was hoping – I was hoping I could see you again, before you leave."

His heart was pounding. "Sure, that would be *great.* I can be at your house in say, twenty minutes."

"No…tonight. After ten o'clock. Could you come then?"

He went completely still and felt his heart beating.

"Sure."

There was a scuffling sound on the other end, a soft sound that might or might not have been a word, and then a dial tone.

CHAPTER TWENTY-FIVE

Brad spent the afternoon in his hotel room, cursing, arguing with himself, and chain smoking. He told himself that he was an idiot, that he should've told the Duchess that he had to leave, that it wasn't fair to Jemima or to himself to drag out a long goodbye. They had no chance, no future, and no good purpose was served by going over to her house at night.

Except that she had *asked* him to come, and apparently, he was her slave, like those three pitiful farm boys.

So he'd gone down to the desk and paid for an extra night on his own dime, like a moron, because the paper had only paid the room until noon. And settled in, and binge-watched the news, and ignored more emails from Delores, mostly to keep himself from speculating about *what Jemima wanted*.

Just to say goodbye, he was sure: but what form would that goodbye take? The possibilities were many and delightful, and sometimes he closed his eyes and let himself imagine them.

The afternoon wore on. Delores sent more emails, hinting that his recent successes did not make him immune to disciplinary action. She informed him that he'd ruined her secretary for any useful work, and suggested that he might want to see some of the packages being sent to his desk by anonymous admirers.

Brad ignored them, as well. He stretched out on the bed with the TV remote in his hand, flipping idly from channel to channel. He had scooped all the other news outlets with his exclusive interview with Jemima, and he was gratified to see that even Wellman at Channel 1 hadn't been able to do much better than awkward interviews with her random acquaintances.

He shook his head and smiled. He had to give them one thing: the Amish were a tight-knit people.

His smile faded. He tried to imagine what was he was going to say to Jemima that night. He could tell her that she was beautiful, that she was amazingly generous, that he genuinely admired the way she lived out what she believed.

That it was a shame that they weren't…

He crushed out his cigarette in the ashtray. No, he wouldn't go there.

The sky began to darken. Brad called room service and had a dinner tray brought up from the kitchen, a big platter filled with chicken and dumplings and fresh green peas and carrots. When it arrived, he sighed and looked down at it affectionately: he was going to miss farm portions when he went back.

The evening news came on. He noticed that Channel 1's coverage of Jemima's trial included his participation. He was surprised to see that somebody had grabbed a clip of him leaving the courtroom.

Wellman's smiling face reappeared on the screen. "It's unusual for a reporter to become part of the story," he smirked, "but Brad Williams of the *Ledger* newspaper has become an integral part of this remarkable tale. We're going to ask people on the street what they think of it."

He stuck a mic into a young woman's face. Brad sat up and scowled. It looked like Wellman had been shooting on the square in downtown Serenity.

The girl giggled. "I think it's romantic!" she chirped. "He's so handsome!"

Brad raised his eyebrows sardonically.

The reporter moved on to a young woman standing nearby. "What's your opinion? Have you heard about Jemima King's trial?"

"Oh yes." The woman looked like a college student and was quite pretty. "I loved that he came to testify for her. I think that was *wonderful*. He can come and do a story on me any day!" she laughed.

Brad shook his head and turned the TV off. *Great.* He was apparently the flavor of the month on the gossip circuit, which would explain some of Delores' recent emails. He made a mental note to tell her that she needn't think he was going to play into that if she was planning it.

The pool lights switched on below, and the ice maker down the breezeway kicked in with a *thrum* as somebody lifted the hatch and raided it.

Brad checked his watch. It was a little past 9 p.m., so he went to the bathroom to shower and shave and dress.

He might not know what he was going to say, but he *was* sure of one thing: he wanted to look his very best when he saw the Duchess for the last time.

Brad pulled his truck up to the spot where he always parked: a little wide space in the dirt road, next to a high bank. He switched off the headlight and pulled the keys out of the ignition.

He took a deep breath and peered through the windshield. It was a beautiful September night, crisp, but not too cold. The moon was a big silver dollar riding high in a dark blue sky, and was so bright that he could walk through the dark without a lantern.

He opened the door and got out. The pale silver light was enough to show the way.

He followed his now-familiar path: over a low split rail fence, into the overgrown field. The last crickets of summer chirped thinly from the bracken, and overhead, the sky was full of stars.

He threw a long leg over the low fence to the King farm, and hopped over, and through the bushes to his usual place. And Jemima was standing there, waiting for him.

He stopped to look at her. The white moonlight touched her with silver: it outlined her little cap, and her hair, it painted the delicate planes of her face, touched her nose, underlined her lips.

He tried to speak, and found that his carefully-considered speech had flown off to the sky. That he had no words.

So he just held out his arms.

To his amazement, Jemima King, the Amish millionaire, the girl whose beauty had enchanted the whole country, came running into them, threw her little arms around his neck.

And *kissed* him.

He stood there, too stunned for the moment to register anything except the luxuriant feel of velvet against his lips.

Then she pressed her cheek against his and held him. "You were so good to come to court," she whispered. "I will *always* remember."

He blinked. A heavy sensation in his chest made it hard to talk. *Oh, right. He was leaving.*

He tried to smile. "No worries, Duchess," he said, though his voice sounded odd, even to him. "I owe you. I'm glad things have turned out okay for you. You deserve to be happy. Have you – have you decided which of those three guys you're going to marry?"

She was still holding him, looking out over his shoulder. She shook her head.

He tried, for the sake of being kind – and he told himself that it *was* kind – to make a joke, to show her that she needed to get on with her life, just as he needed to get on with his. But for the first time in his life, he couldn't summon the right words.

She clutched his shirt. And just as she always did, she astounded him.

"Do you think I should marry one of them?" she asked.

He looked up at the sky in disbelief, then down at the

ground, and then down at her. The correct answer, of course, was: *Yes, you should. They're like you, they can give you what you want, they're part of your world, they understand you.*

But instead -- like a moron -- he shook his head.

Now she was trembling in his arms, like some beautiful, fragile bird. She whispered in his ear, something so soft he could barely make it out.

"Why not?"

Brad set his jaw, squeezed his eyes shut, and willed himself to do the right thing. He opened his mouth to say the right words, the kind words, the words that made sense.

Instead, to his horror, he heard himself saying: *"Because I love you, Duchess."*

Once the words were out, it was too late, too late to take them back, too late to tell her he'd made a hideous mistake, too late to do anything except receive the sweetest, wildest kiss of his entire existence, one that turned his brain to popcorn, made him forget everything, all his objections, all the obstacles, and even his own name.

Everything, in fact, except a brief confusion: he wondered why she was sobbing. But then she put her tiny fingers in his hair and kissed him again, and every question he had ever had flew away to the smiling moon.

THE END

THANK YOU FOR READING!

And thank you for supporting me as an independent author! I hope you enjoyed reading this book as much as I loved writing it! If so, there is a sample of the next book in the series in the next chapter. You can find the next book, An Amish Country Treasure 4, in eBook and Paperback format at your favorite online booksellers.

All the Best

Ruth

AN AMISH COUNTRY TREASURE 4

CHAPTER ONE

Jemima stood, watching and listening, at the property line of her family's farm. She leaned against the fence as Brad Williams clambered over, turned to kiss her one last time, and slowly melted into the darkness beyond. She stood listening as the crunch of his footsteps grew fainter and fainter, until the distant growl of a motor and the faint nimbus of unseen headlights flared, faded and disappeared.

After he had gone, the midnight world was very still and quiet. A solitary owl purred in the distance. Further still, a very faint sound: a train whistle from the crossing beyond town.

Jemima smiled, looked up into the starry sky and hugged herself.

It was turning cool, but the feel of Brad's mouth still

tingled in her own, the warmth of his kisses was still on her lips, her face, her neck. She was trembling slightly. She had never in her life felt so alive. Jemima closed her eyes and replayed every word Brad had pressed into her ear. The way he'd said *duchess* this time made her look forward to hearing it again.

But best of all, better than anything, Brad Williams—the cynical, fast-talking reporter—had made himself completely, gloriously vulnerable.

He'd admitted that he loved her.

Jemima laughed suddenly, took her skirts in both hands and twirled around, making them billow out into the air like a blooming rose.

When she returned to the house, it was dark and still. There wasn't a light even in her parents' window, and the yard and the house were hushed. Jemima entered by the back porch. She opened the door softly, took off her shoes and crept up the back stairs, being careful not to make a sound.

The moon was as bright as day, slanting through the windows and hall floor. Jemima tiptoed past her parents' bedroom and the sound of her father's snores. She crept down the long hall, past Deborah's door. Jemima gave it a wary glance, but there was no light underneath it. Then she slowly twisted the knob to her own door, slid inside and closed it softly behind her.

Once she was safely inside, Jemima smiled and walked to the window. Under that dazzling moon she could see the whole countryside stretching out to the horizon. The dark trees were drawn in charcoal and the rolling hills in white chalk.

She unpinned her cap, unmade her bun and let her silken hair fall free. It cascaded over her hands, over her shoulders and past her waist in shining waves. She brushed it absently, and plaited it into a long braid.

Then she came out of her dress, letting it fall into a heap on the floor. She sat down on her bed, and unrolled her stockings, and tossed them away.

Jemima fell backward onto the bed and stared up at the moonlit ceiling, smiling. Against all odds, Brad Williams *loved* her.

She closed her eyes, savoring the memory. He'd *said* that he loved her. And it was true, she could *feel* it, she could *taste* it. He'd made himself vulnerable, he'd confessed his weakness against his own will. *Oh, Duchess* – the shuddering way he had said it, just before the insanity of those kisses – it was the cry of a man in love.

She knew it, she *knew* it, *she knew it.*

"Do you know what you do to me?" he had breathed into her ear. *"Do you know you make me lose my mind? I should never have come, I should have told you goodbye. This isn't*

right, it won't work, it will only make things harder in the end. I should leave..."

But then he had kissed her like a madman, and pulled her into his arms, and had lost his mind again. And after all the sweet insanity, after the Englischer's wild kisses, after her confusion and his despair, she was sure of only one thing:

Brad Williams might have lost his mind – but he wasn't leaving. He would be coming back, and back again, just as he'd done since the first day they met. Only this time, he wouldn't be after a story.

Jemima smiled again, and bit her nail, and dove under the covers.

The next morning Jemima was up bright and early, neat and trim and pressed. She hummed and smiled over her tasks as she helped make coffee and toast for breakfast. Her parents exchanged a knowing look.

Rachel came up behind her daughter, and slid an arm around her waist. "Well, *you* look happy this morning, Jemima!" she smiled, and kissed Jemima's cheek. "And I think I can guess why."

Deborah was sitting at the table and raised her brows and looked smug but said nothing.

Jemima received her mother's kiss and blushed. "I am, *very* happy," she agreed, and turned her attention to the coffee pot.

Rachel pursed her lips into a knowing smile. "I won't pry into your love life, Mima," she said primly, "but I expect you to tell your father and I *first* – if you have good news."

Deborah choked on her coffee and hacked horribly for a few minutes, but still emerged looking strangely amused. Jemima colored more deeply, and nodded to her mother and said nothing.

Jacob wiped his mouth with a napkin and added: "Well, now that all the nonsense is calming down at last, we can get back to normal. I'm going to clear the drive and put my anvils back in the shop, and about time."

Rachel set a plate of biscuits on the table and sat down next to Jacob. She looked at Jemima and added: "You'll be wanting to go to the bishop today, won't you, Jemima? You can make out a check to the community fund, and then you'll have the whole awful thing behind you."

She looked down mischievously, and smiled: "And certain *young men* will feel free to come calling, I expect."

Jemima sat down at the table and shook out a napkin. "I-I think I'd like to take a few weeks to just – just rest," she stammered. "I don't want to think about anything, right now. Everything has been so hard and – and *trying*."

Jacob looked at his eldest daughter sympathetically. "Yes, my poor girl, you *should* take a few weeks off to enjoy living like a teenager again," he told her. "This business has been more than an adult could've handled, much less a slip of a girl. You can take your time. Go to all the sings and frolics and games you please. Don't worry about the money, for now."

Rachel twitched her brows together, gave her husband a quick look and cleared her throat, but said nothing.

Jemima put a forkful of pancakes in her mouth, and was grateful for her parent's merciful attitude. But she also noticed, to her alarm, that Deborah's amused eyes still watched her all throughout the meal.

CHAPTER TWO

Jemima spent the following week like a hermit. She made no attempt to go out to games or frolics, or even the Sunday night sing. Jacob returned to his work and paid no heed to her seclusion, but Jemima could tell that her mother was puzzled, and a little worried. Rachel had asked no questions so far, but it was only a matter of time.

Jemima noticed her mother watching her at odd moments, and she could almost read the puzzled thought in her mind: *There's nothing standing in the way now. So why doesn't Jemima give the money away, so she can get married?*

It was a reasonable concern, and it was only a matter of time before her mother voiced it.

Jemima bent over her mending, pulling a needle through a torn quilt square. Her mother's warning came back to her: *"I don't know what you feel toward that boy, Mima. But I do know this: That boy is an Englischer. He lives in a different world. He thinks differently from you, he believes different things, and he wants different things. If you lose sight of that, you could be very bad hurt."*

She knew that her mother was right, but it was already too late. She'd lost sight of what she *should* do, or *should* say, or *should* feel. She'd lost sight of everything except what she *did* feel: the intoxication of Brad's lips on hers and of his arms around her.

There were a lot of things that were only a matter of time, and she knew she'd have to address them sooner or later: her mother's confusion, when to give the rest of the money away and what to do when Mark and Samuel and Joseph came to the house and started asking questions of their own.

Jemima pulled the thread taut and tied it off. The thought of hurting her friends was a painful one. She knew that sooner or later, she would have to look into Joseph's eyes, and Samuel's, and Mark's, and tell them what she had just learned herself: *I'm sorry, but I can't marry you. I'm in love with another man.* She couldn't allow herself to dwell on what that would do to them.

She couldn't allow herself to dwell on what she would do *herself,* when the magic faded and Brad inevitably returned to his own life. That, too, was far too painful a thought to dwell on; so she simply pushed it aside.

There would be a price to pay later, she knew. But she had made the decision to pay whatever it might cost her – her friendships, her reputation, her parents' approval. She had pushed the inevitable reckoning into the back of her mind.

All of those hard things were for later. Now, right now, she could only think of Brad.

She pulled her needle through the fabric. Brad had promised to come back on Saturday night, to their usual place. He had to commute all the way from the city to see her – almost fifty miles. It was a long way to travel.

But she was counting the days.

Jemima closed her eyes and leaned back into her chair. Instantly she was with Brad again under the stars. He had taken her hands and warmed them with his own.

"I'll be back again at the same time. Meet me here?"

Brad's blue eyes had glittered in his dark face. Those eyes had looked strange, otherworldly. The moon glanced off them and made them glow. It had been so like the dream she'd once had that it sent a shuddering thrill up her spine.

"Say you will, Duchess."

She'd whispered *yes*, and dug her fingers into his hair. Jemima smiled to herself. Brad's mop of hair was as thick as it looked; it was almost impenetrably dense, but surprisingly smooth and soft. She had dug her hands into that untamable hair, smoothed her hands down behind his ears and cupped them behind his neck.

He had taken her face in his hands and kissed her again, that last time – such a sweet, soft, *good night my love* kiss.

Jemima smiled, sighed and opened her eyes again.

It was only a few days until their next meeting. It was getting chilly at night now, so she'd decided to take a big quilt this time, to wrap around their shoulders. It would be snug and cozy. Maybe they could even sit on the porch swing, if he arrived late enough, after everyone was asleep. A little thermos of hot coffee might also be a nice welcome.

Of course it would be more comfortable indoors, and she toyed with the idea of bringing Brad inside the house, but rejected it as too risky. If her father came downstairs for any reason and saw her sitting there with the Englischer reporter, she trembled to think what he might do.

So for as long as they lasted, her meetings with Brad would have to remain a secret, known only to them.

Jemima's eyebrows twitched together. That is, if Deborah didn't betray them and bring the whole thing crashing down around their ears.

CHAPTER THREE

Jemima folded up the big quilt and carried it up to her bedroom, where she had also stashed a thermos and some cups. She had pushed the family picnic basket under her bed, to be ready when called for.

Jemima put a small finger to her lips, pondering. She couldn't decide if it would be better to have coffee or hot apple cider with caramel. She also planned to fill the basket with some cheese and fresh apples and crackers, and to make some coffee cake.

She reclined on the bed and closed her eyes. She could picture their next meeting already: the two of them snuggling together on the porch swing, toasty warm with the big quilt around them, and each of them warming their hands with a cup of piping hot cider.

And those weren't the *only* ways to stay warm on a chilly evening. Jemima smiled to herself and imagined Brad's arms, strong and tight around her.

A slight noise from the doorway made Jemima sit up suddenly. To her surprise and dismay, Deborah was standing there, eating a piece of pie and wearing an expression that hinted that she'd guessed *exactly* what her sister was thinking.

Deborah glanced back into the hall, and then leaned in through the doorway and drawled: "What's this you're working on – a big quilt? And you're hiding the picnic basket under your bed. Brad is coming back again, I see."

Jemima looked down and tried to assume a neutral expression, but she felt herself going hot with annoyance.

Deborah grinned at her and rolled her eyes to the ceiling in mock innocence. "A lookout *sure would* be handy, huh? You and Brad wouldn't have to worry about Daed coming down and catching you together."

Jemima stared at her grimly. "I don't know what you're talking about!"

Deborah sighed and crossed her arms. "*Sad,*" she replied. "It's *sad* that you don't trust me, because I meant what I said. I could help you."

"This is a change for you, isn't it, Deborah?" she asked coolly. "You like to make fun of Joseph and Mark and Samuel, and of me when I talk to them. Why are you acting so different now?"

Deborah finished the piece of pie she was eating. "Because it isn't Joseph or Mark or Samuel this time," she replied, licking her fingers. "Your life is finally getting interesting – don't jinx it."

"I don't see why you're interested."

"I like Brad Williams. He's kind of cool. I think he'd be good for you," Deborah told her.

Jemima stared at her suspiciously, and Deborah shrugged. "Okay, that's not it. Or at least, not *all* of it. Maybe I *owe* him for something."

Jemima looked up sharply. "*Owe* him? What do you mean?"

"Oh, nothing serious," her sister replied. "Just that I made him pay me 50 dollars once, to bring you out to the garden."

"*What!*"Jemima cried, and stared at her younger sister in outrage. "Oh, Debby – tell me you're joking!"

Deborah nodded her head. "It's true."

"Why – how could you even *think* of such a thing!" Jemima gasped. "You have to give him his money back, right away!"

Deborah smiled, and shook her head. "No, I don't. Because he had it coming. He messed us *all* up. I was just making him pay for it, a little."

"*Of course* you have to give him his money back!" Jemima cried. "What he must think of us! Of all the dishonest, greedy—"

Deborah held up an admonishing finger. "Careful now, Mima. Remember what I know. You don't want me to change my mind about helping you. Right now, I'm willing, but that could change."

"*Oh!*" Jemima pinched her lips into a thin, straight line. "You should pray to God for forgiveness, *pray hard*! And now *I* have to pray that God will make me *willing* to forgive you – you little – you—"

Rachel walked down the hall behind them, and both Jemima and Deborah clamped their mouths shut and looked down at the floor. A few suspenseful seconds passed, and then their mother slowly returned.

Rachel poked her head into the doorway, and opened her mouth as if she was about to ask a question: but one look at Jemima's face made her turn her eyes from one of her daughters to the other.

"What's going on in here? Jemima, why do you look so – so *angry*? Is there something wrong?"

Deborah raised her brows significantly, and smiled.

Jemima bit her lip.

"No, nothing's wrong."

Rachel frowned, and looked from her to Deborah. "Are you sure? Deborah, what did you just say to your sister?"

Deborah regarded her with a kindling eye. "Why does everyone *always* think that if there's something wrong, it has to be *my* fault?" she demanded.

Jemima squeezed her eyes shut and prayed, but Deborah flounced out of the room, sparing her the necessity of a reply.

Rachel watched her go and turned her sympathetic eyes on her oldest daughter. "I don't know what just happened, but whatever it was, forgive your sister," she sighed.

"It's *so* hard, Mamm," Jemima murmured, and her mother nodded.

"I know, dear."

Her mother came over and kissed her, smiled, and put a calming hand to her cheek. Jemima looked up at her mother ruefully.

But after she left, Jemima squeezed her eyes together and stamped her foot on the floor. If it wasn't a sin, she could wish that Deborah would fly away to a desert island somewhere, where she would have to stay until she was thirty years old.

Or at least, old enough to know *not* to play so cruelly with other people's feelings.

Jemima shook her head bitterly. But in the meantime, it looked as if she was in Deborah's power. She could only pray that Deborah was willing to leave her in peace to enjoy what little time she had with Brad.

But given Deborah's actions so far, she had very little hope of it.

CHAPTER FOUR

When Saturday arrived, it dawned clear and crisp and cool under a cloudless blue sky. The rolling countryside around the King farm was as neat and trim as a postcard – white farmhouses, red barns, and green hills spattered with glorious color: fire red, copper orange, lemon yellow.

But Jemima hardly noticed the fine weather. She spent most of the day in the living room mending clothes, and the hours seemed to crawl. Every time she glanced at the old clock on the mantle, the hands seemed frozen to the same position they'd held the last time she looked.

The time dragged to noon. Jacob came in from his workshop, and they all ate lunch: thick slabs of bologna and homemade cheddar between Rachel's sourdough bread, homemade cream of chicken soup with baked butter crackers, a big bowl of potato salad with egg and dill, creamed corn, coffee and tea. Jacob and Rachel talked and laughed together, Deborah looked sour, and Jemima picked at her food, said little and glanced at the clock.

They finished lunch. Jacob kissed Rachel and went back to work. Jemima and Deborah helped their mother clear away the plates and glasses, and Jemima returned to the living room and went back to mending clothes and watching the clock.

A few more hours limped by. At five o'clock they all assembled again for dinner: meatloaf and gravy, biscuits, peas, pickled beets, more potatoes and apple pie with cheddar cheese on top. Jacob and Rachel talked and laughed together, Deborah looked sour, and Jemima picked at her food, remained mostly silent and watched the clock.

After dinner Jemima waited until her parents were occupied, then escaped upstairs. She ducked into the bathroom that she shared with Deborah and shut out the world.

Then she locked the door and ran a hot, fragrant bath.

When the tub was full of steaming water, Jemima peeled off her clothes, stepped gingerly into the hot water, and gradually eased herself into its enveloping warmth.

She sank down into the water until it had closed over her

ears like two hands. The radiant heat slowly drew all the tension and all the frustration of a long wait out of her.

She lathered her hands with a bar of soap until the suds were running through her fingers, then washed her hair and face and body. The soap was deliciously fragrant of honeysuckle, and the aroma filled the tiny room with the last whisper of summer.

Jemima luxuriated in the silky bubbles, breathed the perfume in deeply, and then rinsed it away with cool, clear water. She stepped out of the tub, dried herself, sat down on the edge and smoothed on honeysuckle lotion over her face and neck, all down her arms and legs, and her hands and feet. It felt silky smooth, and to Jemima's delight, the lotion made her skin as soft as a baby's.

After she had he wrapped herself in a bathrobe and her hair in a towel, Jemima slipped into her own room and stretched out on the bed to watch the sun go down through her windows.

The sky gradually melted from pale blue, to blue tinged with pink, to rose red, and then to lavender. Jemima watched it change with rising anticipation. When the sky outside her window deepened from lavender to indigo, she shook her luxurious hair out of the towel and brushed it to a high sheen. Then she pinned it into a coiling bun at the nape of her neck, and dressed in fresh clothes with more than her usual care.

She stood in front the mirror, pinned her cap in place, and

then stared at her own reflection. Her eyes looked dilated, her cheeks were flushed and her lips looked slightly swollen.

She turned to the window and looked out across the fields to the horizon. There was now only the faintest glow where the sun had been. The evening star burned high in the sky.

Behind the closed door, she could hear Deborah stump down the hall, shuffle into her own room and slam the door behind her. Farther away, she could hear the muffled sounds of her parent's voices, then the faint sound of their own door closing.

The sky deepened to dark blue and more stars began to glow here and there. All across the valley, Jemima watched as their neighbors' window lights winked out, one by one.

A deep quiet settled down over the house. The creaks and pops of an old house at night, and the sound of an owl calling outside sounded loud in the silence.

An hour passed...two hours...three. The sound of her father's snores wafted down the hall from her parent's bedroom. Jemima checked her bedside clock, walked to her bed and knelt down on the floor.

She pulled the picnic basket out and set it on the bed. She opened it, gave it one last check and saw that everything was neatly tucked inside. She closed it, locked it and folded the quilt on top of it.

Then she threw a shawl around her shoulders, pulled on

her stockings and shoes, picked up the basket and crept downstairs.

The air was sharp and chill when Jemima stepped out onto the porch. She hurried to the swing, draped the quilt over the seat back, and set the picnic basket down on the floor. Then she turned and took the now-familiar path to their meeting place.

There was only a crescent moon that night, and it was harder to see, but Jemima knew the way: across the lawn, across the bare, fallow ground that had been her mother's summer garden, through the thinning underbrush and on to the fence that divided their farm from the overgrown field next door.

There was little more than starlight, and Jemima leaned forward across the fence, peering out into the darkness. She saw nothing and heard nothing except the night sounds of small unseen animals somewhere in the field beyond – soft *chirps* and *clicks*.

Jemima turned her gaze to the road on the far side of the field. There were no visible lights.

She exhaled in disappointment, and rubbed her hands together under her shawl. The night was deepening, and it was cold.

A tiny sound off to the right made Jemima turn her head.

Suddenly a hand clamped over her mouth, and another

hand slid around her waist. Jemima uttered a smothered scream and rolled terrified eyes to a dark face hovering over her own.

The stranger yanked her to his chest and kissed her. But though she couldn't see his face, Jemima recognized the feel of Brad's kiss. She went limp with relief, then twisted to throw her arms around him.

"*You scared me to death*!" she gasped, but it was all she had time to say before he stopped her mouth with another fierce greeting.

Brad broke off and nuzzled her cheek. "I thought this week would never end! Oh, you smell so good," he murmured, and buried his face into her white neck.

Jemima rolled her eyes up and gasped. She was discovering that she loved the feel of Brad's lips on the tender skin just under her ear; she loved the way his lips teased their way down her neck – and set every spot on fire.

"Come to the house," she whispered, her eyes still closed. "Everyone is asleep, we can sit on the porch. I brought a big quilt, and food."

She slid her hand down his arm, found his hand and clasped it. "It's too cold out here. Come with me."

But he paid no attention. He kissed her again, mussed her hair and knocked her cap askew. Jemima put a distracted hand to her head. Hairpins were falling out everywhere, and now—

"*Oh, my hair—*" she cried softly. The shining skeins unraveled and fell to her waist like rivulets of water. Brad looked down momentarily, and captured one of the skeins with one hand and rubbed it between his fingers like silk.

Jemima took advantage of his momentary distraction. "Come with me, *come*. It's too cold out here."

Still he didn't move, so Jemima pulled out of his arms and, on a mischievous impulse, fled from him.

"*Duchess!*" His exasperated voice hissed out of the darkness, followed by sputtering laughter. "Where did you go? You know this isn't my—"

There was the sound of someone crashing into a bush, and stumbling footsteps. "*When I catch you—*"

Jemima laughed breathlessly, darted to him, grabbed his hand and pulled him across the garden plot and the lawn. He followed, laughing, and they ran up to the brink of the porch steps.

Jemima turned on him and caught him in her arms. "*Hissht! Be quiet, or my father will hear!*"

He stole another kiss before she pulled away again and led him up the steps and to the swing.

CHAPTER FIVE

Brad sat down on the swing and hurriedly wrapped the quilt around Jemima's shoulders, and then around his own.

"*Brrr*! It *is* cold!"

Jemima leaned down and opened up the picnic basket. "I have hot coffee," she told him, and opened the thermos. The scent of fresh-brewed roast curled up into the air.

"You're an angel," Brad told her gratefully, taking the hot cup between his hands. "*Mmmm.* Is that cake? I didn't have time for dinner, and I'm starving."

"Here, here," Jemima told him, and piled treats onto his plate: coffee cake, apple slices, cheese, dried apricots, a wedge of homemade fudge and a beef sandwich. She handed them to him, and he devoured them like a starving man.

Jemima sipped her coffee and watched him, smiling.

"This sure beats TV dinners," he told her, taking a big bite of the sandwich.

Jemima frowned. "Is that what you eat – TV dinners?" she cried. It wrung her heart to think of Brad sitting in his apartment alone, eating skimpy, tasteless portions off a cardboard plate.

He seemed oblivious to her dismay. "Mostly, unless I'm eating out. I'm not much of a cook."

"*Oh!*" Jemima leaned down and quickly made another plate, twice as big as the first. She handed it to Brad.

He took it, but asked: "Aren't you going to eat anything?"

"Oh, I had dinner long ago," she assured him. "Eat, *eat*! I hate to think of you driving for hours hungry!"

"I have to admit, this sure hits the spot," he replied, and made the coffee cake disappear, and all the other things, one by one. Then he leaned back into the swing, and closed his eyes and sighed deeply.

"There's more," Jemima told him, but he shook his head. He tilted his head, turned and stared at her without saying anything. He just sat there with an odd expression on his face, looking at her until she asked:

"*What?*"

For answer he reached out, and took two thick strands of her hair in his hands, and gently stretched them out, like shining ribbons. He wrapped his hands in them and brushed them across his cheek.

Jemima watched him in puzzlement. "What are you doing?" she whispered.

He smiled at her in the darkness. "I didn't know your hair was so *long*," he murmured, looking down at it. "It's beautiful. Soft as silk. I wish it was daylight, so I could see it better."

"If it were daylight, my hair would be pinned up, under my cap," she told him primly. "And we wouldn't be here."

He sighed heavily. "True enough. How do you—" He broke off abruptly.

Jemima tilted her head. "How do I what?" she asked gently.

"Nothing," he replied, but she persisted.

"How do I *bear it*, you mean? All the strict rules? Wearing the same thing every day, putting my hair up under a cap?"

"Look, I—"

"It's all right," she told him. "You're not the first person who's asked me that question. People don't understand. It's natural to be…curious."

"No, I'm sorry, Duchess. You have a perfect right to believe whatever you want. I'm a moron. I admit it." He leaned over, and kissed her apologetically.

Jemima received his apology willingly. His lips tasted of chocolate and apricots, and his arms were as warm as a woolen sweater. She smiled and touched her fingertip to his lip.

"You're not…what you said. You're smart, and you're kind. And I'm not angry."

He sighed, and rested his head lightly on her shoulder. "If I was smart or kind I wouldn't be here," he said, half to himself. "I'd leave you *alone*, Duchess. I'd let you find a husband who *understands*."

Jemima's eyes spangled with sudden tears. "Is that – is that what you *want?*" she cried. "Do you *want* me to marry Mark, or Sam—"

"*Of course not!*" He grabbed her suddenly, looked down at her with that crazy look in his eyes, and kissed her again so savagely that Jemima felt as if she were melting from every place that she touched him.

He buried his face in her neck. "I hate the thought of it!" he told her fiercely. "I *can't stand* to think of you with somebody else!"

Jemima laughed suddenly, and twined her arms around his neck. "Then I don't care," she told him. "That's all that matters. That you *love* me. And I don't want to talk about anything unhappy, not now. This is *our* time. Tell me – tell me about where you live."

"What?"

"*Yes* – tell me about where you live, and what furniture you have, and what pictures are on the wall. And what you read, and, and what you like to eat. All those things. And when you're gone, I'll imagine them in my mind, to help me pass the time until you come back."

He looked down at her, and sighed tenderly: "Oh, *Duchess.*"

"Tell me."

He sighed again. "All right. I live in a studio apartment – oh, that means *small* – in the city. It is *not* as picturesque a neighborhood as yours. I think there's one tree in the parking lot, and it looks as if it's about to croak."

Jemima giggled into his chest, and he looked down at her, smiling. "Is that funny? Yeah, I guess it is. So, there's the croaking tree, and the complex is next door to a fast food place on one side and a pipe shop on the other."

Jemima looked up at him innocently. "What's a pipe shop?"

Brad ran a hand through his hair. "*Ah* – it's a place where – where people buy –*pipes.*"

"Oh."

"I'm on the second floor," he hastened to add, "and my unit's at the end of the row, which is good, because I only share one wall with a neighbor."

"Who is your neighbor?" Jemima asked, looking up at him.

"A guy from Guatemala. He's pretty laid back, but we don't talk much, because I usually come in la— I mean, I don't – don't see much of him."

"Oh."

"My furniture is mostly stuff I bought in a box and assembled. Though I did score a World War I office desk at a yard sale last year. I have a bookshelf crammed with sci-fi and history. I also have a good bit of biography – Disraeli, Lincoln, Eleanor Roosevelt, Einstein, Tesla. I like reading about real people."

Jemima nodded earnestly.

"And as for what's on my walls – I have some posters, mostly groups – I'm into roots music, blues, bluegrass – so mostly obscure stuff. And I don't cook much of anything. I do takeout when I'm tired, and stuff I can microwave when I'm not."

Jemima reached out and caressed his cheek

sympathetically. "You don't eat well, I can see it," she murmured sympathetically. "I'll pack some things for you to take home for tomorrow."

Brad cracked a grin. "*Worried* about me, are you, Duchess?"

She ran her fingers lightly over his bruised chin. "You *know* I—"

But she was cut off with shocking suddenness. The screen door flew open, and they both jumped to their feet in alarm, but it was Deborah's face that peeked out from behind the door.

"*Hide, quick! Daed is coming downstairs!*" she hissed, and darted back inside.

Jemima grabbed up the picnic basket and blanket, and took Brad's hand. They fled down the porch steps and stopped just at the corner of the house, listening.

A light bloomed in the window overhead and gave off a faint yellow glow.

Jacob's voice grumbled: "Deborah – what are you doing down here so early?"

Deborah piped, "Oh, I was hungry, I wanted a snack."

"Is that why I smell coffee?"

Jemima put a hand to her mouth and looked up at Brad in

dismay.

Deborah's voice sounded uncertain, but she answered: "Umm…yes. I got some leftover coffee from dinner."

The floorboards groaned under Jacob's massive footsteps. "How did you heat it without lighting the stove?"

"Ah – it's the *grounds* you smell. I opened the can, but I changed my mind and drank the cold leftovers." There was a quick, rummaging sound. "Do you want me to light the stove now?"

"No, no. There are still hours to sunrise. Eat and go back to bed."

"Why are *you* up so early, Daed?" Deborah queried.

The floorboards groaned again under the sound of heavy footsteps, and to Jemima's dismay, the screen door creaked open.

"I heard a noise and thought I'd check. If I catch one more *verruckt* Englischer sneaking around this house, I'll send him to the blessed God, no matter what your mother says."

Jemima pressed Brad's hand, and looked up at him, but his face was in shadow.

"Oh, now, Daed!" Deborah laughed unconvincingly. "It was only *me*, coming down to the kitchen. Want a piece of pie?"

The screen door closed again. "Just a little piece, and then back to bed, for both of us."

A few more minutes passed, and Jemima held Brad's hand tight. Then the light faded out, and heavy footsteps rang out again, then faded.

When it was silent and dark again, Jemima went limp against Brad's chest, and then lifted her face.

"*You should go. He might come back.*"

He leaned down, found her lips and kissed her. "*When can I see you again?*"

"*Sunday night, next time. I'll meet you at the same place, and the same time.*" She pressed the basket into his hands. "*Take this home with you.*"

"*I can't take this whole....*"

"*Yes, yes.*" She leaned into him, kissed him, pressed her hand over his, and she could feel him relent.

"*All right then, Duchess. I'll bring it back next time, only it'll be my treat then. Deal?*"

"*Just so long as you come back,*" Jemima breathed, twined her hands around the back of his neck, and pulled him to her lips. She poured all her love into that goodbye kiss, all her longing, and was gratified to hear him gasp when their lips parted.

"You shouldn't kiss me like that if you want me to go," he warned.

Jemima instantly replied: *"I don't want you to go!"*

Brad dropped the basket and gave her a lengthy and very communicative kiss in reply. Then he turned away, turned back to give her one more for good measure, and disappeared into the general darkness.

Jemima stared after him for a long time before the pinching cold finally made her give up, and turn to seek her own bed.

CHAPTER SIX

Jemima moaned and turned her face into her pillow. "*Kiss me, Brad!*" she murmured. But instead of Brad placing a tender kiss on her lips, an impatient hand shook her shoulder roughly. She opened her eyes, frowning.

The sky outside was still dark; the glow of a single candle provided the only light in the room. Gradually the dark blob hovering over her resolved into a human face. Deborah held a candlestick high overhead, and leered down at her.

"*'Kiss me, Brad!'*" she simpered. "You'd better be glad it's *me* who's waking you up, and not Mamm!"

"What's the matter? What is it?" Jemima cried, her mind

still clouded by dreams.

"What is it? It's almost *five,* lady of leisure, and Mamm says that if you don't get up, she's going to come and drag you out of bed by your feet. You've overslept!"

"Oh!"

Deborah shook her head and left, but Jemima scrambled out of bed, searching for her clothes. If only they'd let her sleep in, just once! She'd been dreaming the loveliest dream that she was in Brad's arms and that he was just about to ask her...

"JeMIMa!"

Jemima put a hand to her mouth. Her father hadn't used that tone of voice to her in *years.*

"Coming!" she cried, and hurried to put her hair up and dress.

It was Sunday, and they were going to worship at Silas Fisher's, so breakfast was somewhat hurried. Jemima was present in body only, and performed only the bare minimum required of her: a brief *yes, no,* or nod of the head, when she was directly addressed. She had no memory of the meal, or what anyone said – she could only think of Brad.

On the buggy ride to the Fisher farm, Jemima looked out across the fields to the horizon, but what she was seeing was a cramped studio apartment in the city with one tall, bright-eyed occupant. She saw him open the door clumsily in the wee hours of the morning, carrying a big picnic basket on one arm. She saw him set it on the breakfast counter, walk a few big paces across the room, and collapse on a narrow bed pushed up against one wall.

Poor Brad!

She frowned, wishing there was some way she could meet him halfway, instead of him having to make such a long trip at night. But she had no transportation…

"*Jemima*!"

She looked up, startled. Her mother had half-turned and was looking at her in exasperation from the front seat of the buggy. "What did I just say to you?"

Jemima gaped at her in dismay. "Oh…I…"

Deborah rolled her eyes. "Oh, never mind her, Mamm. She's mooning over her boyfriends," she put in unexpectedly. "She's been worthless for *days*."

Jemima gave her sister a glance that was expressive of gratitude – and surprise.

Rachel pursed her lips in exasperation. "Jemima, I asked you if you remembered to bring the book I promised to loan your Aunt Priscilla."

Jemima stared at her guiltily.

"Well – *did* you?"

"No…no, I'm sorry…I forgot."

Her mother looked at her in exasperation. "Child, what will I do with you?" she wailed softly. "But I suppose all young girls are a little distracted when they're…" she bit her lip, smiled faintly and turned back around.

Jemima watched her mother with worried eyes, and then turned to look at her sister. Deborah had saved her last night, and even this morning she was helping her to deflect suspicion. Was it possible that for once in her life, Deborah was trying to be *helpful*?

Deborah felt her gaze, turned and winked at her. Jemima frowned, turned back to her contemplation of the countryside, and remained silent for the rest of the drive.

The Fisher farm was a sprawling complex of four big houses, six barns, and a dozen other outbuildings clustered at the center of acres of corn and wheat. The weather was overcast and cold, but it did not seem likely to rain, so helpers had set up worship benches inside the main barn, and on the lawn outside.

Jacob parked the buggy next to dozens of others lined up on the grass, and they walked down the long road. Jemima kept her eyes on her feet, because she was suddenly stabbed by the fear that Joseph or Mark or Samuel would find her – and she had nothing to give them but heartache.

Jemima followed her mother and Deborah to the main barn, where worship was being held, and sat beside them on the women's benches. She was careful to move to the very end of the row, where she could hide behind Dorcas Hershberger. According to the local grapevine, Dorcas weighed 250 pounds at least. In any case she made an excellent screen; behind her, Jemima didn't have to worry about looking up, and seeing a boy's eyes pleading with her.

As the long, slow hymn singing began, Jemima retreated inside her own mind. It helped her stave off her growing fear that she'd jumped the fence, that she'd strayed into uncharted and dangerous territory.

Jemima gnawed her fingernail. She'd never met anyone who'd gone out with an Englischer – much less fallen in love with one. It just wasn't done.

So what would happen, now that she *had* fallen in love with one?

She closed her eyes. *Hurt.* Yes, a lot of hurt for everyone involved. Pain for her when she had to tell her suitors that she couldn't marry them. Pain for them, because they all loved her. Pain for her parents when their dreams for her didn't come true.

Pain for her and for Brad when they had to part ways at last – because there was no realistic future for the two of them.

Pain for her again, after, when no one else could *ever* be Brad Williams.

Her Mamm had been right: she was going to hurt badly, she was going to hurt other people. The smart thing, the best thing, would be to forget Brad, choose a husband and settle down.

But if she did, which one of them – and how could she choose?

Dorcas Hershberger suddenly leaned down to get something she'd dropped, and for a second Jemima had a clear view of the men's worship benches. Instantly she was aware that three pairs of eyes were looking at her. Jemima's guilty gaze moved from Joseph's hopeful face, to Samuel's questioning glance, to Mark's sad and steady eyes on her.

She felt tears coming to the surface again, and dropped her glance. *No, she couldn't do it.* It would be mean and dishonest to marry Joseph or Samuel or Mark when she was really only *fond* of them. It would be cruel to let one of them pour his whole life into a fantasy.

Because sooner or later, he'd see the truth – and hate her for it.

No, whatever she had to face, it was better to face it and have done. Better to wound a friend honestly, than to poison his whole life with a lie.

Tears sparkled in Jemima's eyes. *Oh Lord*, she prayed, *I*

know I'm not supposed to love an Englisch boy. But please, even if I am doing wrong, help me to tell Mark and Joseph and Samuel what I must. Please comfort them – they're going to be hurt.

Please don't let them hate me for it. I do still love them so!

CHAPTER SEVEN

After worship, Jemima went directly to the Fisher kitchen to help the other girls serve lunch. It was the way things had always been done, and on this particular Sunday, Jemima was glad of the tradition.

She took a platter of pickled beets off the counter, because she knew that Mark and Joseph and Samuel all hated them. She was on the brink of tears and didn't trust herself to face her suitors with equanimity.

When she emerged from the house, Jemima quickly sized up the seating arrangement on the lawn, but to her dismay, her suitors had foiled her. She had hoped to hide in a safe corner, but Joseph was to the left, Samuel was seated in the middle, and Mark was to the right. No matter where she went, *one* of them would be there.

But to Jemima's surprise, Deborah appeared at her elbow, carrying a platter of sandwiches. She turned her head slightly and whispered: *"Don't worry, I'll come with you."*

Jemima couldn't help glancing at her sister in astonishment, but Deborah's freckled face was as placid as dawn. She leaned over again.

"Let's get it over with."

Jemima nodded, and walked down the porch steps. She walked past each table, serving whenever asked. She kept her gaze strictly on the table, spoke only when she was greeted, and answered with a demure smile and downturned eyes.

Her heart began to beat oddly when she approached Joseph's table. She'd never had the chance to talk to Joseph. He still considered them engaged because he'd kissed her one evening. Never mind that it was completely his own idea, and that she'd denied it. *He* believed it, and that was the important thing.

Jemima felt her face going warm, and kept her eyes on the tablecloth as she served the food. But to her dismay, she heard Joseph's voice calling her.

"Good morning, Jemima," he called softly. "Would you give me some beets, too?"

She nodded, but didn't look up. She moved around the table to Joseph's chair, and to her dismay, as she extended her arm to serve him, Joseph surreptitiously slid a small, folded piece of paper up her sleeve.

Jemima lifted her arm at once to keep the paper from falling out on the table in front of everyone, went beet red herself and scrambled to keep the platter from overturning.

"Thank you, Jemima," Joseph murmured, and brushed her sleeve fleetingly with his hand.

Jemima fled back to the house, holding one arm up to keep the paper from falling out onto the ground. She slapped the platter on a countertop, slipped past the other girls lined up outside the kitchen, and found an empty bathroom to hide in. She ducked inside and locked the door behind her, then leaned against it with her eyes closed.

After she had gathered her nerve, Jemima lowered her sleeve and let the paper fall out into her palm. She unfolded it and read:

My maus,

I have heard almost nothing from you in the last few weeks and have missed you very much. Have you given the last of the money away? I will be happy when you do. I am anxious to announce our engagement. I want everyone to know that you are my fiancée!

Jemima put a hand to her mouth and squeezed her eyes

shut to prevent herself from crying.

I have my eye on a house near my brother's farm, for the two of us. I will take you to see it as soon as your business with the money is over. It is small now, but I can add more rooms as we need them.

Jemima shook her head, and choked off a sob. *Poor Joseph!*

When she had calmed down again, she tore the note into tiny pieces and threw it into the trashcan. She couldn't let someone else find it and read it, and nothing poor Joseph said was going to make a difference now, anyway.

Jemima leaned over the sink and splashed her face with cool water. She couldn't afford to advertise that she was upset, not with so many eyes looking at her. She splashed her face again.

After a few minutes her eyes looked more normal, and she had regained a calm expression by sheer will power. She told her reflection that she was going to talk to Joseph, but that *time* and *place* were important, that absolute *privacy* was important and she couldn't bear to do it *now*.

Jemima took a deep breath, smoothed out her skirts, opened the door and walked out again.

But as soon as she had set foot into the little hall outside, something grabbed her and swirled her through the doorway of a neighboring room. She had no sooner recognized the dark blur as Samuel, than he pulled her into his arms and kissed her.

Jemima pulled back from him and turned her face away, blushing. "*Samuel!* What a way to behave – at worship, too!"

He reached for her again. "I've missed you! You've been away for so long, I was afraid you were sick."

Jemima looked down at the floor. "No, no – I haven't been sick," she stammered. "I just needed to, to *rest*, after all the awful things that have happened." She looked up into his face. "I *still* need to rest, Samuel."

His expressive blue eyes registered pity, and then tenderness. "Yes, it has been hard on you, Mima," he agreed, flicking a wisp of her hair with his fingertip. "I'm sorry if I came on too strong, but I just had to see you again. And – I'm still waiting for an answer to my question."

Jemima looked away. She couldn't bear to meet Samuel's eyes, because now they were radiating feelings that she couldn't return. She raised the only objection she could afford to confess.

"I know, Samuel. I *know*. But I still have things to do," she stammered. "I still have so much of the money left."

"When are you planning to give it away, Mima?" Samuel asked, frowning slightly. "I don't mean to pry, but I-I would've thought—"

Jemima bit her lip. "There have been so many other things to do, I haven't had time, Samuel," she replied, and then blushed to think that she'd lied. "I do mean to give it away. I *will*."

Samuel went silent, and Jemima prayed for some distraction to break the awkward silence. And it seemed that God had pity on her, because just then, Deborah's strident voice echoed from the hall outside:

"*Mima*! Where are you? Mamm wants you."

Jemima breathed a prayer of thanks, and looked up apologetically into Samuel's puzzled face. "Oh, I'm sorry, Samuel," she murmured, "I have to go."

"Think about what I said, Mima," he urged, and clasped her hands.

"I will, Samuel, I promise," Jemima told him – and fled.

As soon as she was well away, Jemima gripped Deborah's wrist and pulled her into a little anteroom, away from the sound of voices.

Jemima glared down into her sister's startled eyes. "I want you to tell Mamm that you're feeling sick," she whispered fiercely. "Tell her that you're bad sick to your stomach, that we have to go home. If I don't get out of here now, I'm going to break down. Do you understand? I might not make it even now!"

Jemima's angry façade crumbled suddenly. She put a hand to her mouth to stifle a sob.

Deborah nodded. "All right, I will. We'll go back to the buggy, but we'll have to go out the back way, through the trees. We'd better keep out of sight, or you might get waylaid again."

They escaped out the back door, hurried through the yard, and walked to the buggies behind a long line of thick fir trees that mostly screened them from view.

When they had reached the safety of the buggy, and Jemima was hidden away inside, Deborah looked up into her face and said: "Stay here, I'll bring Mamm and Daed back to you. And try not to bust out crying, will you? It'll make my job easier."

Jemima nodded, and watched her sister disappear into the bushes again. She hugged her knees, and rocked back and forth, and tried to concentrate on her blessings.

But the thing she was most grateful for at the moment, was that her sly, tricky sister was on her side – for *once*.

CHAPTER EIGHT

Although Deborah had helped her escape from her suitors, Jemima soon regretted asking her for help. Because Deborah's help always came with a price tag.

No sooner had they gotten home, than Deborah turned the situation to her advantage. She announced to her startled family that she was *seriously* ill.

"I have to lie *down*," Deborah groaned dramatically. "I feel so *sick*!"

Deborah languished on the living room couch for the rest of that day. To Jemima's surprise and indignation, Deborah's mysterious illness hung on through the next day, and the next.

Deborah told their parents that she was too ill to do any work.

Which meant that Jemima was forced to do both Deborah's chores, and her own. To make things worse, Deborah made Jemima fetch and carry for her like a maid. Jemima grumbled under her breath, but she couldn't very well accuse Deborah, because *she* was the one who'd asked her sister to lie in the first place.

Deborah proved to be extremely fond of a soft couch, and was a frighteningly good liar. When their parents were in the room, Deborah moaned, and rolled her head back and forth on her pillow, and was seemingly racked by spasms of uncontrollable nausea. But after they left, she sat up and laughed wickedly.

She sprinkled water on her face and nightgown to simulate perspiration, she complained constantly of spinning vertigo, and she refused all but the blandest foods.

But when their parents were gone, she made Jemima go to the kitchen and bring up a plate of all of her favorite treats to eat on the sly.

By midweek, Jemima was so heartily sick of this performance that she considered making a confession to her parents; but she was spared the necessity. Whether because she sensed Jemima's rebellion, or because she herself was tired of the charade, Deborah suddenly declared herself much improved and hinted that she could probably eat – if she was fed.

Fortified with all her favorite foods, Deborah recovered from her illness with amazing speed, and started doing her own chores again. Life settled back into its familiar routine, but Jemima decided not to scold her sister.

She didn't have time to quarrel with her, because Brad would return on Sunday night, and she had no room in her heart for anything else.

The remaining days passed slowly. To Jemima, they seemed like years, and she could hardly contain her impatience – but Sunday night arrived at last.

It was a crisp, cold October night, bare of leaves – the wind had stripped the branches of every tree, and even the bushes were mostly bare. The landscape was washed by the light of a full moon, and every star glittered with a sharp, chill brilliance; but, off to the west, clouds scudded across the horizon, and the feel of snow was in the air.

Jemima waited in her bedroom, watching the clock by the light of a single candle. The night was cold, but she had two thick quilts to nestle in, and she had hot cider and coffee in two thermos jugs.

She had also taken the precaution of enlisting Deborah's help. She was reasonably sure, now, that Deborah wouldn't betray them.

She opened her door, crossed the hall, and rapped softly on Deborah's door. It opened, and Deborah's sly face appeared in the crack.

"*Time,*" Jemima whispered.

Her door opened, and Jemima gave her a quilt and a thermos to carry. "*Be quiet,*" she warned, and they descended the front stairs as softly as they could.

Deborah sat down on the couch in the living room to serve as lookout, and Jemima walked out onto the porch.

She breathed in the cold air. It tasted like ice from a silver cup, but the moon was bright and would help Brad find his way. She walked quietly to the swing, arranged the quilts, and set the thermos jugs on the floor. Then she skipped down the porch steps and crossed the lawn.

She could see Brad as soon as she rounded the corner of the house; he was walking across the garden in the moonlight with the picnic basket in one hand. Jemima smiled and ran to meet him.

The shadow stooped, set down the basket, and held its arms wide.

Jemima jumped into them, and two strong arms closed around her, lifted her feet off the ground and spun her through the air.

She buried her face in Brad's shoulder and laughed breathlessly: "*Stop, stop! My head is spinning!*"

But he had no mercy, because no sooner were her feet back

on the ground than he kissed her, braced her back, and bent her away from him until she seemed to be floating out over the ground. She looked up, and could see the stars, winking high overhead. Then he kissed her, and slowly raised her up again. She leaned against his chest, laughing.

"Are you hungry?" he teased her.

She nodded, and he took her hand. "Come on then. I have a basket full of Thai food. You're going to love it."

They ran across the lawn, laughing breathlessly, and stopped just short of the porch. Jemima put her hand on his chest and lifted a finger to her lips.

"Careful! Remember last time," she breathed.

They walked quietly across the porch and settled into the swing. Brad set a small dark lantern on the floor, and a small puddle of light appeared at their feet. Brad knelt down and opened the basket lid. A delicious aroma rose heavenward.

He looked up at her. "Have you ever had Thai food before?"

Jemima shook her head.

"You'll love it. This is courtesy of the little storefront restaurant across the street from my complex. The cook there is an artist."

He lifted the lid off a covered dish, and a fragrant perfume rose up. "Try the cashew chicken. It's amazing." He rummaged in the basket for a cup, a fork and a napkin, and gave them to Jemima with a flourish.

She giggled, and took an experimental forkful. The flavors were unlike anything she was used to – they were spicy and creamy and nutty and sweet, all at once.

It was *delicious*.

She closed her eyes and rolled it luxuriantly in her mouth. When she opened her eyes again, she was embarrassed to find Brad smiling at her, because she had been making involuntary *mmm* sounds. She lowered her eyes in embarrassment but Brad only laughed.

"I told you," he grinned. "Here, have some of mine. This is called pad thai." He held out a heaping forkful of some noodle concoction, and placed it carefully into her mouth. Jemima closed her lips over it and savored the taste.

"*Um Bwad*," she murmured, "*se gud*!"

He found the coffee thermos, poured out two cups and gave one to Jemima. She took it gratefully and gingerly sipped it. The heat from the drink was a welcome relief from the cold.

Brad settled into the swing beside her and began to eat. Jemima watched him, but then cried, "Oh, we forgot!"

He turned to her. "Forgot what?"

"*Grace*," Jemima told him firmly, and bowed her head in

silence. Brad watched her, and waited politely until she raised her head again.

"You don't say grace before you eat?" Jemima asked innocently.

Brad shook his head. "No. I'm an agnostic."

Jemima took another forkful of chicken and ate thoughtfully before replying: "What's an *agnostic*?"

Brad smiled at her and shook his head. "It means I acknowledge that there *might* be a God, but I'm not sure of it."

"Oh."

"Maybe if I'd had a different childhood, I might've," he sighed. "But it's hard to believe in God when your Dad skips out and your Mom is a meth freak." He broke off, and shook his head. "That's all. Maybe there is a God, and He just isn't involved. I don't know."

They ate in silence for a few minutes, and Brad turned to her again and took her hand. "Look, Duchess, the religion thing doesn't matter to me. I don't care what you believe, or if you believe in anything. But – I know it's important to *you*."

He fell silent and looked down. "*How* important is it, Jemima? Could you – ever consider, say – moving away from home, and living somewhere else? Maybe not even being

Amish anymore?"

Jemima looked up at him sharply. "Oh, Brad, don't ask me," she whispered. "I couldn't. I *couldn't,* that's all."

He didn't raise his head. "Is that because of your religion, Duchess, or is it because of one of those guys you told me about? The ones who want to marry you? Have you made up your mind about *them?*"

Jemima fell silent. She looked down at her lap. "I'm not going to marry any of them," she whispered.

Brad nodded. "Why *not?*"

Jemima stared steadfastly at her hands. A wave of shyness washed over her. The silence stretched out.

"Because—"

She closed her eyes and tried again.

"Because I—"

She turned to him suddenly, impatient with herself, and took his face in her hands and kissed him like she had never kissed any boy in her life. She meant the kiss to communicate what she *felt* but could not *say;* but, to her surprise, Brad took her hands in his and pulled back from her lips.

"No, Duchess," he whispered, looking into her eyes. "I know you like to kiss me. What I don't know is *why.*"

Jemima gasped. She was pierced by the guilty insight –

Brad was right. She wasn't being fair to him. In fact, she was doing the *very same thing* to him that Mark and Samuel and Joseph had done to *her*.

Jemima nodded, leaned forward and met his eyes.

"I can't marry them," she whispered, "because I'm in love with another man."

Brad's voice was barely audible. "Lucky guy. Anyone I know?"

Jemima laughed suddenly and rested her brow against his. "Silly! You know."

"Say it," he murmured. "*Say* it, Duchess."

"I love you," she breathed, "I love you, I love you, I *love*—"

But that was as far as she got.

CHAPTER NINE

Brad Williams made the long drive back to the city in the wee hours of Monday morning. It was a challenging drive. The Amish farmland was inked out in a way that only remote countryside can be: there were no street lights and no house lights. There was only the faint glow of his dashboard dials and the headlights of the truck. His headlights suddenly flushed out a deer, and he got a glimpse of a startled buck before the animal bounded across the dirt road, and away.

Overhead, the moon bathed the hills and fields with a ghostly luminescence, and the sky was awash with stars. They seemed sharper and clearer because of the cold, and to Brad, they seemed to smile.

He lit a cigarette, inhaled, and let the smoke curl through the cold air. The Duchess had said that she loved him. He still couldn't believe it.

He cracked a grin. Maybe there *was* a God after all!

He slowed the truck to a crawl and carefully crossed the narrow wooden bridge that spanned the river. The wooden planks made a hollow sound as the truck tires rolled over.

He stopped the truck and turned onto Yoder Road, the paved two-lane that would take him to town. A few ancient-looking street lights made anemic gray puddles here and there.

But he cruised slowly over the deserted road. He wanted to remember what the sleeping fields and darkened town looked like on this *magical* night.

He closed his eyes briefly and relived the passionate kiss the Duchess had given him. He replayed the sound of her melting voice whispering *I love you.*

In the moonlight she had looked almost supernaturally beautiful, like a nymph from some ancient myth. Even the darkness couldn't defeat the preternatural loveliness of those eyes; they had sparkled an icy green, even in the faint light of the moon.

Her lips were like wet velvet, and the sweet things they'd said to him were beyond fantasy. No other girl's kiss had ever sent such an electric sensation crawling up his spine; no other girl's words of love had destroyed and delighted him like hers.

He inhaled deeply from the cigarette, closed his eyes and exhaled slowly.

He was a *very* lucky man.

He opened his eyes again and pulled the truck to a stop. He was now at the one and only red light in downtown Serenity. The streetlights bathed the old brick storefronts in an unearthly orange glow, and all the buildings were blank-faced and locked up tight. There were still two hours between him and his bed. But he would've made the trip a thousand times over to hear and feel what he'd experienced this night.

He nudged the gas pedal, and the truck rolled slowly through the deserted town square. At the stop sign beyond, Brad turned left onto another paved two-lane – the one that eventually funneled into the highway.

He picked up a little speed over the empty road. Of course, there was the *religion* thing, but he hadn't expected Jemima to toss a lifetime of indoctrination over her shoulder in one night. He breathed out smoke and adjusted the heat vent.

But if he kept talking to her, and gave her a chance to see what she was missing, he was reasonably sure that he could get her to leave the green hill country and join the world. Eventually.

Or at least, he *hoped* he could.

He imagined waking up every morning to Jemima's gentle voice whispering in his ear. He closed his eyes briefly.

Good morning tiger, her dulcet voice purred. Jemima's slanting green eyes smiled at him over the bed sheet. One silky leg rubbed sensuously against his.

I never knew it could be like this, she whispered, and then bit his ear, very gently.

A car horn blared and dazzling lights swept across the front of the truck. Brad cursed and yanked the wheel. The oncoming car missed him by inches and disappeared into the night.

He had drifted over the yellow line.

Brad stared wide-eyed at the road, panting and his heart racing. He cursed himself for a fool and gripped the wheel.

But five minutes later, he was dreaming again.

By some miracle, Brad arrived at his own door hours later, at 2 in the morning. He fumbled with the keys, swung the door open, stumbled in and locked the door behind him.

Then he shuffled across the floor to his bedroom, shedding his clothes along the way, and fell back across the mattress.

He stared up at the ceiling. Jemima's angel face smiled down at him and murmured, *I love you, Brad.*

The Duchess *loved* him. He smiled, stretched out his arms,

and crossed them behind his head.

He'd aced those Amish guys, all *three* of them. It was like winning the World Series on the other team's field.

But he was still 50 long miles away, and those guys were right there with her, every day. They lived practically on Jemima's doorstep, and they were all hot to marry her. If he didn't step up fast, *one* of them was sure to move in on the Duchess.

Brad's smile faded, imagining it. He hadn't known he was capable of violent jealousy, but the thought of Jemima in some *other* guy's arms made him think *extremely* uncivilized thoughts.

He needed to make his move. In fact, the sooner he got Jemima *out* of there, the better.

And so, he was back to her religion again. *That* was why she still wanted to stay. *That* was the only obstacle left. How to overcome it?

He turned the problem over in his mind. If he started nagging the Duchess to change her beliefs, she'd probably get mad. No, that would be clumsy and was likely to end badly.

But she might respond if he framed it in a different way. He could promise to learn about *her* religion, provided she agreed to learn about the *Englisch* world.

If he could get her away from the green hill country, and

out into the real world, she'd see that her religion was holding her back. She'd see that modern life was *so* much better than a life of needless hardships and absurd restrictions.

He could show her how much fun living in the Englisch world could be. And then – oh, *baby*.

Brad grinned a sharp, white, ear-to-ear grin, sighed and closed his eyes.

CHAPTER TEN

At noon the next day, Delores Watkins sauntered up behind Brad William's desk chair and glanced at his computer screen. Her eyebrows arched up, but she held her peace.

An instant later Brad sensed her there, and colored to the roots of his hair. He swiveled the chair around and gave her a sheepish grin. "Ah – Delores! I didn't see you there! What can I do for you?"

Delores swept him with her heavy lashes and smiled indulgently. "Don't worry, lover boy," she assured him. "I won't tell anyone that you shop at"—she adjusted her glasses—"*Angel Secrets*. Though I confess—"

"Cut to the chase, Delores," Brad interrupted evenly. "This is my lunch break."

"Yes, you're finally awake! Your bleary mornings are beginning to make sense to me now. I don't object to romance, Brad, but if yours is *newsworthy*, throw the *Ledger* a bone – promise?"

She tossed a report down on his desk, winked at him, laughed at his expression and surged away, like some massive ship.

Brad watched her go grimly, and turned back to his task – but not before closing his office door, to prevent any further intrusions.

He sat down in front of the computer and returned to the *Angel Secrets* gift page. He clicked on a series of lovely, frilly things, the sort of frou-frous all women everywhere loved, and– he'd be willing to bet – even *Amish* women dreamed of, in their weaker moments.

And *weak* was what he was shooting for.

Seduction.

The jewelry page displayed a tiny, elfin gold ring with one delicate emerald chip. It would match the Duchess' eyes to perfection. He clicked on it.

The next page showed a pair of tiny hair barrettes covered in pink, feathery fuzz. Brad lingered over them, fantasizing about what it would feel like to set them in Jemima's flowing hair. He clicked on them, too.

Later on, there were little bottles of perfume, scented soaps and flavored lip gloss with names like '50s Magnolia, Champagne Ice Cream, and Winged Fantasy. Brad chose a small, exquisite vial of a perfume called Moonlight Angel. It was a tiny bottle of cobalt blue glass bearing a blue-and-gold foil label. A tiny gold fringe hung from the bottle neck. He clicked on it, too.

It was the first phase of his campaign to win Jemima away from his last, daunting rival: the Amish church.

He'd start with little gifts of the kind that all girls loved. It would be an innocent gesture, one that men in love were supposed to make – but, hopefully, it would do more than just touch Jemima's heart.

He hoped that it would open her eyes – just a little – to what she was missing. He was confident that, sooner or later, nature would kick in.

It was against nature for a beautiful girl like Jemima to wear drab clothing every day of her life. She should be free to revel in her youth and beauty and enjoy sweet nonsense like—he looked down at the screen—bubble gum lip gloss, and pink nail polish, and even *more* delightfully girly gifts that he was not yet bold enough to give her.

But totally planned to in the near future.

He smiled, imagining Jemima's delight when he presented these frilly nothings. It would probably be the first time she'd ever been given a remotely lover-like gift, and it was going to be fun to watch her face when she opened them up.

He leaned back in his chair and crossed his arms over his head. That Amish asceticism made him kind of *mad*, really – the Duchess was 18 years old, an adult, and had never in her life worn lip gloss, or jewelry or even pretty barrettes in her hair. It was a kind of abuse to make a beautiful girl feel bad about such harmless pleasures – the pretty things that *should* be a beauty's birthright.

Well, he intended to change all *that*.

When he'd finished showering the Duchess with all the pretty things she deserved, as well as the kisses and other delights he had planned for her, she wasn't going to have a thought to spare for all that religious nonsense.

Brad stared grimly at the screen. Yes, the sooner he got her away from the green hill country, the better. All that religious stuff was crushing her down, holding her back. It might even give her some weird complex about *sex*, and that would be a tragedy.

He grinned suddenly. And he certainly intended to do everything in *his* power to make sure *that* didn't happen.

The sound of Delores knocking on his office door burst Brad's pleasant bubble. His lunch break, and his fantasies, were over. It was time to return to the real world.

But to his dismay, Brad found that returning to the real world was an increasingly difficult proposition. He thought of Jemima more than he liked to admit, more than was probably healthy for his ego, or his self-image as an independent bachelor.

That evening, back at his apartment, Brad pushed a TV dinner into his microwave and stared at it hopelessly. Even the "man sized" meat and potato meal was a sorry substitute for the food he remembered from the green hill country. He longed for Jemima's picnic basket with almost physical pain. And the memory of all the meals he'd had in Amish country haunted him – the ham and biscuits and pie and potato salad and chicken fried steak and…

Well, it brought tears to his eyes.

He flopped down at his kitchen table and put his chin on his fists. He thought the Amish were wrong about a lot of things, but food was one thing they got gloriously right.

He glowered at the humming microwave, and imagined the Duchess taking charge of his kitchen. It was a pretty fantasy.

If she did, no doubt the first thing she'd do would be to throw that microwave out as a tool of the devil, which it certainly was. Then she would insist on a brand new gas stove with all the bells and whistles, and would immediately turn his apartment into a home-cooking heaven.

Except that she wasn't *there*.

Brad chewed his lip. The Duchess had always messed with his mind, but to his dismay, her influence on his imagination was approaching critical mass. She was beginning to tint the way he saw the *world*. It used to be that he'd merely missed her when they were apart. But now, he was even beginning to see his apartment differently because of her.

It wasn't the biggest or nicest apartment in the world, that was for sure, but he'd been happy enough with it before he'd met the Duchess. Now, nothing about it seemed right without her.

Not even the microwave oven.

The microwave beeped and Brad rose and pulled the tray out of the oven. He peeled the plastic cover back gingerly.

His dinner stared back at him. It was a brown blob.

Brad leaned his head against the kitchen cabinet, and beat it against the door a time or two before he retired to the kitchen table for his evening meal.

CHAPTER ELEVEN

"Close your eyes now."

Brad smiled down at Jemima indulgently. She sat there with her brows raised, her eyes closed, and her lips slightly open – like a child.

She was *adorable.*

It was half past midnight, and they were huddled together in the office of her father's workshop, because it was snowing and bitter cold outside.

Her father's smithy was an extremely unromantic place – it was an unheated metal structure, and filled with large, heavy tools that looked to Brad like medieval instruments of torture.

But as far as he was concerned, *any* place with the Duchess was a desirable spot, and with blankets draped around them, and practically no space between them, the tiny side office had become very cozy indeed.

Brad reached down into the shiny gift bag he'd brought, and made tantalizing *crinkle* sounds to heighten Jemima's anticipation. "I bought this from a shop called *Angel Secrets*," he teased her, "because it reminded me of you, Duchess. Keep your eyes closed!"

Brad reached into the basket and pulled out a dainty box of gourmet chocolates. It had cost him almost 100 bucks, but each morsel was a work of art, and incredibly delicious.

His past experience with women had taught him, *when in doubt, overspend*. And, he figured that gourmet treats would warm Jemima up to the *other* gifts he planned to give her.

"Open your eyes!"

Jemima's eyes flew open, lighted on the beautiful chocolate box, and the bag brimming with treats, and looked up at him.

"Oh, Brad, they're beautiful!" she gasped. She picked the box up reverently. "Why, they're almost too beautiful to eat!"

"The key word being *almost*," Brad told her. He took the box, carefully removed the cellophane, and smiled at her. "Choose one."

Jemima scanned the box in delight. "I can't, they're all so pretty," she smiled.

"Then I'll choose one for you. *This* one," he murmured, picking out a small square of dark chocolate. Some *artiste* had placed a tiny candy raspberry on top – a delicate purple dot, surrounded by painted flowers.

"Open your mouth."

Jemima smiled and opened her mouth. Brad placed the confection square in the middle of that pink velvet, and Jemima's mouth closed around it.

Her eyes flew open. *"Ohhmm – dwishus!"*

Brad's smile faded. She really *was* just like a sweet, adorable – he shook his head, and the smile returned.

"Let's try this one next." He picked out a creamy white chocolate oval that had been painted with a forest scene, including a graceful deer.

"Here we go!" Jemima closed her eyes and opened her mouth again, and Brad placed the chocolate in her mouth.

"Ha!"

He caught himself up short, and shook his head. He was turning into a complete idi—

"Mmm, mmm," Jemima moaned, and opened her eyes. *"Cinnimum pecan crunch!"*

Brad smiled down at her indulgently. It was just as much fun to spoil Jemima as he'd imagined it would be, and he couldn't *wait* to give her more age-appropriate gifts.

But that was for later – when she'd gotten a little more *used* to delightful gifts.

"What's *this*?" he asked in mock surprise, pulling a bouquet of exquisite lollypops out of the bag. They were tiny, completely clear, and spangled with edible decorations like gold flakes, glitter, flowers, and herbs. They were painted as if they were book illustrations: with flying birds, and smiling cats, and children dancing, and a couple kissing. Jemima reached for them, and spread them out before her like a fan.

"Oh, Brad, where did you *get* these?" she cried. "I've never seen anything like them!"

Brad unwrapped the one with the kissing couple and passed it to her with a smile. "I was kind of hoping it would give you *ideas*," he told her, and Jemima laughed and kissed him, and then pressed her cheek to his.

"You're so *good*, and, and *generous*, Brad!" she murmured fervently.

Brad raised his brows wryly. He probably didn't deserve that kiss, but he was going to claim it anyway. He put his arms around Jemima, and kissed her back.

When they had finished exploring all the contents of the bag, and had traded kisses tasting of champagne marmalade, blackberry crème, and brown sugar pumpkin, Brad decided that it was time to put his broader plan into action. He smiled at Jemima and took her hands between his.

"Duchess, would you be willing to find out a *little* more about the Englisch world, if I was willing to find out more about your religion?"

The green eyes moved to him and held him.

"You want to learn about my religion?" Jemima asked in surprise. "I thought you were a – what was the word—"

"*Agnostic*, yes," Brad told her, smiling. "But I like to think I'm open-minded. I like to learn about what *other* people believe, too. Would you teach me?"

Jemima's eyes widened. "Oh *yes*, Brad," she breathed earnestly, "if you really want to learn."

"Oh, I do," Brad assured her, smiling. "But if I learn about your beliefs, will you listen to mine, too? Would you be willing to – say – learn more about the world?"

Jemima was beaming. "I guess that's only fair," she agreed, slipped a soft hand behind his neck, and kissed him so expressively that Brad forgot his plan. He put his arms around her, and pressed her to his chest, marveling how small and delicate she felt in his arms, and that his fingers *almost* met around her tiny waist.

"I'll give you all the books I can find," she was saying,

"*and* the newsletter, and if you have any questions, I'll do my best to answer them, even if I don't know them all. And if I don't know the answer, I can ask the bishop for you—"

Brad opened his eyes. "Ah ha, no, don't do that, Duchess!" he laughed. "I'm happy just to talk to *you*."

"Oh, yes, of course," Jemima laughed sheepishly. "It's just that I was so – you *really* want to know what we believe, Brad?"

"Yes, I really do, Duchess," he smiled. "We'll learn from each other. Does that sound fair?"

Jemima squeezed her eyes together in happiness. "Oh, *more* than fair!" she cried, and hugged him ecstatically.

Brad received her embrace and smiled up at the ceiling.

"I'm glad you agree," he told her. "I'll read your books, and you can come with me to a movie. Deal?"

She went still in his arms. "A movie?" she faltered. "But – we're not supposed to watch movies."

"Oh, well – I don't want to push you to do anything you aren't supposed to do," he conceded. "How about a trip to see a football game?"

He could feel her relax. "Oh, that would be wonderful," she agreed, in a relieved tone.

He turned his head and kissed her cheek.

"Perfect."

CHAPTER TWELVE

Jemima watched from the window of her father's workshop as the lights of Brad's truck faded down the road. Then she turned and gathered up all the evidence that they'd been there: the glittering bag, the lollypops, the jewelry-box of chocolate and the shiny wrappers.

She watched herself turn down the lantern, walk through the smithy and out into the snow. She saw herself turn and lock the door, walk between the big fir trees and across the yard to the house.

But it was all like a slow motion dream, like the big flakes of snow drifting down from the dark sky. She hardly even felt the cold.

Because Brad wanted to learn about being Amish.

She couldn't believe it!

For the first time, she felt a tiny spark of hope. If – by some miracle of God – Brad were to convert, then...

She closed her eyes. No, she couldn't let herself picture it. It would hurt too much to hope, and then have that hope dashed.

But Brad wanted to learn about being Amish.

She glided through the doorway and up the stairs like a sleepwalker. She entered her bedroom, dropped the quilts on the floor, and hid Brad's gifts away safe in the little nook behind the wall.

She came out of her cap and her dress and pulled on her nightgown. She crawled into bed and watched the big flakes of snow spiral past her window.

It was rare for an Englischer to convert, very rare, but it *had* happened. Oh, what if Brad decided to become Amish, and they got *married*, and they found a house of their own, and— She closed her eyes and smiled, and allowed herself to live in that happy fantasy until sleep took her, and Brad kissed her again in her dreams.

The next morning dawned bright and clear and cold. The sky was a clear, brilliant blue and the countryside was several inches deep in fresh, sparkling snow. By the time the sun was well up, the entire King household had made and eaten breakfast, and had been at work for well over an hour.

But Jacob King was distracted from his work by a troubling mystery. He came back to the house in an attempt to solve it.

"Has anyone been out to my workshop?" he asked.

Jemima had been wiping down the kitchen table, and she froze mid-swipe. She was no good at lying, and Deborah wasn't there to think of a quick excuse. She raised guilty eyes to her father's face.

Rachel shook her head. "I haven't been anywhere near it for the last two days," she replied. "Jemima, were you out there?"

Jemima dropped her eyes to the table. "I-I have no reason to go out there," she said softly. "Why do you ask, Daed?"

Jacob put one big hand to the back of his neck. "They've been snowed over pretty thick, but there are some kind of *prints* on the ground outside the shop. It looks like something was out there last night," he replied.

"Maybe it was an animal," Jemima ventured, but her heart was pounding.

"Maybe," Jacob replied. "But I don't like the idea of a stranger prowling around this house. Maybe it would be a good idea for us to get a watchdog."

Jemima felt her mouth falling open, and quickly closed it.

"Oh, it was probably a deer or a stray, Jacob," Rachel soothed. "Jemima's trouble is over now. Let it go."

Jemima made a desperate attempt to change the subject. "*Yes*, Daed, everything is back to normal now. The Englisch move so fast from one thing to another, they've forgotten all about me!

"When I give the rest of the money away, the last of it will be behind us. In fact, I was thinking – I was wondering – if you would drive me out to the bishop's house today?"

Rachel's eyes lit up. "Oh, what a *wonderful* idea!" she cried. "Did you hear that, Jacob? Jemima is ready to give away the last of the money, and to"—she turned to beam at her eldest daughter—"get back to her own life at last!"

Jacob shook his head. "I'm sorry, Mima. Not today. I have too much work piled up to drive you around the countryside. All this nonsense has put me back six months!"

Rachel's face fell, and she looked uncharacteristically put out. "Well then, if you're behind in your work, Jacob King," she asked him archly, "then why are you worried about a few marks in the snow? I would think you'd be in your shop, instead of here – teasing your poor daughter!"

Jacob looked wounded. "Now Rachel—"

"I'm not upset," Jemima interjected quickly, moving her eyes from her father to her mother. "I can wait, there's no hurry."

Rachel turned to her with her pretty mouth set. "Well, maybe there *should* be a little bit of a hurry, young lady," she retorted. "Those poor boys of yours are wondering when on earth you're going to give that money away. *I* wonder, too!

"And," she added, rounding on Jacob, "I would think that your *father*, of all people, would be willing to help you when it's something as important as your whole future – instead of hunting little snow goblins!"

Jacob crossed his arms. "I know what I saw, Rachel," he told her. "You can come and look at them, there are clear prints!"

To Jemima's astonishment, her mother began to giggle. "*Really*, Jacob," she replied softly, and giggled again.

Her father's face went as red as his hair, and he assumed an air of outraged dignity. He replied: "Laugh all you like, Rachel, but it's a good thing that I'm here to notice such things. There have been strange goings on around this house!"

Jemima lowered her eyes and held her breath, but that was her father's parting shot. He stalked out, and her mother stood silently drying dishes for a few long moments after.

Then she looked up at the ceiling, sighed, wiped her hands

on her apron and followed him outside.

Jemima crept to the window, silent as a mouse, to see if they would look at the telltale tracks she'd left in the snow. She put her ear to the window, and could make out the sound of soft talking. Then there was silence.

Jemima carefully pulled the curtains back, but to her astonishment, her parents weren't concerned with the prints in the snow at all. Her mother was in her father's huge arms, and any hurt feelings were clearly being mended.

Jemima smiled, and let the drapes fall closed, and returned to the kitchen table, but a deep sadness settled over her as she worked. Oh, *if only*, one day, she and Brad could kiss like that – on the porch of their own home!

CHAPTER THIRTEEN

For the next few days, Jemima withdrew from her family and friends in mind and spirit – even in body, when she got the opportunity. She slipped away to her father's study, or to her own bedroom, or to any quiet corner where she could be undisturbed.

Because she mostly didn't know what to do, and she was afraid to do what she *did* know.

She was praying like she'd never prayed before in her life.

Her father's study had always been her favorite retreat, especially on days when snowflakes drifted on the air.

Jemima slipped inside and closed the door behind her. The big red chair was invitingly empty, and a cozy fire crackled in the grate. She sank down into the softness of her father's huge chair, pulled her knees up under her chin, and watched the flames dance in the fireplace.

To Jemima's worried imagination, they seemed to form faces – faces that she knew and loved. She saw Joseph's handsome face break into a shy smile, Samuel's laughing eyes and quick grin, and Mark's quiet, steady gaze.

She closed her eyes and rested her head on her knees. *Oh please Lord*, she prayed, *Help me, I don't want to hurt any one of them. But I must. Show me how to do it the best way, the way that hurts them least!*

And Lord, give them new loves, all three, to heal their hearts. Give them all loving girls who'll adore them, and say yes right away when they propose.

Different girls from me.

She opened her eyes again. The flames crackled and leaped up suddenly, and she saw Brad's magnetic eyes in them, staring down at her. She gazed at them wistfully, but just as suddenly, they disappeared.

Oh Lord, I know I haven't done like I should. I've lied, and I've taken lots of money, and gone out with an Englisch boy who doesn't even believe in You, and all of that was wrong. Please don't be angry, and help me not to lie or do wrong again.

But I can't help seeing Brad, Lord. I love him so much it scares me sometimes, and that used to be wrong, Lord, but things have changed.

Now Brad says he wants to learn about being Amish, and he wants to learn about You. Oh, Lord, if you never hear another prayer of mine in all my life, please hear this one! Please, Lord – open Brad's heart!

Jemima opened her eyes. There was a faint sound from the doorway. The knob turned slightly, and then turned back. Soft voices filtered to her ears.

"No, don't go in, Jacob. Jemima's in there. I think she's praying, and we should let her. She has important decisions to make."

There was more soft murmuring, and the sound of retreating footsteps.

Jemima rested her head on her knees.

Lord, Brad had a terrible childhood, and his parents were very mixed up, and only You know what awful things that did to him. And he didn't have anybody to tell him about You, or to love him except his grandmother, and I don't know anything about her, but anyway, Brad says he's an ag— well, that word that starts with ag. You know!

Oh Lord, only You could ever know how much I want Brad

to become Amish, and to ask me to be his wife. But I would rather lose Brad and stay unmarried all my life, than to think of Brad going through his whole life without knowing how much You love him. Without knowing You at all! It breaks my heart to think of it, Lord, and I know it must break Yours.

Please, please, Lord, open Brad's heart!

And at dinner that evening, when they all bowed their heads to pray, Jemima's head remained bowed so long that Jacob finally had to clear his throat, and that had never happened before.

Jemima looked up quickly, colored faintly, and ate in chastened silence: but she noticed that her parents exchanged an awed look, and that Deborah's keen eyes were watching her narrowly.

She fixed her eyes on her plate and said nothing audibly. But she prayed:

Lord, please, please, open Brad's heart. Let us be married, so that one day I can look across my own table, and see the man I love smiling back at me!

That evening, in her own bedroom, Jemima unfurled her long hair and slowly plaited it, looking out over the snowy fields.

Oh Lord, I know I promised You that I'd give the money away, and I've been slow about that because I was sued, and I know that You know that wasn't my fault. But it's been almost a month since then, and now it is my fault, and I mean to fix that. I'll go to the bishop and give the rest of the money away, just like I promised.

In case You might be upset about that.

Though I don't really think You're worried about a month's delay.

But even so.

She wriggled into her nightgown, and pulled the covers back, and crawled inside, and turned down the lamp. She sighed, and stared up at the ceiling.

Lord, I will go to the bishop and give away the rest of the money. And while I'm there, I'll ask him if he would pray for Brad too, only I'll call him a friend, so the bishop won't know, and if you can't listen to my prayers because I messed up, then maybe You can listen to the bishop's prayers instead, because he's a good man and loves You very much.

Amen.

Jemima uncrossed her hands, and sighed and settled into her pillow.

CHAPTER FOURTEEN

The next day, Jemima rose early, about an hour before her usual time. She turned up the lamp in the freezing kitchen; built and lit a fire in her mother's cast iron stove, and the living room fireplace; and began to make breakfast. By the time her parents came downstairs, the kitchen was alight, cozy warm, and filled with the aroma of coffee and frying bacon.

"Well, well! What's this?" Jacob asked her, leaning over to plant a kiss on her cheek. "It looks like our Mima has come back to live with us."

Rachel opened up a cabinet and took out a frying pan. "Don't discourage her, Jacob. She'll be doing this in her own kitchen soon enough."

Jemima went pink, and smiled faintly, and poured out a cup of steaming coffee for her father. As she leaned over to give it to him, she asked lightly:

"Daed, I was wondering—"

He nodded. "Yes, *here* it comes!"

"—I was wondering, if today might be a better day for you to drive me to the bishop's house."

Jacob looked first at his daughter, and then at his wife, who was staring at him with a look that required no translation. He appeared to deliberate.

"Well – I might." He rubbed his chin with one hand. "I suppose I could find an hour or so to spare."

He was rewarded by his daughter casting herself on his chest with a display of surprising gratitude, and by another, much more pleasant look from his wife – the one that told him he was a *wise man*.

Bishop Lapp was one of the youngest men to ever rise to that position in the local district. He was a big, tall man, with a shock of bright blonde hair beginning to go gray at the temples, and bright blue eyes.

He was splitting wood in his front yard when their buggy

rolled up to his driveway. He paused, and wiped his brow with one arm, and leaned back on his axe handle to await them. His breath was like smoke in the chilly air.

Jemima peeped out of the buggy anxiously. She had seen Bishop Lapp before, but had never spoken to him, and had never been to his house. She looked him up and down, and felt a flicker of anxiety. He was as huge a man as her father. Maybe even a little taller. And he looked busy.

But a quick scan of the front of his house helped calm her flutters. A kind-looking brown-haired woman stepped out onto the porch behind them and waved. A little daughter of about five or six clung to her skirts.

Maybe Joseph Lapp wasn't *quite* as daunting he looked.

They climbed down out of the buggy, and Jacob held out his hand for her, and they walked together to greet the newly-minted bishop.

"Hello, Brother King," the bishop said pleasantly. He extended a hand, and her father shook it warmly. "It's good to see you and your daughter again. Would you like to come in, and have something hot to eat and drink?"

"Thank you, bishop," her father told him. "My daughter was very anxious to come and see you today. You've heard all the things that've happened to our daughter – how she got tangled up with the Englisch, and fell into so much money. Well, she says she wants to close the book on the whole thing, and give the rest of the money to the community fund."

The man's bright eyes moved to her face, and Jemima quickly dropped her own to the ground.

But the bishop's voice was kind. "That's a very generous offer," he said softly, and with a tinge of surprise. "Please, go on in, and make yourselves comfortable. I'll be there directly, and then we can talk."

He turned, and called to the woman on the porch. "Katie, we have company!"

The woman stood back and opened the door invitingly, and they hurried across the snowy yard and into the warmth of the big house.

A few minutes later they were warming their hands with cups of steaming hot chocolate and nibbling off plates filled with syrup-drizzled biscuits, cheese, and ham.

The bishop came in, wiped snow off his boots, and after he'd shrugged out of his coat and muffler, his wife gave him a cup of coffee and he folded himself up in a chair opposite the couch.

He took a long, appreciative sip, and trained those blue eyes on them. "Now, you say that Jemima here wants to give money to the fund. I can take care of that, if you're sure you want to do it, Jemima?"

Jemima raised scared eyes to his face. She nodded mutely.

"Well, then, you can come to my study and we can take care of it."

Jemima spoke up quickly. "Daed, I'd like to talk to the bishop privately – just for a minute," she told her father apologetically.

Jacob looked at her in surprise, but lowered himself back onto the couch. "Very well then, Mima," he told her.

The bishop stood up and extended a hand. "Come then."

Jemima followed the bishop into a large room with a big desk, a bigger chair, and lots of wall shelves, all crammed with books. The bishop pulled out a chair for her, and closed the door behind them.

He walked around to the desk, sat down in the chair and smiled a bit quizzically.

Jemima set her mouth. "I came to give you a check," she said, and reached into her purse. "It's all made out to the community fund – for whoever may need it to pay their emergency bills."

She extended the check in a small hand, and the bishop took it. He placed a pair of glasses over his nose, read the check, and lifted startled eyes to hers.

"This check is for—"

"I know how much it is," Jemima told him firmly. "I-I made a *promise to God*, and I'm here to fulfill it."

The bishop shook his head slightly, and then nodded. "Very well – if you're *sure*. I'll make out a receipt to show that the fund has received the money. I'll deposit it in the fund's bank account tomorrow morning. And I have to say," he added incredulously, "you've been *extremely* generous, young lady!"

He scribbled out a receipt, and handed it to Jemima over the desk. Then he looked a question, and Jemima went red.

"I-I also wanted to ask a favor of you," she said, in a small voice.

"Ask."

She lifted pleading eyes to his face. "First, will you promise me that this will be – just between *us*?"

He nodded. "All right. I won't tell anyone."

"I wanted to ask you to pray for a – a friend of mine," she urged. "This friend doesn't believe in God, but wants to learn more about Him, and – and about becoming Amish. Will you pray for them, bishop? Pray *hard*?"

The vivid blue eyes softened, and the bishop nodded. "Certainly, if you want. Would your friend, by any chance, be a young *man*?"

Jemima lowered her eyes, but could feel her face going bright red.

"I'm not asking you to tell me anything more," the bishop

said gently. "It's just that I once knew a young lady who *also* had a friend. Her friend didn't believe in God, either, and she hoped that he might come around, one day.

"But instead of her friend coming to God, it happened just the opposite. Her friend pulled her *away* from God, and away from her family. She got into more trouble than she could handle, and was very lucky to get away from him in the end."

Jemima kept her eyes glued to her hands, and said nothing.

The bishop sighed, and took off his glasses, and massaged his eyes with his fingers. "I'll pray for your friend, Jemima. But I'll also pray that God gives you the wisdom to put Him *first*."

"Thank you, bishop," she said, in a tiny voice.

He sighed again. "You're a very unselfish young lady, I can see that," he said, eyeing the check. "But sometimes you can be too unselfish for your own good. If your friend really *is* your friend, he won't ask you to do anything that's against what you believe.

"Remember that, Jemima."

"*I will, bishop,*" she replied, in a voice almost too faint to be heard.

CHAPTER FIFTEEN

The lights of the stadium reached high up into the night sky, and far out to each side, with glaring white radiance. Brad pulled the truck into the last parking space left and turned off the motor.

He'd finally convinced Jemima to let him take her out on an *Englisch* date.

He reached back to get the ponchos he'd brought, because the night air was cold, but was struck by the Duchess' expression. She was leaning forward, peering up at the stadium in rapt wonder. He grinned and pulled the ponchos out.

"Pretty big, eh, Duchess?"

"I've never seen anything so big," Jemima breathed. "And the noise, it must be – well, I can hear it through the car door!"

"Yeah, it gets pretty crazy," Brad admitted, and handed her a poncho. "I brought these, because it's going to get cold. Ready?"

Jemima turned her big green eyes to Brad's face. He thought he saw excitement and just a little bit of *fear* in them. He reached out for her hand and gave it a squeeze.

"Come on."

Jemima smiled uncertainly.

Brad gave her a knitted cap to keep her ears warm, a silly little red thing with a long tassle, and thought she looked adorable in it. The big red poncho covered up that black getup she always wore, and for the moment at least, she looked just like anybody else.

Brad stared at her wistfully. If things went as he hoped they would, she'd soon be free to dress as she pleased, and to go anywhere she liked.

Because she'd be with *him*.

He pulled on his own knit cap and poncho, and took her hand.

He'd been careful to get good seats, pretty far down, and close to the 50 yard line. It was a college ball game, between his own school and their closest rivals, and it was getting close to kickoff.

He shouldered across the row of seated people, found their seats and helped Jemima get settled in. She was looking around at everything like a kid, and her eyes were as round as saucers. He smiled and leaned over.

"Do you know how football is played?" he asked.

She smiled and shook her head.

"Well, one team kicks the ball to the other team. And the team with the ball tries to move all the way down the field, to their goal line."

Jemima turned her big green eyes on him.

"Why?"

He felt his mouth slipping open. "Ah – well, to score points, and to win the game. The Miners and the Rockets are archrivals, so it should be a great contest."

"Which one do we want to win?" Jemima asked him, and Brad bowed his head and smiled.

"We're bigtime Rockets fans," he informed her gravely, and she nodded and picked up a plastic pompom.

"Rockets!" she cried.

Brad looked at her affectionately. He was hoping that this would be the first of many evenings out in the real world for Jemima.

He flagged down a vendor, and bought her a big cup of hot coffee and a hot dog, and the same for himself. He laughed at her reaction when the cheerleaders came prancing out on the field in their scanty outfits.

Her eyes got round, and her cheeks went pink and she was adorably embarrassed. To be fair, though, she was right – they had on very little, and it *was* cold. But for *his* money, not one of those glamour girls could compete with the Duchess, because their beauty depended on heavy makeup and a flashy wardrobe – things that seemed oddly garish, now that he'd grown used to her fresh-faced beauty.

The teams jogged out onto the field to the roar of the crowd, and everyone stood up and screamed. Brad laughed to see Jemima put her hands over her ears as the roar built like a wave to the point of kickoff – and then subsided.

Near the end of the first quarter there was a crushing tackle, and a man was down on the field. The medics and trainers rushed out onto the field, and Jemima stood up with one hand clapped to her mouth.

"Oh, Brad, something's wrong!" she cried. "They hit him too hard, he's *hurt!*"

Brad looked around them, smiling apologetically at the

people sitting behind them. "Yes, they're taking care of him, Duchess," he soothed, and slid a hand under her elbow. "You don't need to be upset."

Jemima allowed him to press her back into her seat, but insisted: "He's still down! Why do those boys play this game if it can hurt them?"

"He's all right – look, he's standing up now."

The player stood up slowly and was escorted off the field, to the applause of the crowd. Jemima seemed mollified, but when he glanced at her again, her head was bowed and her eyes were closed.

"What is it, Duchess?" he asked. "Are you feeling okay?"

She moved her lips, and then opened her eyes and looked up at him. "Yes, I'm all right."

"What were you doing?"

"I was praying for that boy who got hit," she replied earnestly. "And the others. I didn't know football was such a *dangerous* game!"

He couldn't help laughing, and leaned over and kissed her cheek, because he couldn't help that, either. "Of *course*," he laughed.

After the game was over and the Rockets had won, and Jemima had enjoyed her first ever football game, and he'd been more entertained than he'd been in years, he'd had to drive her right back to her house. It was a long way back, and she had to get up at an insane hour.

But their farewell in the car had been warmer than ever, and more tantalizing. And before she had gone, he'd given her the little gold ring with the emerald chip. Her expression had been worth every penny of what it had cost him, and then some.

"*Oh, Brad*," she'd gasped, and then rewarded him with another, very appreciative kiss. "Oh, I could never wear this, but I'll *always* treasure it. It's *so*—"

And she'd kissed him again.

That night, he lay awake on his bed, reliving it. He blew smoke rings toward the ceiling, and they magically transformed themselves into likenesses of Jemima. The way she'd looked in that silly red cap, the way she laughed at the dancing mascots and her mesmerized fascination with all the sights and sounds.

He could only hope that he was making headway, so that when it came time to ask her to leave home – to come away with him – he'd have a shot.

He turned on a little bedside light, sighed and picked up one of the many books the Duchess had given him as part of their deal. They were black and thick, and were crammed with hundreds of pages of tiny type and looked like they were a century old, at least.

There was also a copy of the local Amish newsletter. He leafed through it. It was filled with weather reports, crop news, recipes and livestock advice.

Yes, he was in love with the Duchess.

Nothing less than *love* could've made him crack such boring books, but he tilted up the cigarette, opened the first one and began to read.

CHAPTER SIXTEEN

The next weekend, Brad took Jemima out on another date to a county fair, and did all the things that a guy was supposed to do when he took his girl out to the fair: bought her cotton candy, won a stuffed animal to give her, and took her through the Tunnel of Love as often as she as willing to go.

Jemima screamed with laughter on the whirling teacups, had clung to him like a frightened kitten in the Fun House, and had gasped and whispered sweet things in his ear in the Tunnel of Love.

He'd given her the little vial of perfume, and she'd made all kinds of fuss over it, and then over him, and they had to move to a hidden spot, and had stayed there for a few delightful minutes.

A curling tendril of hair had escaped from under her cap, and he brushed it back, and asked her: "Having a good time, Duchess?"

She beamed at him. "Oh, Brad, the best time of my *life!*"

"We could do this sort of thing all the time, you know," he said casually – and waited. He didn't want to push his lady-love too much, or too soon. But to his dismay, she seemed not to take the hint.

Or what was more likely – she was being *polite.*

He smothered a sigh, and then smiled at her. "Ready for the House of Doom?"

"Oh, Brad," she whispered, and looked up at him with such serious dread that all his frustration vanished. He laughed, and kissed her, and promised: "Don't worry, I won't let anything *get* you."

And so he had saved her from the evil scarecrow and the clown with the maniacal laugh, and had smiled when she'd thrown her arms around him and buried her face in his shirt.

"Why do people even come to these *awful* haunted houses?" she'd wept, and he'd tightened his arms around her, and kissed away her tears, and forbore to point out the obvious.

The next week, he finally talked her into attending a movie

with him, but she had made him promise not to take her to something that involved people getting hurt, or stealing, or basically breaking any of the commandments. He had ended up taking her to a children's movie about a lost dog, and she had loved it.

After the movie, when he had driven to a pretty, moonlit spot and they were sitting together in his truck, he'd asked her to take her hair down again, and she had pulled out the pins that held it. That glorious, coppery hair had tumbled down like a waterfall, and he had taken it between his fingers, held it up to his mouth and inhaled its fragrance.

"I love your hair this way," he told her. "I wish you'd wear your hair like this *all* the time, Duchess. You *could*, you know," he added, and stared at her meaningfully.

Then he had presented her with the fluffy pink barrettes, and had begged to put them in her hair. She had blushed, and looked at her hands, and finally said *yes*; so he had slowly and reverently placed them in her silky hair.

They had been even prettier than he'd imagined, and he couldn't help wondering what Jemima would look like, if she dressed like any other woman. She'd be breathtaking – but a part of him was almost glad that she didn't.

He had *enough* competition already.

He raised his hand to caress her cheek, and she turned to him suddenly. She looked into his eyes so intently that he thrilled with the hope that she was going to throw herself into his arms. But instead, she knocked him completely off balance by asking the most unromantic and off-topic question he could imagine.

"Brad, did you—did you ever have time to – read the books and the magazine I loaned you?"

He raised his brows, sputtered a little and was glad that he'd taken the time, because he was able to say that he had.

She got shy suddenly, and looked down at her hands. "What did you *think* of them?" she asked.

He'd hesitated over his answer. He reminded himself that this was a *very* big deal for Jemima, and that it was important to be politic.

"Well, I think I got my head around the big picture," he told her cautiously. "I think I understand the main points of what you believe. And a lot of it is – is admirable. Really, I don't have a problem with most of it, because it's mainly the Golden Rule, and minding your own business, and working hard, and – all that kind of thing."

He stopped, and rubbed the back of his neck, and cast about in his mind for a way to change the subject. Religion always made him uncomfortable.

He looked over at Jemima, to see how his answer had gone down with her. She was still looking at her hands.

"I'm glad that you took the time to read them," she said at last, in a small voice. 'That was *very* sweet of you, Brad. I know you think – differently."

She looked at him just then, with something almost like hero worship in those big eyes, and he allowed himself to bask in the glow of her admiration – just a little.

He shrugged. "I try to keep an open mind," he told her nonchalantly. "It's part of my training as a reporter."

The part of his brain that policed idiocy struck him smartly upside the head. He caught himself and winced, imagining what Delores would've made him suffer, if she'd caught him preening about his "training as a reporter."

But of course, Jemima knew no different. She beamed at him.

"Oh, Brad, it really is so good of you to – to see our side," she told him warmly, taking his hand. "Most people on the outside don't even try," she added sadly. "They just laugh, and make fun of us, or, or seem to be *fascinated*, which is almost as bad. They ride by our house sometimes on tour buses and point at us, as if we're some kind of exhibit in a museum."

Her eyes looked unbearably forlorn, and he leaned over and kissed the sad look away and stroked the softness of her hair.

"Not cool," he told her sympathetically. "*So* not cool."

"I really appreciate that you try, Brad," she sighed, pillowing on his chest. "That at least you take the time to *try* to understand why we're different. It means a lot to me."

"Anything to oblige," he murmured, and caressed a silky skein of that amazing hair.

"I *mean* it," she answered, and turned to look at him. She held his face in her hands and looked into his eyes. Her expression was serious.

"I pray for you *every* day, Brad," she whispered. "I pray a *long* time. I pray that one day, you really will understand. That you'll know God for *yourself*."

He sighed, and looked down at her. It was adorably sweet, and it melted his heart; and it simultaneously made him intensely uncomfortable. So he'd stopped Jemima's mouth with a kiss.

That sweet, silky mouth had made all the words slide away, made them the only two people in the world, made his hands itch to wander, but he forced himself to exercise restraint. *That* part had always been hard, and now it was approaching torture, but something else, something stronger, held him back.

Love, yes – but more than love. The dawning suspicion that the delight of discovery was keenest, most intense, when it was achingly *gradual.*

He was falling in love with Jemima by delicious inches, a

little more every time they were together. He felt privileged to witness her delight as she turned her face to the world for the first time – like a flower opening up to the sunlight. She was blooming into womanhood before his eyes, like a young rose.

Brad looked down at her as their lips parted. She beamed up at him, laughing, her beautiful eyes alight.

He wanted to be the one to carry her through that last door. It would be a supremely tender moment, and even in imagination, it was precious to him. He'd planned it a hundred times, but had always turned away.

Because he was coming more and more to the conclusion that he wanted to marry Jemima. And for once in his life, he wanted to be unselfish.

He wanted to give Jemima what *she* had imagined.

CHAPTER SEVENTEEN

That evening Brad lay on his bed, shirtless, wearing a rumpled pair of plaid pajama bottoms. It was almost 2 a.m., but he was wide awake – smoking and assessing his plans for the future.

He shook his head. A year ago, if anyone had told him that he'd *long* to get married, he would've laughed. He was probably the world's unlikeliest candidate for matrimony.

He'd never felt the smallest temptation to follow his parents' example. Their marriage had been a case study in dysfunction. His memories of his father were few and dim – a pair of unhappy blue eyes, looking down at him, hands that held him carelessly and echoes of shouted obscenities and slamming doors.

His father had been a loud, unpleasant haunting in their home. And then one day, just like *that*, he'd disappeared like a ghost, leaving Brad and his mother to live in an ever-widening pool of silence.

Brad blew a contemplative smoke ring toward the ceiling, thinking that it really was kind of a miracle that he didn't have a complex toward women, after all his Mom had put him through. Her meth addiction had turned him into a seven-year-old adult who knew way too much about booze and drugs and whose biggest talent wasn't baseball or soccer, like other kids, but a knack for hustling money from people who didn't pay attention.

His mom had spent most of his childhood in a drugged stupor, and when the state had finally stepped in and taken him away from her, he'd felt nothing but sorry for her – and relieved for himself.

A few months later, she was dead.

He'd lived with his grandmother for awhile, and he'd been fond of her. She had been a stern, strong old woman with a booming voice and no patience for nonsense. But she'd provided him a stable home, and as much affection as it was in her nature to show.

She'd encouraged him to find a trade, to start work, to make something of himself and to stop trying to take advantage of other people. He smiled to himself. That teaching had only *half* taken. He'd been doing it for so long that he didn't know how to stop.

But when he'd had a chance to get a scholarship from a local school, his grandmother had encouraged him to apply. And when he'd won, she had put up some of her own money to send him. Yeah, she'd kind of saved him.

She was dead now, too, and he missed her.

He inhaled deeply, and the embers of the cigarette glowed.

Now, he'd met the Duchess, and maybe had a chance to build something like a family with her. If he could convince her to marry him, and to live with him.

Jemima couldn't possibly be the angel that she *seemed* to be. He wasn't *that* far gone. But she was still the most unselfish, sweet-tempered person he'd ever met. Her beauty made those qualities even rarer, and more to be admired.

It was kind of like that verse he'd read out of the hotel room Bible, the one about the good woman who was worth more than rubies. The writer might've been talking about Jemima. She really was a rare jewel.

If only she wasn't so *religious*. That, *that* was the only thing that still stood between them, and it was the one thing that might still ruin his chances.

Their last few months together had been nothing short of

amazing, and he was tempted to call them a success. Jemima had told him that she loved him. She gave the impression that she was walking in a dream when they were together. She'd expressed nothing but delight when she was with him, and had been appreciative of even his smallest effort to please her.

When he took her out to experience a world she didn't know, she didn't seem to suffer culture shock. She'd never objected to any place he'd taken her. She had a childlike openness to new experiences, as long as they weren't forbidden by her church.

He frowned, sputtered smoke, and tamped out his spent cigarette.

But in spite of all of that, he had the sense that his relationship with Jemima had reached an impasse. He reached over to the nightstand and pulled out a fresh cigarette.

After weeks of retail romance, he had to conclude that flowers and candy and gifts hadn't been enough to move her.

Jemima was humoring him, he could *feel* it. She never expressed any curiosity about the Englisch world. She never asked questions about it, she never begged him to show her more of it, and she still wore her traditional dress, even when they went out together.

In spite of all his efforts to win her over to the world, Jemima hadn't shown the slightest sign that she'd be willing to abandon her beliefs, or leave her home for him.

In short – he was *in trouble*.

He sighed. Every time he'd tried to gently suggest a different life for her, she'd looked at him with that blank, polite expression that promptly ended the discussion. He didn't get the sense that she was trying to be coy – she was the most genuine person he'd ever met.

Maybe the trouble was that he'd been too general, too vague. Maybe she didn't yet understand *exactly* what he'd been trying to say.

He chewed his lip. If he asked her to *elope* with him, to leave her home, there'd be no doubt in her mind what he was asking. Her choices would be clear.

It was a long shot, he knew that, but he told himself that it wasn't *impossible*, that some people *did* leave the Amish church. There were whole *TV shows* built around them.

But on the other hand – it would be risky. If Jemima said *no*, there would be no alternative, nothing left for him to suggest. There was no way that he could be part of her world.

It would be *over* between them.

And that was why he was chain smoking in his bed at 2 a.m.

Brad sighed, crushed out his cigarette, and turned off the bedside light. Then he folded his arms behind his head and stared up at the dark ceiling for awhile.

On an impulse, he prayed: *God, if you exist, I could use a little help here.*

Then he laughed at himself, shook his head, and closed his eyes.

CHAPTER EIGHTEEN

Jemima slipped into the house through the back door and closed it softly behind her. She had just returned from a date with Brad. It was after midnight, and her shoes were dangling from her hands as she tiptoed up the stairs and down the long moonlit hall to her own bedroom door.

She slipped safely inside and placed her shoes carefully under the bed. Then she trimmed the lamp, and lit it, preparing to undress.

But to her surprise, she wasn't the only one up late. There was a soft tap at the door. Jemima's heart quickened in alarm, and she padded to the door and pressed her face to the crack.

"Who is it?" she whispered.

"It's *me,* stupid."

Jemima opened the door, Deborah stood there in her nightgown. She pushed in as soon as the door was open.

Jemima closed the door behind her, and looked at her sister with some irritation. "What is it? Why are you up at this hour?"

Deborah gave her a shrewd look. "I could ask *you* the same question! You've sure been sneaking out a lot lately. I'm surprised how much you're pushing your luck."

"It's late, Deborah," Jemima told her. "What do you *want*?"

"You're skating on such thin ice that I just want to review some facts before I skate out on the ice with you. You've decided on the *Englisch* boy, that's your final decision? You're *sure* you're not sneaking out with Samuel or Joseph or Mark?"

Jemima pinched her lips into a thin line. It was a crazy hour of the night to have this conversation, it was none of Deborah's business *who* she loved, and she had no idea why Deborah was interested *anyway.*

But she didn't dare tell her so. Deborah had too much *on* her now to be challenged. She took a deep breath, and nodded. "I've decided. It's *Brad.*"

Deborah looked oddly relieved. "Well, what are you going to do with the others? It won't take long for word to get out that you've given away all your money. All three of those guys are going to be coming here to court you again. You're not going to be able to put them off for long."

Jemima bit her lip. Deborah was right, but for the wrong reason. She should've told her friends the truth as soon as she knew it herself. It was cruel to keep them in suspense.

"I'm not going to try to put them off," she answered. "I'm going to tell them all. It isn't fair to them to delay."

"I agree," Deborah mused. "Go ahead and tell them – the sooner the better! But it's going to be harder to meet your Englisch boy on the sly once you've cut them all loose," she added. "You have to be prepared for that. Mamm is holding Daed off because she thinks you're meeting *Mark* or *Samuel* every weekend. She's *covering* for you – or haven't you noticed?"

Jemima gasped and looked at her sister in dismay. Deborah shook her head.

"You really *are* in your own little world, aren't you?" she marveled. "But you better wake up quick, if you don't want things to blow up on you. You have to be extra careful. If Daed catches you with that Englisch boy, *then* there'll be fireworks!"

Jemima shuddered. "Don't even *say* it!" she murmured

fervently.

Deborah bit one thumbnail. "Daed might kill him," shrugged. "I'd give it fifty-fifty odds."

Jemima sat down on the bed, and brushed her hair a little harder than necessary. "You all talk like Brad is some, some kind of *housebreaker*. He's a *fine* man. He says he wants to learn about becoming *Amish*," she said.

Deborah glanced at her, but said nothing.

"He really *is* interested!" Jemima added defiantly.

"So *you're* not going to be the one to change?" Deborah frowned. "I thought you were going to, I don't know, run away with him and get married and live with the Englisch. Do you really think he could live like us?"

Jemima stopped brushing and stared into space. She really didn't know the answer to *that* question.

"If I were you, which God forbid," Deborah said devoutly, "I'd be thinking about how I was going to meet Brad after you set all those other boys free, because Mamm will be so mad at you for throwing them away that not *only* will she stop holding Daed back, she'll be watching you *herself*."

Jemima's eyes widened. She hadn't thought of *that*.

"Oh, *Debby*," she gasped.

"*Mmm-hmm.* So, you need to be setting things up *now*,

before you let the others go, so Mamm can okay your outings before she knows what they're really *for*."

Jemima hung her head sadly. "Oh, Deborah, you make it sound so – so *sneaky*."

"Do you want to see him, or not?"

"Oh, I *have* to see him!"

Deborah sighed and looked at her ruefully. "You are my sister, Jemima, but *honestly*. God knew what he was doing when he made you beautiful," she mused, "because you are the woolly lamb of the *world*. You're lucky I'm here to hold your hand, or things would've gone bad for you long before now."

Jemima looked up at that, and eyed her sister doubtfully. "Why *are* you helping me?" she asked. "You never gave me an explanation that made any sense. Why do you care if Brad and I get together?"

Deborah gave her a shrewd look, as if she was weighing her answer. After a long moment, she shrugged.

"Because I'm in love with *Mark*, that's why!"

"*What?*"

"If you'd been paying any attention at all, you would've seen it," Deborah told her, shaking her head.

"Oh, Debby, I didn't dream—" Jemima wailed softly.

"Why didn't you *tell* me?"

Deborah gave her such a wry look that Jemima felt her own face going hot. "*Oh – yes.* I guess it would have been – very awkward."

"I know it's a hopeless case," Deborah sighed forlornly, flopping down on the bed, "but I figured that if you didn't want him *yourself,* maybe you could put in a good word for me – here and there."

Jemima pursed her lips and nodded. *Now* the mystery was solved. *That* explained everything. But, even if Deborah *was* a scheming little imp, and bad-tempered and rude and not above lying, and lazy and manipulative and generally not to be trusted – she still *was* her sister.

Though to tell the truth, she didn't know if there was much good she could honestly tell Mark about Deborah. But – then again – maybe Debby had been all those wrong-headed things because she'd been in love with Mark, and had to watch him fall in love with someone *else.* It must have been *very* trying.

She decided to give Deborah the benefit of the doubt.

"Well, Debby," she said softly, "here's what I can do, and I think it will work out the best. I'll tell you what kind of girl Mark likes, and maybe you can – try to be more like *that.*

"Mark is very conservative. He likes a girl who has a *sweet, pleasant personality*, who says *nice* things about other people, who doesn't *complain*."

Deborah gave her a dry look, but said nothing.

"He likes to be the one to lead. He likes modesty, and a girl who holds to traditional ways." She gave Deborah a meaningful look.

"And most of all – *Mark hates lying*, and can smell it a *mile* off!"

"*Hmmm*," Deborah said primly. "I guess we're *both* in trouble, then."

CHAPTER NINETEEN

Jemima sat sewing on the couch in the living room. The sound of a horse's hooves on the road outside made Rachel walk to the front door and peek out the glass pane, but Jemima continued to sew.

"Why, it looks like Joseph Beiler," she murmured. Then she pursed her lips, and turned to her daughter.

"But that wasn't news to you, was it, Mima?" she asked, and then nodded knowingly. "Yes, I can see that it wasn't. I'll make sure that no one interrupts the two of you," she smiled.

Jemima didn't look up. "Thank you, Mamm," she murmured.

But after her mother was gone, Jemima sighed deeply. She'd decided to take Deborah's advice and break it off with her admirers, at last.

She'd written Joseph a short note a few days ago, asking him to come to the house. She dreaded this meeting, and hated to hurt Joseph – sweet, *smitten* Joseph – but she couldn't let him go on thinking that she was going to marry him.

She heard him park the buggy into the yard, and after a few minutes, the sound of his footsteps crunched over the snow. She almost smiled. Joseph had such *big* feet.

The porch steps creaked under him, and his knock at the door sounded loud in the stillness. Jemima put away her sewing, and rose to answer it.

Joseph was standing in the doorway, his dark eyes shining. His cheeks were rosy with the cold, and Jemima stared at him wistfully. He really was *so* handsome.

She tried to smile. "Come in, Joseph," she murmured, and held the door open.

Joseph took off his hat, and scraped the snow off his boots politely, and stepped in.

"Come and sit with me," she invited, and motioned toward the couch.

He sat down quickly, and she sat down beside him. He

searched her face with his eyes, and his smile faltered.

"What's this I see?" he said quietly, and took her chin gently in his hand. "You look – *sad*."

Jemima turned her head, and his hand fell away. "I *am* sad, Joseph," she answered softly. "I have to tell you something that will hurt you, and I hate to do it. We've been such good friends, and I wouldn't hurt you for the world."

His eyes registered confusion. "What could make my *maus* sad?" he asked, and reached for her hand, but she wouldn't let him take it.

Jemima closed her eyes. She couldn't bear to see his reaction.

"I asked you here to tell you – that I can't marry you, Joseph," she said simply. "I can't let you make plans, and buy a house, and – and go on thinking that we're engaged."

There was no sound at all. Jemima took a deep breath, and when she opened her eyes, Joseph was looking down at his hands. Her heart ached for him.

He shook his head, once. "How can that be?" he asked brokenly. "How? After all that's passed between us?"

"Joseph, I-I've always been so *fond* of you, but – I've searched my own heart, and I'm not in love with you, at least, not enough to be your wife. I can't marry you. It wouldn't be fair," she whispered.

"But – but why *not?*" he asked.

If it had been a less painful conversation, she might almost have sputtered out a fond laugh. Joseph was so sweet and naïve – like a child, sometimes.

When she didn't answer, he looked up, and there was a tinge of anger in his eyes. "There's someone else, isn't there, Mima?" she asked.

Tears blurred her eyes, and she looked away. He nodded.

"You don't have to tell me – I can *see* it," he growled. "Who is it, Mima? *Who* stole you away from me?"

"Joseph, please—"

"No, Mima, I have to know. Because I'm not going to give up so easy. I'm going to fight to keep what's mine!"

"Joseph—"

He stood up suddenly, looked up at the ceiling, then down at her. "If you won't tell me, I'll find out myself. No matter what I have to do, this isn't over. Somehow, I'll make you change your mind, Mima."

Jemima put her hands over her face and shook her head. "Oh, Joseph, *don't,*" she cried, but he had already stalked out. The sounds of his receding footsteps were followed by the crack of a buggy whip, and the sound of his horse's hooves clattering over the snow.

Jemima turned into the sofa cushions and cried brokenheartedly. After awhile her mother came in softly, took one look, and sat down beside her on the couch. Jemima went wordlessly into her arms.

"So it wasn't Joseph," her mother soothed, rocking her back and forth. "My poor girl. Telling a friend you're *not* going to marry him is one of the hardest things a woman must do."

She turned her head and kissed her daughter. "But I know that you did it as kindly as you could, my Mima," she soothed.

"Oh, Mamm," Jemima sobbed, "you should have heard him! He wouldn't accept what I told him! He says he's not giving up so easy, and he's going to *fight*!"

"He'll come to accept it, Mima," her mother answered calmly. "He will, eventually. Right now he's hurt and confused. But when he's had time, he'll be all right. You'll see."

"I feel so awful," Jemima sobbed, "like I've *murdered* him somehow. I don't know how I'm going to do this—"

Jemima gasped, and caught herself just in time. She had been on the brink of saying, *I don't know how I'm going to do this – two more times.*

"You've been so sought after, Mima," her mother sighed. "And this is the hard part. But once it's over, the easy part comes. The joyous time comes, when you can say *yes* to the boy you love."

Jemima stared over her mother's shoulder, wide-eyed. "Will it?" she whispered.

"*Of course*, dear," her mother soothed.

CHAPTER TWENTY

Jemima gave herself a few days to recover from her painful parting from Joseph. She spent her days in quiet, repetitive work that required no mental concentration. She washed and ironed, she mopped and dusted, and she helped her mother make dough for baking.

She shunned society, and whenever she was able, she stole away to her own bedroom, or her father's study. She had never felt in such urgent need of prayer; but she also felt a growing sense of guilt over her delay.

She planned to tell Samuel next. But telling *him* was going to be even harder than telling *Joseph*.

Because she loved Samuel, had loved him since they were children. It was impossible *not* to love the mischievous blond boy with the twinkling blue eyes and ready charm. He'd been a fixture at their house for years – swinging his legs over their porch rail, sitting at their table, snitching cake from the fridge.

Filling the house with the sound of his jokes and laughter.

It was going to be *lonely* when he wasn't there anymore. But Jemima told herself that such thoughts were selfish. So she gathered her strength and mailed Samuel a note.

He arrived on the afternoon of the next day. It was a greeting-card November afternoon, with big flakes of snow falling from a leaden sky.

She had chosen to talk to him in her father's cozy study, where they could be alone. She'd prepared cups of hot coffee and built a crackling fire, in the forlorn hope that the *warmth* at least would be of some comfort to him.

She sat in the study, listening to the sounds of his progress to the house and then the jaunty rapping that was his familiar knock at the door. The sound of her mother's greeting, and his own respectful reply.

The sound of his footsteps across the floorboards of the living room. Samuel had a quick, light step.

The sound of a second rapping – softer this time – on the study door.

She lifted her head. "Come in, Samuel."

The door opened and Samuel filled the space inside it. He was holding his hat, and his mop of blond hair caught the firelight and glistened like gold. Jemima looked up at him wistfully, forced herself to smile, and motioned toward her father's chair.

"Please sit down, Samuel. I have coffee, if you're cold."

Samuel accepted the cup gratefully, warmed his hands on it and took an appreciative sip. "Thanks Mima," he grinned. "It's cold outside. Coffee just hits the spot."

She let him warm himself. She listened wistfully as he told a funny story about a fox that burst out of the bushes and spooked his horse on the way over, and how he'd almost set a world record, until he could get it under control. She smiled sadly, watching him, thinking: *It's the last time.*

When he'd finished his story she smiled, and bowed her head, and prayed: *Lord, help me do this. I don't know if I can.*

Samuel laughed again, and took another sip of coffee. "So why did you ask me over, Mima? A note, too! It sounded *official.*"

He turned to look at her, and the smile gradually faded from his eyes.

Jemima prayed again, and looked up into his eyes.

"I wanted to talk to you alone, Samuel," she murmured. "I

need to let you know – that I've made a decision." Her eyes filled with tears.

"I'm *sorry*, Samuel," she went on, "but I can't marry you. I'm in love with another man."

Samuel's beautiful blue eyes widened. Jemima watched as a dozen emotions chased each other across their swirling surface – hurt, disbelief, shock, and – loss. Samuel bowed his blond head, and his hands hung limply over the edge of the armrests.

"Samuel, I'm *so*—"

His sandy brows rushed together. "Who is it, Mima?" he asked huskily. "Not Joseph, surely. So it must be Mark."

Jemima dropped her gaze to her lap and said nothing, but to her relief, Samuel didn't press her.

"I hope the two of you are – very happy together. I mean that, Mima." He turned to her, leaned over, and kissed her cheek.

Jemima put a hand to his face as he kissed her. "Oh, Samuel, I hope that when – when some *time* has passed, we can go back to being friends," she whispered, turning pleading eyes to his face. "I've always been *so* fond of you."

He looked down, shook his head, and smiled crookedly. "It might not be right away, Mima," he said softly.

"Just so long as we *can* still be friends," she replied. "But I can't see it being very long, Samuel," she murmured fondly. "You're too sweet and handsome to be without a girl for long."

He looked at her and smiled gallantly. "You're probably right, Mima," he rallied, and in spite of her tears, Jemima laughed a little.

"I know I'm right. Miriam Zook has had her eye on you for years," she told him, "and I'll probably still be jealous if I see the two of you together. But I'll just have to live with it."

Samuel looked up at her. "Mark is a lucky man," he told her ruefully. "I hope he understands that."

Jemima looked down and made no reply.

Samuel nodded. "I hope you won't think I'm rude if I leave a little early," he told her. "I think I need to go home and lick my wounds for awhile." He turned, looked at her affectionately, and caressed her cheek with his hand.

"Best of luck, Mima."

"And you, Samuel," Jemima told him, with tears in her eyes.

She watched him as he walked out of the room, so tall and straight and handsome, and was stabbed by a sense of terrible loss. There had been no other way – but *even so*.

The tiny crackle of the fireplace suddenly sounded loud in his absence.

Jemima listened for Samuel's voice as he said his farewells to her parents in the living room. She heard the screen door creak open and slap shut. She heard Samuel's slow footsteps fade gradually across the yard.

The thought that she would never hear them coming back, was almost too sad for her to bear.

Dinner that evening was subdued and mostly silent. Jemima was oppressed with a heavy sense of sadness and said almost nothing, and Deborah spoke only on command, but Jacob and Rachel exchanged knowing glances. Rachel maintained a silence that was respectful of Jemima's melancholy mood, but it was clear that she was *glowing* with suppressed excitement.

Deborah's wary eyes flitted occasionally to her mother's face, and then to her father's, and then to Jemima's – but she said nothing.

CHAPTER TWENTY-ONE

The next morning after breakfast, Rachel bustled around the house, humming happily. Occasionally her voice welled up into song.

"Sister dear, never fear, for the Savior is near, With His hand He will lead you along; And the way that is dark Christ will graciously clear, And your mourning shall turn to a song."

Jemima looked up from her mending and met her mother's happy eyes. Rachel dimpled at her, and turned back to her work.

"For that home is so bright, and is almost in sight,

And I trust in my heart you'll go there."

Jemima lowered her eyes submissively, but couldn't endure her mother's cheerfulness for long. She excused herself, pleading a headache, and went upstairs to her bedroom where she could think in peace.

She closed her bedroom door behind her and walked to the window overlooking the countryside. The porch roof, the yard and the hills beyond were covered with snow, and in the predawn light, they had taken on a pale blue cast. Here and there, in the folds of the hills, smoke rose faintly from their neighbors' chimneys.

It was nearing Thanksgiving, and Jemima knew that she had *many* things to be thankful for. But it was hard to remember them, because the dread of her final duty weighed on her like a lead weight.

She had to tell Mark that she couldn't marry him, and it would be the hardest thing she'd ever done in her life. Of all her suitors, she was the closest to Mark. She and Mark understood one another so well that sometimes they didn't even need to say anything.

Some people expected them to get married because of that. Some people had *already* assumed that they were engaged.

And that was why she had to talk to Mark, whether she felt like it, or not. Otherwise, her mother might let slip what she was clearly thinking, and *that* would be terrible.

Jemima leaned her brow against the freezing window pane, praying for guidance; but the sky didn't open, and no clear instructions formed in her mind.

But when she opened her eyes, a small, dark figure below made her stand up straight. It was a man in dark coat and hat, walking across the yard to the porch.

Jemima's heart sank. *It was Mark.*

She closed her eyes. She didn't need to ask why he'd come, she knew it in her bones. He'd come to get his answer, and it was just like him to take the initiative. He never could endure waiting.

The living room was directly below her, and she could hear and *feel* Mark climbing the porch steps, stomping the snow off of his boots, and knocking at the door.

Jemima brushed her hand across her eyes, and smoothed back her hair. She had to get Mark out of the house, or her parents would know at once that they weren't engaged, and weren't *going* to be, and she wasn't ready for that scene. It would also spare Mark the necessity of having to make small talk with her family.

She quickly put on her heavy cape, then turned and went swiftly downstairs.

"Well, good morning Mark!" Rachel was saying.

"Good morning," Mark replied. His eyes met Jemima's

over Rachel's shoulder as she came quickly down the stairs.

"Good morning, Mark," Jemima said, as cheerfully as she could. She turned her face to her mother's. "Mark promised to take me on a buggy ride this morning through the snow," she smiled.

Mark's expression revealed no hint of surprise, and Jemima blessed him silently.

"Why, that sounds lovely," Rachel smiled, and kissed her daughter's cheek. "Try to be back by lunch!"

"We will," Jemima said over her shoulder. She took Mark's arm, and shuttled him out of the front door almost as fast as he'd come in.

They walked down the porch steps, and across the yard, and Mark helped her up into the buggy before asking: "What was that all about?"

Jemima couldn't meet his eyes. "I wanted to talk to you alone," she replied softly. "I wanted to get out of the house."

Mark climbed up into the buggy and turned to her. "Where do you want to go?"

"It doesn't have to be far," Jemima answered, and he shook the reins.

They turned right off the lane, and the buggy rolled over the snow better than any car could have. Soon the high banks blocked the King farmhouse from sight, and the last window faded from view.

Mark pulled the buggy around the big curve, and past the fallow field where, unbeknownst to him, Brad had cut many a path coming to see her. They rounded the curve, and to Jemima's chagrin, Mark parked the buggy in the very spot where Brad always parked his truck.

He pulled the horse to a stop, looped the reins over the dash. He sat without saying anything for a few long moments. Finally he turned to her, with those sapphire eyes that saw so clearly. Jemima felt her throat tightening, because the truth was in those eyes.

Mark knew.

"I just thought I'd come over. I got tired of waiting, Mima," he said at last. "Better to just get it over with."

She couldn't meet his eyes. "*I'm sorry,* Mark," she whispered.

He was still looking at her steadily. "It's the Englisch guy, isn't it, Mima," he asked, "the reporter?"

She still couldn't meet his eyes, and couldn't deny it. He nodded.

"I had a feeling," he said slowly. "I could tell by the way you were acting. You never acted that way with me, and I never saw you act that way with anybody else. And when I saw you *looking* at him in the courtroom that day, I knew you'd decided. When you wouldn't talk to any of us after, I was sure."

Jemima shook her head. "I'm sorry, Mark," she whispered. "I should've told you sooner, I should've let you know. It's just that – I didn't know myself at first. It happened so fast, and I still don't know how it will end. It makes no sense to love an Englisch boy, but I can't help it. I *can't*. I'm sorry."

He looked at her, and his expression didn't convey whether he was feeling sad or angry or merely empty.

He reached out and took her hand. "I won't lie, Mima. It hurts. But I don't blame you, and I'm not mad. You have a right to fall in love with any guy you like. Even if he's – not me."

Jemima looked up at him through red eyes. "Don't hate me, Mark. I never meant to hurt you!"

He looked faintly surprised. "Hate you, Mima? No, that's impossible. I've already tried, and I can't do it."

"Oh, *Mark*!" she sobbed, and he lifted a gloved hand, and brushed the tears off her cheek.

"A girl as beautiful as you should never have to cry," he told her softly. "And if it doesn't work out between you and that guy, Mima, you know where I am," he told her.

He raised his dark brows and smiled.

"One last time," he murmured, and before she could react,

Mark's lips were warm on hers – as always, communicating with actions what he could not say in words.

CHAPTER TWENTY-TWO

Brad picked up his jacket and shrugged into it. It was freezing outside, and he'd forgotten to bring his lunch, so it was time to make the punishing trek from the front doors of the *Ledger*, to the warm, steamy interior of Mama Wong's Chopstix Heaven, two blocks down on Main.

He shouldered through the revolving door in the lobby and was hit immediately with an icy blast. He dug his hands into his pockets and put his head down against the wind.

He got about halfway there, and had to wait at a street crossing for the light to change. There was a jewelry store on the corner, just a little hole in the wall, really, but the display in the window caught his eye.

There was a delicate diamond ring glittering under a spotlight. It was tiny, elfin, and as it turned back and forth on a revolving stand, it threw off sparks of pure white light.

Brad stared at it, and kept staring, even after the light changed. But when the people waiting beside him started to move, he followed quickly. It was too cold to window shop.

Brad crossed the windy street, dove into the restaurant on the other side, and was glad when the heavy doors of Mama Wong's closed behind him. Warmth and noise reached out and enveloped him. He followed the waitress to a booth in the back, pulled out his smart phone, and settled in.

The waitress soon reappeared with warm coffee and a menu, and he ordered a big bowl of noodle soup and a platter of Mongolian beef. The girl took his menu and disappeared.

Brad checked his messages, searching for a call from a Lancaster County prefix, but there was none. He sighed and scrolled back up to the top.

Junk, junk, spam. More spam, junk, one laughable email from an English "estate lawyer," a threatening message from Delores.

He backed up and read that one.

Brad, I don't know why you're evil with Eddie, but if you send him out to take photos of a sewage treatment plant, you'd better have a good reason next time, or it's coming out of your paycheck.

He grinned and scrolled down further. More spam, a magazine article he'd never read, and – an email from Sheila. His brows went up. He hadn't expected to hear from *her* again.

The waitress returned with the soup and the platter. She set them on the table in front of him. They looked delicious, and they were fragrant of soy sauce, shallots and braised beef. Brad turned off the phone and turned his attention to his lunch.

A few minutes later, after he'd taken the edge off his hunger, his mind began to wander again. To Jemima, as it inevitably did, when there wasn't some other urgent interruption.

He wondered what she was doing at that moment, and wished for the thousandth time that he could call her, but she'd refused to accept a cell phone, refused even to use one. Some silliness about being *connected to the world*. Which, apparently, was a mortal sin.

He frowned. The cell phone was a small thing, but it was one more disturbing sign that he was in trouble. It was a reminder that every time Jemima had to choose between him and her religion – he *lost*.

He pulled his mouth to one side. Out of all the women in the world, he had to fall in love with the most religious one. It was maddening. He'd met nuns who were more liberal than Jemima.

His expression softened. But Jemima was also the most beautiful girl on the planet, and the sweetest. And – she really loved him. Even if she hadn't told him so, he would've known. He could tell.

He could *feel* it.

He took a sip of coffee. He was ready to make his next move, but he had to go carefully. He was at a disadvantage in many ways: he was from the wrong culture, he held the wrong beliefs, he had the wrong career, and probably had the wrong *personality* thrown into the pot, too – just for good measure.

He shouldn't have had a snowball's chance with a girl like Jemima. But somehow, miraculously, he did. And he didn't intend to waste that chance.

He patted his lips with his napkin, motioned for the waitress and paid his bill.

He was going to go back to Lancaster County, red roses in hand, and pitch Jemima like he'd never pitched anyone in his life. Harder than he'd pitched the college admissions board, harder than he'd pitched Delores…harder than he'd even pitched *Jemima* before.

He was going to make love to her eyes, to her mind, to her heart. He was going to make the best pitch he'd ever made in his life – the best case a man ever made to a woman.

Because he was going in with two strikes against him –

and he knew it.

He put his card back into his wallet, turned up the collar on his coat, and shouldered out through the restaurant's big double doors. He walked to the corner and waited, shivering, until the light changed.

He paused for a moment in front of the jewelers', looked at the delicate ring sparkling in the window – and then walked inside.

CHAPTER TWENTY-THREE

Brad parked the truck in his usual spot, put on the parking brake and killed the motor. It was a few minutes before midnight, and Jemima was expecting him. He reached for a glossy cardboard bag on the driver's seat, reached in, and pocketed a small velvet box.

Then he grabbed a bouquet of red roses, and another box of the painted chocolates that Jemima had loved, and stepped outside.

The cold pinched his cheeks, his nose and his fingers. He sputtered, and could see his own breath in the frosty air. Lucky for him, there was a bright moon.

He chose to take the road this time, figuring that no one would be out in the snow at that hour. He also had no desire to wade through the brown brambles when he wanted to look his very best.

He walked briskly, and within minutes he was on the moonlit porch. He rapped cautiously on the front door, and it opened instantly. Jemima was standing there, smiling. She was framed by the muted light of a single lamp.

"Come in," she whispered.

They had decided to risk the house this time, partly because it was too cold for anything else, and partly because Brad had the strong sense that a marriage proposal should be made from the warmest, most favorable spot possible.

He held out the roses and smiled. "These are for you, Duchess."

"*Oh, Brad!*" She leaned over to kiss his cheek. "They're *beautiful!*"

She took his hand and led him to the couch, and they sat down. She leaned close and whispered in his ear: "We have to be *very* quiet. Deborah is watching upstairs, but if someone comes, we won't have much time."

"I'm not worried," he told her, and smiled again – as big and bright as he could.

"I was out shopping the other day, and happened across

these," he told her, and presented the box of chocolates. Jemima giggled and kissed him again.

He pulled off her cap, tangled his hands in her hair, and mussed it so badly that she pulled away from him, laughing, and pulled out the pins herself. That red gold tumbled over her shoulders and glowed in the lamp's warm light.

He played with a strand of her hair. "I can't stay away, Duchess," he told her. "You're the most beautiful woman I've ever met."

She colored, and dropped her gaze, but he took her chin in his hand and made her look at him. He held her eyes.

"*I love you, Jemima.*"

The smile faded from her lips and her eyes widened. She stared at him, searched his eyes.

"You don't have to check to see if it's true," he reassured her tenderly. "I mean it. Can't you tell? Doesn't *this* give you a hint?"

He took her by the shoulders and kissed her savagely, felt her gasp, and melt in his arms, and then open up to him like the rose that she was. She began to respond, to return his kisses, even to—

He checked himself, closed his eyes, pressed his cheek to hers.

"*Do you love me, Duchess?*" he breathed.

"Oh, darling – with all my heart!" she breathed. She twined her arms around his neck, as if to prove it, and pressed her lips to his ear.

It was a *good* sign. He took a deep breath, and decided to go for it.

"I came here tonight to ask you a question, Duchess," he smiled. "I hope you'll be kind to me."

He turned and kissed her again, and she murmured uselessly, and then put her hands in his hair.

When they parted again, they were both breathless. Brad smiled, and looked at her, and reached into his pocket. He opened his palm, and presented the little velvet box, and was gratified to see her beautiful eyes widen.

"Open it, Duchess," he told her. "This is for *you.*"

She took the box reverently in her hands, and opened the little lid. Then she gasped and put a hand to her mouth.

Her voice was almost inaudible. *"Oh, Brad!"*

He leaned forward and put his hand on hers. "Will you *marry* me, Duchess?"

Those magical green eyes glowed with unbelievable fire. They met his, pooled with sparkling emerald tears.

"Oh, *yes,*" she breathed fervently. "Yes, Brad. *Yes!*"

He sputtered with relief, cracked into a wide smile, put his arms around her, held her tight and rested his head against hers. *He couldn't believe it. It was a miracle!*

They kissed again, softly, deliciously. It was going to be the first of a lifetime of kisses, a glorious...

"Hissht!"

Jemima pulled back from him suddenly and turned to look at the stairs. A sharp, sly face appeared for an instant, and then was gone. It was followed by the unmistakable thunder of heavy footsteps, and they were travelling fast.

Jemima turned to him. "It's my father," she gasped, "Go, *quick*! I don't know *what* he'll do if he finds—"

Brad stood abruptly, but couldn't bring himself to leave. He'd only *just* won Jemima's agreement to marry him, and he figured it was bad luck to begin their engagement by treating Jemima to the sight of his back, running away.

Even if running away made *perfect sense.*

Jemima leapt up and clutched his arm just as Jacob King burst onto the scene like a giant from some fairy tale. His red hair was sticking out at all angles, he was barefoot, and—

Brad goggled at him. He was wearing a nightshirt. Even their pajamas were from the 1800s!

Jacob's outraged eyes took in the scene – Jemima's flowing hair, all undone, her rumpled dress, the bouquet of roses, the chocolates – and then they turned to *him.*

Jacob's red eyebrows descended in a thunderous scowl. His face gathered darkness, and he drew himself up until he towered over them like a storm cloud.

"I *knew* something strange was going on!" he burst out. "So! This is what my daughter does when she thinks her parents are asleep! She *cavorts* with a strange Englischer – in my very *living room!*"

Jemima burst into sobs and cast herself on her father's chest. She raised her hands to his neck, beseeching him in anguished German, but Jacob put her aside without a glance.

He turned his awful gaze full-bore on Brad.

Brad squared his shoulders, met the giant's eyes, and put out his hands in a calming gesture. "Mr. King, before you jump to *conclusions—*"

For answer, two massive hands grabbed him by his coat lapels and hoisted him up into the air. Brad suddenly found himself looking down into Jacob King's blazing blue eyes, and Jemima's horrified green ones, from just under the ceiling.

He dangled there for what seemed like eternity. Jemima was on her father's chest again, shrieking the word *verlobter* over and over again, to no effect, when a pretty blonde woman hurried into the room, dressed in a nightgown and a shawl.

She looked up at him with horrified eyes, rushed to the red

giant's side, and spoke to him in urgent German. For the first time, Jacob's menacing expression cracked. He turned his head and spoke a few terse words to her in German, and then raised his eyes.

Brad looked down into them and ventured diplomacy. "Mr. King, there's no reason for you to be angry. Jemima and I are *engaged.*"

The word seemed to set his future father-in-law on fire. He jerked him higher, and his head bumped smartly against the ceiling.

"No daughter of *mine* is going to marry with a weaselly little Englischer reporter who makes his name off the misfortunes of others!" he thundered, "a fortune-hunting, fame-hungry, night-sneaking, fast-talking, dirt-eating, *schmutzig, wehleidig kleiner wurm!*"

With that, the red giant surged across the room, kicked open the door, took a running start across the porch and flung him into the blind night like a sack of potatoes. Brad sailed through the icy air, burst through a snowdrift, rolled over the edge of the lawn, fell onto the driveway, rolled a few more times, and came to a lumpy halt.

He raised his head painfully and looked back at the house through his hair. The door was still open, and he could see Jemima in it.

"*Brad*!" she shrieked, and made as if to run out after him, but someone pulled her back inside, and the door closed with a *bang*.

CHAPTER TWENTY-FOUR

The next morning Brad rose early, showered, shaved, bandaged his many scrapes and scuffs, and dressed smartly. Then he called in sick to work, and drove right back out to the King farm.

He pulled the truck up into the driveway, got out, walked stubbornly across the lawn to the front door, and rapped on it like a fearless man.

The sly-faced girl opened the door. She goggled at him for an instant, then drawled: "Well, you're brave – I'll say *that* for you."

"Where's Jemima?"

"Upstairs."

"Go tell her I'm here."

The girl shook her head and disappeared. Brad looked back over his shoulder, toward the workshop. The sound of vigorous hammering wafted through the open door.

There was a soft rushing sound inside, and Brad turned just in time to receive Jemima on his chest. She threw herself into his arms and covered his face with kisses.

"Oh my *darling!*" she cried, "Are you hurt?" She ran her small fingers over his face, and her mouth crumpled at the sight of a scrape across his jaw.

"Oh, Brad," she mourned, "I'm so *sorry!*"

Brad took Jemima by the shoulders. "Go get your things," he told her. "You're coming with me. I'm taking you back to my apartment until we get married."

But Jemima looked down at the floor and made no reply. Instead, the blonde woman that he assumed to be her mother appeared out of the kitchen, and invited him in.

"Why don't you come inside, Brad, and sit down?"

Brad shook his head. "I'm not here for a social visit," he told her, and turned back to Jemima. "Listen, Jemima, you're eighteen now, you don't need your parent's consent to be legally married. They can't hold you here against your will."

Jemima looked up at him pleadingly. "Come and sit down, Brad," she asked, "*please.*"

The older woman beckoned, and after a long hesitation, he allowed himself to be led into the living room.

"I'm sorry for what happened last night, Brad," she told him. "My husband will be, too, when he's had time to cool down. Please, make yourself comfortable. I'll get something for you."

Brad sat down next to Jemima on the couch and turned to her, frowning, but she kissed the question right off his lips.

Mrs. King came back and set two cups of coffee down on the table before them, and a plate of peanut butter cookies. Brad glanced up at her with a look that communicated his sense of deep irony, but her manner remained placid and unruffled. She took a seat in a rocking chair across from the couch.

"You'll have to forgive us," she said quietly, "but last night was the first time that my husband and I even *knew* that you were courting with our daughter. It was quite a surprise to us. We assumed that Jemima would marry an Amish boy."

Her eyes moved to Jemima, and Jemima dropped her glance instantly. Then her eyes moved to Brad's.

"That's because, if Jemima marries a non-Amish boy, like you, it means that she will *not* be able to join the Amish church."

Brad turned to Jemima. She looked up at him pleadingly, and he read the truth of it in her eyes.

"It means that she will lose her place in this community, and her decision will be seen by others as a sign that she has turned her back on her faith. She will, in fact, be burning the only bridge that connects her to her faith, and to her God," Rachel explained.

Brad stirred and looked up at her. "I understand that's what *you and your husband* believe," he told her, with some heat, "but I don't share your views and I don't see why Jemima has to, either. If her family and friends think they should be able to pick who she *marries*, then maybe she's better off without them!"

Jemima turned toward him. "Brad, *please*," she murmured.

The older woman regarded him calmly. "Brad, when you ask Jemima to marry you, it isn't at all the same as asking an Englisch girl. You're asking Jemima to make a complete break with her past life. To abandon everything"—her voice cracked slightly, and she paused for an instant before going on—"and *everyone* she ever knew in her past. You might not have understood that, but we feel it *very* much. That's why her father was so – upset – last night."

Brad fell silent. He couldn't honestly say that he *had* understood that part. Jemima's eyes held unshed tears, and anger died out of his heart as he looked down at her. He hadn't really understood, until now, just *how much* he'd been asking her to give up. He felt his face going warm, and was struck with a sudden sense of his ignorance of Jemima's culture.

The sound of the front door opening made them all look up. Jacob King stepped inside and looked around for his family. When he caught sight of them all in the living room, he froze, wide-eyed.

Rachel was on her feet in an instant. "Jacob, *Jemima's fiancé* has come to pay us a call."

Jacob's voice seemed to rise up like a geyser, from deep underground. "*What is he doing here?*" he demanded, and began walking toward them.

A dark blur rushed past Brad's right shoulder. In an instant Jemima had moved between him and her huge father, and was staring up at him like a kitten challenging a bear.

"Daed, this is the man I've *chosen*," she quavered, "and I'm sorry if you don't *like* it, but Brad is my fiancé, and, and if you lay a hand on him *again*, I-I'll leave with him now and *never come back*!"

It was the only threat Jemima had uttered in her short life, but it froze Jacob in his tracks. He looked down at her, and then over at his wife.

"Come and sit down, Jacob," Rachel said softly, and touched his shoulder fleetingly with her hand. "I've been telling Brad about what it will mean to Jemima – and to us –

if Jemima marries with him."

Jemima returned to her place beside Brad on the couch, and reached for his hand. Jacob sat down in a big overstuffed chair, and regarded the two of them grimly.

"The only way I could *ever* approve of such a marriage," Jacob rumbled, "would be if the Englischer converted to the church. Then he and Jemima could *both* join, and be married. Only then."

Rachel nodded, and they both turned to look at him. To his horror, Brad felt Jemima's shy gaze on him as well. Surely *she* didn't expect him to convert, too?

Brad felt his mouth dropping open, and closed it. He sputtered incredulously, but the elder couple's grim expressions told him that no one in the room was joking.

Brad clawed at his collar, because suddenly it felt as if the room was closing in on him. He turned to Jemima.

"Jemima, this is crazy. I *love* you, and I'll marry you tomorrow if you get in the truck and come with me. But if you're expecting me to join your family's *religion*"—he threw out his hands—"I just – I can't *do* it. I don't believe in *any* God, and I could never live like *this*"—he gestured to the room around him—"like it was a *hundred years* ago!"

He reached for her hand and took it. "Let's get out of here," he urged softly. "Don't even worry about your stuff, I'll buy you new things. *Just come with me.* I love you,

Jemima. Come with me, *now*."

Jemima looked up at him with anguished doe eyes, and then looked at her parents.

"*Think* about what you would be doing, Jemima," her mother urged softly, "what you would be giving up *forever!*"

Jemima's eyes moved to her father's face. He looked at her with deep sadness. Tears shone in his weary blue eyes, and he rubbed them away with a big hand.

To Brad's dismay, Jemima put her hand over her mouth and burst into tears.

He leaned back into the sofa, stunned.

Once again, when it came to a choice between him and Jemima's religion – he'd *lost*.

CHAPTER TWENTY-FIVE

"Earth to Brad? Seriously – *wake up!*"

Brad snapped out of his daydream and looked up into Delores Watkins' disgusted face. She shook her head. "I don't know what's gotten into you, wonder boy, but it's reached the point that I don't care. If you don't start paying attention, I'm going to be the one sending *you* out to the sewage treatment plant!"

Brad shook his head. "Sorry, Delores. What was that again?"

She sputtered in exasperation. "I'll just send you an email. Assuming you still read *those*?" she snapped, and swept out of his office. The door slammed impressively behind her.

Brad closed his eyes. Delores was right, he was going to have to come back to his own life sooner or later. Sooner, if he wanted to keep his job.

He massaged his brow with one hand. He had an interview with the city mayor at 1 p.m., and he had to crank out a 1,000-word story after for the evening edition.

And he didn't know how he was going to do it. He was a *wreck.*

It had been a week since he'd driven the truck away from the King house, and he hadn't gone back. But yesterday he'd received a tearstained letter from Jemima.

He reached into his pocket, unfolded it on his desk, and read it again for the thousandth time.

Dear Brad,

I wanted to tell you I'm so sorry for all the bad things that have happened since you asked me to marry you. Please don't think hard thoughts about Daed, he is going to church tomorrow to repent and he is truly sorry.

Brad put a hand to his head and massaged the little throbbing spot between his eyes.

I didn't know what to say when you asked me to come with you. I love you with all my heart, and I want to marry you, but I love my parents too, and I love God, and I don't know what to do. It's true that you might not understand what it means for me to marry you, and how could you, you're not Amish, and I didn't want to harp on it or make you feel bad.

I wouldn't blame you if you never came back, or if you decided to break our engagement and find another girl. Like that bionde girl I saw you with once in town. She was very pretty and I could tell that she liked you a lot.

This part of the letter was heavily smudged, and was marred with watery blotches and signs of many revisions. Brad ran his thumb softly over the fuzzy lines.

I don't know what to do now, except to tell you that I will love you until I die. And to give you back the beautiful ring. I wouldn't be able to wear it anyway, because we don't wear jewelry, but I kept it under my pillow and looked at it a lot. But you might want to give it to some other girl, someday.

Brad sighed and reached into his pocket. He pulled out the little ring. Jemima had enclosed it in her letter. He turned it between his fingers, and it winked at him forlornly.

So if I don't see you again, I will understand, and I will pray that God sends you a beautiful Englisch girl who makes you very happy, and also that maybe someday you come to know Him, because that's what I have always prayed since I first knew you, and is the best thing that could happen.

So, if that is what you decide, I hope you go ahead with your own life, and forget you ever met me, and find someone who makes you happy. And I will go on, too, but I will always be glad that I found the George Washington letter, in spite of all the trouble it caused me, because it brought us together for awhile.

Love,

Jemima

Brad folded the letter carefully, put it back into his pocket, and pulled his hands over his face.

That evening, he stumbled through his front door and dropped his backpack on the floor. He'd been sitting all day, but he was bone tired. He stretched, massaged his back, and walked to the refrigerator. He pulled out a TV dinner, peeled back the plastic cover, and stuck it in the microwave.

The microwave beeped, and he pulled the tray out, stirred the contents, and brought it over to the table.

He looked down at his dinner. It was a disgusting brown blob.

Brad sank into a chair and poked at his food. He couldn't help wondering what Jemima was doing at that moment. Having dinner with her family? Or maybe, not *just* with her family. Maybe one of those Amish guys was there, too.

He picked up a plastic knife and fork and jabbed the meat patty. It wouldn't be long before they were all back at her house. Jemima's letter had made it clear that she was setting him free, and by implication, getting free herself. *That* news would travel fast.

He paused, staring vacantly into space. The thought of some other guy putting his hands on Jemima made him want to claw his own eyes.

But if he wasn't right for her, maybe he should be big enough to wish her happiness with someone else. Like she'd been trying to do for him.

He speared a chunk of meat and put it in his mouth.

After dinner, Brad went straight to bed and lay in his bed, staring at the ceiling. He was exhausted, but couldn't go to sleep for a long time. And when he finally did nod off, he was wracked by terrible nightmares.

He tossed and moaned on his pillow. He was back at the King farm again, and he was begging Jemima to come away with him, but it was like he was a ghost. No matter how he shouted and shook her, she gave no sign of having seen or heard him. She sat in her chair, sewing placidly, as if he wasn't there. Her parents sat beside her, reading, and no one paid any heed to him at *all.*

Then the door opened, and the dark-haired Amish guy came in smiling with a bouquet of roses. He presented them to Jemima. She took them shyly, and smiled back at him.

Brad ground his teeth, and *shook* her arm, and tried to get her to *hear* him, but instead, she stood up, and took the boy's hand, and they walked to the center of the room.

An elder appeared out of nowhere, an old Amish guy with a long white beard and a Bible. Jemima and the dark-haired guy stood before him, heads bowed, as he prayed over them. To Brad's horror, he pronounced them *married*, and Jemima's parents rushed over to kiss Jemima, and shake the boy's hand.

Then the smiling groom swung Jemima up in his arms, and carried her up the stairs and out of sight.

Brad sat bolt upright in bed, and yelled out hoarsely.

It took him a long time to realize that he was in his own apartment, and that it had just been a dream.

CHAPTER TWENTY-SIX

Brad went to work the next day and sleepwalked through his tasks. When he returned to his own apartment at the end of the day, he couldn't say that he'd accomplished much.

But even his own apartment had ceased to be a refuge. Brad tried to stave off the emptiness he felt by smoking; watching television, which he soon found unbearably irritating; and reading a book, which bored him.

He went to replace the book on its shelf and noticed his old photo album crammed in between a biography of Buckminster Fuller and a history of baseball. The album was skinny – he had very few photos of his own childhood, or of his parents. Most of the pictures had been given to him by his grandmother, or had been taken by her, and were relatively recent.

Brad opened the album, sat down on his bed, and sputtered out a wry laugh.

There was a wedding photo of his parents that his grandmother had kept. He stared at it, thinking that it must've been the only day in their married lives that they didn't fight. His Dad was wearing a brown tuxedo and a yellow boutonniere, and his Mom was wearing a white satin slip dress. She was holding a bouquet of yellow roses. They were both smiling, and his Dad's arm was around his Mom.

Then there was his own baby picture. He'd never liked that photo. He didn't know why his Mom thought it was cute to take a picture that he'd have to spend the rest of his life denying, but there he was, smiling up at the camera from a fake bearskin rug. His face hadn't been the only thing shining. He flipped the page.

There was the one school photo of him when he'd been in fourth grade, the one with his hair sticking almost straight up. He'd been wearing a goofy striped shirt that he'd had to pick out himself. To make things worse, the colors had faded strangely, and the photo looked almost pink now. He sputtered and shook his head.

That was the year Bobby Jenkins had tried to bully him, and he'd taught Bobby the definition of "left cross."

Brad moved the fingers of his left hand, and turned the page.

Then there was a picture of him and his grandmother. It had been taken by a friend of hers, not long after he'd gone to live with her. They'd been standing out in front of her little white house, on the lawn. He shook his head, thinking how skinny he looked, and his grams – he let his gaze linger on her face. She was scowling, her hair was pulled back into a severe bun, and her dress was a blue print bag.

He flipped the page, and smiled faintly. His grandfather's service medal was stuck in between the next pages. His grams had given it to him one day, long before he'd had any idea how big a deal that was for her.

"You never knew your grandfather," she had told him gruffly. "He grew up real poor. But he worked hard, and he *made* something of himself. See this? This is his service medal. He rose to the rank of a major in the Navy. It goes to show you what *you* can get, if you work hard."

She had pressed it into his palm, and leaned over and stared at him with an almost crazy intensity in her eyes.

"You take this. Maybe it'll remind you that you can make something of yourself, too."

He smiled faintly.

Yeah.

He flipped the page. There was his high school graduation photo of him standing there in his cap and gown. His grandmother had been by his side, but he'd had to hold her arm to keep her steady. By that time she'd been sick, and a month later, she'd been gone.

He still missed her.

He cut off that line of thought abruptly, flipped the book shut, and stretched out on the bed. He blew smoke contemplatively toward the ceiling.

The milestones of his life, in five photos.

But it was what had happened between the milestones, and the carefully posed portrait shots, that had shaped his life most. The things he didn't want to remember.

The things that had made an agnostic of him. He frowned.

Things like the recurring nightmare he'd had as a child, except that it had been *real*: the sound of his father screaming, of him knocking things off the kitchen table and yelling at his Mom. His earliest memories were of hiding behind the couch as his parents fought.

He took a pull at his cigarette. When he'd been very small, he'd prayed to God – he supposed because his Mom had taught him a bedtime prayer once and put the idea in his head. But if there *was* a God, He hadn't chosen to listen to those prayers. His parents' fights got more frequent and even more frightening.

One night when he was six years old, his old man had come home drunk and had beaten his Mom up. The sound of her screaming had driven him into the darkest corner of his bedroom closet, where he'd stayed all night with his hands clamped over his ears.

The next morning everything was deathly quiet. His Mom had been curled up in bed with a bruised face and cuts on her hands.

His Dad had gone, and he never returned.

Anger whisked up in him, like sparks from a lighter. He glared up at the blotchy ceiling of his apartment and prayed his first prayer in years. All the pent up resentment and rage of his childhood came pouring out suddenly, like flood waters breaking through a dam.

Why?

If You exist at all, why did You let all that happen? Why did you let my Dad take his issues out on Mom, and then leave us both alone? Why did You stand by when she started doing meth? Why didn't you save her?

Why didn't my Dad ever call me, even once? He didn't even come to Mom's funeral! If you're a God of love, why did You let all that mess happen?

Brad's mouth twisted down bitterly. *You abandoned us before Dad did.*

He lifted blazing eyes to the ceiling, and his face contracted in fury. *And how can you let an innocent girl like Jemima believe in the fairy tale, and sacrifice her own happiness because of it, when one day something will go so wrong that she'll see the truth? She'll see that there's nothing to all those stories she was told. But then it'll be too late to get back what she lost. It'll be too late to get back her life!*

What did she ever do to You?

If this is the kind of God you are, then You're a God of hate, not a God of love, and I want nothing to do with You!

Brad shook his head, and leaned over, and crushed out the cigarette.

CHAPTER TWENTY-SEVEN

"Darren! Darren -- don't!"

Brad moaned and tossed on his pillow. His mother's anguished screams filled his mind. He was a four-year-old again, hiding behind the couch as his parents fought.

There was a heavy, scraping sound, like heavy furniture being moved. Then another shrill scream, and a heavy crash, like someone falling to the floor.

More screams, worse than before, and the sound of heavy blows.

His dad's voice was thick, bleared, and rang out to the accompaniment of his mother's sobs. "I told you what I'd do if my dinner was cold again," he announced. "You've only got yourself to blame! I work my hands raw to put food on this table. The least you can do is make sure it's hot when I get home!"

"*Oh don't!*" his mother screamed, and his child-self clapped his hands over his ears again.

Brad moaned and tossed on his bed, and dug his face into the pillow.

His parent's living room melted, changed. The shouting faded to silence. The dull yellow lamplight gradually lightened to a wintry sky.

He was standing on the little stoop outside their back door. It was bitterly cold, but his mom was sitting on the steps, her shoulders slumped against the railing. And at seven years old, he knew what was wrong – when his Mom was crashing, she got so sleepy she practically passed out.

It was hard to move her, but he'd had practice; he opened the door, grabbed her feet, and slowly dragged her back inside again.

He had to stop and catch his breath. His Mom lay there on the kitchen floor with her arms splayed out, unconscious. Her face was gray, her lips were shriveled and dry, and her teeth were brown.

She looked older than his grandmother.

He'd crouched down and put his hand to her cheek, grieving for her. For the mother he should've had, and didn't. A hard lump burned in his throat.

He moaned in his sleep, hunched his shoulders over and settled onto his side.

The nightmare convulsed again, and now he was standing on a windswept hillside with his grandmother. It was cold and overcast, and he couldn't feel his fingers.

His grandmother had looked down at him, and for once, the look in her eyes had been soft. "You can *cry*, boy," she whispered, and squeezed his hand. But he'd cried himself dry long before he'd ever met his grandmother.

A minister stood in front of a big hole, and was praying over his mother's casket. And he had bowed his head, but he wasn't praying. He looked down into the hole and decided that there was no God, in spite of what his grandmother told him. No one could look down on that raw, gaping hole in the ground and believe in such a thing.

But he frowned, and thrashed, and prayed in his *sleep*.

Why.

Why.

Why.

Brad tossed, turned over on his back, and settled down with a sigh.

The dream vanished – and then began playing all over again. Brad gasped in his sleep, and thrashed.

No, no. No more.

He was back in his parent's living room. *"Darren! Darren – don't!"*

His mother's screams began again, and once again, he was a terrified four-year-old hiding behind the couch.

But this time, the dream was different. This time, he sensed the presence of a new participant. He raised his brows, and his eyes rolled underneath their lids.

There was light in the room now, not the dull yellow light of the lamp, but brilliant light – blue-white, dazzling. It blotted out the sight of his parents fighting, blotted out the sounds of his father's shouts and his mother's screams. It drowned everything else into oblivion – even his fear.

He saw his four-year-old self hiding behind the couch. And he saw a man standing beside him. The man reached down and put his hand on his head. He saw his child-self look up and smile.

He felt the old pain pouring out of his heart like black smoke, to be instantly swallowed up by the light.

Joy flooded his heart, and he didn't know why.

The light filled his whole mind, and the dream changed again. Gradually it resolved to the little stoop outside their back door. Once again, it was cold, and his Mom was slumped against the railing, in the throes of withdrawal.

And the light surged in like the sea. It streamed through the bare oak branches, consumed the ugly black railing, the concrete steps, his mother, and even him. And the man was there again, and looked down at him.

Unreasoning joy swelled in his heart, strained it, threatened to burst it – and the man laughed.

The old pain and the heavy grief burst out of his chest and flew away over the housetop like a flock of wild birds. And the joy threatened to overcome him.

An answering joy radiated from the man's face, and Brad looked at him in wonder.

The light blotted everything out and made his mind go white and blank. Then shape and color slowly returned. Once again, he and his grandmother were on the gray, windswept hill, and the minister prayed, and his child self looked down into the gaping hole in the ground. But now the man came and stood at his side, and wiped the face of the hillside with his hands. Light blurred the minister, blotted out the casket, filled the hole with light as if with water.

And then another white shape came and stood beside the man. Brad looked at the face that slowly resolved through the whiteness, the familiar eyes, and the smiling mouth – not shriveled now, not blighted, but young and radiant with life.

He fell to the ground and hugged his knees and moaned, crying like he'd never cried before – deep, wracking sobs. And the bitter anger spiraled up through his chest, was expelled with those sobs, and consumed by the light.

Brad woke sobbing. He sat up and reached wildly into the air with both his hands. The joy still glowed in his heart like a star.

But his apartment was dark and still. *It had been a dream.*

Brad sat in the dark, wide-eyed and panting. No, *not* just a dream. Because the old hurt, the old pain and fear were gone, as if the sea had poured through him and washed them away.

Even his *doubt* was gone.

He got up and turned on the light. He scrabbled over his bedside table for the one souvenir he'd brought from the green hill country: the plain brown book from his hotel room table.

He took it, and it fell open to a spot near the back. He looked down, and read:

"For God so loved the world, that he gave his only begotten Son, that whosoever believeth in him should not perish, but have everlasting life. For God sent not his Son into the world to condemn the world; but that the world through him might be saved."

Brad stared at the page through tear-filled eyes. The words pierced him, in their terrible beauty; his heart had been broken by joy, and emptied of grief, and now it was tender enough to be filled.

He bowed his head, and shook it in wonder. "You *are* real," he prayed in amazement. "I can't explain how, but I *feel* Your presence, and I know You're real."

He shook his head. "The pain is gone. It's *gone*. I don't know how – what did You do? – but I guess that part doesn't matter. The point is, I asked if you were real, and You showed me. I *believe* now."

Tears filled his eyes. "I may weaken later, but take my heart *now*, if you want it. It's not much, but I'll give it to You."

The joy came again, an echo of the joy in his dream, and he had the sense, somehow, that God was smiling. Brad closed his eyes and warmed himself in that glow. Then a new thought prodded him, and he smiled wryly.

Brad Williams – the *Christian*.

Who would've thought.

CHAPTER TWENTY-EIGHT

Brad pulled his truck to a stop in front of the King house. It was early twilight, a few days before Christmas. Snow covered the whole landscape, and the house looked like something from a holiday card. In the early dusk, the old homestead was a pale lavender, and warm golden light beamed from the windows.

There was a buggy parked in the front yard. Brad stared at it, frowning, and climbed out of the truck.

He knocked softly at the door and waited. He could hear the sound of many voices, and the scent of cinnamon escaped from inside.

The door opened, and Rachel King stood in the opening. Her eyes widened at the sight of him and her expression was one of surprise.

"I hope I haven't come at a bad time," Brad told her quickly, "but I'd *really* like to talk to Jemima."

Rachel hesitated for an instant, and then nodded. "Please come in."

Rachel opened the door and led him to where the chatter and laughter were coming from – a small room off the living room. Brad stepped in and drew a sharp breath.

The scene before him was straight out of his nightmare. Jemima was sitting in a big red chair, and there beside her was the dark-haired guy from his dream. Jealousy stabbed him. His rival sure hadn't wasted any time!

They both looked up as he entered. Jemima gasped and cried "Brad!" The smile faded off the other guy's face.

"Jemima, you have a visitor," her mother said quietly, and left.

The dark-haired guy stood up and turned to Jemima. "I'll go and see if Deborah has that book you were talking about," he said, and slowly walked out of the room.

They eyed one another uncomfortably as he walked past, and then he was gone.

Brad turned back to Jemima. Those huge eyes were on his

face and glowing like emeralds in the firelight.

"Come and sit down," she murmured.

He walked over and sat down in the chair beside her. The situation felt strained and awkward, but he plunged in.

"Jemima, I came here because I wanted to talk to you. I hope I haven't"—he tried not to grind his teeth—"*interrupted* anything?"

Jemima shook her head, and said nothing more. Her eyes were on his, as if she were trying to read them.

"I, um – I got your letter," he mumbled. "And I understand what you were trying to do. It was, it was very unselfish of you, Duchess. It was a beautiful gesture."

Jemima bowed her head, and looked down into her lap.

"But I came here to tell you that I don't *want* to be free. I want us to be married. More than anything in the *world*."

He reached over and took her fingers in his. They were trembling, and still she didn't meet his eyes.

"That is, if you still want to marry *me*."

She looked down at his hand. "But how, Brad?" she asked, in a small voice. "You don't want to live like me, and I can't live like you. How can we be married, if we can't live together?"

He ran his thumb gently over her fingers.

"Um…something happened this week, Jemima. Something happened to me that – well, I still don't how to describe it, but it – it made me see things differently. It made me think that maybe I can see things more like you. It made me – it made me—"

It was harder to say than he'd imagined. He closed his eyes and made himself do it.

"It made me believe that there *is* a God, after all. It helped me to trust Him. I, um, I-I met *Jesus*. As odd as that sounds."

Jemima's mouth had dropped open slightly, and she shook her head. "It doesn't sound odd *at all*," she cried, and tears spangled her eyes. "Oh, Brad, I've been praying for that for *months*!"

She threw her arms around him, and buried her head in his shoulder. To his amazement, she was crying. He put his arms around her.

"I just wanted to tell you that maybe we aren't that far apart anymore, in what we believe. At least *that.*

"And I've thought a lot about the other stuff. About my life, and my home, and my job. And, um"—he looked up at the ceiling in embarrassment, because there were tears in his eyes—"*none* of those things are as important to me as you are, Jemima. If I have to give them up for us to be married, I *will.*

"I'm not making any *promises*," he added quickly, in

response to her glad cry, "I can't promise that I'll be able to do it, Jemima. Just that I'm willing to *try*. I'm willing to start. If you'll help me."

"Oh, Brad," Jemima sobbed into his shirt, "*Help* you? Anything, anything, *anything!*"

Then she turned and gave him such a kiss, that he suddenly felt that he'd be able to live in a house on the *moon* – much less in a house off the grid.

Jemima laughed and took his hand. "Now come and talk to my family, and meet Mark. The two of you are going to be great friends."

He allowed her to lead him along, and they walked into the kitchen together, where their news was received by the family with joy, and a good bit of surprise. The sly-looking kid raised her eyebrows, as if she was out a bet; the mother burst out crying, and hugged Jemima; and the old man gave him a narrow look, grunted, stood – and stuck out his hand.

He had taken it, and tried not to wince when his hand was almost crushed.

He even took the dark-haired guy's hand, when he stuck it out.

"I'm Mark Christener," the guy had said.

He tried to think of something polite to say. "Nice right," he replied, and rubbed his jaw.

CHAPTER TWENTY-NINE

A year later, Jemima stood in her parent's living room, in her brand-new blue wedding dress. Bishop Lapp smiled down at her, and his bright blue eyes were full of the same joy that filled her heart. She looked over at Brad, so handsome in his black suit and bow tie, and with his shock of sandy hair.

It was their wedding day. Under usual circumstances, it never should have happened.

But *nothing* about their story had been usual.

As the bishop intoned the words of the blessing, Jemima thought back over the last year: all the things that had happened to make this day come true. Her Daed had built

Brad a little apartment addition onto the workshop, and let him live there while he was learning. He'd taught Brad how to help him in the shop, and so many other things: how to dress, what to do in worship, and what was expected of him as an Amish man.

It hadn't always been easy. They had fought *often*. Her father had threatened to throw Brad into the pond for his smart mouth, and his disrespect for tradition, and his rebellious attitude. And three times Brad had thrown down his hammer, and said he was going back to the Englisch.

But neither one of them had carried out their threats.

Maybe, she considered, the fighting had been necessary to make them respect each other. And then, to *like* one another. Jemima looked over at her father. He was sitting just behind them, wiping his eyes with a big brown hand.

Her mother had quickly come to love Brad. When she'd told her mother about Brad's childhood – or *lack* of one – Rachel had taken him to her heart immediately. And she knew he was fond of her, too.

As for Deborah – she still hadn't paid back the fifty dollars she'd wangled from Brad. But he didn't seem to hold it against her. In fact, Brad seemed to understand Deborah better than anyone else did, and even to *like* her. Which she had to admit, was kind of a rare quality.

She looked over at Brad, and caught his glance and smiled.

He gave her a look that promised great things later, and she lowered her eyes primly.

Brad had promised her nothing when he'd first come to live with them. But he'd stuck to his intentions more stubbornly even than she'd hoped. She'd probably never know how hard it had been for him to change to their ways. When he first came to live with them, Joseph had challenged him to a fight, and Samuel had accidentally knocked him into a pig pen.

But *none* of it had made him change his mind.

Gratitude welled up in Jemima's heart, followed quickly by joy. She closed her eyes.

Thank you Lord, she prayed. *Thank you for giving me the George Washington letter, because without it, I would never have met Brad. I couldn't see what You were doing at the time. I thought it was about the money, and I was unhappy for all the trouble it'd brought. But You never gave me the letter to make me a millionaire.*

You gave me the letter to make me rich in another way. To make us all rich.

She looked over at Brad again. He met her eyes, smiled mischievously and winked.

EPILOGUE

Former Reporter Marries Amish Millionaire

Serenity, PA – In a private ceremony conducted at the bride's home, Jemima King, best known as the Amish Millionaire, and Brad Williams, formerly of the *Ledger Enquirer*, were married this Tuesday. King first came to the attention of the public when the *Enquirer* broke the story of her rare find – a previously unknown letter from George Washington to his wife. King subsequently sold the letter at Brinkley's Auction House for $1.6 million.

Williams, at the time a *Ledger* reporter, met King in the course of reporting her story, and he also testified on her behalf when she was unsuccessfully sued for the money.

Williams resigned his post as an up-and-coming reporter for the *Ledger*, and has renounced modern life to convert to the Amish faith. He is one of the few people who have successfully made the transition to that way of life.

His former colleagues at the *Ledger* wish him, and his lovely bride, every happiness.

THANK YOU FOR READING!

And thank you for supporting me as an independent author! I hope you enjoyed reading this book as much as I loved writing it!

In the next chapter, there is a FREE sample of my new Christmas book, A Lancaster County Christmas Yule Goat Calamity.

If you like the sample, you can look for the rest of the book at your favorite online booksellers.

All the Best

Ruth

A LANCASTER COUNTY CHRISTMAS YULE GOAT CALAMITY

RETURN TO THE WORLD OF LANCASTER COUNTY SECOND CHANCES WITH ANNIE MILLER, A FIFTEEN-YEAR-OLD WILD CHILD WITH A GOAT-LOAD OF PROBLEMS!

Meet Annie Miller, a fifteen-year-old wild child with a Goat-Load of problems! After losing her mamm when she was only six-years-old, 15-year-old Annie Fisher and her family have managed to find some peace and happiness – even as Annie is viewed as a wild child by the rest of the community. But when Annie starts helping her daed out in his shop, things go from bad to worse when Annie accidentally wins an auction for five Nubian goats. Unable to return them or gain a refund, will this wild child find a way to sell the goats and rescue Christmas for herself and her family?

Find out in A Lancaster County Christmas Yule Goat Calamity by Ruth Price. This book is set in the same world as Lancaster County Second Chances.

CHAPTER ONE

The little bell over the shop door tinkled loudly, a current of cold air poured in, and Annie Miller stopped playing with a little ball and cup toy to see who was coming into her father's store.

Annie's bright blue eyes peeped out from behind the handmade brooms, but their expectant look quickly dimmed. It was only her cousin, Emma Lapp. Emma was nice enough, but she was *courtship* age. And that meant only one thing.

Poor Emma had *lost her mind.*

Annie gave her cousin a pitying look. All Emma ever talked about, all she cared about lately, was *boys.* She was dull as dirt – that was for sure!

Annie shrugged and went back to seeing how many times she could flip the ball into the cup. She was pushing a new record – 200 – and if she got it, she'd be sure to lord it over

Samuel Stauffer, because his record was 180, and he never let anyone forget it.

"Good afternoon, Emma."

Annie glanced up momentarily. Her father's redheaded employee, Daniel Gingerich, was standing at attention behind the counter and gazing down at Emma with that goofy look he always got when she came in. Annie frowned. She liked Daniel, but he'd turned into a real *goober* lately, and Emma was to blame. Not only was she boring, herself – she was spreading the infection to others.

"Good morning, Daniel."

"More of your friendship bread, I see! Your loaves just *fly* off the shelves during the holidays."

There was a soft simpering sound, and Annie rolled her eyes, and then spat out an exclamation, because she'd taken her eye off the ball and missed her shot – just shy of the record, too!

"I made an extra loaf for you, Daniel."

"Thank you, Emma."

A crinkling sound advertised the transfer of the gift from Emma's hands to Daniel's. Annie peeped at the counter from her hiding place and was astonished to see that Daniel's hand lingered on Emma's...*on purpose.*

She shook her head. It was a rotten shame: Daniel was a

sport and pretty good fun when he wasn't mooning over Emma, but bad was quickly turning into worse. The next thing you knew, he'd probably get all serious and start traipsing off to Emma's house, and stop joining snowball fights after work with the rest of them.

Annie calculated that it would probably be smart for her to start looking for next year's softball catcher too, before Daniel bailed, because she could see it coming. She made a mental note to choose a younger player next time, too, so she could count on at least a *few* steady years before the madness took hold.

"Are you coming to the sing this Sunday, Emma?" Daniel asked softly.

"Oh yes."

'Then I'll be there, too."

Emma giggled. "Oh, Daniel."

Annie, feeling she could stand no more, stepped out into the center aisle nonchalantly, but conspicuously. Daniel looked up and colored.

"Oh, there you are, Annie! I was wondering where you'd gotten off to," he said hastily.

She gave him a quick look, thinking that he should be ashamed to tell such a honking whopper, but only shrugged.

Emma turned and smiled at her. "Annie, Mamm has been

asking about you. She said that if I saw you, I was to ask you to come over for dinner this weekend."

Annie goggled at her pretty cousin in dismay. She had to think of an excuse, quick, or else her daed would make her go to her Aunt Katie's. But every time she went over there, they tortured her with soap and shampoo and brushing and braiding and all manner of foofy nonsense that made her wish that she could just run away into the woods.

"I-I'm sorry, I can't," she stammered, "I feel a cold coming on!"

She put a hand to her mouth and coughed. And then, because there were no excuses that worked better than her own feet, she turned and fled.

Daniel turned to Emma apologetically. "I'm sorry, Emma. She behaves more like a little squirrel than a little girl."

Emma stared at the shop door and shook her head. "Mamm is worried about her," she replied thoughtfully. "When Aunt Elizabeth died, there was no one left to teach Annie the things a girl should learn. And now she's 15, almost courtship age, and – look at her. Her hair coming loose, her dress all stained with grass and dirt from climbing and running. She doesn't even wear shoes until it gets cold."

She turned her lovely brown eyes back to Daniel. "What boy would ever want to court with Annie?" she wondered aloud. "She doesn't know the first thing about being a woman!"

Daniel shrugged and smiled. "Oh, she'll come around, Emma," he assured her. "When Annie decides she *wants* to court, she'll do what it takes to learn."

Emma shook her head. "Then she'll have to learn fast," was her worried assessment...

THANK YOU FOR READING!

If you enjoyed this sample, feel free look for the rest of the book in eBook and Paperback format at your favorite online booksellers.

All the Best,

Ruth

ABOUT THE AUTHOR

Ruth Price is a Pennsylvania native and devoted mother of four. After her youngest set off for college, she decided it was time to pursue her childhood dream to become a fiction writer. Drawing inspiration from her faith, her husband and love of her life Harold, and deep interest in Amish culture that stemmed from a childhood summer spent with her family on a Lancaster farm, Ruth began to pen the stories that had always jabbered away in her mind. Ruth believes that art at its best channels a higher good, and while she doesn't always reach that ideal, she hopes that her readers are entertained and inspired by her stories.

Made in the USA
Lexington, KY
16 December 2016